J. G. BALLARD was born in 1930 in Shanghai, China, v   : his father was a businessman. Following the attack on Pearl Harbor, Ballard and his family were placed in a civilian prison camp. They returned to England in 1946. After two years at Cambridge, where he read medicine, Ballard worked as a copywriter and Covent Garden porter before going to Canada with the RAF. He started writing short stories in the late 1950s, while working on a scientific journal. His first major novel, *The Drowned World*, was published in 1962. His acclaimed novels include *The Crystal World*, *The Atrocity Exhibition*, *Crash* (filmed by David Cronenberg), *High-Rise*, *The Unlimited Dream Company*, *The Kindness oj Women* (the sequel to *Empire of the Sun*), *Cocaine Nights*, *Super-Cannes*, *Millennium People* and *Kingdom Come*. His autobiography, *Miracles of Life*, was published to great acclaim in 2008. J. G. Ballard died in 2009.

D1628199

521 175 14 9

By the same author

J. G. BALLARD

The Kindness of Women

FOURTH ESTATE • *London*

Fourth Estate
An imprint of HarperCollins*Publishers*
77–85 Fulham Palace Road
London W6 8JB
4thestate.co.uk

This edition published by Fourth Estate in 2014
1

First published in Great Britain by Harper Collins in 1991

A catalogue record for this book is available from the British Library.

ISBN 978-0-00-654701-3

Set in Minion by FMG using Atomik ePublisher from Easypress

MIX
Paper from
responsible sources
FSC www.fsc.org   **FSC™ C007454**

FSC™ is a non-profit international organisation established to promote the
responsible management of the world's forests. Products carrying the FSC label
are independently certified to assure consumers that they come from forests
that are managed to meet the social, economic and ecological needs of
present or future generations, and other controlled sources.

Find out more about HarperCollins and the environment at
www.harpercollins.co.uk/green

Contents

Introduction

by Michel Faber

Like many men scarred by war, J. G. Ballard spent much of his life determined not to talk about it. Had he died in his early fifties (not such an improbable fate, given his intake of alcohol and tobacco) only one short story, 'The Dead Time', would have existed to pay direct witness to his wartime experience. He preferred to divert the memories into more fantastical conceptions: drowned worlds, concrete islands, terminal beaches, atrocity exhibitions.

It wasn't until the 1980s that he commanded his fiction to shine a documentary torch into his own life, to illuminate and perhaps exorcise his Shanghai ghosts. He confronted them first in *Empire of the Sun*, tackled them again from another angle in *The Kindness of Women*, and finally – just before he died – offered a conventionally 'truthful' account in his autobiography, *Miracles of Life*. The author who'd built his reputation on a 'never explain, never apologise' attitude seemed increasingly concerned that people should understand what he'd gone through and how it had affected him.

Empire of the Sun was not the book to achieve that, partly because it didn't show what happened 'afterwards' to the boy who saw corpses littering the streets of his city and spent several years in a Japanese internment camp, partly because the public's view of the novel was filtered through the lens of Steven Spielberg's sentimental, soaringly upbeat movie adaptation. *The Kindness of Women*, marketed as a 'sequel', steered back towards the provocative style of Ballard's earlier work, exploring the psychic fallout of horror and violence. The scene where young Jim watches four somnolent Japanese soldiers slowly murder a

Chinese prisoner with telephone wire is a masterpiece of understate-
ment and baleful resonance: even as Jim negotiates his own escape, we
know that, on a deeper level, there is no escaping from such a sight.

As in *Empire of the Sun*, Ballard erases his real-life parents from the
Lunghua camp, turning Jim into an orphan for dramatic purposes.
Other than this, the events of the earlier book are handled quite differ-
ently, with a different cast of characters. Seventeen novella-like chapters fictionalise the key phases of Ballard's life from 1937 to 1987,
starting with his childhood in Shanghai where the rich, perpetually
tipsy Westerners play tennis, go shopping and sidestep the growing
mound of refugee bodies felled by hunger, typhus and bombs. 'To my
child's eyes, which had seen nothing else, Shanghai was a waking dream
where everything I could imagine had already been taken to its extreme.'
Those last fifteen words serve as a manifesto for all of Ballard's novels.

Ballard was enthralled by the Surrealists, and felt that his discovery
of their paintings gave his fiction its distinctive aura. The Shanghai we
encounter in *The Kindness of Women* evokes a gallery full of unknown
masterpieces by Dalí, Magritte, Delvaux and so on. The dead Chinese
lying outside the bombed amusement park are 'covered with white
chalk, through which darker patches had formed, as if they were trying
to camouflage themselves' – an image worthy of De Chirico. Severed
hands are eerily described as 'mislaid'. Chauffeurs ferry the expats to
abandoned battlefields where open coffins protrude 'like drawers in a
ransacked wardrobe', spent rifle shells create 'a roadway covered with
pieces of gold' and dead infantrymen lie in 'drowned trenches, covered
to their waists by the earth, as if asleep in a derelict dormitory'. Forced to
spectate upon such scenes in the company of well-dressed ladies 'fanning
away the flies', Jim gets a nightmarish education in the emotional and
moral disconnects that would define the 20th century.

If the strangeness of Shanghai is meant to foreshadow Auschwitz,
Vietnam and the contextless chaos of modern media, Jim's medical
studies in post-war England tell us a lot about Ballard's values as a
prose-writer. When he begins to dissect a cadaver, a friend warns him:
'You'll have to cut away all the fat before you reach the fascia.' It's an
appropriate metaphor for Ballard's clinical approach to narrative, an

odd mixture of focus and nonchalance. While he liked to set himself apart from oh-so-literary avant-gardists by insisting that he was 'an old-fashioned storyteller at heart', he was impatient with the conventions that had underpinned respectable mainstream fiction since the Victorians. Surrealism's emphasis on the inexplicable and Sci-Fi's tolerance for haphazard characterisation and unnaturalistic dialogue suited his own inclinations, even if some readers might find these things alienating.

It is in the area of physicality – especially sex – that Ballard's style jars most with the conventions of British fiction. It's hard to imagine another English author who could come up with a sentence like 'Her small, detergent-chafed hands, with their smell of lipstick, semen and rectal mucus, ran across my forehead.' Frequent references to penises, labia, pelvises and prostates underscore Jim's contention that 'Gray's Anatomy is a far greater novel than Ulysses.' Even in a chapter that celebrates the miracle of birth and the love between a husband and wife, we see Jim pushing Miriam's prolapsed rectum back into her anus during her uterine contractions. Readers who discover Ballard via the Booker-shortlisted, essentially sexless Empire of the Sun might find such explicitness repellent; indeed, once Ballard was famous, he began to receive letters from disgruntled people who regretted reading his other books. Yet, though Ballard shares William Burroughs' disregard for 'good taste', his focus on the visceral is not a mere shock tactic. Unable to believe in an immortal soul or any of the transcendent mysticism that offers comfort to more 'spiritual' writers, he is unashamedly fascinated by the flesh – every pore, blemish and scar of it. The scenes in The Kindness of Women where Jim dissects the woman's carcass inspire some of Ballard's most tender, most respectful, most reverent writing.

For all his modernity, however, Ballard was formed by the fashions of a previous age; he could never quite shake the values instilled in him by Biggles and Boy's Own. His ambivalent fascination with soldiers, his disdain for the defeatism of the British in Singapore, and his lifelong love affair with fighter planes set him apart from the long-haired peaceniks of later generations. It was not Ballard's date of birth per se that caused this disjunct: Burroughs and Timothy Leary were both much older, but it's impossible to imagine them standing shoulder-to-shoulder with Jim and the RAF 'honour guard' at the funeral of a Spitfire pilot. As this scene from *The Kindness of Women* shows, Ballard could be cynical about many things, but not the tragic dignity of fallen soldiers.

Much of *The Kindness of Women* is set in the 1960s and early 1970s, when Ballard hatched the stories that made his reputation as a social anatomist. His relationship with the times was atypical. Indifferent to music, immune to the charms of psychedelia, and bemused by the idealism of hippies, he felt less enamoured of the 1960s than many of his fellow experimenters. He approved of the shake-up of the class system, and celebrated the rise of the literary counterculture that promoted his work, but in *The Kindness of Women* he chooses to present the sixties as an era driven to psychosis by a steady diet of drugs, assassinations, war trauma and TV. 'The demise of feeling and emotion, the death of affect, presided like a morbid sun over the playground of that ominous decade.'

If society is insane and the world has turned toxic, what hope is there? The kindness of women? Is it through female nurture that Jim (and his author) survives and thrives? So the book's title invites us to think. Closer examination renders that notion dubious: Jim's mother is absent; his sulky nanny is employed merely to mind him; Jim's occasional lover Sally Mumford seems bent on addictive self-destruction; and even his wife Miriam, for all her support, is restless for change, regarding marriage as a 'cul de sac ... a detour from the main road'. In any case, just like Ballard's own wife Mary, she dies suddenly, leaving him to bring up three children on his own. The novel might have been more appropriately titled *The Allure of Closure*. Certainly in the final chapters, the contrived sex scenes in which any remaining significant women from Jim's past pop up to make love to him suggest a last-ditch authorial attempt to bind everything together with artificial dialogue and genital fluids. If any females can truly be said to have rescued Jim (and J. G.), it is, I think, his daughters, who provided their boozy, bereaved dad with all the stability, solace, love and happiness he needed.

Ballard was not an emotionless man and he did not write emotionless fiction. The coolness which many critics have characterised as archetypically 'Ballardian' is not as chilly as it seems. In *The Kindness of Women*, warm feelings – of pity, of passion, of parental love, of fond friendship – course richly beneath the surface of the skin but, like veins that retreat or collapse when a hypodermic needle seeks to penetrate them, they elude the forensic approach of Ballard's pen. *The Kindness of Women* is a curious hybrid, combining – not always successfully – the merciless thematic rigour of his earlier, more fantastical work and a new humanity that dispelled the deviant cyborg of myth. Many years before, when *Crash* was rejected by a publisher whose editorial assistant had branded him 'beyond psychiatric help', Ballard took the comment as encouraging proof that he'd hit a nerve. By 1991, he no longer revelled in such opprobrium.

In truth, Ballard's basic decency was always there, even in his most outrageous tales. He wanted people to grow up well-loved and safe in families like the one he maintained in suburban Shepperton, rather than descending into madness and cannibalism like the trapped hordes in *High-Rise*. It is a measure of how obtuse the guardians of public morality continue to be that Ballard was ever accused of being a nihilistic pervert or a champion of orgasmic car crashes. Like all satirists, he assumed that humans should behave compassionately and morally. Grieved by their failure to do so, he expressed his alarm – not with earnest hand-wringing, but by ushering us straight to a dystopian fait accompli. In short, he shanghaied us.

Us? I have to admit that for me, Ballard's work was an oddly recent discovery. I say 'oddly' because he was so integral to the other cultural phenomena I investigated during my formative years that it's hard to believe I could have passed him by. As a fan of underground comics, I was intimate with Gaetano Liberatore's surreally cruel, visceral dystopias – *Crash* on steroids. I evangelised on behalf of Phoebe Gloeckner, who, in one of the few works of hers I didn't possess, crafted anatomical phantasmagoria for a revised edition of *The Atrocity Exhibition*. I swayed to Throbbing Gristle's 'Hamburger Lady' (pure Ballard in sonic form), chilled out to Paul Schütze's 'Vermillion Sands', and sang along to Hawkwind's 'High Rise'. David Cronenberg was one of my favourite directors. I was hugely impressed by the Industrial Culture handbooks issued by Re/Search in the 1980s, rereading them many times but somehow never getting around to the ones devoted to Ballard.

Looking back on it now, my avoidance is inexplicable. Was I subconsciously worried that his fiction would unduly influence mine? In my own output, the occasional short story like 'Explaining Coconuts' strikes me as intoxicatingly Ballardian and I feel a peculiar pleasure to have explored such territory independently of his lead. But still I feel the poignancy of his absence from my life while he was alive. I would have liked to send him a letter praising him for his uncompromising vision and his often beautiful prose. Maybe this is it.

Fearn by Tain, 2014

PART I

A Season for Assassins

1

Bloody Saturday

Every afternoon in Shanghai during the summer of 1937 I rode down to the Bund to see if the war had begun. As soon as lunch was over I would wait for my mother and father to leave for the Country Club. While they changed into tennis clothes, ambling in a relaxed way around their bedroom, it always amazed me that they were so unconcerned by the coming war, and unaware that it might break out just as my father served his first ball. I remember pacing up and down with all the Napoleonic impatience of a 7-year-old, my toy soldiers drawn up on the carpet like the Japanese and Chinese armies around Shanghai. At times it seemed to me that I was keeping the war alive singlehandedly.

Ignoring my mother's laughter as she flirted with my father, I would watch the sky over Amherst Avenue. At any moment a squadron of Japanese bombers might appear above the department stores of downtown Shanghai and begin to bomb the Cathedral School. My child's mind had no idea how long a war would last, whether a few minutes or even, conceivably, an entire afternoon. My one fear was that, like so many exciting events I always managed to miss, the war would be over before I noticed that it had begun.

Throughout the summer everyone in Shanghai spoke about the coming war between China and Japan. At my mother's bridge parties, as I helped myself to the plates of small chow, I listened to her friends talking about the shots exchanged on July 7 at the Marco Polo bridge in Peking, which had signalled Japan's invasion of northern China. A month had passed without Chiang Kai-shek ordering a counter-attack, and there were rumours that the German advisers to the Generalissimo were urging him to abandon the northern provinces and fight the Japanese nearer his stronghold at Nanking, the capital of China. Slyly, though, Chiang had decided to challenge the Japanese at Shanghai, two hundred miles away at the mouth of the Yangtse, where the American and European powers might intervene to save him.

As I saw for myself whenever I cycled down to the Bund, huge Chinese armies were massing around the International Settlement. On Friday, August 13, as soon as my mother and father settled themselves into the rear seats of the Packard, I wheeled my bicycle out of the garage, pumped up its tyres and set off on the long ride to the Bund. Olga, my White Russian governess, assumed that I was visiting David Hunter, a friend who lived at the western end of Amherst Avenue. A young woman of moods and strange stares, Olga was only interested in trying on my mother's wardrobe and was glad to see me gone.

I reached the Bund an hour later, but the concourse was so crowded with frantic office workers that I could scarcely get near the waterfront landing stages. Ringing my warning bell, I pedalled past the clanking trams, the wheel-locked rickshaws and their exhausted coolies, the gangs of aggressive beggars and pickpockets. Refugees from Chapei and Nantao streamed into the International Settlement, shouting up at the impassive facades of the great banks and trading houses along the Bund. Thousands of Chinese troops were dug into the northern suburbs of Shanghai, facing the Japanese garrison in their concession at Yangtsepoo. Standing on the steps of the Cathay Hotel as the doorman held my cycle, I could see the Whangpoo river filled with warships. There were British destroyers, sloops and gunboats, the USS *Augusta* and a French cruiser, and the veteran Japanese cruiser *Idzumo*, which my father told me had helped to sink the Russian Imperial Fleet in 1905.

Despite this build-up of forces, the war obstinately refused to declare itself that afternoon. Disappointed, I wearily pedalled back to Amherst Avenue, my school blazer scuffed and stained, in time for tea and my favourite radio serial. Hugging my grazed knees, I stared at my armies of lead soldiers, and adjusted their lines to take account of the latest troop movements that I had seen as I rode home. Ignoring Olga's calls, I tried to work out a plan that would break the stalemate, hoping that my father, who knew one of the Chinese bankers behind Chiang Kai-shek, would pass on my muddled brain-wave to the Generalissimo.

Baffled by all these problems, which were even more difficult than my French homework, I wandered into my parents' bedroom. Olga was standing in front of my mother's full-length mirror, a fur cape over her shoulders. I sat at the dressing-table and rearranged the hair-brushes and perfume bottles, while Olga frowned at me through the glass as if I were an uninvited visitor who had strayed from another of the houses in Amherst Avenue. I had told my mother that Olga played with her wardrobe, but she merely smiled at me and said nothing to Olga.

Later I realised that this 17-year-old daughter of a once well-to-do Minsk family was scarcely more than a child herself. On my cycle rides I had been shocked by the poverty of the White Russian and Jewish refugees who lived in the tenement districts of Hongkew. It was one thing for the Chinese to be poor, but it disturbed me to see Europeans reduced to such a threadbare state. In their faces there was a staring despair that the Chinese never showed. Once, when I cycled past a dark tenement doorway, an old Russian woman told me to go away and shouted that my mother and father were thieves. For a few days I had believed her.

The refugees stood in their patched fur coats on the steps of the Park Hotel, hoping to sell their old-fashioned jewellery. The younger women had painted their mouths and eyes, trying bravely to cheer themselves up, I guessed. They called to the American and British officers going into the hotel, but what they were selling my mother had never been able to say – they were giving French and Russian lessons, she told me at last.

Always worried by my homework, and aware that many of the White Russians spoke excellent French, I had asked Olga if she would give me a French lesson like the young women at the Park Hotel. She sat on the bed while I hunted through my pocket dictionary, shaking her head as if I were some strange creature at a zoo. Worried that I had hurt her feelings by referring to her family's poverty, I gave Olga one of my silk shirts, and asked her to pass it on to her invalid father. She had held it in her hands for fully five minutes, like one of the vestments used in the communion services at Shanghai Cathedral, before returning it silently to my wardrobe. Already I had noticed that the White Russian governesses possessed a depth of female mystery that the mothers of my friends never remotely approached.

'Yes, James?' Olga hung the fur cape on its rack, and slipped my mother's breakfast gown over her shoulders. 'Have you finished your holiday book? You're very restless today.'

'I'm thinking about the war, Olga.'

'You're thinking about it every day, James. You and General Chiang think about it all the time. I'm sure he would like to meet you.'

'Well, I could meet him ...' As it happened, I did sometimes feel that the Generalissimo was not giving his fullest attention to the war. 'Olga, do you know when the war will begin?'

'Hasn't it already begun? That's what everyone says.'

'Not the real war, Olga. The war in Shanghai.'

'Is that the real war? Nothing is real in Shanghai, James. Why don't you ask your father?'

'He doesn't know. I asked him after breakfast.'

'That's a pity. Are there many things he doesn't know?'

Still wearing the breakfast robe, Olga sat on my father's bed, her hand stroking the satin cover and smoothing away the creases. She was caressing the imprint of my father's shoulders, and for a moment I wondered if she was going to slip between the sheets.

'He does know many things, but ...'

'I can remind you, James, it's Friday the 13th. Is that a good day for starting a war?'

'Hey, Olga ...!' This news brightened everything. I rushed to the window – superstitions, I often noticed, had a habit of coming true. 'I'll tell you if I see anything.'

Olga stood behind me, calming me with a hand on my ear. Much as she loved the intimacy of my mother's clothes and the ripe odour of my father's riding jacket, she rarely touched me. She stared at the distant skyline along the Bund. Smoke rose from the coal-burning boilers of the older naval vessels. The black columns jostled for space as the warships changed their moorings, facing up to each other with sirens blasting. The darker light gave Olga's face the strong-nosed severity of the mortuary statues I had seen in Shanghai cemetery. She lifted the breakfast robe, staring through the veil of its fine fabric as if seeing a dream of vanished imperial Russia.

'Yes, James, I think they'll start the war for you today ...'

'Say, thanks, Olga.'

But before the war could start, my mother and father returned unexpectedly from the Country Club. With them were two British officers in the Shanghai Volunteer Force, wearing their tight Great War uniforms. I tried to join them in my father's study, but my mother took me into the garden and in a strained way pointed to the golden orioles drinking from the edge of the swimming pool.

I was sorry to see her worried, as I knew that my mother, unlike Olga, was one of those people who should never be worried by anything. Trying not to annoy her, I spent the rest of the afternoon in my play-room. I listened to the sirens of the battle-fleets and marshalled my toy soldiers. On the next day, Bloody Saturday as it would be known, my miniature army at last came to life.

I remember the wet monsoon that blew through Shanghai during that last night of the peace, drowning the sounds of Chinese sniper fire, and the distant boom of Japanese naval guns striking at the Chinese shore batteries at Woosung. When I woke into the warm, sticky air the storm had passed, and the washed neon signs of the city shone ever more vividly.

At breakfast my mother and father were already dressed in their golfing clothes, though when they left in the Packard a few minutes later my father was at the wheel, the chauffeur beside him, and they had not taken their golf clubs.

'Jamie, you're to stay home today,' my father announced, staring through my eyes as he did when he had unfathomable reasons of his own. 'You can finish your *Robinson Crusoe*.'

'You'll meet Man Friday and the cannibals.' My mother smiled at this treat in store, but her eyes were as flat as they had been when our spaniel was run over by the German doctor in Columbia Road. I wondered if Olga had died during the night, but she was watching from the door, pressing the lapels of her dressing gown to her neck.

'I've already met the cannibals.' However exciting, Crusoe's shipwreck palled by comparison with the real naval disaster about to take place on the Whangpoo river. 'Can we go to the Tattoo? David Hunter's going next week ...'

The Military Tattoo staged by soldiers of the British garrison was filled with booming cannon, thunderflashes and bayonet charges, and recreated the bravest clashes of the Great War, the battles of Mons, Ypres and the Gallipoli landings. In a sense, the make-believe of the Tattoo might be as close as I would ever get to a real war.

'Jamie, we'll see – they may have to cancel the Tattoo. The soldiers are very busy.'

'I know. Then can we go to the Hell-drivers?' This was a troupe of American dare-devil drivers, who crashed their battered Fords and Chevrolets through wooden barricades covered with flaming gasoline. The sight of these thrillingly rehearsed accidents for ever eclipsed the humdrum street crashes of Shanghai. 'You promised ...'

'The Hell-drivers aren't here any more. They've gone back to Manila.'

'They're getting ready for the war.' In my mind I could see these laconic Americans, in their dashing goggles and aviator's suits, crashing through the flaming walls as they answered a salvo from the *Idzumo*. 'Can I come to the golf club?'

'No! Stay here with Olga! I won't tell you again ...' My father's voice had an edge of temper that I had noticed since the labour troubles at his cotton mill in Pootung, on the east bank of the river. I wondered why Olga watched him so closely when he was angry. Her toneless eyes showed a rare and almost hungry alertness, the expression I felt on my face when I was about to tuck into an ice-cream sundae. One of the communist union organisers who threatened to kill my father had stared at him in the same way as we sat in the Packard outside his office in the Szechuan Road. I worried that Olga wanted to kill my father and eat him.

'Do I have to? Olga listens all the time to French dance music.'

'Well, you listen with her,' my mother rejoined. 'Olga can teach you how to dance.'

This was a prospect I dreaded, an even greater torture than the promise of unending peace. When Olga touched me, it was in a distant but oddly intimate way. As I lay in bed at night she would sometimes undress in my bathroom with the door ajar. Later I guessed that this was her way of proving to herself that I no longer existed. As soon as my parents left for the golf club my one intention was to give her the slip.

'David said that Olga—'

'All right!' Irritated by the ringing telephone, which the servants were too nervous to answer, my father relented. 'You can see David Hunter. But don't go anywhere else.'

Why was he frightened of Shanghai? Despite his quick temper, my father easily gave in, as if events in the world were so uncertain that even my childish nagging carried weight. He was too distracted to play with my toy soldiers, and he often looked at me in the same firm but dejected way in which the headmaster of the Cathedral School gazed at the assembled boys during morning prayers. When he walked to the car he stamped his spiked golf shoes, leaving deep marks in the gravel, like footprints staking a claim to Crusoe's beach.

Even before the Packard had left the drive, Olga was reclining on the verandah with my mother's copies of *Vogue* and the *Saturday Evening Post*. At intervals she called out to me, her voice as remote as the sirens on the river buoys at Woosung. I guessed that she knew about my afternoon cycle rides around Shanghai. She was well aware that I might be kidnapped or robbed of my clothes in one of the back alleys of the Bubbling Well Road. Perhaps the terrors of the Russian civil war, the long journey with her parents through Turkey and Iraq to this rootless city at the mouth of the Yangtse, had so disoriented her that she no longer cared if the child in her charge was killed.

'Who did your father let you see, James?'

'David Hunter. He's my closest friend. I'm going now, Olga.'

'You have so many closest friends. Tell me if the war begins, James.'

She waved, and I was gone. In fact, the last person in Shanghai I wanted to see was David. During the summer holidays my schoolfriends and I played homeric games of hide-and-seek that lasted for weeks and covered the whole of Shanghai. As I drove with my mother to the Country Club or drank iced tea in the Chocolate Shop I was constantly watching for David, who might break away from his amah and lunge through the crowd to tap me on the shoulder. These games added another layer of strangeness and surprise to a city already too strange.

I wheeled my cycle from the garage, buttoned my blazer and set off down the drive. Legs whirling like the blades of an eggbeater, I swerved into Amherst Avenue and overtook a column of peasants trudging through the western suburbs of the city. Refugees from the countryside now occupied by the Chinese and Japanese armies, they plodded past the great houses of the avenue, their few possessions on their backs. They laboured towards the distant towers of downtown Shanghai, unaware of everything but the hard asphalt in front of them, ignoring the chromium bumpers and blaring horns of the Buicks and Chryslers whose Chinese chauffeurs were trying to force them off the road.

Standing on my pedals, I edged past a rickshaw loaded with bales of matting, on which perched two old women clutching the walls and roof of a dismantled hovel. I could smell their bodies, crippled by a lifetime of heavy manual work, and the same rancid sweat and hungry breath of all impoverished peasants. But the night's rain still soaked their black cotton tunics, which gleamed in the sunlight like the rarest silks on the fabric counters in the Sun Sun department store, as if the magic of Shanghai had already begun to transform these destitute people.

What would happen to them? My mother was studiously vague about the refugees, but Olga told me in her matter-of-fact way that most of them soon died of hunger or typhus in the alleys of Chapei. Every morning on my way to school I passed the trucks of the Shanghai Municipal Authority that toured the city, collecting the hundreds of bodies of Chinese who had died during the night. I liked to think that only the old people died, though I had seen a dead boy of my own age sitting against the steel entrance grille of my father's office block. He held an empty cigarette tin in his white hands, probably the last gift to him from his family before they abandoned him. I hoped that the others became bar-tenders and waiters and Number 3 girls at the

Great World Amusement Park, and my mother said that she hoped so too.

Putting aside these thoughts, and cheered by the day ahead, I reached the Avenue Joffre and the long tree-lined boulevards of the French Concession that would carry me to the Bund. Quick-tempered French soldiers guarded the sand-bagged checkpoint by the tramline terminus. They stared warily at the empty sky and spat at the feet of the passing Chinese, hating this ugly city to which they had been exiled across the world. But I felt a surge of excitement on entering Shanghai. To my child's eyes, which had seen nothing else, Shanghai was a waking dream where everything I could imagine had already been taken to its extreme. The garish billboards and nightclub neon signs, the young Chinese gangsters and violent beggars watching me keenly as I pedalled past them, were part of an overlit realm more exhilarating than the American comics and radio serials I so adored.

Shanghai would absorb everything, even the coming war, however fiercely the smoke might pump from the warships in the Whangpoo river. My father called Shanghai the most advanced city in the world, and I knew that one day all the cities on the planet would be filled with radio-stations, hell-drivers and casinos. Outside the Canidrome the crowds of Chinese and Europeans were pushing their way into the greyhound arena, unconcerned by the Kuomintang armies around the city waiting to attack the Japanese garrison. Gamblers jostled each other by the betting booths of the jai alai stadium, and the morning audience packed the entrance of the Grand Theatre on the Nanking Road, eager to see the latest Hollywood musical, *Gold-Diggers of 1937*.

But of all the places of wonder, the Great World Amusement Park on the Avenue Edward VII most amazed me, and contained the magnetic heart of Shanghai within its six floors. Unknown to my parents, the chauffeur often took me into its dirty and feverish caverns. After collecting me from school, Yang would usually stop the car outside the Amusement Park and carry out one or other of the mysterious errands that occupied a large part of his day.

A vast warehouse of light and noise, the Amusement Park was filled with magicians and fireworks, slot machines and sing-song girls. A haze of frying fat gleamed in the air, and formed a greasy film on my face, mingling with the smell of joss-sticks and incense. Stunned by the din, I would follow Yang as he slipped through the acrobats and Chinese actors striking their gongs. Medicine hawkers lanced the necks of huge white geese, selling the cups of steaming blood to passers-by as the ferocious birds stamped their feet and gobbled at me when I came too close. While Yang murmured into the ears of the mahjong dealers and marriage brokers, I peered between his legs at the exposed toilets in the lavatory stalls and at the fearsome idols scowling over the temple doorways, at the mysterious peep-shows and massage booths with their elegant Chinese girls, infinitely more terrifying than Olga, in embroidered high-collared robes slit to expose their thighs.

This Saturday, however, the Great World was closed. The dance platforms, dried-fish stalls and love-letter booths had been dismantled, and the municipal authorities had turned the ancient building into a refugee camp. Hundreds of frantic Chinese were forcing their way into the ramshackle structure, held back by a cordon of Sikh police in sweat-stained khaki turbans. Like a team of carpet-beaters, the Sikhs lashed at the broken-toothed peasant farmers with their heavy bamboo staves. A burly British police sergeant waved his service revolver at the monkey-like old women with bound feet who tried to push past him, their callused fists punching his chest.

I stood on the opposite sidewalk, listening to the sirens sounding from the river, a great moaning of blind beasts challenging each other. For the first time I guessed that war of a kind had already come to Shanghai. Buffeted by the Chinese office clerks, I steered my cycle along the gutter, and squeezed past an armoured riot van of the Shanghai Police, with its twin-handled Thompson machine-gun mounted above the driver's cabin.

Breathless, I rested in the doorway of a funeral parlour. The elderly undertaker sat among the coffins at the rear of the shop, white fingers flicking at the beads of his abacus. The clicks echoed among the empty coffins, and reminded me of the superstition that Yang had graphically described, snapping his fingers in front of my nose. 'When a coffin cracks, the Chinese undertaker knows he will sell it ...'

I listened to the abacus, trying to see if the coffins gave a twitch when they cracked. Soon a lot of coffins in Shanghai would be cracking. The old man's fingers flicked faster as he watched me with his vain, dreamy eyes. Was he adding up all those who were going to die in Shanghai, trying to reach my own number, somewhere among the cracking coffins and clicking beads?

Behind me a car horn blared into the crowd. A white Lincoln Zephyr was forcing its way through the traffic, hemmed in by the rickshaw coolies and refugees clambering into the entrance of the Amusement Park. David Hunter knelt on the rear seat beside his Australian nanny, blond hair in his eyes as he squinted at the pavement. Forgetting the coffins and the clicking abacus, I pushed my cycle along the gutter, aware that David would see me once the traffic had cleared.

An air-raid klaxon sounded from one of the office buildings, overlaid by a heavy, sustained rumble like a collapsing sky. A shouting coolie strode towards me, bales of firewood on a bamboo pole across his shoulders, from which the veins stood out like bloated worms. Without pausing, he kicked the cycle out of my hands. I bent down to rub my bruised knees, and tried to reach the handlebars, but the rush of feet knocked me to the ground. Winded, I lay among the old lottery tickets, torn newspapers and straw sandals as the white Lincoln cruised past. Playing with his blond fringe behind the passenger window, David frowned at me in his pointy way, unable to recognise me but puzzled why an English boy in a Cathedral School blazer had chosen this of all moments to roll about in a filthy gutter.

The klaxon wailed, keening at the sky. Chinese office workers, women clerks and hotel waiters were running down the Nanking Road from the Bund. An immense cloud of white steam rose from the Whangpoo river behind them, flashes of gunfire reflected in its lower surface. Around it circled three twin-engined bombing planes, banking as they flew through its ashen billows.

A squadron of Chinese aircraft were bombing the *Idzumo* and the Japanese cotton-mills at Yangtsepoo, little more than a mile from the Bund across the Garden Bridge. The boom of heavy guns jarred the windows of the office buildings in the Thibet Road. A tram clanked past me towards the Bund, its passengers leaping into the road. High above them, on the roof of the Socony-Vacuum building, stood a party of unconcerned Europeans in white tennis clothes, binoculars in hand, pointing out details of the spectacle to each other.

Had the war really started? I was expecting something as organised and disciplined as the Military Tattoo. The planes lumbered through the air, as if the pilots were bored by their targets and were circling the *Idzumo* simply to fill in time before returning to their airfield. The French and British warships sat at their moorings near the Pootung shore, signal lights blinking softly from their bridges, a vaguely curious commentary on the bombing display down-river.

Mounting my cycle, I straightened the handlebars and brushed the dust from my blazer – the officious junior masters at the school liked to roam the city in their spare time, reporting anyone untidily dressed. I set off after the empty tram, steering between the polished rails. When it neared the Bund the conductor dismounted, swearing at the driver and waving his leather cash bag. The tram's warning bell clanged at the empty street, watched by groups of Chinese clerks pressing themselves into the doorways of the office buildings.

A water-spout rose from the choppy waves beside the bows of the *Idzumo*, hovered for a second and then surged upwards in a violent cascade. Arms of hurtling foam punched through the air and soared high above the radio aerials and mast-tops of the ancient cruiser. A second squadron of Chinese bombers swept in formation down the Whangpoo, midway between the Bund and the Pootung shore, where my father's cotton mill lay behind a veil of greasy smoke. One of the planes lagged behind the others, the pilot unable to keep his place in the formation. He rolled his wings from side to side, like the stunt pilots at the aerobatic displays at Hungjao Airfield.

'Jamie, leave your bike! Come with us!'

The white fenders of the Lincoln Zephyr had crept behind me. David's Australian nanny was shouting to me, her arms stretched across the shoulders of the nervous Chinese chauffeur. Steadying her straw hat with one hand, she waved me towards the car. Nurse Arnold had always been easy-going and friendly, so much more pleasant to me than Olga, and I was surprised by her bad temper. David had recognised me, a gleam of triumph in his eyes. He brushed the blond hair from his forehead, aware that he was about to make the first capture of our marathon game of hide-and-seek.

The *Idzumo* was laying smoke around itself. Scrolls of oily vapour uncoiled along its bows. Through the sooty clouds I could see the tremble of anti-aircraft fire, the sounds lost in the monotonous drone of the Chinese bombers.

'Jamie, you stupid …!'

I pedalled away from them into a wall of noise and smoke. Glass was falling from the windows of my father's building in Szechuan Road. Office girls darted from the doorways, their white blouses speckled with fine needles. My front wheel jolted over a piece of masonry shaken loose from a cornice. While I straightened the pedals a low-flying bomber veered away from the Japanese anti-aircraft fire. It flew above the Bund, exposed its open bombing racks and released two bombs towards the empty sampans moored to the quay.

Eager to watch the water-spouts, I mounted my cycle, but a pair of powerful hands gripped my armpits. A uniformed British police sergeant whirled me off my feet. He kicked away my cycle and crouched by the steps of the Socony building. As he held me against his hip the metal hammer of his revolver tore the skin from my knee.

Exploding debris burst between the hotels and department stores of the Nanking Road and filled the street with white ash. A wave of burning air struck my chest and threw me to the ground beside the sergeant. Chinese office workers with raised hands ran towards us through the billows of dust, blood streaming from their foreheads. One of the stray bombs had fallen into the Palace Hotel, and the other into the Avenue Edward VII beside the Great World Amusement Park. The buildings in the Szechuan Road rocked around us, shaking a cascade of broken glass and roofing tiles into the street.

Beside the kerb a matronly Eurasian woman stepped from her car, blood running from her ear. She touched it discreetly with a silk hand-kerchief as the police sergeant propelled me towards her.

'Keep him here!' He jerked my shoulders, as if I were a sleeping doll, and he were trying to wake me. 'Lad, you stay with her!'

When he ran towards the Nanking Road the Eurasian woman released my hand, waving me away and too distracted to be bothered with me. Blood seeped down my leg, staining my white socks. Looking at the thin trickle, I noticed that I had lost one of my shoes. My head felt empty, and I touched my face to make sure that it was still there. The explosion had sucked all the air from the street and it was difficult to breathe. Gesturing to me in an absent way, the Eurasian woman wandered through the debris, wiping the dust from her leather handbag. The blood ran from her ear as she stared at the broken glass, trying to recognise the windows of her own apartment.

Far away, police sirens had begun to wail, and an ambulance of the Shanghai Volunteer Force drove past, the glass spitting under its tyres. I realised that I was deaf, but everything around me was deaf too, as if the world could no longer hear itself. Two hundred yards from the Great World Amusement Park I could see that most of the building had vanished. Smoke rose from its exposed floors, and an arcing electric cable sparked and jumped like a swaying firecracker.

Hundreds of dead Chinese were lying in the street among the crushed rickshaws and burnt-out cars. Their bodies were covered with white chalk, through which darker patches had formed, as if they were trying to camouflage themselves. I walked among them, tripping over an old amah who lay on her back, pouting face covered with powder, scolding me with her last grimace. An office clerk without his arms sat against the rear wheel of a gutted bus. Everywhere hands and feet lay among the debris of the Amusement Park – fragments of joss sticks and playing cards, gramophone records and dragon masks, part of the head of a stuffed whale, all blanched by the dust. A bolt of silk had unravelled across the street, a white bandage that wound around the lumps of masonry and the mislaid hands.

I waited for someone to call to me, but the air was silent and ringing, like the pause after an unanswered alarm. I could no longer hear my feet as they cracked the blades of broken glass. I walked back to the Hunters' Lincoln Zephyr. The chauffeur stood in his pallid uniform by the open driver's door, brushing away the dust that covered the windshield. David sat alone in the back, hands pressed to his mouth.

He ignored me and stared at the torn seat-cover with fixed eyes, as if he never wanted to see me again.

I looked through the broken windows at Nurse Arnold, who was lying across the front seat. Her hair fell across her face, forced by the explosion into her mouth. Her hands were open, white palms exposed, displaying to any passer-by that she had washed them carefully before she died.

Later, when he visited me in Shanghai General Hospital, David asked me about the blood on my leg. Curiously, this was the only blood that he had seen on Bloody Saturday.

'I was wounded by the bomb,' I told him.

I had begun to boast in a small way, but more truthfully than I realised. One thousand and twelve people, almost all Chinese refugees, were killed by the high-explosive bomb that fell beside the Great World Amusement Park. As everyone constantly repeated, proud that Shanghai had again excelled itself, this was the largest number killed by a single bomb in the history of aerial warfare. My own trivial injury, caused by the police sergeant's revolver, numbered me among the thousand and seven who were wounded. Although not the youngest of those injured, I liked to think that I was No. 1007, which I firmly inked on my arm.

Months of fierce fighting took place around the International Settlement before the Japanese were able to drive the Chinese from Shanghai, during which tens of thousands of soldiers and civilians were to perish. But the Avenue Edward VII bomb, dropped in error by a Chinese pilot, had a special place in the mythology of war, a potent example of how mass death could now fall from the air.

At the time, as I rested in my bed at Shanghai General, I was thinking not of the bomb beside the Amusement Park, but of my army of toy soldiers on the floor of my playroom. Even as the rescue workers of the Shanghai Volunteer Force carried me to their ambulance through the dusty streets I knew that I needed to rearrange their battle lines. I had seen the real war for which I had waited so impatiently, and I felt vaguely guilty that there were no models of dead Chinese in my boxes of brightly painted soldiers. Now and then my ears would clear for a brief moment, and the eerie sounds of Japanese artillery drumming at the hospital window seemed to call to me from another world.

Within a few days, however, my memories of the bombing had begun to fade. I tried to remember the dust and debris in the Szechuan Road, but the confused images in my head had merged with the newsreels I had seen of the Spanish civil war and the filmed manoeuvres of the French and British armies. The fighting in the western suburbs of Shanghai veiled the window with curtains of smoke which the autumn winds drew aside to reveal the burning tenements of Nantao. The nurses and doctors who tested my ears with their tuning forks, Olga and my school-friends, my mother and father on their evening visits, were like actors in the old silent films that David Hunter's father screened for us against his dining-room wall. The bomb that destroyed the Amusement Park and killed more than a thousand people had become part of those films.

It was three months before I could go back to Amherst Avenue. Artillery shells from the rival Chinese and Japanese howitzers at Siccawei station and Hungjao were passing over the roof of our house, and my mother and father had moved to an apartment in the French Concession. The battle for Shanghai continued around the perimeter of the International Settlement, shaking the doors of our apartment and often jamming the elevator. Once Olga and I were trapped for an hour in the metal cage. She, who was usually so silent, spent the time delivering a torrent of words at me, well aware that I could hear not a single one. I often wondered if she was accusing me of starting the war, though in Olga's eyes that would have been the least of my crimes.

In November the Chinese armies began to withdraw from Shanghai, retreating up the Yangtse to Nanking. They left behind them the devastated suburbs, which the Japanese occupied, ringing the International Settlement with their tanks and machine-gun posts. We were then safe to return to Amherst Avenue. While my parents talked to the servants I ran up to my playroom, eager to see my army of toy soldiers again.

The miniature battle of Shanghai had been swept aside. Broken soldiers lay scattered among my train set and model cars. Someone, perhaps Coolie or Number 2 Boy, had used my *Robinson Crusoe* as an ash tray, stubbing his half-smoked cigarettes into the cover as he watched nervously from the windows. I thought of reporting him to my father, but I knew that the servants had been as frightened as I was.

I gathered the soldiers together and later tried to play with them, but the games seemed more serious than those that had filled the playroom floor before Bloody Saturday. When David and I set out our rival armies it worried me that we were secretly trying to kill each other. Thinking of the severed hands and feet I had seen outside the Amusement Park, I put the soldiers away in their box.

But at Christmas there were new sets of soldiers to take their place, Seaforth Highlanders in khaki battle-kilts and Coldstream Guards in bearskins. To my surprise, life in the International Settlement was unaffected by the months of fighting around the city, as if the bitter warfare had been little more than a peripheral entertainment of a particularly brutal kind, like the public strangulations in the Old City. The neon signs shone ever more brightly over Shanghai's four hundred nightclubs. My father played cricket at the Country Club, while my mother organised her bridge and dinner parties. I served as a page at a lavish wedding at the French Club. The Bund was crowded with trading vessels and sampans loaded with miles of brightly patterned calico which my father's printing and finishing works produced for the elegant Chinese women who thronged the Settlement. The great import-export houses of the Szechuan Road were busier than before. The radio stations broadcast their American adventure serials, the bars and dance halls were filled with Number 2 and Number 3 girls, and the British garrison staged its Military Tattoo. Even the Hell-drivers returned from Manila to crash their cars. While the distant war between Japan and Chiang Kai-shek continued in the hinterland of China the roulette wheels turned in the casinos, spinning their dreams of old Shanghai.

As if to remind themselves of the war, one Sunday afternoon my parents and their friends drove out to tour the battlegrounds in the countryside to the west of Shanghai. We had attended a reception given by the British Consul General, and the wives wore their best silk gowns, the husbands their smartest grey suits and panamas. When our convoy of cars stopped at the Keswick Road check-point I was waiting for the shabby Japanese soldiers to turn us back, but they beckoned us through without comment, as if we were worth scarcely a glance.

Three miles into the countryside we stopped on a deserted road. I remember the battlefield under the silent sky, and the burnt-out village near a derelict canal. The chauffeurs opened the doors, and we stepped on to a roadway covered with pieces of gold. Hundreds of spent rifle cartridges lay at our feet. Abandoned trenchworks ran between the burial mounds, from which open coffins protruded like drawers in a ransacked wardrobe. Scattered around us were remnants of torn webbing, empty ammunition boxes, boots and helmets, rusting bayonets and signal flares. Beyond rifle pits filled with water was an earth redoubt, pulverised by the Japanese artillery. The carcase of a horse lay by its gun emplacement, legs raised stiffly in the sunlight.

Together we gazed at this scene, the ladies fanning away the flies, their husbands murmuring to each other, like a group of investors visiting the stage-set of an uncompleted war film. Led by my father and Mr Hunter, we strolled towards the canal, and stared at the Chinese soldiers floating in the shallow water. Dead infantrymen lay everywhere in the drowned trenches, covered to their waists by the earth, as if asleep in a derelict dormitory.

Beside me, David was tittering to himself. He was impatient to go home, and I could see his jarred eyes hidden behind his fringe. He turned his back on his mother, but the dead battlefield surrounded him on every side. Deliberately scuffing his polished shoes, he kicked the cartridge cases at the sleeping soldiers.

I cupped my hands over my ears, trying to catch the sound that would wake them.

2

Escape Attempts

All day rumours had swept Lunghua that there would soon be an escape from the camp. Shivering on the steps of the children's hut, I waited for Sergeant Nagata to complete the third of the day's emergency roll-calls. Usually, at the first hint of an escape attempt, the Japanese sentries would close the gates with a set of heavy padlocks – a symbolic gesture, as David Hunter's father remarked, since anyone planning to escape from Lunghua hardly intended to walk through the front gates. It was far easier to step through the perimeter wire, as I and the older children did every day, hunting for a lost tennis ball or setting useless bird-traps for the American sailors.

Symbolic or not, the gesture served a practical purpose, like so much of Japanese ceremony. Closing the gates was a sign to any Chinese collaborators in the surrounding countryside that a security alert was under way, and told the few informers within the camp – always the last to know what was going on – to keep their eyes open.

However, the gates hung slackly from their rotting posts, and the sentries stamped their ragged boots on the cold earth, even more bored than ever. Almost all the Japanese soldiers, like Private Kimura, were the sons of peasant farmers, so poor that they regarded Lunghua, with its two thousand prisoners and its unlimited stocks of cricket bats and tennis rackets, as a haven of affluence. The unheated cement dormitories at least received an erratic supply of electric power, an unimagined luxury for the Japanese peasant.

I whistled through my fingers, trying to attract Kimura's attention, but he ignored me and gazed at the Chinese beggars waiting patiently outside the gates for the scraps that never came. As if depressed by the untended paddy-fields, Kimura frowned at the steam that rose from his broad nostrils. I imagined him thinking of his mother and father tending their modest crops in a remote corner of Hokkaido. Neither of us had seen our parents during the years of the war, though in many ways Kimura was more alone than I was. In the panic after the Japanese seizure of the International Settlement I had been separated from my mother and father when we left our hotel on the Bund. Nonetheless, I was confident that I would see them again, even if their faces had begun to fade in my mind. But Kimura would almost certainly die here, among these empty rice fields, when the Japanese made their last stand against the Americans at the mouth of the Yangtse.

I lined my fingers on his shaven head, as if aiming Sergeant Nagata's Mauser pistol, and snapped my thumb.

'Jamie, I heard that.' A tall, 14-year-old English girl, Peggy Gardner, joined me at the doorway, her thin shoulders hunched against the cold. She nudged me with a bony elbow, as if to make me miss my aim. 'Who did you shoot?'

'Private Kimura.'

'You shot him yesterday.' Peggy shook her head over this, her face grave but forgiving, a favourite pose. 'Private Kimura is your friend.'

'I shoot my friends too.' Friends, surprisingly, made even more tempting targets than enemies. 'Besides, Private Kimura isn't really my friend.'

'Not half. Mrs Dwight thinks you're an informer. Why do you have to shoot everyone?'

Sergeant Nagata emerged from D Block, scowling over his roster board, the British block commander behind him. Peggy pushed me against the door and forced my hands into my back. Glaring suspiciously at every blade of grass, Sergeant Nagata would not appreciate serving as my practice target. I leaned against Peggy, glad to feel her strong wrists and smell the cold, reassuring scent of her body. She was always trying to wrestle with me, for reasons I was not yet ready to explore.

'Why, Jamie? You've shot everyone in Lunghua by now. Is it because you want to be alone here?'

'I haven't shot Mrs Dwight.' This busybodying missionary was one of the English widows who supervised the eight boys and girls in the children's hut, all war-orphans separated from parents interned in the other camps near Shanghai and Nanking. Rather than make sure that we had our fair share of the falling food ration, Mrs Dwight was concerned for our spiritual welfare, as I heard her explain to the mystified camp commandant, Mr Hyashi. For Mrs Dwight this chiefly involved my sitting silently in the freezing hut over my Latin homework – anything rather than the restless errand-running and food-scavenging that occupied every moment of my day. To Mrs Dwight I was a 'free soul', a term that contained not a hint of approval. Spiritual well-being seemed to be inversely proportional to the amount of food one received, which perhaps explained why Mrs Dwight and the other missionaries considered their pre-war activities in the famine-ridden provinces of northern China such a marked success.

'When the war's over,' I said darkly, 'I'll ask my father to shoot Mrs Dwight with a real gun. He dislikes missionaries, you know.'

'Jamie …!' Peggy tried to box my ears. A doctor's daughter from Tsingtao, she was a year older than me and pretended to be easily shocked. As I knew, she was far more protective than Mrs Dwight. When I was ill it was Peggy who had looked after me, giving me some of the younger children's food. One day I would repay her. She ruled the children's hut in a firm but high-minded way, and I was her greatest challenge. I liked to keep up a steady flow of small outrages, but recently I had noticed Peggy's depressing tendency to imitate Mrs Dwight, modelling herself on this starchy widow as if she needed the approval of an older woman. I preferred the strong-willed girl who stood up to the boys in her class, rescued the younger children from bullies, and had a certain thin-hipped stylishness with which I had still to come to terms.

'If your father's going to shoot anyone,' Peggy remarked, 'he should start with Dr Sinclair.' This vile-tempered clergyman was the headmaster of the camp school. 'He's worse than Sergeant Nagata.'

'Peggy …?' I felt a rush of concern for her. 'Did he hit you?'

'He nearly tried. He always looks at me in that smiley way. As if I was his daughter and he needed to punish me.'

Only that afternoon one of the ten-year-olds had come back to the hut with a stinging red forehead. Our real education at the Lunghua school came from learning to read Dr Sinclair's moods.

'Did you tell Mrs Dwight?'

'She wouldn't listen. Just because they're kind to us, they think they can do anything. She's more frightened of him than I am.'

'He doesn't hit everybody.'

'He'll hit you one day.'

'I won't let him.' This was idle talk, and my next Latin class could prove me wrong. But so far I had avoided the clergyman's heavy hands. I had noticed that Dr Sinclair left alone the children of the more well-to-do British parents. He never hit David Hunter, however much David tried to provoke him, and only cuffed the sons of factory foremen, Eurasian mothers or officers in the Shanghai Police. What I could never understand was why the parents failed to protest when their children returned to their rooms in G Block with ears bleeding from the clergyman's signet ring. It was almost as if the parents accepted this reminder of their lowly position in Shanghai's British community.

Bored with it all, and deciding to show off in front of Peggy, I picked up a stone from the step and hurled it high into the air over the parade ground.

'Jamie, you're in trouble! Sergeant Nagata saw that ...'

I froze against the door. The sergeant was standing on the gravel path twenty feet from the children's hut. As he stared at me he filled his lungs, his face bearing the weight of some slow but vast emotion. However complicated the British at Lunghua seemed to me, there was no doubt that Sergeant Nagata found them infinitely more mysterious, a stiff-necked people whose armies in Singapore had surrendered without a fight but nonetheless acted as if they had won the war. For some reason he kept a close watch on me, as if I were a key to this conundrum.

Why he should have marked out one 13-year-old boy among the two hundred children I never discovered. Did he think I was trying to escape, or serving as a secret courier between the dormitory blocks? In fact, most of the adults in the camp shied away from me when I loomed up to them, eager to play blindfold chess or offer my views on the progress of the war and the latest Japanese aerial tactics. My nerveless energy soon tired them and, besides, I was forever looking to the future. No one knew when the war would end – perhaps in 1947 or even 1948 – and the internees coped with the endless time by erasing it from their lives. The busy programme of lectures and concert parties of the first year had been abandoned. The internees rested in their cubicles, reading their last letters from England, roused briefly by the iron wheels of the food carts. Mrs Dwight was not the only one to see the dangers of an overactive imagination.

'Jamie, look out …' Mischievously, Peggy pushed me through the doorway. I stumbled on to the gravel, but Sergeant Nagata had more pressing matters on his mind than a head-count of the war children. Slapping his roster-board, he led his entourage back to the guard-house. I was sorry to see him go – I enjoyed squaring up to Sergeant Nagata. There was something about the Japanese, their seriousness and stoicism, that I admired. One day I might join the Japanese Air Force, just as my other heroes, the American Flying Tigers, had flown for Chiang Kai-shek.

'Why isn't he coming?' Disappointed, Peggy shivered in her patched cardigan. 'You could have escaped – think what Mrs Dwight would say. She'd have you banished.'

'I am banished.' Not sure what this meant, I added: 'There might be an escape tonight.'

'Who said? Are you going with them?'

'Basie and Demarest told me.' The American merchant seamen were a fund of inaccurate information, much of it deliberately propagated. As it happened, escape could not have been further from my mind. My parents were interned at Soochow, far too dangerous a distance to walk, and the British in charge might not let me in. They were terrified of being infected with typhus or cholera by prisoners transferred from other camps.

'I would have gone with them, but Basie's wrong.' I pointed to the guard-house, where Private Kimura was saluting the sergeant with unnecessary zeal. 'They always close the gates when Sergeant Nagata thinks there's going to be an escape.'

'Well ...' Peggy hid her pale cheeks behind her arms and shrewdly studied the Japanese. 'Perhaps they want us to escape.'

'What?' This struck me with the force of revelation. I knew from the secret camp radio that by now, November 1943, the war had begun to turn against the Japanese. After the attack on Pearl Harbor and their rapid advance across the Pacific, they had suffered huge defeats at the battles of Midway and the Coral Sea. American reconnaissance planes had appeared over Shanghai, and the first bombing raids would soon follow. Along the Whangpoo river Japanese military activity had increased, and anti-aircraft batteries were dug in around the airfield to the north of the camp. Lunghua pagoda was now a heavily armed flak tower equipped with powerful searchlights and rapid-fire cannon. The Korean and Japanese guards at Lunghua were more aggressive towards the prisoners, and even Private Kimura was irritable when I showed him my drawings of the sinking of the *Repulse* and the *Prince of Wales*, the British battleships sent to the bottom of the South China Sea by Japanese dive-bombers.

Far more worrying, the food ration had been cut. The sweet potatoes and cracked wheat – a coarse cattle feed – were warehouse scrapings, filled with dead weevils and rusty nails. Peggy and I were hungry all the time.

'Jamie, suppose ...' Intrigued by her own logic, Peggy smiled to herself. 'Suppose the Japanese want us to escape, so they won't have to feed us? Then they'd have more to eat.'

She waited for me to react, and reached out to reassure me, seeing that she had gone too far. She knew that any threat to the camp unsettled me more than all the petty snubs. What I feared most was not merely that the food ration would be cut again, but that Lunghua camp, which had become my entire world, might degenerate into anarchy. Peggy and I would be the first casualties. If the Japanese lost interest in their prisoners we would be at the mercy of the bandit groups who roamed the countryside, renegade Kuomintang and deserters from the puppet armies. Gangs of single men from E Block would seize the food store behind the kitchens, and Mrs Dwight would have nothing to offer the children except her prayers.

I felt Peggy's arm around my shoulders, and listened to her heart beating through the thin wall of her chest. Often she looked unwell, but I was determined to keep her out of the camp hospital. Lunghua hospital was not a place that made its patients better. We needed extra rations to survive the coming winter, but the food store was more carefully locked than the cells in the guard-house.

As the all-clear sounded, the internees emerged from the doorways of their blocks, staring at the camp as if seeing it for the first time. The great tenement family of Lunghua began to rouse itself. Listless women hung their faded washing and sanitary rags on the lines behind G Block. A crowd of children raced to the parade ground, led by David Hunter, who was wearing a pair of his father's leather shoes that I so coveted. As he moved around the camp my eyes rarely left his feet. Mrs Hunter had offered me her golfing brogues, but I had been too proud to accept, an act of foolishness I regretted, since my rubber sneakers were now as ragged as Private Kimura's canvas boots. The war had led to a coolness between David and myself. I envied him his parents, and all my attempts to attach myself to a sympathetic adult had been rebuffed. Only Basie and the Americans were friendly, but their friendliness depended on my running errands for them.

Mrs Dwight approached the children's hut, her fussy eyes taking in everything like a busy broom. She smiled approvingly at Peggy, who was holding a crude metal bucket soldered together from a galvanized-iron roofing sheet dislodged by the monsoon storms. With the tepid water she brought back from the heating station Peggy would wash the younger children and flush the lavatory.

'Peggy, are you off to Waterloo?'

'Yes, Mrs Dwight.' Peggy assumed a pained stoop, and the missionary patted her affectionately.

'Ask Jamie to help you. He's doing nothing.'

'He's busy thinking.' Artlessly, with a knowing eye in my direction, Peggy added: 'Mrs Dwight, Jamie's planning to escape.'

'Really? I thought he'd escaped long ago. I've got something new for him to think about. Jamie, tomorrow you're moving to G Block. It's time for you to leave the children's hut.'

I emerged from one of the hunger reveries into which I often slipped. The apartment houses of the French Concession were visible along the horizon, reminding me of the old Shanghai before the war, and the Christmas parties when my father hired a troupe of Chinese actors to perform a nativity play. I remembered the games of two-handed bridge on my mother's bed, my carefree cycle rides around the International Settlement, and the Great World Amusement Park with its jugglers and acrobats and sing-song girls. All of them seemed as remote as the films I had seen in the Grand Theatre, sitting beside Olga while she stared in her bored way through *Snow White* and *Pinocchio*.

'Why, Mrs Dwight? I need to stay with Peggy until the war's over.'

'No.' Mrs Dwight frowned at the prospect, as if there was something improper about it. 'You'll be happier with boys of your own age.'

'Mrs Dwight, I'm never happy with boys of my own age. They play games all the time.'

'That may be. You're going to live with Mr and Mrs Vincent.'

Mrs Dwight expanded on the attractions of the Vincents' small room, which I would share with this chilly couple and their sick son. Peggy was looking sympathetically at me, the bucket clasped to her chest, well aware of the new challenge I faced.

But for once I was thinking in the most practical terms. I knew that I would be easily dominated by the Vincents, the morose amateur jockey and his glacial wife, who would resent my presence in their small domain. I might try to bribe Mrs Vincent with the promise of a reward for being kind to me, which my father would pay after the war. Unhappily, this choice carrot failed to energise the Lunghua adults, so sunk were they in their torpor.

If I was going to bribe the Vincents I needed something more down to earth, the most important commodity in Lunghua. Ignoring Mrs Dwight, I seized my cinder-tin from beneath my bunk, shouted a goodbye to Peggy and set off at a run for the kitchens.

Spitting in the cold wind, the glowing cinders seethed across the ash-tip behind the kitchens. Naked except for their cotton shorts and wooden clogs, the stokers stepped from the steaming doorway beside the furnace,

ashes flaming on their shovels. Now that the evening meal of rice congee
had been prepared, Mr Sangster and Mr Bowles were raking the furnace
and banking the fires down for the night. I waited on the summit of the
ash-tip, enjoying the sickly fumes in the fading light, while I watched
the Japanese night-fighters warming up at Lunghua airfield.

'Look out, young Jim.' Mr Sangster, a sometime accountant with
the Shanghai Power Company, sent a cascade of cinders towards my
feet. The ashes covered my sneakers and stung my toes through the
rotting canvas. I scampered back, wondering how many extra rations
had helped to build Mr Sangster's burly shoulders. But Mrs Sangster
had been a friend of my mother's, and the horseplay was a means of
steering the most valuable cinders towards me. Small favours were the
secret currency of Lunghua.

Two other cinder-pickers joined me on the ash-tip – the elderly Mrs
Tootle, who shared a cubicle with her sister in the women's hut and
brewed unpleasant herbal teas from the weeds and wildflowers along
the perimeter fence; and Mr Hopkins, the art master at the Cathedral
School, who was forever trying to warm his room in G Block for his
malarial wife. He poked at the cinders with a wooden ruler, while Mrs
Tootle scraped about with an old pair of sugar tongs. Neither had the
speed and flair of my bent-wire tweezers. A modest treasure of half-
burnt anthracite lay in these cinder heaps, but few of the internees
would stir themselves to scavenge for warmth. They preferred to huddle
together in their dormitories, complaining about the cold.

Squatting on my haunches, I picked out the pieces of coke, some no
larger than a peanut, that had survived the riddling. I flicked them into
my biscuit tin, to be traded when it was full for an extra sweet potato
or a pre-war copy of *Reader's Digest* or *Popular Mechanics*, which the
American sailors monopolised. These magazines had kept me going
through the long years, feeding a desperate imagination. Mrs Dwight
was forever criticising me for dreaming too much, but my imagination
was all that I had.

As I knew, criticising everyone else was a full-time British occupation.
Sitting on the ash-tip, while Mrs Tootle and Mr Hopkins scratched at
the spent clinkers in their doomed way, I looked down at the camp. The

British had nothing to which they looked forward, unlike the Americans, whose world was always filled with possibilities. Every American was an advertisement for confidence and success, like the vivid pages in the *Saturday Evening Post*, while every Englishman was a sign saying 'trespassers prosecuted'. One day, my father had told me, I would go to school in England. Already I feared that the England I visited after the war would be a larger version of Lunghua camp, with all its snobberies and social divisions, its 'best' families with their strangled talk of 'London town' brandished about like the badges of an exclusive club, a club I would do my best to avoid joining. The last heat faded from the cinders below my feet. The night air was chilled by the flooded paddy fields and the maze of creeks and canals around Lunghua. I watched the exhaust of the Japanese fighters, warming myself with the thought of their powerful engines. Mr Hopkins had wandered away from the ash-tip, carrying his few coals back to his invalid wife, but Mrs Tootle still stabbed at the dead clinkers. There was an evening curfew at Lunghua, but the Japanese made little effort to enforce it. In the unheated huts and cement buildings of the former teacher-training college the internees went early to bed, assuming that they had ever got up in the first place. Mrs Dwight and the missionary ladies were used to my roving the adult dormitories with my chessboard, gathering the latest rumours of war.

I slid down the slope towards Mrs Tootle and selected three choice pieces of coke from my tin.

'Jamie ... I can't take those.'

'You keep them, Mrs Tootle. Tell your sister I gave them to you.'

'I will ...'

A cup of herbal tea already brewing in her mind, she drifted off into the darkness. I felt sorry for her, but I needed her out of the way. When I was alone on the ash-tip, screened from the camp buildings by the kitchen roof, I crawled across the cinder slope to the brick wall of the annex.

Here was stored Lunghua camp's food supply for the coming week – sacks of polished rice and cracked wheat, and straw bales of grey sweet potatoes. Crouching by the rear wall of the annex, I reached inside my jacket and withdrew a crude knife I had fashioned from a broken Chinese bayonet. All but two inches of the blade were missing when I found the weapon in a disused well behind the camp hospital, but I had honed it into a useful tool. During the hours I spent on the ash-tip, waiting for the next consignment of spent coals, I had noticed that the mortar surrounding the brickwork was little harder than dried mud. Either the Japanese engineers responsible for equipping Lunghua camp had never known that they were being cheated by the Chinese contractors, or they had not expected the war to last more than a few months before America sued for peace.

Selecting the lowest course, I scraped at the mortar, the sound of the blade lost in the rumble of engines at the airfield. Within ten minutes I had loosened the first brick. Carefully, I withdrew it from the wall, slid my fingers into the dark space and touched the coarse straw sacking of a bale of sweet potatoes.

The next two bricks fell into my hands, as if the entire wall of the annex was about to collapse. They lay beside me, like gold bars in the darkness. Later I would return them to the wall, using the white coal-dust as a substitute mortar. With any luck I would be able to revisit the food store without arousing the suspicions of Mr Christie, a former manager of the Palace Hotel, who guarded these mildewed potatoes and warehouse sweepings with fanatic zeal. If Mr Christie had his way, the food reserves of Lunghua camp would be larger than the Sincere Company's department store, and all the internees would be dead.

I pulled the bricks from the soft mortar, steadily enlarging the aperture. The distant lights of the airfield threw silhouettes of the perimeter fence-posts on to the wall above my head. A straw sack filled most of the opening, but in the sweeping searchlight I could see the airless interior of the store-room, a mysterious inner world like the dwarfs' cottage in *Snow White*. The heavy sacks slumbered against the walls, and their comforting bulk reminded me of a family of dozing bears. My few doubts about stealing the food were forgotten. Already I thought of crawling into the store-room and sealing the wall behind me. Peggy and I would sleep there, out of the cold, safe among the great drowsing sacks ...

*

A signal flare exploded in the night sky. Its amber light trembled in a halo of white smoke. It fell slowly towards the open ground between the perimeter fence of the camp and the airfield boundary, reflected in the surface of a flooded paddy field.

Without thinking I stood up, my shadow leaping across the wall of the annex. Fifty feet from me four figures were caught by the intense light, their orange faces like lanterns in the darkness. Two of the men had already climbed through the wire, and a third knelt with one leg through the sagging strands. They shouted to each other above the spitting flare, and the man caught in the wire tore off his shirt and stumbled through the grass towards the paddy field. His shirt hung on the wire like a ragged flag.

Torches veered across the ground on both sides of the fence. Armed Japanese soldiers stood in the deep grass between the perimeter fence and the airfield. Already the would-be escapers had stopped and were waiting for the Japanese to approach them. The fourth figure stood by the wire, and began to disentangle the tattered shirt. When he looked up I recognised the blond hair and pinched face of David Hunter.

The signal flare fell into the paddy field and was swallowed by its black surface. Taking my chance, I scrambled from the ash-tip and darted past the rear door of the kitchens. I tripped over my cinder-tin, scattering the precious coke, and stumbled into a torch-beam that filled my face. Rifle raised, Private Kimura blocked the path leading to the children's hut, the night mist rising from his nostrils. Beside him stood Sergeant Nagata, the beam of his torch tapping my head as he watched his men round up the escaping prisoners. When they had been knocked to the ground, Sergeant Nagata beckoned me to him. I waited for him to slap me, but he stared into my face as if he had difficulty in recognising me, and found it scarcely conceivable that I, of all the internees in Lunghua, should want to escape.

Later we sat on one side of the wooden table in the guard-house. The Japanese soldiers stood against the wall, their boots covered with wet grass. The camp commandant, Mr Hyashi, roused from his quarters in the staff bungalows, paced up and down, doing his best to control himself. A former diplomat at the Japanese Embassy in London, he was a small and precise man of painstaking nervousness, the only Japanese civilian in the camp and as frightened of Sergeant Nagata as any of the prisoners. Long pauses interrupted his interrogation, as he formulated the necessary phrases in his laboured English.

Bored by this time-wasting, Sergeant Nagata strolled behind us, slapping our heads at random. My ears rang, as they had done after the bomb in the Avenue Edward VII. I was sure we would soon be too deaf to understand Mr Hyashi's halting questions.

At one end of the wooden bench, his chest and face bruised by the rifle stocks, was a 29-year-old Londoner called Mariner. After being discharged from the Shanghai Police for robbing a rickshaw coolie he had become a foreman at the Shell terminal, and had scarcely stirred from his bunk since entering the camp. Beside him were the Ralston brothers, stable lads who had come out from England to work at the Shanghai racecourse. They joked nervously with David Hunter, who sat between them with his head lowered, blond hair streaked with blood.

Why David, with his caring parents, should have tried to escape from Lunghua puzzled me, and clearly puzzled Mr Hyashi.

'You walked … through the … fence?' He pointed at Mariner. 'You?'

'We didn't walk, no. We *climbed* through the fence,' Mariner explained half-facetiously. 'You know, stepped like …'

The older Ralston inclined his head, dripping blood on to my arm, and said in a stage-whisper: 'I knew I got these cuts somewhere.'

Both Ralstons tittered, and Sergeant Nagata stepped behind them and slapped their heads with his hard fist. They fell forward across the table, dazed but still smiling in a cracked way, and unable to hear Mr Hyashi's next question for which they were punched again.

I frowned at David, warning him to keep a straight face, but he was caught up by the Britishers' horseplay. Without thinking, David began to titter with them, tears streaming across his cheeks. He avoided my eyes, as if he was glad to be caught and was prepared to be punished. Like the Chinese, they laughed because they were frightened, but to Mr Hyashi and Sergeant Nagata they were being deliberately insolent in a peculiarly British way, never more arrogant than when they had blundered into defeat.

Baffled by them, Mr Hyashi took up his position at the head of the table, forced to preside over this deranged meeting for which his diplomatic training at the Foreign Ministry in Tokyo had not prepared him. He stood a few inches from me, and I could feel him trembling as Sergeant Nagata slapped the laughing Ralstons. I was so frightened that I, too, wanted to laugh, but already I was wondering what would happen when the sergeant discovered my attempt to break into the food store.

Mr Hyashi gazed down at me, noting my lowered eyes. Relieved to find one small point of sanity, he placed his unsteady palm on my head, as if to reassure himself that I was real.

'You not ... trying to escape?'

'No, Mr Hyashi.'

'Not?'

'Mr Hyashi, I like Lunghua camp. I don't want to escape.'

For the first time Mr Hyashi raised his hand to restrain Sergeant Nagata. 'Not escaping. Good.' He seemed immensely relieved.

The older Ralston leaned against me, his eyes dazed by the blows. 'Look after yourself, lad. You're on your own here.'

'Everyone in Lunghua ...' Mr Hyashi began, as if addressing the assembled camp. He searched for a phrase, and then let the air leak from his lungs, visibly resigned that he would never master this strange language and its stranger people. Covered in blood, Mariner was lying across the table, but the Ralstons were still uncowed, ready to provoke the Japanese and force them to do their worst. I admired them for their courage, as much as I admired the Japanese. I never understood why the only brave Britishers were the ones I was never allowed to meet, while the officers my mother and her friends danced with at the Country Club had surrendered without a shot at Singapore.

Mr Hyashi pointed to me, and turned a wavering forefinger towards the door. Five minutes later I was back in the children's hut, regaling Peggy and an astonished Mrs Dwight with the saga of my attempted escape.

On the following day the first American daylight raid took place over Shanghai. Flying from airfields near Chungking, Fortress bombers attacked the dockyards at Yangtsepoo. At last the war was coming home to the Japanese. As they strengthened the anti-aircraft defences of Lunghua airfield all concern for the escape attempt was forgotten. After a night in the guard-house cells the three men returned to convalesce on their bunks in E Block. A shocked David Hunter, his face still bruised, watched me from the window of his parents' room, refusing to wave back to me as I stood on the parade ground.

To my relief, no one learned of my attempt to break into the food store. The Japanese cemented the bricks into the wall, assuming that the escaping prisoners had tried to supply themselves with rations for their long cross-country walk to the Chinese lines four hundred miles away.

To anyone who would believe me, I pretended that I had joined the escape party at the last moment. Mrs Dwight expected nothing less, but Peggy shook her head over my boasts in her kindly, sceptical way. She knew that I was too wedded to Lunghua to want to leave it, that my entire world had been shaped by the camp, and that I had found a special freedom which I had never known in Shanghai.

One day the war would end, but for the time being I was busy learning to cope with the stony couple whose room I shared. Around my bunk I constructed a small hutch, where I tried to recreate the peaceful interior of the food-store. Sitting on the ash-tip as Mr Sangster tossed the evening's coals at my feet, I waited for the American bombs to set fire to the sky, and thought of the white dust and the cracking coffins in the Avenue Edward VII.

Below me the fresh mortar marked the outline of a secret door into an interior world. Far from wanting to escape from the camp, I had been trying to burrow ever more deeply into its heart.

3

The Japanese Soldiers

Everyone was shouting that the war had ended. Prisoners leaned from their windows, waving to each other across the parade ground and pointing to the sky. Peggy Gardner and a delegation of missionary women gathered outside the guard-house and peered through the door at Sergeant Nagata's ransacked desk. I stood by the open gates of the camp, looking at the dusty road that followed the long arm of the Whangpoo river towards the south. The August sky was veiled by layers of haze that enclosed the empty landscape like an immense mosquito net. Threads of cloud ran through the pearly light, stitching the sky together. Vapour trails left by the American reconnaissance planes dissolved over my head, the debris perhaps of gigantic letters spelling out an apocalyptic message.

'What do they say, Jamie?' Peggy called to me. 'Is the war really over?'

'Ask Sergeant Nagata. I'm going to the river.'

'Sergeant Nagata's not here any more. You can go back to Shanghai now.' She plucked at the patches on her dress, sorry to see me leave but not yet sure that I had the necessary nerve. 'If you want to …'

'I'll come back tonight. Wait for me at the hut.'

For all the excitement, no one was in any hurry to evacuate the camp, as Peggy had noticed. For days we had listened to rumours that the Americans had dropped a new super-bomb on Japan, destroying the cities of Nagasaki and Hiroshima. Some of the prisoners even claimed to have seen the bomb-flash. The squadrons of B-29s had broken off their attacks on Lunghua airfield, but armed Japanese soldiers still waited by the anti-aircraft guns. One morning we woke to find that Mr Hyashi and the guards had vanished, slipping away under the cover of the night curfew. We stood by the perimeter wire, like children abandoned by their teachers and unsure whether to leave the classroom.

All day we watched the Shanghai road, expecting a convoy of American vehicles to speed towards us out of the dust, though everyone knew that the nearest Americans were hundreds of miles away on the island of Okinawa. Bored by this stalemate, a few men from E Block stepped through the wire and stood in the deep grass. Staring at the silent air, they seemed oddly self-conscious, as if they had forgotten who they were.

Showing off to Peggy, I climbed through the fence behind G Block and walked towards a burial mound two hundred yards from the camp. I mounted the stairway of rotting coffins, with their small skeletons asleep under quilts of silky mud. Standing in the overbright air, I signalled to Peggy as she pressed against the wire, breathlessly waiting for me to be shot. I could see the burnt-out hangars and cratered runways of Lunghua airfield, surrounded by the wrecks of fighter aircraft, and the unchanged skyline of Shanghai that had formed the horizon of my mind for the past three years. Despite myself I kept glancing over my shoulder at the camp, seeing the cement buildings and wooden huts for the first time from this strange perspective.

By leaving the camp I had stepped outside my own head. Had the atom bombs in some way split the sky, and reversed the direction of everything? I felt uneasy in the open air, a tempting target for some brooding Japanese sentry. I jumped down from the coffins, leaving my ragged footprints in the soft quilts, and ran to the safety of the wire. Ignoring Peggy's angry eyes, I went back to G Block and lay behind the curtain of my cubicle, glad for once to hear Mr Vincent's voice, complaining to his wife about the failure of the allied authorities to notify us properly of the war's end.

But did I want the war to end? The next day, when the Japanese guards returned to Lunghua, I felt secretly relieved. Already there were signs that life in the camp was breaking down. Led by the Ralston brothers, a gang of men had tried to break into the kitchens, while others had looted the guard-house. The food-stocks were almost exhausted, and our daily ration was down to a bowl of congee. The American bombing raids had imposed a kind of order, which both the prisoners and their guards had respected. Now the sky was empty and exposed, a house without its roof.

Fortunately, the Japanese commandeered the guard-house and posted sentries outside the kitchens. But the soldiers were pale and uneasy, and Private Kimura avoided my eyes, aware now that he would never see his family again. Even Sergeant Nagata was subdued, waving me away when I hovered around the guard-house, trying to think of something to encourage him. He sat stiffly at his rifled desk, and ignored the English and Belgian women who stood outside his window in their tattered cotton dresses, screaming abuse at him until necklaces of spit glistened on their breasts.

At last came the Emperor Hirohito's broadcast, calling on his armies to lay down their weapons. At the time I laughed aloud at this. No Japanese would ever surrender. As long as he had a bayonet and grenade, or a rifle with a single round, he would fight to the end. Like everyone else, I took for granted that the Japanese forces in China would make their last stand against Chiang Kai-shek and the Americans at the mouth of the Yangtse, well within sight of Lunghua.

But the first American reconnaissance planes appeared in the sky, cruising a few hundred feet above the camp, and the anti-aircraft guns at the airfield remained silent. Sergeant Nagata and his men, who had only returned to Lunghua in the hope of finding food, once again abandoned us, marching off into the night. The next day at noon, the two Shanghai Water Company engineers who had operated the clandestine radio throughout the war placed the battered bakelite set on the balcony above the entrance to F Block. Then at last we heard the recorded victory speeches of Truman and MacArthur.

So, I told myself, the war had ended. But as I stood by the open gates I was still not convinced. The missionary women had wandered away, and Peggy gave a last hopeless shrug and went back to the children's hut, leaving me to hover between the rotting posts. Everything within the camp was unchanged, but beyond the fence lay a different world. The wild rice growing by the roadside, the blades of sugar cane and the yellow mud of the abandoned paddy fields were touched by the same eerie light, as if they had been irradiated by the bomb dropped on Nagasaki, 400 miles across the China Sea. The drowned canals and the grave-mounds, the forgotten ceramics works by the river, looked like an elaborate stage-set. I stepped forward, but the curving ruts which the supply truck had cut into the earth steered me back into the camp.

I knew, though, that it was time to leave. My mother and father would soon return to our house in Shanghai, and I wanted to meet them while there was still a faint chance that they remembered me. Shanghai was eight miles away, across a silent terrain of rice fields and deserted villages. In my pockets were a bottle of water that Peggy had boiled for me and a sweet potato I had saved. Settling them into my khaki shorts, I stepped through the gates on to the open road.

I set off along the dusty verge, trying to fix my eyes on the Shanghai skyline. Within the barbed wire another day in Lunghua was unfolding. The war might have ended, but the women worked over their washing and the men lounged on the entrance steps to the dormitory blocks. David Hunter and a group of younger children played one of their hour-long skipping games, jumping together as David whipped the ground under their feet, as always carried away by his wild humour.

Outside the children's hut Peggy sat with one of the four-year-olds, teaching him to read. I called to her, but she was too engrossed in the book to hear me. Peggy's parents would take weeks to travel from Tsingtao, and I would be back to look after her. If Lunghua was my real home, Peggy was my closest friend, far closer now than my mother and father could ever be, however hard the missionary women tried to keep us apart. We often quarrelled, but in the dark times Peggy had learned to rely on me and control my leaping imagination.

I passed the kitchen garden behind the hospital, with its rows of beans and tomatoes. Peggy and I had grown them to eke out our rations, fertilising the ground with buckets of nightsoil that we hoisted from the G Block septic tank, the only useful product of the Vincents' existence. Mrs Dwight stood on the hospital steps, lecturing a young Eurasian whose father had been chauffeur to the Dean of Shanghai Cathedral. A reluctant orderly at the hospital, he would once have deferred meekly to Mrs Dwight, but I could see from his bored stare that he was no longer impressed by her moralising talk. British power had waned, sinking like the torpedoed hulks of the *Repulse* and the *Prince of Wales*, and he could choose to become a Chinese again. As David's father often reflected during our chess games, the Japanese attack on Pearl Harbor had marked the first revolt by the colonised nations of the east against the imperial west. Shanghai, which had endured throughout the war, might have changed more than I realised.

Leaving the road, I turned my back on the camp and stepped into the deep grass that ran towards the canal marking the southern perimeter of the airfield. A cloud of mosquitoes rose from the stagnant water, greeting me as if I were the first person to enter this empty world. Dragonflies hunted the lacquered air, swerves of electric blue reflected in the oil leaking from a bombed freighter at Nantao.

A sunken Japanese patrol-boat lay in the canal, its machine-gun pointing skywards from the armour-plated turret. Already sections of the wooden decking had been chopped into firewood by the returning Chinese villagers. Strafed by the American Mustangs before the crew could take cover, the craft was dissolving into the soft mud of the canal bottom. Only the Japanese soldier lying face down in the shallow water was still himself, the brass buckles of his canvas webbing polished by the stream. I stood on the bank above him and watched the water lift the hairs from his scalp. I could see each of the ulcers on his neck, and the swollen stitching of his coarsely woven shirt. Water-beetles raced between his fingers, sending shimmers of light into the air, as if this dead soldier was tapping the underside of the surface and sending out some last message.

The canal turned to join the Whangpoo half a mile away. I left the bank and strode through the waist-high grass towards the circular rim of a flooded bomb crater. A white snake swam through the milky water, exploring this new realm. Beyond the crater was the boundary road of the airfield, roofless hangars standing beside the bombed engineering sheds.

Caught by the last of the American air-raids, a Chinese puppet soldier lay by the embankment of a single-track railway line. Bandits had looted his body, stripping his pockets and ammunition pouches, and he was surrounded by scraps of paper, pages from his pass-book, letters and small photographs, the documentation of a life he might have laid out beside himself as he waited to die.

Envying him all these possessions, I climbed the earth embankment, a spur of the Hangchow–Shanghai railway which ran towards the north-west, losing itself in the misty light. I strode between the polished rails as they hummed faintly in the heat, adjusting my step to the wooden sleepers. I searched for Lunghua camp, but its familiar roof-lines had vanished. An intense light, more electric than solar, lay over the derelict fields, as if the air had been charged by the energy radiated by that sombre weapon exploded across the China Sea. I stared at my hands, wondering if I had been affected, and tasted the tepid water in my bottle. For the first time it occurred to me that everyone in the world outside Lunghua might be dead, and that this was why the war was over.

Half an hour later, when I had walked a further mile into the haze, I approached a small wayside railway station. It stood beside the track with a modest waiting room and ticket office, faded time-tables hanging in the air. Sitting on the concrete platform were four Japanese soldiers. They were fully armed, rifles beside them, and wore canvas webbing and ammunition pouches over their shabby uniforms. A unit of field infantry, they were perhaps waiting for their orders at this rural station, orders that would now never come. They had cooked a simple meal on a makeshift stove, using strips of wood torn from the walls of the waiting room, and were resting in the mid-day heat.

Smoking their handmade cigarettes, they watched me walk towards them between the rails. I slowed my step, unsure whether to make a detour around the Japanese. Below the embankment was an anti-tank ditch partly filled with water, in which lay a dead water-buffalo. The carcase of this docile beast was somehow reassuring, and I stopped to catch my breath before sliding down the embankment.

Then I noticed that one of the Japanese had raised his hand. I stared back at him, my feet slipping in the soft earth. I decided not to make a run for it – there was nowhere to go, and the Japanese would shoot me without a moment's thought. Walking up to the platform, I stopped by the private soldier who had beckoned to me. Grunting to himself over the last of his meal, he squatted beside his rifle. With his heavy workman's hands he was coiling the telephone wire which he had cut from the wooden pole above the station.

Sitting with his back to the telephone pole, hands tied behind him, was a Chinese youth in a white shirt and dark trousers. Bands of wire circled his chest, and he breathed in empty gasps. His quick mouth and composed eyes reminded me of the clerks who had worked for my father before the war. He seemed out of place on this rural railway platform, unlike the soldiers and myself. The Japanese corporal lashing him to the telephone pole tightened the cords as if to anchor him firmly to this desolate terrain.

The Chinese choked, his throat knotting while he fought for air. Trying to ignore him, I faced the soldier coiling the wire. All my experience of the Japanese had taught me never to comment on anything they were doing, nor to take sides in any dispute involving them. I told myself that the Chinese was an important prisoner, and that they had tied him up before taking their afternoon sleep.

One of the older soldiers was already dozing in the shade of the waiting room, head on his knapsack. The other sat by the stove, carefully reaming out the mess-tins. Their faces were empty of all feeling, as if they were aware that the war had ended but knew that, for them, this meant nothing.

Only the first-class private coiling the wire showed any interest in me. I guessed that they had been up-country, fighting the Kuomintang armies, and had seen few Europeans. Their food rations would have been as meagre as those in Lunghua, but the private's broad temples were still fleshy, his cheekbones swollen like a boxer's at the end of a hard-fought bout. He flicked his lips with a blackened finger and cleared his throat in a forced way, as if releasing to the air a stream of thoughts that no longer concerned him.

Exhausted by the long walk, I leaned against the platform, unsure whether to risk eating my sweet potato. The corporal securing the

Chinese youth to the telephone pole was a short, starved man with a war-hardened face. As soon as I touched my pockets he began to watch me in a hungry way. The smells of burnt fat from the stove made my head swim, and I drew the water bottle from my trousers.

With a brief grunt, the private put out his hand. I released the cap, took a quick gulp and handed the bottle to him. He drank noisily, spoke to the corporal and passed the bottle back to me, disappointed that it contained nothing stronger than water. He tossed the coil of wire on to the platform beside the prisoner, and then turned his attention to me. A wistful smile appeared on his roughened lips, and he pointed to the sun and to the sweat staining my cotton shirt.

'Hot?' I said. 'Yes, it's the atom bombs … you know the war's over? The Emperor—'

I spoke without thinking. The only sound in the silent landscape, marooned in its haze, came from the Chinese. As another coil of telephone wire encircled his chest he tried not to breathe, and then began to pant rapidly, his head striking the wooden pole. His eyes were loosening themselves from his face. The corporal knotted the wire and tightened the noose with a wristy jerk. Drops of bloody saliva fell from the youth's lips, staining his white shirt. He looked at me, and gasped a word of Chinese, like a warning shout to a dog.

The first-class private scowled knowingly at the sun, urging me to drink. He appeared to be busy with his own thoughts, but every few seconds his eyes fixed on a different point in the surrounding fields. He was watching the drained paddy beside the embankment, the burial mound at its north-west corner, the stone footbridge across a canal. Did he know that the war was over, that his Emperor had called on him to surrender? Among the canvas packs and ammunition boxes piled against the waiting room was a field radio only issued to specialist troops. Perhaps they had heard that the war was over, but this simple statement, so meaningful to civilians far from the front line, meant nothing to them. Within a few weeks the American forces would reach Shanghai, and the Chinese armies they had fought for so many years would take control of this derelict realm in which they waited, their minds already far beyond any future in store for them.

I decided to eat my sweet potato while I still had the chance. The private watched me approvingly, brushing a fly from my shoulder. His ragged uniform was a collection of tatters held together by the straps of his webbing, from which the smell of sweat emerged in almost intact layers. While I ate the potato skin he pointed to a piece of pith that clung to the back of my hand, and waited until I returned it to my mouth.

As he smiled at me in his simple way I felt an uneasy sense of pride. Despite myself, I admired this Japanese soldier, with his swollen temples and bruised face. He was no more than a labourer, but in his way he had risen to the challenge of the war. His heavy shoulders, marked by patches of eczema and scores of flea-bites, were bursting through the fabric of his shirt, his chest restrained like an animal by the canvas webbing. He was one of the few strong men I had met, completely unlike the officers in the British forces and most of the adults in Lunghua. Only Mariner and the Ralston brothers would have been a match for this Japanese warrior.

I finished the potato and wiped my fingers on my lips, watching the sweat running from his neck into the hollows of his collar bones. I wished that I had learned enough Japanese from Private Kimura to explain that the war was over. The Chinese prisoner on the platform was now scarcely able to breathe, his ribs crushed by the coils of telephone wire. Bruises filled with congested blood stared from his forehead. Tired by the effort of knotting the heavy wire, the corporal tossed the cable on to the concrete floor and strolled stiffly along the platform.

The private's fingers flicked at his lips, tapping a message to himself. He grimaced over some memory bothering him like a mosquito. Deciding to take the risk, I slid my clasp knife from my hip pocket. With the blade closed, I offered it to the private, hoping that he would want to test the blade, and might cut the telephone wire binding the Chinese prisoner.

But the blade was of no interest to him. He cut away a canvas flap that hung from his ragged boot, and turned his attention to the clasp. He smiled at the cowboy motif carved into the mother-of-pearl handle. His thick fingers traced out the ranch-hand in stetson and high-heeled boots, and the twirling lasso that resembled the telephone wire he had been coiling at his feet.

The railway lines hummed in the heat, a sound like pain. The Chinese slumped against the pole, his neck so flushed that it was almost blue. He raised his head and looked at me in a fevered way, as if we were fellow passengers who had missed our connection. He was four or five years older than I was, his hair cut neatly in a way that Mrs Dwight had always urged on me. Was he a Kuomintang agent, one of the thousands in Shanghai, or an office clerk working for the Japanese occupation authority who had fallen foul of the kempetai?

The corporal stepped on to the track and gathered sticks for the fire. I searched the railway line, hoping that an American patrol might be approaching. From the moment I left Lunghua all the clocks had stopped. Time had suspended itself, and only the faraway drone of an American aircraft reminded me of a world on the other side of the pearly light.

The private gestured to me to empty my pockets. The corporal stood at the end of the platform, relieving himself on to the track. The drops of urine hissed as they struck the rail, sending up a fierce cloud of yellow steam. The corporal walked back wide-legged to the Chinese prisoner. He had cut his hands on the wire, and shook his head ruefully as he bent down and picked up the coil, ready to return to his work.

Hurriedly I dug into my pockets and handed my tie-pin to the private, hoping that the silver buckle might distract the corporal. The private's gaze brightened again as he examined the worn image of a long-horn cow. With his thumb-nail he cleared away the flaking chrome, then placed the pin against the brass clip of his ammunition pouch. Keen to display his new insignia, he shouted over his shoulder, puffing up his chest. The corporal nodded without expression, too busy with his cumbersome knots. He wrenched at the wire, spreading his legs like a rancher trussing a steer.

The private returned the tie-pin to me, catching sight for the first time of the transparent celluloid belt looped through the waist-band of my cotton shorts. This belt, which I had nagged out of one of the American sailors, was my proudest possession. In pre-war Shanghai it would have been a rarity eagerly sought after by young Chinese gangsters.

As I released the buckle the private stared at me cannily. I guessed that he was weighing in his mind the small duplicity represented by this transparent belt, virtually invisible against my khaki shorts. He inspected the belt, holding it up to the light like the skin of a rare snake, and tested the plastic between his strong hands. He blew through the crude holes that I had gouged, shaking his head over my poor workmanship.

'Look, you keep the belt,' I told him. 'The war's over, you know. We can all go home now.'

By the telephone pole the Chinese had ceased to breathe and I knew that he would soon be dead. The corporal worked swiftly, coiling lengths of wire around the Chinese and knotting them with efficient snatches of his wrists. The youth's arms were pinned back by the wire, but his hands tore at the seat of his trousers, as if he were trying to strip himself for his death. When the last air left his crushed chest he stared with wild eyes at the corporal, as though seeing him for the first time.

'Listen, Sergeant Nagata ...'

The belt snapped in the private's hands. He passed the pieces to me, well aware from my trembling that I had willed myself not to run away. His eyes followed mine to the second telephone pole at the western end of the platform, and the wire that looped along the embankment. The resting soldiers lay against their packs, watching me as I rolled up the celluloid belt. One of them moved his mess-tin from the stream of urine crossing the concrete from the heels of the Chinese. None of them had been touched by the youth's death, as if they knew that they too were dead, and were matter-of-factly preparing themselves for whatever end would arrive out of the afternoon sun.

A hooded rat was swimming around the carcase of the water buffalo in the anti-tank ditch. Despite the sweet potato, I felt light-headed with hunger. The haze had cleared, and I could see everything in the surrounding fields with sudden clarity. The world had drawn close to the railway station and was presenting itself to me. For the first time it seemed obvious that this remote country platform was the depot from which all the dead of the war had been despatched to the creeks and burial mounds of Lunghua. The four Japanese soldiers were preparing us for our journey. I and the Chinese whom they had suffocated were the last arrivals, and when we had gone they would close the station and set out themselves.

The corporal tidied the loose coils of wire, watching me as I steadied myself against the platform. I waited for him to call me, but none of the Japanese moved. Did they think that I was already dead, and would continue my journey without their help?

An hour later they let me go. Why they allowed a 15-year-old boy to witness their murder of the Chinese I never understood. I set off along the track, too exhausted to stride between the sleepers, waiting for a rifle shot to ring out against the steel rails. When I looked back, the station had faded into the sunlit paddy fields.

The railway line turned towards the north, joining the embankment of the Shanghai–Hangchow railway. I slid down the shingle slope, walked through a deserted village and set off towards the silent factories on the western outskirts of the city. As I neared Amherst Avenue I recognised the cathedral at Siccawei and the campus of Chiao Tung University, the wartime headquarters of the puppet army raised by the Japanese.

I pressed on through the quiet suburban roads, past the tree-lined avenues of European houses, with their half-timbered gables and ocean-liner facades. Groups of Chinese sat on the steps, waiting for their owners to return from the camps, like extras ready to be called to the set of an interrupted film production. Time was about to get off its knees. But for a few moments Shanghai, which I had waited so patiently to revisit, had lost its hold on me.

On the next day, August 14, I at last saw my parents again. Throughout the war our house had been occupied by a general of the Chinese puppet armies. A single unarmed soldier was standing guard when I reached the front steps after the long walk from Lunghua. He made no attempt to resist as I pushed past him, and vanished half an hour later. I wandered stiffly around the silent house, with its strange smells and musty air. There were Chinese newspapers on my father's desk, and a Chinese dance record on the turntable of the gramophone, but otherwise not a carpet or piece of furniture had been disturbed, as if the house had been preserved in a quiet bypass of the war. Even my toys lay at the bottom of the playroom cupboard, my papier mâché fort and Great War artillery guns. Holding them in my hands, I could hardly believe that I had ever played with them, and felt vaguely sorry for the small boy who had taken them so seriously.

The refrigerator was filled with bowls of boiled rice and the remains of the last meal which the puppet general had interrupted before he discarded his uniform and disappeared into the alleys of the Old City. I helped myself to the cold noodles and pickled pork, startled by the taste of animal fat, and drank the dregs of rice wine in the stone jars. Exhausted, I sat on the verandah and stared at the jungle of the garden and the drained swimming-pool, which had been used as a garbage tip.

Slightly drunk, and with my stomach painfully stretched by this huge banquet, I roved around the house. I lay on my mother's mattress, smelling the general's sweet hair oil, and stared at the imposing bathrooms, like white cathedrals, that I had forgotten how to use. I was trying out my past self, but it seemed too small and confined for me, like the toys in the playroom cupboard. I fell asleep in my father's armchair in the panelled study. The heavy leather furniture and dark walls reminded me of the food-store at Lunghua which I had dreamed of sharing with Peggy.

At noon the next day my parents arrived, in a taxi covered with the yellow dust of the Lunghua road. They had driven to the camp hoping to collect me. Smiling cheerfully, they embraced me as if we had been separated for no more than a few days. Did they really recognise me? I was happy to be with them, but we were like actors playing parts presented to us at short notice. We played the roles of parents and son, and in a few days were word-perfect and genuinely glad to be together. I remembered my mother's voice, and her mouth and cheeks, but her eyes belonged to an older woman who had never known me.

Meanwhile, life in Shanghai resumed without a pause, as if the war had never occurred. Yang, the chauffeur, and most of the servants reappeared, and I almost expected Olga to arrive and tell me that it was time for bed. Sitting in my uneasy new clothes at my parents' dinner parties, I began to remember the Shanghai of my childhood. My parents entertained their old French friends, rich Chinese businessmen and

officers of the American occupation army. I listened to the talk of the
latest London and Broadway plays, real estate values in Hong Kong and
California, and the flood of antiquities which impoverished Chinese
families were releasing on to the market.

The war had already been absorbed into the extraordinary history
of Shanghai, along with the Avenue Edward VII bomb, the Japanese
attack on the city and the years of brutal occupation. The assets of the
Axis powers, the Japanese cotton mills and the German engineering
works, were swiftly appropriated and put to use. The great trading
houses opened their doors. The port of Shanghai was crammed with
freighters unloading merchandise for the department stores of the
Nanking Road. Thousands of bars and nightclubs lit the afternoon sky.
American servicemen swarmed ashore, an army of war embraced by
an even more disciplined army of peace, the Chinese pimps and their
massed ranks of White Russian, Chinese and Eurasian prostitutes, who
welcomed them eagerly as they stepped on to the Bund.

But from all this activity I felt set apart, as if I had landed in an
unfamiliar future. So much had happened that I had not yet been able
to remember or forget. There were too many memories of Lunghua
that were difficult to share with my parents. Over breakfast my father
and I talked about our experiences, as if we were describing scenes
from the films showing in the Shanghai theatres. My sense of myself
had changed, and I had mislaid part of my mind somewhere between
Lunghua and Shanghai.

Strangest of all, Japanese soldiers were still patrolling the streets of
Shanghai. As Yang and I drove in the puppet general's Buick to a garden
party at the British Consulate I pointed to the Japanese sentries in faded
uniforms, standing with their long rifles on the steps of the Mayoral
Office. Yang sounded his horn, forcing the Buick through the pedicab
drivers, beggars and office clerks, shouting to the Japanese to clear the
way. I stared at the faces hidden under their peaked caps, hoping to
recognise the first-class private and the corporal I had left behind on
the railway platform.

Other Japanese sentries, at the request of the American and
Kuomintang authorities, guarded key government buildings around

the city. My father told me that the Free French occupying Indo-China had recruited units of the Japanese army in their fight against the communist Viet Minh. For all this, whenever I saw the armed Japanese I thought of the isolated railway station in the countryside south of Shanghai. I almost believed that the Japanese soldiers guarding the city were preparing the bar-keepers, prostitutes and American servicemen for a longer journey that would soon set out from that rural platform.

The first of a long series of war crimes trials were held in October, and the senior Japanese generals who had ruled Shanghai during the war were charged with an endless catalogue of atrocities against the Chinese civilian population. Almost in passing, we heard that the Japanese had planned to close Lunghua and march us up-country, far from the eyes of the neutral community in Shanghai. But for the sudden end of the war, they would have been free to dispose of us, and only the atomic bombs had saved our lives. The pearly light that hung over Lunghua reminded me for ever of the saving miracle of Hiroshima and Nagasaki.

Once a week I visited the camp, where several hundred of the British internees were still housed. They survived on the rations parachuted by B-29 Superfortresses identical to those that had bombed Nagasaki. The dead and the living had begun to interbreed. As Yang drove south along the Lunghua road I searched the paddy fields for any sign of the railway station, expecting to see its platform crowded with new arrivals.

I tried to explain all this to Peggy, while she waited for her parents to sail from Tsingtao. I gave her the presents of clothes that I had bought at Sincere's, the latest American lipsticks, nylon stockings and a box of Swiss chocolates. I was happy to be with her again in the children's hut, watching her try on her new make-up. Through the rouge and lipstick a vivid woman's face appeared, more beautiful than all the prostitutes at the Park Hotel. I wanted to embrace her and thank her for everything she had done for me, but we knew each other too well. Already I felt that she had begun to free herself from the camp, and that we would soon grow apart.

Casually, I described the death of the young Chinese. When I finished, hiding my feelings behind a liqueur chocolate, I realised that I had made him sound like myself.

'Jamie, you should never have gone.' Peggy settled a small child into its cot. 'We did try to stop you.'

'I had to go back to Shanghai. You know, I was really looking for Sergeant Nagata ...'

'Those soldiers might have killed you.'

'They didn't need to – I wasn't ready for them.'

'Jamie, they didn't touch you! You walked away from them.'

'I suppose I did – I keep thinking I should have stayed. Peggy, they wouldn't have hurt me.'

Already she could see that I was disappointed.

At the end of October, as I left the Cathay Hotel after lunch with my mother, I shared a taxi with two American navy pilots who were trying to find the Del Monte Casino. I guided the Chinese driver to the Avenue Haig, only to find that the casino had been ransacked by the Japanese in the last days of the war. As we left the taxi, looking at the shattered windows and the broken glass on the steps, I noticed David Hunter hailing the driver from the lobby of Imperial Mansions, a run-down apartment building across the street in which several brothels operated.

David, like me, was dressed in a pale grey suit and tie, which he wore in the faintly shifty way shared by all the former Lunghua boys, as if we had been released after serving a sentence at a corrective institution. At times we would meet every day, but often I would do my best to avoid him. He had recovered from Sergeant Nagata's slaps on the evening he tried to escape, but his swerves of dangerous humour exhausted me. Often I saw him on the steps of the Park Hotel, staring in a strained, smiling way at the Eurasian women waiting for the Americans. Once he lured a suspicious 14-year-old Chinese prostitute into his father's Studebaker, which he borrowed to take us to the jai alai stadium. In the car park she squatted expertly across David's lap, embroidered gown around her waist, shouting over her shoulder at the Chinese chauffeur. Dazed by her energy and nakedness, I let David order me into the night air, but twenty minutes later, when the chauffeur and I returned, she was kicking David in a fury of Chinese obscenities and trying to escape through the passenger window. David was laughing generously, his hands on her waist, but under his ruffled pale hair the flush of his cheeks resembled the bruises left by Sergeant Nagata's hand.

I listened to my feet cracking the broken glass outside the Del Monte. Deciding to give David the slip, I left the American pilots with their taxi and stepped into the entrance of the casino. Gilt chairs lay heaped against the walls of the foyer, and the red plush curtains had been torn from the windows. Like chambers in an exposed dream, the gaming rooms were flooded with sunlight that turned the dance floor into the scene of a traffic accident. A roulette table lay on its side, gaming chips scattered around it, and the gilded statue of a naked woman with upraised arms that supported the canopy of the bar had fallen across a collapsed chandelier, a princess frozen in a jewelled bower.

A Chinese waiter and a young European woman were straightening the overturned chairs and brushing up the plaster that had fallen from the ceiling. As I walked past them the woman turned and followed me, pulling my arm.

'James! They said you were back! You remember your Olga?'

Olga Ulianova, my pre-war nanny, pinched my cheeks with her sharp fingers. Unsure whether she had recognised me, she felt my shoulders, running her brightly varnished nails over the lapels of my suit.

'Olga, you really scared me. You haven't changed.' I was glad to see her, though time seemed to be running in all directions. If I was three years older, Olga was both in her early twenties and late thirties. A procession of faces had been let into the bones of her face, layers of paint and experience through which gleamed a pair of pointed and hungry eyes. I guessed that she spent her days fighting off American sailors in the backs of the Nanking road pedicabs. Her silk suit was torn around the armpit, exposing a large bruise under her shoulder blade, and a smear of lipstick marked the strap of her brassiere. As she looked me up and down I knew that she had already dismissed my own experiences of the war.

'So ... such a smart suit. Mr Sangster said you had a good time in Lunghua. I guess you miss it.'

'Well ... a little. I'll take you there, Olga.'

'No, thanks. I heard enough about those camps. All those dances and concerts. Here it's been real hell, I can tell you. The things my mother had to do, James. We didn't have the Japanese looking after us.' She sighed headily, swayed by the memory. She was sober, but I guessed that for the past three years she had been slightly drunk.

'Do you work here, Olga? Are you the owner?'

'One day. Bars, hotels, sing song parlours, everywhere. Believe me, James, these American boys have more money than Madame Chiang ...'

'I hope they give you plenty, Olga.'

'What? Well, we won the war, didn't we? Tell me, James, is your father still rich?'

'He definitely isn't.' The thought of money had rekindled her waning interest in me. 'He's been in Soochow camp all through the war.'

'He can still be rich. Take it from me, you can find money anywhere. Just look hard enough and give a big pull.'

She wiped the lipstick from her teeth, appraising me anew. Already I felt aroused by Olga, as confused as ever by her changes of temper. In every sense she was more wayward and exciting than the women in Lunghua. Before the war, when I undressed, she had glanced at my naked body with the off-hand curiosity of a zoo-keeper being shown a rare but uninteresting mammal. I took for granted now that no male body would rouse even a flicker of interest. Yet her eyes were sizing me up as if she were about to place a large physical burden on my shoulders.

'I can see that you're still a dreamer, James. I'm thinking about your father. He can make a good investment right now, while the Americans are here. There's a small restaurant in the Avenue Joffre, only six tables ...'

She stepped forward on her high heels, stumbling across the cut-glass pendants of the chandelier. She steadied herself, holding my arm in a strong grip. Her hip pressed against mine, trying to remind me of something I had forgotten. A potent scent of sweat and powder rose from her shabby dress, a quickening odour that I had noticed in the women's huts at Lunghua.

I let her lean against me as we walked across the dance floor, our shoes breaking the glass. A rush of ideas filled my head as she worked her thigh into my leg. The war had accelerated everything, and I felt that I was surrounded by moving trains all beyond my reach. I wanted to have sex with Olga, but I had no idea how to approach her, and I knew that she would enjoy laughing at my gaucheness.

At the same time, something more than shyness held me away. Part of her attraction was the thought of going back to my childhood, but if I was certain of anything it was that I was no longer a child, and that the games of hide-and-seek through the streets of pre-war Shanghai were over for ever. Being brought up by servants, supposedly the gift of privilege, in fact exposed a child to the most ruthless manipulation, and I had no wish to be manipulated again, by sex or hunger or fear. When I made love for the first time it would be with Peggy Gardner.

I listened to the pendulum-like motion of the waiter's broom. Olga's free hand had slipped under my jacket and was pressed against my abdomen. She was hesitating, as if aware that she might find herself cast again as my governess, reminded of her parents' penury in their pre-war tenement and the boring hours she had spent looking after this little English boy with his cycle and free-wheeling imagination.

From the hollows of Olga's neck and the enlarged veins in the skin of her breasts I guessed that she had eaten as little as I had in the past three years. I put my arm around her shoulder, suddenly liking this tough young woman with her rackety ideas. Only the first-class private at the railway station had looked at me so intently. I wanted to tell Olga about the dead Chinese, but already the lost Japanese patrol was moving into the rear of my mind.

'Are you going back to England, James?'

'After Christmas – I'm sailing on the *Arrawa* with my mother.' This troopship, a former refrigerated meat carrier, would repatriate the British nationals in Shanghai. 'My father's staying on here.'

'He'll stay? That's good. I'll talk to him about my restaurant. Will you study in England?'

'If I have to.' On an impulse, I said: 'I'm going to be a doctor.'

'A doctor? That's very good. When I'm sick you can look after me. It's your turn now.'

As I left, promising to introduce her to my father, Olga said: 'Now you can play hide-and-seek in the whole world.'

A week after Christmas I left Shanghai for ever. Some six hundred former internees, mostly women and children, sailed for England in the converted meat carrier. My father and the other Britons staying behind in Shanghai stood on the pier at Hongkew, waving to us as the *Arrawa* drew away from them across the slow brown tide. When we reached the middle of the channel, working our way through scores of American destroyers and landing craft, I left my mother and walked to the stern of the ship. The relatives on the pier were still waving to us, and my father saw me and raised his arm, but I found it impossible to wave back to him, something I regretted for many years. Perhaps I blamed him for sending me away from this mysterious and exhilarating city.

When the last of the banks and hotels faded into the clouds above the Bund I carried my suitcase to one of the men's mess rooms. At night we slung our hammocks across the open decks where the refrigerated carcases of New Zealand meat had hung. In the darkness the hundreds of sleeping bodies swayed together like sides of lamb packed in canvas.

After our evening meal I returned to the stern rail, almost alone on the deck as the *Arrawa* neared the entrance to the Yangtse. Shanghai had vanished, a dream city that had decided to close itself to the world. The rice fields and villages of the estuary stretched to the horizon, with only the sea to separate them from the nearest landfall at Nagasaki.

The *Arrawa* paused at Woosung, readying itself to join the great tide of the Yangtse as it flowed into the China Sea. As we waited on the swell, edging closer to the eastern bank of the Whangpoo, we drifted past a large American landing craft beached on the shore. A tank-landing vessel scarcely smaller than the *Arrawa*, its flat prow lay high on the streaming mud-flat, as if it had been deliberately beached on this isolated coast. The *Arrawa* was in no danger of striking the craft, but a signal lamp flashed from its bridge. American military police patrolled its decks, their weapons levelled as they waved us away.

A fetid stench floated on the air, as if vented from an exposed sewer filled with blood. Leaning from the stern rail, I saw that the hold of the

landing craft was filled with hundreds of Japanese soldiers. They sat
packed together in rows, knees pressed against each other's backs. All
were in a bad way, and many lay down, crushed by the mass of bodies.
They ignored the *Arrawa*, and only a group of handcuffed NCOs turned
their eyes towards the ship.

A loudspeaker barked from the bridge of the landing craft, and the
American guards shouted at the British officers in the wheel-house.
Clearly the *Arrawa* had appeared at an inconvenient moment. The
Japanese armies in China were being repatriated, but I wondered how
this large body of men, almost a brigade in strength, would ever survive
the three-day voyage to the Japanese mainland.

Then, on a cliff above the mud-flats, another group of armed soldiers
caught my eye. Hundreds of Kuomintang infantry, in their peaked caps
and leggings, bayonets fixed to their rifles, stood on the grass-covered
slopes, waiting for the *Arrawa* to move away.

A siren thundered over my head, almost splitting the funnel. Its
echoes hunted the vast brown swells of the Yangtse. We steered ahead,
the single propeller churning the water and sending its spray into my
face. The forward ramp of the landing craft was being lowered from the
prow, and the first Japanese soldiers were stumbling on to the mud-flat.

PART II

The Craze Years

4

The Queen of the Night

Women dominated my years at Cambridge – fellow medical students, the cheerful Addenbrookes nurses I took drinking on the Cam and the moody demonstrators in the Physiology Department, forever polishing their cracked nails behind the jars of embryos – but none more than Dr Elizabeth Grant. During my first term at the university I saw her naked every day, and I knew her more intimately than any other woman in my life. But I never embraced her.

I remember the October morning in the Anatomy Department when I first met Dr Grant. With the hundred freshmen joining the medical school, I took my seat in the amphitheatre for the welcoming address by Professor Harris, the head of anatomy. I sat alone in the topmost row, marking my distance from the other undergraduates. Exempt from military service, and rugby fanatics to a man, they were mostly the sons of provincial doctors who in due course would take over their fathers' practices. Already I was depressed by the thought that in forty years' time, when I needed their help, it would be these amiable but uninspired men who held my life in their hands. But in 1950 I knew nothing about medicine, and had yet to learn that inspiration and amiability played next to no part in it.

Professor Harris entered the theatre and stood at the podium. A small, puckish Welshman, he gazed at the tiers of beefy young men like an auctioneer at a cattle market. He spotted me sitting alone under the roof, asked for my name and told me to put out my cigarette.

'Come and join us – there's no need to be standoffish. You'll find we need each other.'

He waited as I crept red-faced to the seats below. Despite the humiliation, I admired Harris. He and his brother, both now eminent physicians, had been born to a poor Swansea family, and each had worked
for six years to support the other until he qualified. Despite the late start,
Harris had rapidly propelled himself to the professorship of anatomy
at Cambridge. His idealism and lack of privilege struck me as unique
in the university, and I identified myself closely with him. Needless to
say, the privileges of my own childhood escaped me altogether.

Welcoming us to his profession, Harris took us through a brief
history of medicine from the days of Vesalius and Galen, stressing its
craft origins and low social standing – only in the present century, in
response to the emotional needs of his patients, had the physician's
status risen to that of the older professions, and Harris warned us
that in our own lifetimes its status might fall. In China, I remembered,
physicians were paid only while their patients enjoyed good health. The
payments were suspended during illness and only resumed when the
treatment succeeded.

Lastly, Harris stressed the importance of anatomy as the foundation stone of medicine, and warned that a small number of us would
be unable to face the long hours of dissection. Those repelled by the
sight of a cadaver should call on him privately, and would be assigned
to other degree courses.

How many did? None in my own year. I can remember the sudden
silence, and uneasy jokes, as we entered the dissecting room, part
nightclub and part abattoir, with an illuminated ceiling of frosted glass.
Waiting for us, lying face up on the dissection tables, were some twenty
cadavers. Steeped in formaldehyde, they were the colour of yellow ivory.
More than anything else, the richness of their skins marked out the
dead, as if their personalities had migrated hopefully to the surface of
their bodies. Every kind of blemish stood out in the harsh light, moles
and operation scars, warts and faded tattoos, an amputated big toe
and a pair of supernumerary nipples on the barrel chest of a cadaver
with a prize-fighter's physique. Each body was an atlas recording the
journeys of an entire life.

I took my place at the glass-topped table assigned to me, and set out my dissection manual and instruments. Already I noticed a few curious stares. Alone among the cadavers, mine was that of a woman. For purposes of dissection, the human body was divided into four sections: thorax and abdomen; head and neck; arm; and leg. Each would occupy a term, and be dissected by a team of two students. I knew no one at the medical school whom I could partner, apart from Peggy Gardner, now in her final year at Cambridge, and decided to select a cadaver at random. Then, scanning the list of numbers I noticed that one was identified as '17F'. Without hesitating, I wrote my name alongside.

Sure enough, I found myself sitting beside the bald head of a strong-shouldered woman who had died in her late middle age. Fine blonde hairs rose from her shaved eyebrows, lips and pubis, and her face had the firm set of a headmistress or hospital matron. In most respects she was indistinguishable from the male cadavers – her breasts had subsided into the fatty tissue of her chest wall, while the genitalia of the males had shrivelled into their groins – but she was already an object of attention. Most of the students had spent the war in their boarding schools relocated far from the bombed cities, and had probably never seen a naked body, let alone that of a mature woman.

Only Peggy Gardner was unimpressed, when she entered the dissecting room and found me working with my partner, a Nigerian dentist in his thirties, who was taking an anatomy degree.

'There's a lot more work there,' she said reprovingly. 'You'll have to cut away all the fat before you reach the fascia.'

'It was the luck of the draw.' Embarrassed, I added: 'For some reason I got the Queen of the Night.'

'Rubbish. And that's awfully flippant, Jamie. You're still trying hard to be different. You haven't changed since Lunghua.'

'Peggy, that sounds like a death sentence.'

I might not have changed, but Peggy had transformed herself from the thin-shouldered 16-year-old who had sailed to England with me on the *Arrawa*. I remembered how she had started to mimic the fine-stitched mannerisms of the widowed Mrs Dwight. Peggy had spent her first years in England in a world without men. Behind her handsome stride I could see the self-confident spinsters who had taught Peggy at her boarding school near Brighton. Stylish but well-buttoned, she sailed through the young demonstrators who tried to flirt with her.

But Peggy, at least, seemed at home in England, which for me was a zone of transit between my past life in China and a future that, annoyingly, showed no signs of arriving. I was marooned in a small, grey country where the sun rarely rose above the rooftops, a labyrinth of class and caste forever enlarging itself from within. The English talked as if they had won the war, but behaved as if they had lost it. My years at school had made me realise how much I was an outsider – the other boys were friendly, but left me alone, as if they found me threatening in some undefined way. I thought all the time of going back to Shanghai, but that escape route had closed in 1949 with Mao Tse-tung's takeover of China.

Soon after arriving at Cambridge I invited Peggy to my rooms at King's, with their windows on to the noisy, organ-weary chapel. Happy to see her again, I watched her stalk around my sitting-room, shaking her head over the Magritte and Dali reproductions on the mantelpiece, and the novels by Camus and Boris Vian. I remembered our days together in the children's hut at Lunghua when she had carefully explained, in at least twelve stages, the right way to sew a button on to my shirt. Sensible housewifery could hold any demons at bay, any hunger.

'Why do you read all this stuff? You aren't going to the Sorbonne. Nobody's heard of them here.'

'Peggy, they haven't heard of anything in Cambridge. The dons are only interested in their damned madrigals and getting on to the Brain's Trust. The whole place is fake gothic pageant with a cast of thousands of bicycles.'

'It isn't gothic and it isn't a fake.' Peggy turned the novels face down on to the mantelpiece, clearly worried for me. 'When they built King's Chapel it was more modern than Corbusier, and stood for something weird enough even for you to believe in. Go to the Cavendish – Rutherford split the atom there.'

'You make it sound like Anne Hathaway's cottage. I have met E. M. Forster – he tottered into the Provost's sherry party yesterday. Whiskery old gent with sad eyes, like a disappointed child-molester.'

'Good.' Peggy nodded approvingly. 'At last you're meeting the real King's. Did he put his hand on your knee?'

'I waited, but no luck. The real King's, all right. If you listen carefully you can hear the choir-boys sobbing. That's why they play the organ all day long.'

'You're too old for him, that's all. Those Addenbrookes nurses are more your line. They'll completely corrupt you ... all this brave talk about psychoanalysis.'

'Psychoanalysis? If I talk about it ever, it must be to myself. Here they see it as a rather strained kind of mittel-European joke.' I stared through the window at the American tourists outside the chapel. 'Yesterday I saw a Chevrolet in the Psychology Department car park – it must be the only Chevvy in Europe. God, it made me think of Shanghai and all those Americans.'

'Why? Stop thinking about Shanghai and Lunghua. It's all over.'

'I don't think about it, actually. But it isn't over.'

Peggy took my shoulders, as if we were back in the children's hut and she was warning me not to provoke Sergeant Nagata. 'Jamie, try to remember – you're here, in England.'

'Yes ... in a weird way Lunghua was a small version of England. I used to wonder why no one tried to escape.'

'Where would they have escaped to?'

'That wasn't it. Lunghua reminded them of home. Remember all those signs? "Waterloo Station", "Piccadilly Circus", "The Serpentine"? That was a stagnant pond that gave everyone malaria.'

'It kept people's spirits up. Besides, you've forgotten that some people did escape. You were the one who wanted the war to go on for ever. While David and the Ralstons were trying to break out, you were trying to break in. People thought it was very funny.'

'The food store? So everyone knew? I wanted us to live there for ever. Hansel and Gretel, I suppose. God, I loved you so much ...'

But when I placed my hands on her waist, trying to thank her for all she had done in Lunghua, she slipped away from me. I sat down in my armchair, as the organ blared insanely from the chapel, thinking of the elderly lechers who had made Peggy's last year in the camp such a trial.

Something about my books and reproductions disoriented her; perhaps she feared that Cambridge might be dismantled like the Tsingtáo of her childhood. The French novels and my feigned world-weariness were not merely frivolous and adolescent, but dangerous, like my decision to dissect a female cadaver. Peggy had been my first love, but sadly not my first lover. She had known me too closely in Lunghua, washing and feeding me when I was ill, and sharing too much emotional stress, to want us to come together again.

During the following weeks, as I began to dissect the dead woman, I realised that my decision had been correct. I took part in undergraduate life, getting drunk on the river with the Addenbrookes nurses, playing tennis with my fellow Kingsmen, but in every other sense the university remained a foreign city. Sometimes I would wake in my rooms, roused by one of the endless voluntaries, and be unable to remember where I was. Then I would smell the faint traces of human fat and formalin on my hands and think of the woman in the dissecting room. I imagined her lying on the darkened table, as deep as pharaoh in her dream of death. Her calm presence presided over the cadavers and students alike. Exposing herself to young men with knives in their hands, she set a kind of order on my memories of the dead Chinese and Japanese I had seen during the war.

As the four student teams began to dissect this unknown woman, opening flaps of skin in her limbs, neck and abdomen, she seemed to undress in a last act of self-revelation, unpacking herself of all the mortal elements in her life. Sitting beside her, I pared back the skin of her shoulder, dividing the muscles and exposing the nerves of her brachial plexus, the strings that had once moved her arms as she caressed her husband, brushed her hair, cradled her child. I tried to read her character in the scars beneath her chin, traces perhaps of a car accident, the once broken bridge of her strong nose, and the mole on her right temple which she might have disguised with a handsome blonde wave. Pretending to read my Cunningham, the dissection handbook whose pages were now stained by the dead woman's skin, I stared at her matronly hips, and at the calluses on her left fingers, those of an amateur cellist ...? As we opened the doors of her body, students and demonstrators working on other cadavers would pause behind us, drawn to this solitary woman among the dead men. She alone was treated to none of the lewd dissecting room humour.

Hoping to identify her, I talked to the assistants in the preparation room, and learned only that she had once been a physician. Almost all the cadavers were those of doctors who had donated their bodies before their deaths – it moved me to think that these dying men and woman had bequeathed themselves to the next generation of doctors, a great testimony to their spirit.

Aware of her hold over me, and eager to get out of Cambridge for a few hours, I bought a Triumph motorcycle and began to ride into the flat countryside to the north of the city, a realm of fens and water-courses that vaguely resembled the landscape around Shanghai. Behind the hedges lay forgotten wartime airfields, from which the bombing offensive against Germany had been launched, but there were new and larger bases where nuclear bombers were parked in their fortified dispersal bays. American military vehicles patrolled the runways, and the stars and stripes flew from the flagstaffs by the gates. Chryslers and Oldsmobiles cruised the country lanes, sudden dreams of chromium, driven by large, pensive men and their well-dressed wives, who gazed at the surrounding fields with the confident eyes of an occupying power. From their closely guarded bases they were preparing England, still trapped by its memories of the Second World War, for the third war yet to come. Then the atomic flash that I had seen over Nagasaki would usher these drab fields and the crumbling gothic of the university into the empire of light.

Every afternoon, as I left the dissecting room, I passed the blue Chevrolet parked outside the Psychology Department, owned perhaps by some visiting Nobel Prizewinner from Harvard or MIT. Admiring the car, and the Stan Kenton gramophone record on the rear shelf, I noticed a windshield sticker inviting volunteers to take part in a new experimental project. Almost all the department's volunteers were medical students, who could be counted on to walk the treadmills with electrical leads taped to their chests, and ride exercise bicycles without gagging into the mouthpieces.

I hesitated before pushing back the swing doors of the designated office, wondering if I would rather spend the afternoon with one of the physiology demonstrators and her cracked nails. A lecturer knelt on the floor, hard at work repairing an electric coffee percolator. He ignored me until he had finished, and handed the machine to a tall, dark-haired schoolgirl in her late teens who was standing beside the secretary's desk.

'Good ... Coffee first, psychology second.' Looking up at me, he asked: 'Another victim? We need all the volunteers we can get. Miriam, fill out his death certificate.'

Already I had recognised the rising star of the Psychology Department, Dr Richard Sutherland, presumably the owner of the Chevrolet and the Stan Kenton record. More like a film actor than a Cambridge don, he was a handsome Scotsman with a shock of red hair that he combed out to maximum effect. He wore basketball sneakers, tartan shirt and jeans, clothes only seen in Cambridge on off-duty American servicemen. On the wall behind him were the wooden propeller of a Tiger Moth, a New Jersey licence plate and a framed photograph of himself with von Neumann. Sutherland had taken his doctoral degree at Princeton, and it was even rumoured that he had appeared on television, inconceivably fast behaviour for a Cambridge academic.

He cast an affable eye over me, as if he already had a serviceable grasp of my motives. 'You're a first-year med ...? How did I guess? The formalin – you all smell like Glasgow undertakers. Let me show you what we're testing.'

Watched by the schoolgirl's approving but arch eyes, he took me rapidly through the experiment, which would test the persistence of after-images in the optical centres of the brain.

'You'll find it fascinating – you can actually see the brain working – assuming you medicos have a brain, something Miriam inclines to doubt. First we'd like you to fill out this questionnaire. We need to get an idea of your psychological profile. Do introverts have more persistent after-images than extroverts? Nothing personal, we don't need to know if you lusted after your grandmother.'

'She lusted after me.'

'That's the spirit. Miriam, take over, he's ready to confess.'

'I'm looking for the thumbscrew, Dr Richard.'

Sutherland lifted an American ski-jacket from the door-peg. 'Miriam's in the sixth form at the Perse School, she's helping out while my secretary has a baby. See you after my lecture.'

He left us while Miriam took me through the questionnaire. She read out the entries in a mock-solemn voice, strong eyes watching me without expression as I fumbled over my replies. Her fingers played with the beads of her bracelet, as if adding up her first impressions of me. A modest score, I guessed. Despite the school uniform, she was only a year younger than me, and in complete command of the office, handling the bulky folders like an experienced book-keeper. Her loosened school tie, creased tunic and the laboratory stain on her cotton shirt gave her a kind of dishevelled glamour. Had she just left the unmade bed I could see in the inner office? Already I wondered if she and Dr Sutherland were lovers.

Only when she checked the details of my birth in China did she properly notice me for the first time.

'Shanghai? Were you there during the war?'

'I was interned by the Japs. Do you know Peggy Gardner?'

'Of course – we're all in awe of her.'

'She was in the same camp.'

'Peggy? How strange. Why doesn't she talk about it?'

'Nothing very much happened.'

'I can't believe that. How long were you and Peggy there?'

'Three years. I never think about it.'

'Perhaps you should.' Using an American ball-point pen shaped like a silver rocket ship, she checked off my entries, eyebrows raised as her fingers flicked through the beads. 'Then you came to England and went to the Leys School – I can imagine how you felt about that.'

'It was fine. Just like the camp, only the food was worse.'

'God, I know, school food. I refuse to eat ours. I practically led a riot last week.' She lowered her voice. 'I only come here for Richard's chocolates. He calls me his Hershey bar girl.'

'Why do you work for him?'

She picked at the stain on her tunic, showing off her breast for me. 'I used to hang around here after school – it's easily the most interesting department. I go to a lot of lectures – Leavis, Ryle, Leach. Richard's are the best. One day he gave me a lift in his car.' She smiled at the memory.

'You're going to read psychology here?'

'No fear! I've spent enough time in Cambridge. My father's the bursar at Fitzwilliam Hall. I want to be a cocktail waitress in New York, or live on a desert island with three strange men. Anything to get out of here.'

'I have a motor-bike. Why don't you?'

'I will!' Aware that I might be sceptical, she said with some pride: 'I tried to join the RAF. Richard's taken me up in his Tiger Moth and says I have a real flair for flying. The RAF had the nerve to turn me down, something about the lack of toilet facilities in the V-bomber force. Jesus, if I can fly a plane I can learn to pee in a milk bottle.'

'Well ... Professor Harris says anatomy is the basis of everything.'

'He's right. So why are you doing medicine?'

'I've forgotten already. I thought that I wanted to be a psychiatrist.'

'But why? What do you need to cure? Something to do with the war?'

I hesitated, unsettled by this bright schoolgirl and her shrewd questions. 'That might be true. I haven't found out yet.'

'Well, you will.' She spoke with a robust confidence in me. 'And now you're cutting up your first corpse. Treat him with respect.'

'Of course. In fact, it's a woman.'

'A woman?' She whistled through a chipped tooth. 'You're my first necrophile.'

'In a way, that's not far from the truth.'

'Go on. This is being secretly recorded.'

'Nothing. You can get very close. It turns into a sort of weird marriage.'

'Hold on! Professor Harris is going to be bailing you out of the local clink.' She leaned back and put her feet on the desk, revealing her long legs and the white skin of her thighs through the holes in her black school stockings.

'So?' I asked.

'Instead of the dead, why don't you try the living?'

In her teasing way, this intelligent schoolgirl had seen through my under-graduate banter and realised that I was still preoccupied by wartime events that now seemed to be reimposing themselves on the calm Cambridgeshire landscape. The students poled their punts on the Cam, talked endlessly in the coffee houses and debated the issues of the day at the Union, mimicking the tones of the House of Commons. Meanwhile, on the airfields that ringed the university, American bombers were massing for a final nuclear countdown.

On Sunday afternoons I drove Miriam on my motorcycle to Cambridge airfield, where we watched Richard Sutherland circle the field in his Tiger Moth. Later I took Miriam out to the great American bases at Lakenheath and Mildenhall, and we walked together through the November wind to stare at the nuclear bombers. Once we came across a run-down British air-base where World War II Liberators sat in parking bays far from their hangars. As Miriam kept watch, I climbed through the wire and approached one of the unguarded bombers. I swung myself through the ventral hatch into the equipment-cluttered fuselage. As the wind drummed at the bomber's hull and flexed its heavy wings I imagined myself taking off towards the east.

'Jim, you're trying awfully hard to get arrested,' Miriam told me when we returned to King's. 'Where is your father now?'

'He's still in China.'

'You won't feel at home until he comes to England.'

'He's stuck in Shanghai for a while. The communists put him on trial. Luckily, he'd read more Marx and Engels than the peasant judges, so they let him off.'

'There's a moral there ...' Miriam took my arm as we stood by the fire, running her eye along the surrealist reproductions. 'Ernst, Dali, the Facteur Cheval ... they're your real syllabus. Don't let Peggy Gardner rubbish them. Hang on to your imagination, even if it is a bit lurid.'

'Miriam ...' I had heard this too often at school. 'The world *is* lurid. You've never had to rely on your imagination, thank God.'

'Any moment now, he's going to start tunnelling ...'

I had described my attempt to break into the food-store at Lunghua, which Miriam thought comical but oddly touching. Already I was infatuated with this quick-witted schoolgirl, with her bold gaze and outrageous enthusiasms. At times she would lose interest in me, preoccupied with some grudge against one of the women teachers at the Perse, or after the endless rows with her mother about her drinking in the undergraduate pubs. The proctors had complained to her father that Miriam had been seen in a punt with a crowd of Trinity men, threatening them with a pint of beer in each hand.

Every moment with her produced some surprise. She told me that the optical experiments devised by Richard Sutherland were no more than a blind, part of a larger test to determine the psychological profiles of students who volunteered to take part in medical experiments. Research workers had always assumed that casually recruited volunteers formed a typical cross-section of the student population.

'But that isn't true. Richard says that the only ones who apply are either aggressive extroverts or neurotic introverts.'

'And where are the sane ones?'

'They never apply. They're either getting drunk or necking on the river.'

'Call Professor Harris ...' We were lying in bed together, and I searched below the sheet. 'Where does that leave me?'

Miriam pressed my head to the pillow and brushed the hair from my eyes. 'Jim, you're a war criminal.'

'What?'

'Or you think like one. Richard and I were talking about you.'

'Another bogus test ...'

'Listen, if you take away the war you behaved just like a schizophrenic child. Richard has a patient whose son was schizophrenic. He spent twenty years quietly trying to kill himself. It's all he wanted to do.'

'And?'

'I forget. Anyway, you aren't going to kill yourself. I need you for at least the next three weeks.' She sat up on one elbow, laying her right breast on my chest, and drew lines with her fingernail around her nipple. 'Tell me, is it strange to dissect a woman? You say she's the only one there.'

'Speak softly, she's the queen of the dead.'

'I know she's my biggest rival. Can you imagine dissecting me? Where would you start?'

Smiling, I turned to face Miriam, drawing back the frayed sheets so that the firelight warmed her broad hips and rib-cage. 'I don't know ... in a way, dissection is a kind of erotic autopsy. We could start with the cervical triangle, save me having to wring your neck ...' I kissed the small mole under Miriam's chin, savouring the taste of her mother's perfume. 'Or a nasal re-section, you have been getting a little toffee-nosed ...' I pressed my tongue into her nostril with its scent of decayed lavender until she snorted with laughter. 'Or what about an augmentation mammoplasty, not really necessary in your case ...' I ran my lips from the musky sweet hollow of her armpit to her full breast with its heavy nipple. Veins ran below the white skin, asps waiting to sting a princess. I tasted the skin of her breasts, hunting for the scent glands, running my tongue against the hard pippin of her nipple. I moved down to her abdomen. 'Your navel smells of oysters ...'

'Wait a minute. You haven't dissected the abdomen yet.'

'The only tool I need here is a slice of lemon.'

'So this is what you get up to in the DR. My mother always warned me about unqualified doctors ...'

I embraced her, pressing my lips against her nipple. The only women I had made love to, apart from David Hunter's Chinese girl-friends in Shanghai, were the middle-aged landlady and her daughter who ran the small hotel in west London where I had stayed during my mother's return to the Far East, and a Cambridge prostitute who thought I was an American serviceman posing as an undergraduate, a shrewd guess in the circumstances. With Miriam, sex for the first time brought with it a sense of the future. I hoped that she and I would make love many other times, and that an unlimited store of affection lay waiting for us in some bonded warehouse of the heart.

Miriam's fingers were snipping across my chest, scissoring at my breast-bone. She tapped down to my stomach, by-passing my navel with an elegant swerve, and with a cry caught my testicles in a lobster's claw. Laughing, I raised her thigh and placed it across my hip. She sat astride me and rested her vulva against my penis, teasing me as she held the tip between her labia. I entered her vagina, needing her so much that I could happily have dissected her. I imagined a strange act of love performed by an obsessed surgeon on a living woman, in a deserted operating theatre in one of those sinister clinics in the Cambridge suburbs. I would kiss the linings of her lungs, run my tongue along her bronchi, press my face to the moist membranes of her heart as it pulsed against my lips ...

'Jim ...' Miriam paused, a forefinger on my nose. 'What are you thinking about?'

'It's probably illegal.'

'Well, stop ...'

I held her tightly, forgetting the dissecting room and its cadavers, the nuclear bombers and the November fens.

Soon after, Miriam returned to her Trinity friends and her work for Richard Sutherland. She was unsettled by my obsessive visits to the American bases, and aware that I was still ensnared in a past from which I made little effort to free myself. She realised, too, that I was under the sway of a woman whose body I knew even more intimately than her own. Concerned for me, she tried to make me talk about Shanghai and the war, and even asked another medical student to smuggle her into the dissecting room, ready to confront her rival. But I cared for Miriam too much to risk exposing her to the past.

So, in her wise and kindly way, she kissed me against the mantelpiece, formally turned my surrealist paintings to the wall, and with a friendly wave closed the door of my rooms behind her.

I was sorry to see her leave, but she was right in thinking that a strange duel was taking place between herself and the dead physician who had begun to dominate my waking hours in Cambridge. Through the milky eyes of this silent woman I felt that I was joined once again to the Shanghai I had left behind, but which I still carried with me like a persistent dream that gripped my shoulders. Inside my head hung the facades of the Bund and the Nanking Road. When I looked from the windows of the Anatomy Library at the flat Cambridgeshire countryside, with its American air-bases and their glowing vision of a third world war, I could see the abandoned paddy fields near Lunghua. The railway lines that carried me back to Cambridge after my weekend visits to London seemed to lead to the small country station where the four Japanese soldiers still waited for me.

Without speaking to me, the woman doctor on her glass table had identified herself with all the victims of the war in China, and with the young Chinese clerk I had seen murdered against the telephone pole. By dissecting her, exploring her body from within, I felt that I was drawing closer to some warped truth which I had never been able to discuss with anyone since sailing from Shanghai on the *Arrawa*. Its refrigerated meat-holds had carried a secret cargo back to England. I had left Shanghai too soon, with a clutch of insoluble problems that post-war England was too exhausted and too distracted to help me set aside.

The British had known their own war, a conflict with clear military and political goals, so unlike the war in China. They had coped with its unhappy memories and their reduced status like the adults in Lunghua camp. Over the rubble of bombed streets and the deflated hopes of a better world they had imposed a mythology of slogans, a parade of patriotic flags that sealed the past away for ever, far from any searching eye.

Even the ex-servicemen I met in London bars, who had experienced real combat during their years in the British forces, seemed to have taken part in a different war, a bloody pageant not too far removed from the Military Tattoos which one or two of them, bizarrely, had helped to stage in Shanghai. But war, which had widowed and maimed so many of them, had never touched their imaginations. In Shanghai, from 1937 to the dropping of the atom bombs, we had been neither combatants nor victims, but spectators roped in to watch an execution. Those who had drawn too close had been touched by the blood on the guns.

I tried to shut my eyes, dozing in the cramped flats of the hard-drinking physiology demonstrators, but the past endured. More and more, the cadavers in the dissecting room reminded me of the severed limbs I had seen in the Avenue Edward VII.

On the last Thursday in November I drove out to Cambridge airfield. I knew that Miriam often skipped her sports afternoon at school, and sneaked away to watch Richard Sutherland practise aerobatics in his Tiger Moth. As I guessed, she was waiting in the Chevrolet when I arrived, running the car's powerful heater. Cheerily, she waved me towards her, and threw open the passenger door. Glad to be with her again, I sat next to her in the car, listening to the exhilarating drone of aircraft engines.

Comfortable in her untidy school uniform, Miriam held my cold hands. Her breasts trembled as the antique biplane flew over the car park, propeller wash drumming at the Chevrolet's windshield.

'So, how's everything in the dissecting room?' she asked. 'There must be some news from the dead.'

'I'm still working on the arm – I'd like to get away from the place, but it has a kind of hold ...'

'Jim, have you thought of giving up medicine?'

'Not yet. This is my first term. I'll wait until I've finished the head and neck.'

'That might be too late. See your tutor, say that you want to read English.'

'After medicine? Why bother? *Gray's Anatomy* is a far greater novel than *Ulysses*.'

'It's making you worse, not better. Cutting up all those bodies – it reminds you of the war.'

'Miriam ...' I squeezed her shoulders reassuringly. 'Real bodies don't look like dissecting room cadavers. They look like the living – that is what's so strange.'

'I want to help, Jim. But there's nothing I can do.'

'Maybe not.' I watched Richard step from the Tiger Moth and stride towards us in his yellow flying suit. 'I'll take up flying.'

'Good – then you can teach me. I need to fly!'

She kissed me and stepped from the car, holding Richard's helmet as I straddled the Triumph. We made a curious trio, the aviator, the schoolgirl and the medical student. Richard watched me with his friendly actor's smile. Thinking of Miriam's American underwear, I wondered if this spunky young woman had been his gift to me, part of another experiment. He was always glad to see me, asking about the war in a casual but faintly prurient way, as if I were some kind of laboratory specimen exposed to too many images of violence. Sometimes in his office, while I waited for Miriam to finish her typing, he would watch me turning the pages of *Life* magazine with its graphic photographs of the Korean War. Despite all this, I liked him for his energy and openmindedness, for Miriam and for his American car. He and his sister had been evacuated to Australia before the London blitz, and he had sprung free from the Sydney suburbs, a man with no past and only the present.

'Jim – Miriam says you're going to take up flying. Come out next week and I'll give you a spin. You can try some circuits and bumps.'

'Thanks, Richard. You trust me at the controls?'

'Of course.' Once, to his irritation, Miriam and I had overtaken him on the Triumph as he flew along the Newmarket road. 'By the way, you've been to Lakenheath? The big American base?'

'A few times.'

'He goes every weekend.' Miriam took my arm, pressing her cheek to my leather jacket, as if trying to read the wind in its bruised seams. 'Jim will be the first to know when the war comes.'

'Absolutely. I've always taken that for granted. Jim, there's a chance of visiting the base, part of some Anglo-American community project, so that we don't feel left out when armageddon begins. Come along – we might wangle a look at a nuclear bomber.'

'I'll pass, Richard.' I guessed that I was being tricked into another experiment, and remembered the term 'imposed psychopathy' that he had used in the lecture I attended. He had moved around the podium like an actor delivering Hamlet's soliloquy, ignoring the twenty students in the front rows of the auditorium and addressing himself exclusively to me as I sat high at the back under the fanlights, deliberately smoking under the 'no smoking' sign. Yet already he was appealing far beyond the empty seats, to a greater audience he had glimpsed from the air.

He watched me encouragingly while I kick-started the Triumph's heavy engine. Miriam waved as I drove between the parked aircraft.

'See you tonight, Jim! You can take me to a flick. And keep away from that woman!'

However, it was that dead woman doctor who set me free. As the weeks of dissection continued, the teams of students cut away the superficial muscles of their cadavers and reached the underlying bones. For convenience, each body was then divided into its constituent parts. The Nigerian dentist and I detached the woman's arm from her thorax, and stored the limb in one of the wooden chests at the end of the dissecting room.

Arriving one morning, I was surprised to find that she was without her head. I hunted the tables, and at last found the head at the bottom of a storage cabinet. It lay among a dozen detached heads, the name-tags of their students stitched through their ears. The advanced stages of dissection had pared away the skin of her face and the flaps of facial muscles, so that each muscle layer folded back like the page of a book. I held her head in my hands, looking into the eyes still set in the dissected orbit. Someone nudged my arm, and the book of her face fell open to reveal her hungry bones and notched teeth, warning me away.

The doctor demonstrating the female urino-genital system asked the students at our table to detach the remaining arm and legs, and soon only the thorax and abdomen remained. The womb, fallopian tubes and pelvic basin were displayed like a miniature stage set, a boudoir framed by the curtains of the abdominal muscles. The unneeded blood-vessels and nervous tissue were discarded into a scrap pail. I tied together her shoulder blade and arm bones, and attached my name to her identification tag. I held her dissected hand, whose nerves and tendons I had teased into the light. Its layers of skin and muscle resembled a deck of cards that she waited to deal across the table to me.

On the last day of term she had gone. The tables were cleared, and the assistants polished the glass tops. When we returned after Christmas a new set of cadavers would lie under the overlit ceiling, and we would begin the dissection of a second body part.

Searching for a scalpel I had mislaid, I stepped into the preparation room, where the chief assistant was tying together the bones of each cadaver. Later they would be individually cremated or interred. Little more than clutches of gristle and joint, they lay on the work-benches like the remains of so many Sunday roasts.

I scanned the benches, and recognised a familiar hand tied with a stout string to her ribs and hip bones. Together, they made up a parcel that might have slipped into a small suitcase. I read the name tag: *Dr Elizabeth Grant*. This dead physician had not only offered her body for dissection, but had reduced herself to a heap of fatty sticks as if deliberately dissolving whatever power she held over me.

I threw my gown into the laundry basket, emptied my locker and set out to find Miriam. If I needed to woo her from Richard Sutherland I would buy an American car, take up flying, cast myself as her Lindbergh, ready to fly the Atlantic with nothing but a packet of sandwiches and my own will.

5

The Nato Boys

As always, the sound of engines in the morning sent the slipstream racing through my mind long before I steered the Harvard from the parking apron. Snow lay across Moose Jaw airfield, draped like overnight laundry on the windsocks and the grilles of the landing lights. But the sky was a crystal summer blue, lit by needles of high-altitude ice, the flying weather of which we trainee pilots had dreamed as we waited among the dog-eared magazines in the flight room.

For four days the Saskatchewan fogs had put an end to all flying, and now every serviceable Harvard at the Nato training base was on the apron. The ground crews moved along the line of aircraft with their battery carts. The signal lamps flashed in a green fever from the control tower, and the first planes taxied towards the runway. As each engine choked and stuttered into life another layer of sound stiffened the air, the bull-throated roar of exhausts and intakes. The windows of the Canadian officers' mess and the cadet barracks trembled with the noise of propeller steel setting its edge against the wind.

A ground crew moved their battery cart under my starboard wing. Muffled like arctic explorers in oilskins, goggles and ear-muffs, they plugged their cable into the starter motor. I completed the take-off check, signalled to them through the canopy and pressed the worn brass ring of the ignition button.

The heavy engine snuffled and kicked, the cylinders trying to clear their throats, and the propeller threw a slice of wet ice across the windshield. The blades lurched in unwieldy staggers against the air. I cracked the throttle, increasing the fuel supply to the carburettors, and felt the harness pulling at my shoulders as the cylinders fired together. The slipstream whirled the ice from the windshield and buffeted the yellow wings and tailplane, jarring the control column against my knees. An organ loft of noise filled the aircraft and reached out to the frozen deserts of Saskatchewan, driving everything from my mind. As I waited for the battery cart I had been thinking of my overdue letters from Miriam, the drunken brawl earlier that week at the Iroquois Hotel in Moose Jaw and the penalty hours cleaning aircraft in the hangar, and the fifty dollars I owed David Hunter for stripping the second gear from his Oldsmobile. But all this was forgotten when the engine came to life and the Harvard thrust itself against the brake pedals.

To my left Captain Hamid of the Turkish Army moved from the apron. He scowled at the odour in his open face mask, remembering the unspeakable ham and egg breakfasts in the mess. He steered his Harvard with a heavy hand, forcing the plane to left and right like a stupid horse on a parade ground. But I could eat the breakfasts and take the eventless winter wheatlands in my stride. Behind me a sharp-tempered Frenchman urged me on, flicking his flying gloves against the windshield. Harvards were taking off and making right-hand circuits of the airfield, solo trainees and student pilots with their instructors in the back seat, the junior air arm of Nato preparing itself for the even colder and more crowded high-altitude space above the north German plain. Within hours of my first solo I had decided to transfer to Bomber Command after my jet training. I saw myself at the controls, not of this antique World War II trainer, but of a nuclear, delta-winged Vulcan as it sped over the marshy forests of Byelorussia armed with pieces of the sun ...

'Air Force two niner niner one ...' A Canadian flight controller leaned against the tower windows, watching me through field glasses. Behind me a line of Harvards waited their turn to reach the runway, engines aimed at the back of my head.

'Moose Jaw tower, this is Air Force—' A crackle of squawks interrupted me. However clearly I spoke, trying to disguise my English voice and assume a Canadian accent, the RCAF flight controllers deliberately

made their intercom messages as garbled as possible, venting all their
irritation with the Nato training programme. The French, Norwegian
and Turkish pilots, despite the hours spent in the English language
classes, had virtually no idea what their instructors were saying to them.
World War III could have broken out and ended before we disentangled
ourselves and climbed through the babel of the Canadian skies.

Aligned at the foot of the runway, I waited for the tower's final signal,
and eased the throttle to its maximum setting. Released from its brakes,
the Harvard lumbered forward like a short-sighted rhino, hunting for
every crack in the worn concrete. At full throttle, the engine seemed
to tear itself from the fuselage spars, and I waited for the elderly craft
to disintegrate at the end of the runway. But the Harvard had trained
generations of American fliers. I pushed the stick forward to raise the tail
off the ground. At 70 knots I drew back on the column and the aircraft
rose comfortably into the air, its broad wings breasting the thermals that
rose from the heated runways. I climbed to three thousand feet, trimmed
the elevators and set the engine for cruise. The winter fields of southern
Saskatchewan, its frozen lakes and empty highways, stretched to the
horizon. Beyond Saskatoon, the vast wildernesses of northern Canada
extended to the planet's edge, touched only by the aurora borealis and
the condensation trails of military jets surfing on the upper limits of the
atmosphere. Here the great radars of the Norad chain and the Russian
defence system bayed at each other like lions staked to the ice.

Loosening my harness, I listened to the steady drone of the engine
and watched the white land shift beneath me. Officially, I was to practise
stalls and spins, and navigate a course to Swift Current before returning
to Moose Jaw, but like most of the trainee pilots I had no intention
of following my instructions. The evening at the Iroquois had left me
with a two-day hangover and an infected shoulder bite. Neither would
be helped by being thrown around thousands of feet of overlit air. As
always, I went up into the sky to calm myself, to think of Miriam, to
rest and to dream.

Flying, which had obsessed me since the war years in Shanghai, had
brought me to this remote town in the Canadian west. I had left

Cambridge after two years, completely cured of any need to become a doctor. Despite the Cavendish laboratory, the university was excluded from the more urgent world of the American nuclear bombers flying from their Cambridgeshire airfields, readying themselves for the final global war. The Berlin Airlift, the Korean War, a re-arming Europe belonged to a realm I had seen born over the paddy fields of the Yangtse estuary. Dr Elizabeth Grant had freed me from my dreams of the dead, but a far greater army of casualties was preparing itself for the planetary dissecting room.

I sat with Miriam in the Cambridge cinemas, compulsively watching the newsreels of the hydrogen bomb-tests. The sight of these immense explosions at Eniwetok stirred and enthralled me, and often I had to steady my trembling hands to avoid frightening Miriam. The mysterious mushroom clouds, rising above the Pacific atolls from which the B-29s had brought to Nagasaki the second day of apocalypse, were a powerful incitement to the psychotic imagination, sanctioning everything. Fantasies of nuclear war fused for ever with my memories of Shanghai, reminding me of the white dust in the Avenue Edward VII, down which I had walked like a child straying into a preview of the future.

Working as a copywriter for an advertising agency in London, I thought constantly of the pioneers of aviation – Lilienthal and the Wrights, Lindbergh and even little Mignet, who ended his days in poverty, camping in disused hangars under the wing of his beloved Flying Flea. In my mind all the romance and ascensionist myths of flight were linked to weapons of destruction and the greater possibilities that lay beyond them.

At a reunion of Shanghai friends at the Regent Palace Hotel, I saw David Hunter for the first time since our arrival at Southampton in 1946. Despite the seven years he had scarcely changed, eyes under his pale fringe still watching the doors and windows as if he had just escaped from a penal institution. After a few years of working for his father, an import-export agent in the City, he had been a tennis instructor, a trainee actor and even, briefly, a Jesuit novice. We began to see each other for lunch, drawn together by that sense of an unresolved past which we shared. He was nearly always drunk, but at the same time almost pedantically sober, unable to make sense of his own life but certain about the right course for mine. When his face was flushed with gin I could see the bruises rising through his skin.

'Psychiatry wasn't right for you, Jim,' he told me frankly, waving aside an entire career. 'You'd have spent all your time analysing yourself.'

'Why? I didn't know there was anything to analyse.'

'You could have fooled me, dear sport. Your patients would never have left the waiting room.' David glanced at me in the same irritating and knowing way that Richard Sutherland had sometimes watched me in his office at the Psychology Department, as if waiting for some sudden insight into my character. 'Tell me, do you still think about Shanghai?'

'Less than I used to. We might as well forget it – Shanghai's forgotten us.'

'Unsettling, that. Strange city, but it does have a kind of claim on us. All those poor bloody Chinese. What was Cambridge like?'

'I didn't see that much of the place. It's a glorified academic gift-shop for American universities, where they can buy some quaint little professor for a few dollars. You need to be a tourist or an au pair girl to get the most out of it.'

'I took a course of lessons at the flying school. For some reason I wanted to go crop-spraying in British Guiana. It's curious the delusions one has.' David shook his head at himself. 'A girl and I went on the river in a punt. Cambridge seemed a good place to be.'

'The Americans have their nuclear bases there. Advanced jets sit on the runways loaded with hydrogen bombs, while huge quartermaster-sergeants cruise the country lanes in their Chryslers, looking for turkey farms.'

'Nuclear bases – I imagine you spent a lot of time hanging around them?'

'A little. Better than singing madrigals every hour of the day and night, or pretending to be Rupert Brooke.'

'Only in a way. You should have gone to Yale – though I wouldn't put it past them to be singing madrigals there as well.' David stared at his hands, holding them up as if he had just discovered a new weapon. 'You know, we ought to join the American air force. You'd look great in a USAF uniform, Jim, driving around Cambridge in a Chrysler. It's really what you've always wanted to do. You could lay all the girls who haven't already been laid by the boys in USAF uniforms. Jim, *think* about it.'

'David, I am thinking about it. It's quite an idea – in fact, the first new one I've heard for years.'

'And not just for the girls ...' David steadied his cutlery, glancing around the tables as if he wanted to straighten all the knives and forks in the restaurant. He was smiling at me with the excited but reassuring eyes I remembered from our afternoons in Shanghai, when he invited the wary Chinese bar-girls to the apartment he rented from a Russian dentist in Imperial Mansions. As usual, he had soon provoked these young prostitutes into abusing him. Sex, for David, was as close as he could get to that terrifying evening in the guard-house with Sergeant Nagata and Mr Hyashi.

A career as a military pilot offered an even more direct entry to the realm of violence for which we hungered. For both of us the war years in Shanghai still set the hidden agendas of our lives. David dreamed of violence, in his concerned and thoughtful way, while I was looking for a means of recreating the pearly light I had seen over the rice-fields of Lunghua beside the railway station, and which seemed to hover so promisingly over the American air-bases near Cambridge.

During the next weeks we met again and talked around the possibilities of a flying career. I was bored by my job as a copywriter, and there were fewer weekend visits to Cambridge now that Miriam was working for her history of art degree. Still the mutinous sixth-former, she had become one of the star turns of undergraduate life, scandalising the first-year men with her powerful motorcycle, acting in a pornographic play by Apollinaire that the proctors had banned, smuggling boyfriends overnight into her room at Girton. She was always happy to see me, fiercely holding my shoulders as if ready to marry me that afternoon. But she was waiting for me to come to terms with the war and find my real compass bearing.

Flying in the American bomber force, now readying itself for a nuclear attack on the Soviet Union, seemed to fulfil all those dreams, a make-or-break challenge that would force me to face myself. However, the US Embassy, in a misguided fit, declined to recommend us for pilot training. David was stunned by the rejection, remonstrating with the polite but weary officials, who clearly regarded us as complete madmen and strongly urged us to join the RAF.

'No Chrysler for you, Jim, more like some gravel-rash MG.' David patted my shoulder as we stood outside the RAF recruitment office in Kingsway, after enlisting on short-service commissions. 'But at least you'll get a ringside seat at World War III.'

Needless to say, this shrewd guess summed up my real reasons for joining the RAF. During our three months of basic training at RAF Kirton in Lincolnshire, as we learned the rudiments of meteorology, scaled hangar walls on assault courses and fired submachine-guns at the rifle range, I never once lost my belief that at last the real elements of my life were coming together. I was preparing myself, in the most practical way, for the third world war which had already begun at Nagasaki and Hiroshima, and whose first instalments were the Berlin crisis and the Korean war. Somewhere over the skies of central Europe armageddon would wake me from my dreams.

As it happened, we fledgling pilots were sent, not to a front-line base in West Germany, but to one of the remotest corners of the world, RCAF Moose Jaw in Saskatchewan. As part of the Nato agreement, the aircrews of its European members received their flight training in Canada. We crossed the Atlantic in the *Empress of Britain*, a pre-war liner of the Canadian Pacific fleet, sitting under the baroque ceilings of the vast state-rooms. Miriam drove her motorcycle up to Liverpool to see me off, and stared with awe at the magnificent gilt furniture and attentive stewards, as if I were going off to some strange and lavish war in which every private soldier travelled to the front in his own Rolls-Royce. When she embraced me on the gangway she had clearly taken for granted that she would never see me again. I waved from the rail long after the Liver building had dropped below the horizon.

Surviving the Atlantic, a subarctic realm of vertical seas, deranged ice and voracious sea-birds, we landed at Montreal, and began a pleasant, month-long acclimatisation period at a Toronto air-base, being prepared for the social and psychological hazards of a waffle-and-turkey lifestyle that David and I eagerly embraced. Even the endless hours of propaganda and VD films – which carried the message that the entire female half of the human race was dedicated to infecting us – failed to cool our pleasure at being in north America.

At last, after a four-day train journey from Toronto, we arrived at Moose Jaw, Saskatchewan. We stepped from the train with our suitcases and stared at the small prairie town, a mixed group of suspicious Turks, stoical Norwegians, hungover Britishers and impatient Frenchmen.

'I wish Miriam could see this.' I gazed at the immensity of the Saskatchewan plain. 'Where does it end? This is the wrong planet.'

'If visitors from outer space ever land on earth they will choose this place,' David reflected gloomily. 'Moose Jaw, Saskatchewan, will remind them of home.'

But Moose Jaw was more interesting than we realised. Beyond the 49th parallel were the great cities of the American mid-west. The re-arming United States of the Eisenhower years enjoyed a confidence and prosperity unknown in Europe. Fleets of baroque vehicles soared along its highways, as if a race of interplanetary visitors were landing on a recreational visit. On our second day David bought a used Oldsmobile, and we began to take long drives in any direction. The Canadians were a hospitable and tolerant desert people, living on the edge of a wilderness of snow and permafrost. Winnipeg, Regina and Saskatoon were cities of the northern desert, Samarkands of ice. At the end of every street there were white horizons of emptiness. My mind leapt, expanding to fill the void ...

A shadow veered across the Harvard, darkening its wings. I woke as a blare of engine noise drummed at the canopy. A pilot of the French training flight swept past in a shallow dive, so close that the torque from his propeller almost rolled the Harvard into a high-speed stall. I secured my harness, put out the cigar I was smoking and prepared for a chase, when a second Frenchman dived past my starboard wing, climbing away into a steep half-spiral that would put him back on to my tail. The two planes had crept behind me as I cruised over the snow-covered wastes of Deer Lake, listening to the country music broadcast from a Medicine Hat radio station.

For the next five minutes we hauled the ageing trainers around the sky in a mock dog-fight, and only scattered when a dual-control Harvard with a Canadian instructor in the rear seat sped towards us from the south. Deer Lake was out of bounds, while mock air-battles and unauthorised low-flying were court martial offences. The mink-farmers of Saskatchewan, a powerful political lobby, were our sworn enemies, and their farms were marked on our maps like so many German ball-bearing factories in World War II. We liked to overfly their farms, so low that the angry farmers were unable to photograph our identification numerals, engines so loud that the frantic beasts tore down their cages and scattered to the safety of the snow.

However illicit, these air games helped to sustain us. The Frenchmen swung away to the south-west, heading towards Medicine Hat, and the Canadian instructor set off after me. I took for granted that he was shouting at me over the R/T, but my tanks were lighter by fifty gallons and I soon pulled away from him. Gradually he fell behind, then gave up and returned to Moose Jaw.

Scanning the snow-covered wilderness, I searched for a railroad line or highway that would give me my bearings. I was now some 70 miles to the north-west of Moose Jaw, above a featureless terrain of snow-covered lakes. Under the needle-like sunlight the snow had begun to melt, and the pools of darker water resembled bowls of black sherbet. A mile to starboard a grain silo rose from the white plain, like a silver sculpture erected beside the embankment of a railway line. I turned towards it, one eye on my fuel gauge, following the Harvard's shadow across a curious turtle-shaped lake. In one of its arms I saw a submerged structure that resembled a sunken cabin with a flat yellow roof.

Or a Harvard trainer lying inverted in fifteen feet of water? Too short of fuel to make another circuit of the lake, I followed the railroad spur towards Swift Current and set course for Moose Jaw. But as I faked the navigation course on my knee I was thinking of the Turkish pilot, Captain Artvin, who had disappeared two months after our arrival.

Of all the Nato trainees, the Turks were the most unhappy. Older and more senior than the young Canadian instructors, they mustered no more than a few words of English between them. They pooled their pay and bought a second-hand Ford from a Moose Jaw dealer, only to find that there was nowhere to go. They sat silently around the mess tables in their green, American-style uniforms, gold bars gleaming on their shoulders, as the blizzards swept horizontally past the windows. When the snow ceased they stared at the watery skies and the triple suns, as if these optical illusions produced by the vast mists of ice crystals were a signal to some desperate action.

Unable, perhaps, to cope with this arctic world of snow and mirages, Captain Artvin had disappeared on a training flight. Every Canadian instructor took to the air and searched the wintry landscape within a 100-mile radius. His fellow Turks refused to assist the enquiry, but none showed the slightest surprise. Curiously, Artvin had taken with him all his possessions, his spare uniforms, his newly purchased electric razor and American radio. Everyone assumed that Artvin had defected to the Russians, but I was convinced that he had simply had enough of RCAF Moose Jaw and decided to fly home.

But the captain's Harvard was never found. Had he managed to land on isolated airfields in Alberta and the North-West Territories, refuel with the help of Soviet sympathisers and somehow make his way across Alaska to the Bering Strait? It seemed unlikely, and I preferred to think that Captain Artvin had set off towards the east, ignoring his fuel gauges, and flown on into his own dream.

'Artvin? Poor bugger,' David commented when I told him of the possible sighting. The submerged cabin with its yellow roof had certainly resembled a Harvard. 'Are you going to report it?'

'Naturally. "Sorry, Group Captain, just happened to be over Deer Lake, all these damned Canadian lakes look the same, you know ..."'

'What about the Turks?'

We were changing out of our flying suits, and David passed me the bottle of bourbon he kept in his parachute locker. I watched Captain Hamid stowing his boots, overall and helmet in the same neat way that I imagined Artvin packing his radio and electric razor. These impressive and over-controlled men reminded me of the Japanese, hovering perpetually on the edge of a mental crisis. The Danes and Norwegians were self-contained, the British blurry with drink, in the air as on the ground. The French, for their part, were forever staging mutinies, refusing to obey their senior officers until the French military attaché flew in from Ottawa and arranged some concession that briefly calmed them down. North American cooking, the waffles and turkey drumsticks and jugs of milk were a constant intellectual challenge.

But it was these sombre Turks who would run amok one day. As we sat together in the meteorology theatre during our current affairs classes, watching the propaganda newsreels and the endless VD films with their demonstrations of how to soap and wash the male genitalia after intercourse, I expected the Turks to seize all the weapons in the armoury and slaughter the English-speaking world to a man.

'Tell the Turks?' I reflected. 'That might not be good for the nerves. I don't want to wake up and find my testicles inside my mouth.'

'I'm glad you've still got testicles, dear sport. It's Friday night and we're heading for the Iroquois.' David took a sip from his bottle, scarcely bothering to disguise it from a Canadian instructor who walked past. 'Hard cheese on Artvin. He didn't make it to Mother Russia after all.'

'I don't think he was trying. He didn't defect to the Soviets.'

'So what was he doing?'

'He was flying home. He'd had it here.'

'Well, he didn't get very far.'

'Far enough.'

'Jim?' David was about to hand me the bourbon, but put the cork into the bottle. 'What did that mean? I can see the Lunghua look in your eye.'

'There's no Lunghua look.'

'Artvin's sitting upside down in fifteen feet of iced water. That isn't flying home.'

'It's a figure of speech – people create their own mythologies.'

'You should have sung more madrigals. Never mind, we're off to the Iroquois tonight.' David steadied himself against me. Completely

sober for a fleeting moment, he said: 'When you fuck Yvette and Brigid
promise me you'll think of Miriam ...'

Four hours later I lay on a bed in the Iroquois Hotel, my hands gripping the candlewick bedspread. The room rotated around me like a
slowly processing gyroscope. Beyond the room a larger carousel circled
in a clockwise direction, carrying the elderly hotel and its shabby ceilings, the noise from the bar downstairs, the streets of Moose Jaw with
their filling stations and hardware stores, and beyond those the snow-
covered fields and the old bison slumbering by the railroad creek in
their overcoats of wallows mud. For some reason I was at the centre
of this rotating system, which had begun to tilt, as if banking into a
power dive. I was flying the world ...

'Jim, are you still with us?' David was calling to me through the glare
of the bedside lamp. 'Oh, my God! Don't look at him ...'

I was trying to open the pillow case, needing desperately to be sick.
My trousers lay on the floor beside the bed. Too dazed to think, I vomited
into them. Tears welled from my nose and eyes as shreds of turkey and
bourbon streaked with blood lay inside the vent like a rancid haggis.

'Jesus, what a spectacle,' David exclaimed from somewhere behind
me. 'I hate to say it, girls, but there's no sight more disgusting than the
British officer class with its pants down. It was men like him who did
the dirty on us at Singapore. No wonder the Japs slapped their faces ...'

I dropped the trousers to the worn purple carpet and rested against
the quilted headboard, stained with the hair-oil of a thousand anonym-
ous salesmen. The room had steadied itself, and I could see David lying
naked on the next bed, laughing in his happy but slightly crazed way
at the two young women who knelt across him, taking turns to suck
his penis. In a firm baritone he sang:

'With his mixture rich and his carb heat cold
He got the highest pressures on his manifold ...'

One of the women was a strong-shouldered blonde, naked except for
the silk stockings rolled down to her ankles. The other, kneeling with

the grubby soles of her feet towards me, wore a black slip around her waist. It rode over her buttocks, which David parted with his left hand as he fondled the dark hair and pink combs of her vulva.

'God, yes, Yvette, yes … watch those teeth, for Christ's sake, this isn't a lunch counter. I'm going to have to take a leak. Jesus, that stink …'

The women ignored him and continued their efforts over his flagging erection, all the while keeping up a brisk conversation about a local beauty parlour that had spurned their custom. I could feel the bites on my penis, and the pain in my anus where an untrimmed finger-nail had almost stripped away the mucous membrane. I vaguely remembered having sex with the blonde girl, Yvette, while David played one of his odd little games in the bathroom, urging Brigid to slap his buttocks with the soles of her high-heeled shoes as he dropped dollar bills into the toilet.

Friday night at the Iroquois was taking its familiar course. First there were two hours of forced drinking in the bar crowded with Nato trainees and railroad workers, our shirts soaked with the beer that swilled across the counter. Then we took Brigid and Yvette to the two rooms on the second floor. As usual, I was so drunk that I could scarcely separate the floor from the walls. Flat surfaces, some carpeted and others with lamps and switches bolted to them, were forever veering at me and striking my face.

For reasons clear only to David, we always had sex in the same room – he needed to watch and to be watched. Brigid sat across me, wearing her little slip like a masonic apron, steering my penis inside her with one hand as she squeezed my testicles with the other. Yvette at last made me come while she lay on her back, breast held to my mouth as she forced her finger into my anus. In turn, David liked me to watch him on the adjacent bed. His eyes would be fixed on mine in a curiously innocent and trusting way. Shoe-marks flushed his thighs, and Yvette sat across him, smearing my semen from her vulva on to the pillow. His hands thoughtfully massaged the stretch-marks of her heavy abdomen. One evening he had taken photographs which no one in Moose Jaw would develop. The flash lights irritated the women's eyes, but in the sudden glare their faces, so empty of expression when they had sex, at last came alive, and I saw two blue-collar housewives who had ditched their husbands and aspired to the most bourgeois of lives.

'You Nato boys sure need your liquor,' Yvette opined. She grimaced as David carried my trousers into the bathroom. 'How come they ever let him into the air force?'

'It's all part of the communist conspiracy,' David explained. He began to wash out the trousers in the hand-basin, picking at the shreds of turkey. 'Don't you listen to Senator McCarthy? Nato is a plot to overthrow the US of A. We're so busy fighting each other we'll have no time to take on the Russkies.'

'I can believe that. It beats me you're ever fit to climb inside those airplanes.'

'Yvette, let me tell you. A few drinks make those old tubs really sit up. Jimmy boy's planning to start World War 3 on his own.'

'Looks like he's already finished.' Brigid, the dark-haired girl in the black petticoat, sat on the bed beside me. Her small, detergent-chafed hands, with their smell of lipstick, semen and rectal mucus, ran across my forehead, trying to find a surviving personality. A flicker of concern crossed her eyes, and then faded into the vast indifference that separated her from all men. Her small, bony face had the seriousness of a determined child's. She helped me into the bathroom and watched without comment as I sat on the edge of the bath, washing my face in the basin. David had rinsed out my trousers and hung them over the radiator. When I finished she stood in front of the mirror and began to bathe her breasts, trying to soap away the marks left by David's teeth.

I led her into the spare bedroom and sat beside her on one of the beds. Music drummed through the wall, shaking the Victorian dresser. Looking at Brigid's reflection in the full-length mirror, I realised that she was pregnant. I lifted her petticoat and stared down at the plump curve of her abdomen. I held her breast, almost expecting to feel the milk gathering inside its heavy globe, then gently touched her stomach.

'Hey, you're too young for that stuff.' She pushed me away. 'It's okay to fuck me but anything else is off limits.'

'Don't worry.' It had not occurred to me that sexual games could be played with an unborn child. 'How many months are you, Brigid?'

'The doctor thinks four, but I say five.'

'That's good. What about the father? Does he know?'

'What father?' She glanced at me as if I had not yet learned the facts of life. 'She doesn't have a father.'

'It could be a boy.'

'It's a girl.' She spoke with complete certainty, then lay on the bed and raised her knees to expose her vulva. I knelt in front of her, drawing her buttocks onto my thighs, and eased my penis into her vagina, moved by the thought of sharing this private space with her unborn infant. For the child's sake, I hoped it was not a son.

'Just take your time. You won't hurt her.'

Who was the father – one of the Danes or Norwegians, or some Canadian railroad worker waiting for her in the trailer town behind the grain elevators?

'Did Captain Artvin ever come here?'

'Who's that again?'

'Artvin – the Turkish pilot who disappeared.'

'They all disappear, believe me. I went with some of the Turks. Yvette likes them, but I couldn't get to them. What did this one look like?'

'I never met him. He took off one day and flew away.'

'Sounds like a great idea. Next time he can ask me to go with him.' She held my scrotum, drawing on my testicles. 'Come on, baby, more now … that's it, push for momma …'

Later I lay beside her, gazing at the curve of her abdomen. One day soon, a midwife would be using similar words to her. Accepting that I had no prurient interest, she let me raise the petticoat and put my hand on her skin. I was surprised by the size of the child. Now and then a small tremor moved the surface, as if it recognised my hand.

'You come from England?' Brigid asked. 'I always wanted to visit there. Maybe I'd see the king and queen.'

'The king died. But I've seen them – they came to my college.'

'On the level?'

'Sure. A big limousine pulled up and four little people stepped out, the king and queen and the princesses. They looked as if they were landing on the Earth for the first time.'

'That's something. Did you really get to meet them?'

'Almost ...' As an undergraduate prank I had taken off my academic gown and laid it in a pool of water under the wheels of the approaching Daimler. Describing the incident, I realised that I had impressed Brigid at long last. When I entered her body she saw me as working for her, doing my bit to help the unborn child, but now I was more than 20 Canadian dollars.

In the next room David and Yvette were asleep. I was glad that David had calmed himself and was able to embrace Yvette without needing some elaborate ruse. Flying, and these matter-of-fact women with their direct view of the world, had settled him.

Brigid lay on her side and pressed my hand to her abdomen. 'It doesn't bother you?'

'I used to be a medical student.'

'Then you know about it. Yvette says it's going to be hard in the last months. You can attract the wrong kind of guy.'

I was massaging the small of her back, in a way I imagined young husbands caring for their pregnant wives. I felt the child stir, as if woken by the music. The likelihood of Captain Artvin being the child's father was remote, but something bound them together in my mind. Assuming that Artvin was dead, and that I alone knew his resting place, as a fellow pilot I had some notional responsibility for this infant. I tried to think of Miriam, but her letters had become more and more infrequent.

'Tell me, Brigid, would you like to go to England?'

'Sure. I could meet the queen – you can introduce us.'

'I mean it. I have enough money.'

'So?'

'So we go together. You can stay with me there.'

'Together?' She turned from me and lay on her back, moving my hand from her abdomen. She pulled down the black slip.

'Why not?' I waited for her to reply. 'You think I'm too young?'

'Just a little. You Nato boys ... you're going to be flying around with your atom bombs, making the world a safer place. Let's get to sleep while there's still time left ...'

Her coolness hurt, however naive my drunken scheme seemed in the uneasy light of the next day's hangover. A week later, flying over

Deer Lake, I tried to remember the position of the drowned Harvard.
Somewhere to the north-west I had seen the turtle-shaped lake, but
it had vanished into the featureless landscape. Warmed by the late
February sunlight, the surface ice was beginning to melt, and the lakes
were changing shape as the snow retreated to the original shorelines.
Abandoning my navigation exercise, I flew back and forth across the
white land, past the isolated water-towers and grain elevators.

An hour later, when I found the Harvard, I had almost run out of
fuel. The turtle lake had become a long ellipse, one of a cluster of small
lakes separated by yellowing meanders. Algae covered the fuselage, but I
could see the blurred numerals on its wing. Circling the lake at 500 feet,
I fixed its map position – once the lake warmed in the early spring, a
month before we moved to the jet school at Winnipeg, I would rent an
inflatable dinghy and show the Turks where their comrade was buried. I
hoped that they would decide to leave him in the lake, sealed away from
the world in his cocoon of algae, still embarked on his solitary flight.

Twenty miles from Moose Jaw the fuel tanks were empty. By luck I
found an empty stretch of road between two deserted wheatfields. At
the last moment, as I came in to land, I saw the fencing posts beneath
their upholstery of snow. The Harvard touched down in a storm of icy
mud that sluiced across the silent fields. It lost its starboard wing-tip,
then ground-looped and careened to a halt in the ditch beside the road.

Fifteen minutes later a mink-farmer in a slush-covered Cadillac
drove up as I sat stunned in the cockpit. He stared calmly at the blood
leaking from my helmet, and drew on his cigarette with his hard lips.
At last he raised his window and rolled away. I learned later that he
had never contacted the airfield, perhaps hoping that I would freeze
to death behind my cracked windshield.

The senior Canadian officers hearing my case openly admitted their
bafflement. I had been seen over Deer Lake, but they were puzzled that
I had managed to consume the Harvard's ample reserves of fuel. They
had already decided that I should cease training and be returned to
England, but they examined and re-examined my flight plan, suspecting
that I had been navigating a secret course of my own.

Did they think that I might be planning to defect, and was rehearsing the same escape flight made by Captain Artvin? In a sense they were right, as David was well aware. He made no attempt to intervene on my behalf, knowing that it was time for me to leave the air force. Whatever mythology I constructed for myself would have to be made from the commonplaces of my life, from the smallest affections and kindnesses, not from the nuclear bombers of the world and their dreams of planetary death. By revealing the location of the lost Harvard I might have persuaded them to alter their decision, but I had seen enough of the RAF. I wanted to forget Shanghai and the Avenue Edward VII and the flash of the Nagasaki bomb, and there was a simple way of doing so.

I would never lead the Moscow run to the Third World War. The unborn child in the Iroquois Hotel had given me my new compass bearing. Miriam had written to say that she had taken a job on a Fleet Street newspaper, and I wanted to be with her again and be amazed by her American underwear. I was sorry to leave David, endlessly driving the long roads of Saskatchewan in his second-hand Oldsmobile, but he was happy now and had his own destinations. Flying had helped to free him from the past, and already he talked of leaving the RAF at the end of his initial engagement period and becoming a commercial pilot. For the time being he was right to stay in Moose Jaw and do his best to cheer up the Turks. The Nato boys would stage their mutinies and fill the bar of the Iroquois, while the VD films played in the meteorology theatre and Captain Artvin continued his long flight home.

6

Magic World

'Shall we go to Magic World?' I asked the children.

'Magic World! Yes!' Four-year-old Henry was already at the gate, rattling the iron catch. He shouted to the neighbours' dozing retriever: 'Polly, we're going to Magic World!'

Three-year-old Alice skipped down the path, admiring her shiny shoes. 'Magic World, Magic World ...!'

Miriam leaned against the door while I hunted for sunglasses in the clutter of toys and unread bills on the hall stand. She waved to the children, smiling at them as if she would never see them again and wanted to remember this moment for ever. When we returned from the walk Alice and Henry would have changed in a hundred small and marvellous ways, leaving their present selves somewhere in the woods. Parents were nostalgic for every second of these lost lives.

'Keep an eye on them.'

'They'll keep an eye on me. We'll be gone for an hour – you're sure nothing's going to happen before then?'

'I don't know ...'

In the last month of her pregnancy time seemed to slow for Miriam, stretching her smallest gesture – a hand raised to ease her heavy breasts, the lipstick drawn absent-mindedly across her mouth. She was moving into the timeless realm of the child in her womb; mother and child would begin life together. She pressed against me, knowing that I liked to feel the warm bulk beneath her smock, and lightly patted my penis.

'Just making sure you have everything you might need on the walk.'

'Sh ... Midwife Bell will hear you. She disapproves enough of me already.'

'She adores you. Without you she'd be out of a job.'

I embraced Miriam, breathing the familiar heady scents of baby talc, basil, gloss paint and washing powder that clung to her smock. On its hem was a brown potty stain left by one of the children, taking its place among the countless stains and smells of our little house, a realm of soft armpits and swollen nipples in which I had spent an entire life.

'Rest, now. Don't start rebuilding the bedroom.'

'Bring me back some magic.'

With a last wave, I latched the gate and set off with Henry and Alice down the sun-filled street. Polly the retriever had decided to join us. He trotted beside Alice, now and then detouring to quiz and spray a lamp-post. The modest houses in Charlton Road sat in their quiet suburban gardens, but seeing them through the dog's and the children's eyes transformed the rose bushes and rockeries, the freshly painted front doors and forgotten roller skates. They became more vivid, as if aware that Polly and the children would soon forget them, and were urging themselves more brightly into existence. Our own house was as modest as the others – my salary as assistant editor of a scientific journal barely matched the small mortgage – but Miriam, Henry and Alice turned it into an endless funfair of noise and cheer. Behind other doors in Charlton Road were other Miriams. Young wives and their children strolled the streets of Shepperton and played in their gardens like agents of an exuberant foreign power.

The number of children always surprised me – this small Thames-side town was a life-engine. When we reached the end of Charlton Road we had already collected a sandy-haired boy on a tricycle, two ten-year-old girls and the infant daughter of the local builder. The splash meadow was filled with children playing on the grass and fishing for minnows along the reedy banks of the stream. I could almost believe that the bright summer frocks, fishing nets and children's voices were a dream conjured from this placid stream asleep beneath the willows.

Alice and Henry ran towards the bank, where two mothers kept watch on a park bench. I took off my tennis shoes and walked in bare feet through the cool pelt of the meadow. Beyond the willows lay the calm surface of a gravel lake, its giant excavator rising like the gantries at Cape Canaveral.

Water surrounded Shepperton – the river, the gravel lakes and the reservoirs of the metropolitan water board whose high embankments formed the horizon of our lives. Once I told Miriam that we were living on the floor of a marine world that had invaded our minds, and that the people of Shepperton were a new form of aquatic mammal, creatures of a new *Water Babies*.

'You're Tom, the poor sweep,' she told me, as if placing me for the first time. 'Poor Tom ...'

'And who are you – Mrs Do-as-you-would-be-done-by?'

'I don't think so, somehow. More like Mrs Do-as-you-would-like-to-do-with ...'

But we were all water babies. Alice was shrieking at the green slime that Henry flicked with a stick from the stream. I showed them a dead water-beetle, but they were more interested in an aerosol paint-can that floated between the reeds. It still held some of its propellant gas, and Henry fired a burst of spray at a dragon-fly that veered too close.

Trying to repaint the air, we moved through the willows to the water-splash that crossed the road. The water ran clear over the worn pebbles, but cars taking a short cut to Shepperton often stalled there. The exasperated drivers would look up to find a beaming audience of mothers and their children curious to see what they would do next. It was here that the water-splash sequence from *Genevieve* had been filmed. Whenever Miriam and I watched the scene of the stranded antique car we could see ourselves, Henry and Alice out of shot as we leaned on the polished rail of the footbridge.

Led by the retriever, we set off along the upper arm of the stream, collecting more children on our way. The rectangular stages of Shepperton film studios rose above the trees. Their presence dominated the town as much as the marine world of the reservoirs. Many of the programmes we watched on television were filmed in the streets of Shepperton, and its leafy avenues stood in for locations all over

England. In Henry's intense four-year-old mind, Shepperton had begun to colonise the whole country.

These confusions of image and illusion gave Shepperton its special charge, as if true reality rested in the merging of the two. Next door to us lived a married couple whose daughter was a minor television actress. Twice a week the children watched her appear in one of their favourite series, and sometimes would turn from the screen to see her in Charlton Road, stepping from her car on a family visit. Henry and Alice would rush out to greet her, taking for granted that her real character lay somewhere between her fleeting street-self and the far more solid broadcast figure on the screen. Many of our neighbours worked as extras in feature films made at Shepperton studios, and I sometimes felt that Miriam and I were playing our parts in some happily chaotic sitcom whose script we extemporised as we went along.

The children squatted on the edge of the gravel lake and stared at a submerged motor car resting on the sandy bed. The lake had been stocked by a local fishing club, and rainbow trout swam through the open windows. These drowned cars never failed to intrigue Alice and Henry.

'Henry, where's the car going?' Alice asked.

'Going a long way,' he told her. 'Going to China.'

Miriam had explained that a hole dug deep enough in our garden would emerge somewhere in China. The gravel pit was the largest lake that Henry had ever seen, and he often tried to convince me that it was this hole that went all the way to Shanghai. Once when I dived into the lake he watched me as if I were about to set off for ever to the world of my childhood.

'Daddy, are you going to swim to China now?'

'Well, it's too far to swim before tea. Let's go to Magic World instead.'

I waited for Polly to round up the children and led them towards a screen of fir trees. Mattresses and rusting bicycles lay among the pine cones, and we followed the dark path to an enclosed meadow behind the film studios. The sunlight played by itself on the knee-deep grass, and the children ran ahead of me, their faces bobbing like lanterns.

Standing in the grass was a collection of stage props abandoned by the companies shooting television commercials. A candy bar the size of a small car lay in the sun, its papier mâché wrapper peeling from the wooden frame. Beside it were a detergent pack my own height, its plywood sheeting warped by the rain and sun, and a fibre-glass ketchup bottle painted in red enamel. Canvas peeled from the shampoo sachets and toothpaste tubes, but this never dismayed Alice and Henry. They ran squealing through the grass, fascinated as ever by the magnified versions of the objects that made up their domestic world.

Pride of place in their affections was taken by a ten-feet-high replica of a pink toilet roll. On earlier visits Henry had pulled back a flap of the rotting canvas, and through this small door the children crawled one by one. I could hear them shrieking with delight at this notion of a toilet roll large enough to live in. They waved their arms through the canvas, shouting to Polly, who was frantically trying to nose his way into the dim interior.

'Let's have a party!' someone shouted.

'Party, party …' Alice was skipping inside the giant roll, eyes on her shiny shoes in case they vanished from her feet.

I lay back in the grass, thinking contentedly that there would soon be another child to dance in this enchanted meadow. I was glad that our third child would be born here, as much from the stream and the splash-meadow as from Miriam's womb. Her first labour, at the nearby maternity hospital, had been over before I returned home, expecting to be called the next day. Our huge son, solemn as any alderman, was asleep in his mother's arms when I reached the ward. But the infants were separated from their mothers for long periods of the day, bellowing together in their cribs behind a heavy door, and Miriam vowed to have her future children delivered at home, in our own bed.

So we conceived and slept beside the growing Alice as she came to term, and made love an hour before the labour began. Miriam lay back on her own pillows, hands grasping the headboard with its erratic reading light, surrounded by the wardrobe and her familiar clothes, her mother's photograph and her friends' flowers and greetings cards on the dressing-table. In this warm midden with its utter lack of hygiene she had swiftly given birth to Alice as I stood weeping behind the capable shoulders of Midwife Bell. That night we slept together with Alice in her cot beside us, as Polly the retriever nosed the dustbin, snuffling for the placenta in its parcel of newspaper. The next day Miriam was up to welcome her friends and see me off to work.

Not only was I glad that our child would be born in Shepperton, but I almost believed that I too had been born there. The past had slipped away, taking with it my memories of Cambridge and Canada, of the dissecting room and the snow deserts of Saskatchewan, and even of Shanghai. The warm light over Shepperton reminded me of the illuminated air that I had seen over the empty paddy fields of Lunghua as I walked along the railway line, but the light that filled the splash-meadow came from a kinder and more gentle sun. The children Miriam had borne and the others who played by the stream had taken the place of the dead Chinese lying in the Lunghua creeks and canals.

For the first time I was living in an endless present that owed nothing to the past. The skies over Shepperton were crossed by airliners taking package tourists to the holiday beaches of Corfu and the Costa Brava. Soon the whole planet would be on vacation. At Cape Canaveral, the Americans were readying themselves to fly into space. On television we watched Richard Sutherland reporting from the space centre, the Florida sun gleaming through his blow-dried hair. He was now a presenter of popular science programmes, one of the new breed of media academics who taught the world to feel at ease with itself. His upbeat commentaries dovetailed perfectly with the commercials for candy bars and fabric conditioners. Past and future had been annexed into a present as depthless and cheerful as a child's colouring book.

I woke in the sleepy heat of the meadow grass, aware that the children were fighting inside the toilet roll. A light aircraft soared overhead, its propeller catching the sun. A single-engined Piper, it had flown from the west, where Fair Oaks airfield lay in the woodland beyond Chertsey. It turned in a wide circle above the studios, flaps lowered as if the pilot were trying to land in this secret meadow.

The children broke off their quarrel. Alice ran to me as I knelt in the grass and hid in my shoulder.

'Is that a bad plane, Daddy?'

As always, I was surprised by her shrewdness. She had seen me frowning at the aircraft and its camera pylon mounted behind the passenger door.

'No, it's a good plane – it might bring you a present.'

Henry sat against my knee, pushing Alice's hand from my chin. 'Daddy, has it got a bomb?'

'A bomb? Who would want to bomb Shepperton?'

'Uncle David might. He has a bomb, Daddy. He told me.'

'Not any more. Besides, he's much too fond of you and Mummy. Home, everybody ...'

David Hunter came to see us that afternoon. He had left the RAF at the end of his short-service commission, after active service against the terrorists in Kenya and a last tour flying the Vulcan nuclear bomber. 'Think, Miriam,' he liked to remind her, 'if that Turk hadn't defected to the Russians, your husband and I could have dropped the first hydrogen bomb on Moscow. How does it feel to be married to a man who might have started World War 3?'

His scatty charm still protected him, but he had the edginess of a man who expected the past to come up behind him and tap him on the shoulder with some absurd but nagging inquiry. For a year he had drifted along the fringes of private aviation, and then bought a small company specialising in aerial photography. He would be away for months, photo-graphing industrial complexes in Brazil or hotel developments in the Seychelles. For the past week he had been based at Fair Oaks, making a cine-film of the pre-war Brooklands motor-racing circuit.

As rootless as ever, he never ceased to be amazed by my quiet domesticity, suspecting that I had repressed a large part of my true nature. Aware that Miriam felt uneasy at any talk of Shanghai, he rarely referred to our war years together.

He arrived with presents for the children, a bottle of whisky for me which he promptly opened and began to drink, flowers for Miriam and lavish compliments she was too delighted to resist.

'Why are pregnant women so erotic? Tell me, Miriam. In my bones I know we'll get married one of these days.'

'There's a queue forming,' Miriam warned him. 'Richard Sutherland, Henry, Jim … You'll have to fight your way down the aisle.'

'God, woman, I'm kneeling by the altar.' He placed his hands on Miriam's smock. 'It must be due any moment – if it comes this afternoon, can I watch?'

'Only if you can prove that you're the father.' Miriam loved his attentions, as she loved those of other men, revived by their compliments far more than by mine. She had always been a flirt, but five years of marriage and children made the lightest flirtation seem a serious business. To a mother of two children, sex was all or nothing. I knew that sometimes she longed to get away, to live on her desert island with three strange men – though with husband and children tucked into a decent pension in the next bay – and that she encouraged my writing as a way of being adventurous by proxy. I dimly guessed that one day she would have affairs and this second childhood would be over. I had learned that a woman could love her husband and children but still feel restless enough to want to leave them.

As we stumbled around the broken toys in the garden, David came to the point.

'I'm off to Hong Kong at the end of the month. All expenses paid. We're filming a housing project in Kowloon for a Chinese developer.'

'What a plum. There are lots of old Shanghai hands you can look up.'

'I'll avoid them. I want to go up to Shanghai itself.'

'Think of me as you stroll down the Bund.'

'As it happens, I wondered if you'd like to come?'

'To Hong Kong?'

'Shanghai, mostly. You could take a month's leave. We need to go back and see the place for ourselves.'

'David, I can't. Even if I wanted to, there are Miriam and the baby. You'll find someone in Hong Kong.'

'No, thanks. Those old Shanghai hands, and all that talk of tiffin and mah-jong and how many servants they had – nothing to do with what really happened. That's why you and I should go.'

'Nothing did happen.'

'For a start, Jim, we happened. That railway station you were always talking about in Moose Jaw. We ought to find it for you.'

'That was a killing. Sad for the Chinese, but it meant nothing.'

'You used to say he was trying to tell you something. You need to get away from this – it's potty botty doo-doo all the day ...'

'David, it's the only time I've been happy.'

'But you shouldn't be too happy, Jim.'

After David had gone I mentioned his offer to Miriam.

'David's a fool!' She thumped her saucepan on to the kitchen table, where the children had set up a miniature replica of their Magic World. 'You haven't flown for years. He'd have you killed the first time you tried to take off.'

'He doesn't want me to fly. He needs me to go to Shanghai with him, walk the streets where we played hide-and-seek. Sometimes I think he's still playing there by himself. He's like those old Shanghai hands he hates so much.'

Miriam knew that I had no intention of going, but held my shoulders reassuringly. 'Dear, forget about it – you've put all that behind you.'

'One day I might write about the war – it would help to have been there.'

'It won't. If you don't go back anything you write will be far more true. When I visit Mother and Dad in Cambridge I look around the house and can't believe I was ever a child there. It's like a film set with these two old actors ... even they can't remember the script.'

Later, in bed, when the children were asleep and the old retriever had barked at the moon for the last time, I massaged Miriam's tired shoulders. Strange scents hovered over her ears and armpits, quickening odours of hormones rising and falling, overrunning each other's cycles. I touched her tender nipples, damp with some secretion I remembered from her earlier confinements.

'Tasty?' Miriam asked, finishing the glass of wine that helped her to sleep.

I touched my fingers to my lips, savouring the racy flavours, closer to the taste of her vulva than to the milk massing within her breasts.

'Colostrum ... in fact, men don't like the taste of their wives' milk.'

'Good news for baby. Nature's way of making sure he gets his share. Have you tried anyone else's milk?'

'No ...' I thought of the pregnant whore at Moose Jaw who had wanted to meet the queen. 'Ask your friends at the clinic for a sample.'

'Midwife Bell would love that.'

'Tell her we're going into the dairy business. Mother's Pride Milk Products. Slogan: "Putting Shepperton's breasts to work."'

'"Butter freshly churned from mother's milk." Oh, my God, yoghurts and milk-shakes. Jim, think ...'

'We'd have a range of cheeses, flavoured by cigarette brand, lipstick and toothpaste ...'

'Policemen's wives would give a sturdy goat-like cheese.' Miriam loved her flights of fantasy, and had a healthy interest in the more wayward possibilities of human anatomy and physiology; she had always seen the mischief and humour in the surrealists. Shepperton bored her a little, and she liked to provoke its domestic norms. As the secretion from her nipples moistened my hands she extemporised happily: 'Vegetarians would make bland and mimsy cheeses, West End actresses over-ripe Camembert, queens and princesses a high royal Stilton ...'

'We'll stage a cheese-tasting for all our friends ...'

'I can just see Peggy Gardner!' Miriam sat up, smothering her laughter in her pillow, abdomen heaving, the baby riding a roller-coaster of snorts and guffaws.

Fifteen minutes later her labour began.

'We'll make you tidy, dear. We want baby to find a nice bedroom.'

Midwife Bell moved expertly around the room, stirring up the dust and old talc as she ran a damp towel over the dressing-table. She hung Miriam's maternity smocks in the wardrobe like a theatrical dresser stowing away unwanted costumes at the end of a season. Beneath the bed she found a one-legged teddy bear and a child's potty, ancient contents fossilised in place, and handed them to me with a refined grimace. She had arrived after midnight, soon after Miriam had finished her bath, but insisted on shaving and bed-washing her again. She changed the sheets as Miriam lay on the bed, employing a series of complex folds like a conjuror demonstrating a trick of large-scale origami.

Now that mother and bedroom met with Midwife Bell's satisfaction, the child could be born. On the bedside table were her instrument case, gloves and gas cylinder, everything except the legendary hot water, not a drop of which had I ever been asked to boil.

Disturbed by the noise, Alice had begun to cry in her sleep. Henry woke and shouted at her, rocking his cot against the wall. Miriam lay quietly, her large eyes on Mrs Bell's composed face, waiting for her next contraction. I went off to settle the children, played a small word-game with Alice that she enjoyed and then handed Henry his comforter, an ancient baby blanket that was a universe of friendly smells.

By the time I returned to the bedroom Miriam's contractions were coming every other minute. Nightdress rolled back to her breasts, she filled her lungs with deep, measured breaths as Mrs Bell sat beside her, listening to the child's heartbeat with her stethoscope.

'You can hold your wife's hand – I know she'd like that ...'

I pressed Miriam's fingers. She smiled briefly, but I could see that she had already withdrawn from me. Only the midwife and the child were properly in the room with her. She moistened her lips, staring at the shadowy ceiling and the frayed lampshade on the headboard, as if this was the only delivery that had ever taken place, the primeval birth from which all life had sprung. As Miriam released my hand I felt that she and Midwife Bell had returned to a more primitive world, where men never intruded and even their role in conception was unknown. Here the chain of life was mother to daughter, daughter to mother. Fathers and sons belonged in the shadows with the dogs and livestock, like the retriever growling at Midwife Bell's unfamiliar car from the window of my neighbours' living room.

Nonetheless, I was glad that Miriam had overruled Mrs Bell and insisted that I be with her during the delivery. Richard Sutherland, for all his sense of the modish, had squeamishly declined to be present when Miriam half-jokingly invited him to watch the birth. He claimed that the ordeal of a woman in the *extremis* of labour, exposing her genitalia and gasping with pain, unconsciously mimicked the act of rape and diminished the wife in her husband's eyes, as if he had witnessed her assault by an invisible stranger. Not for nothing did the world's oldest cultures segregate women during confinement, preserving the mystery of the wife's body.

By contrast, I felt my closest to Miriam during these last minutes. Everything bonded me to her: the sweat on her thighs, the mole above her navel, her freckles and pearly stretchmarks, the shaved skin of her pubis and the bright petals of her labia, her engorged clitoris with its endearing leftward tilt, the childhood riding scars on her knees and the spots on her bottom, the damp talc gleaming on her breasts and shoulders.

She farted lustily, and reached up to grip the headboard. Midwife Bell averted her nose, but the air was heavy with the smell of anaesthetic gas.

'We'll be waking the whole street if we go on like that. Push again now, dear. Baby's ready. Push harder ...'

Miriam frowned at the headboard, concentrating as she waited for the next contraction. Panting, she clenched her fists.

'God Jesus! My piles are killing me ...!'

I knelt down and placed my hand between her buttocks, pressing my fingers against her swollen anus. The bloated lining of her rectum ballooned outwards, and I pushed the spongy cushion into her anus, then held it there as the last contractions came.

'One last push, it's coming now, another push for the head ...'

Miriam's vulva had expanded and the crown of a minute head had appeared between her legs. The black hairs were moist and neatly parted, as if a thoughtful nature had groomed the child for its first appearance in this world.

'Push now, we're almost there ...'

The whole face had emerged, a high forehead, miniature nose and mouth, and closed eyes, streamlined as if by time, by the aeons that had preceded this child down the biological kingdom. Waking into the deep dream of life, it seemed not young but infinitely old, millions of years entrained in the pharaoh-like smoothness of its cheeks and its ancient eyelids and nostrils. Its lips were composed, as if it had patiently endured the immense journey across the universe to this modest house with its waiting mother.

Suddenly it was young again; in a last rush of fluid a pink and hair-less puppy bundled itself into Midwife Bell's arms. As the tears wept from my eyes I felt Miriam's fingers grip my hands. The dawn light was filling the spaces between my neighbours' roofs. After a few hours away from me, Miriam had returned and was a wife again.

Miriam slept during the morning, the baby girl in the wicker-work cot beside her. At noon Midwife Bell called, bathed the baby and pronounced herself satisfied, as if willing to accept the formal entry of our child into the mundane world of time and space. Before leaving, she handed Miriam her make-up case, hair brush and mirror. Midwives sat close to the fire, busy with their washings and breaking of the waters, drawing life into the light. By contrast Miriam's local physician, Dr Rogers, with his jovial humour and misplaced advice, resembled a light-headed tour guide searching none too confidently for the sacred spring.

Alice and Henry crept into the bedroom and inspected the baby, curious but faintly disapproving.

'Will she stay with us?' Alice asked.

Miriam laughed at this. 'Don't you want her to stay?'

'I might ...'

Henry was more interested in the remnants of the midwife's equip-ment, the foil caps, spare swabs and mouthpiece. Miriam sat up and hugged them tightly. Later I drove them to spend the afternoon with local friends of Miriam, and they were already planning games and initiation ceremonies for their new sister. Seen through my sleepless eyes, Shepperton had changed. The air was more vivid, as if the town was being lit for some large-budget production at the film studios. The women sitting under the driers at the hairdressers, the cashiers behind the counter at the bank, resembled extras recruited to play the roles of ordinary suburbanites. At any moment the action would begin, and I would find that I had a walk-on part and lines of dialogue I had forgotten to learn.

When I returned home Miriam called to me from the bedroom. She had put on a fresh nightdress, combed her hair, and rouged and powdered her face. The slash of lipstick on her mouth was a pennant flying proudly above the debris of this quiet room.

I looked down at the baby. She had changed yet again, more puckered and more alive, her lips moving while she slept, as if she were trying to remember a message entrusted to her by the unseen powers of creation. Within a few hours she had recapitulated her roles, from archaic messenger to slippery water sprite baptised in her mother's caul, and then a dreamy swaddling whose skin flinched at the light and air.

'Lucy?' I suggested.

'Yes ... Lucy.' Miriam beckoned me to the bed. 'You must be exhausted. Come and lie down for an hour.'

I undressed and lay beside her, my hand against her shoulder. The faint, smothering odour of anaesthetic gas clung to the pillows, and I felt myself drifting back into the heady night from which Lucy had emerged.

'Hold me ...' Miriam pressed my hands to her waist. She lowered the neck of her nightdress and exposed her breasts, their swollen nipples already quickened by the baby's lips. She pushed back the sheet and drew the nightdress to her hips, reached down and held my penis in her hand. Knees in the air, she smiled as I massaged her feet and calves, and caressed her thighs.

'Come into me ...'

Lying on my side, I gently entered her vagina. Already its walls had contracted, and it held me in a firm embrace.

Lucy stirred, her larynx clicking. Miriam smiled at her, her hands on my shoulders as I moved softly within her. Life-magic breathed over us, over the sleeping child, over everything in the sunlit town.

7

The Island

I was swimming strongly, four hundred yards from the beach at Santa Margarita, when I saw the Estartit ferry steering towards me. Loaded with holiday-makers on their way to Cadaques and the Dali mansion at Port Lligat, it cut through the dark water where the Bay of Rosas met the open sea. Bolts of foam jumped from its bows and swept the passenger rail, cooling the legs of the German and Scandinavian girls gazing through their sunglasses at the lizard-backed hills.

A yacht passed me, its main-sail only inches from the water. A middle-aged French couple sat on the side-decking in their yellow life-jackets, watching me in a sceptical way. A pedalo driven by two teenage boys was as far from the beach, but I was well beyond the limit of most holiday swimmers. I had set out to swim across the bay from Santa Margarita, little more than a mile in all, but the French pair clearly took for granted that I was not going to make it.

Ignoring them, I swam on through the black, sunlit water, now and then glancing at the balcony of our apartment. After breakfast I had announced my decision to challenge the bay, and the children had been seized by the vastness of the project.

'Daddy, that's at least … seventeen lengths!' Alice cried, thinking of the public swimming pool near Shepperton.

'More like a hundred,' I told her. 'Or two hundred, if I swim back.'

'Two hundred! Daddy, you're making up fibs again …'

An impromptu arithmetic lesson followed, one of the few in which they had ever taken an interest. They watched me walk into the water, convinced that their father would never return. I could see them on the beach below the apartment, sitting in a row on the rubber inflatable, arguing over my exact position. I waved to them, and saw Miriam, in sun hat and black bikini, wave back, then a semaphore of little arms. My heroic status was guaranteed at least until tea-time.

I pressed on towards the cape, carried to the west by the strong counter-clockwise current that circled the bay. The Estartit ferry was less than a hundred yards away, turning towards the quay at Rosas where it would collect its last batch of sightseers. The helmsman stood behind the open windows of the bridgehouse, surveying the pedalo-filled waters like a hunter at a turkey-shoot. He noticed me trailing my small wake, and then altered course straight towards me.

Was he drunk? I waited for him to spin his wheel, but the bars of his moustache were fixed on me like the arms of a range-finder. The ferry captains of the Costa Brava had been deranged by the endless tourists, like the waiters and taxi-drivers, hovering all summer on the edge of a mental explosion. An isolated swimmer impaled on his bows would be no more than a butterfly on a windshield. The ferry sped towards me, the dull murmur of its propeller carried through the water. Switching to my fastest crawl, I swam at right angles to the vessel's path. Passengers were leaning on the forward rail, waving to me as if I were determined to kill myself.

The ferry passed within a dozen feet, a clamour of engine noise and clinking beer bottles, its wash sending a cloud of diesel fumes into my face. Exhausted, I lay in the rocking wake. The beach was six hundred yards away, and a row of unfamiliar hotels faced me across the water. Our apartment house had moved along the bay, and Miriam and the children were lost behind the lines of umbrellas and beached pedalos. The current had carried me beyond the concrete mole that marked the end of the Santa Margarita beach. Already I could see the undeveloped shoreline of Ampuriabrava, an area of grass-covered dunes, creeks and mosquito inlets.

Giving up any hope of swimming across the bay, I rested on the current, and began the long swim to the empty beach. The concrete mole cut off my sight of Santa Margarita, and I wondered if Miriam had seen me apparently disappear under the ferry's lethal bows.

Twenty minutes later, when I reached the beach, I was too tired even to crawl. I lay in the shallow water, my hands resting on the corrugated sand, my face nudged by the curious waves. A speedboat swept past, two men towing a 15-year-old girl on water-skis. They soared away, leaving behind a blare of pop music.

Untouched by the feet of holiday-makers, the white sand was like fluffed sugar. I stepped out of the water and sank into its soft quilt. I had nearly been chopped into bloody fillets under the critical gaze of hundreds of tourists clutching their Dali guide-books. Somewhere beyond the mole there was the sound of the inflatable's outboard. Miriam had seen me, and was speeding towards the shore.

She expertly beached the craft as Henry jumped onto the sand.

'Are you all right?' Miriam knelt beside me. 'What are you doing here? I'm married to a madman.'

Henry scowled at me. 'Is he dead?'

'He's pretending awfully hard.'

'Being dead must feel like this.' I sat up, glad to see the sun. 'It was like trying to cross the Styx – a ferryman almost ran me down.'

'What a nerve! We'll report him to the Guardia Civil.'

'They're probably in league.'

'How many lengths did you swim?' Henry asked.

'About a thousand.' I leaned against Miriam, resting my chafed chin against her sea-cool shoulder. 'What about Alice and Lucy?'

'They're with the Nordlunds – they spotted you from their balcony. Henry, we'll get Daddy back to the boat.'

'Hold on – let's explore a little. This is some sort of island.'

'A real desert island, Daddy? With cannibals?'

'Definitely cannibals …'

We had come ashore on a long sandbar, separated from the dunes of Ampuriabrava by an arm of shallow water. Some fifty yards wide, the sandbar followed the curve of the bay, rising in a series of grass-covered hillocks. As we walked along the firmer ground we passed the remains of a rusting shack. Wine bottles, an old portable radio and a bicycle wheel lay half-buried in the sand beside this terminal hut. In the hollows between the dunes small fires had been lit during the winter. Across the inlet the scrubland of creeks and inlets extended as far as the Figueras road, but already property developers' signs stood by their marker posts, announcing a new resort complex of hotels, marinas and apartment houses.

As we strolled along, my arm around Miriam's waist, Henry rushed back to us through the long grass.

'There's a Wendy house! It's got a door and windows – and guess what? A real toilet!'

'A Wendy house with a toilet.' Miriam took his hand. 'Are you sure?'

'Yes – I used it!'

At the western end of the island the dunes rose twenty feet above the beach. An old sea-wall had collapsed into the inlet, and the stones had been carried ashore. Standing on a makeshift patio was an ornately gabled cabin that had once been an Edwardian bathing machine, and had probably served for years as a chicken coop in some Rosas back garden. A tattered parachute canopy hung from a trellis of wooden poles and formed a shaded verandah.

I pushed back the cabin door and glanced at the interior. There was a rudimentary kitchen with a stone sink, bottled gas cooker and chemical toilet. Sand covered the wooden floor, blown through the weather-boarding.

Miriam lay back in a wicker chair below the canopy, while Henry and I set out to explore the dunes. We found burnt-out fireworks, beer cans and even, mysteriously, an old portable typewriter. When I carried it back to the patio Miriam nodded approvingly.

I sat beside her and blew through the sandy keys. 'Well, I guess I'm ready to start work. It's not quite the Villa Mauresque, but so what …'

'Good for you.' Miriam closed her eyes, listening to the waves. 'It's lovely here – who owns all this stuff?'

'Local beatniks? Nothing's locked and everything's broken.'

'That sounds more like Shepperton. I always thought we were Shepperton's beatniks without realising it.'

'We still are.' I rested my feet on the typewriter, all notions of work already forgotten. 'I hate to mention it, but the apartment is going to cost us a fortune in dilapidations.'

'I'll talk to Señor Robles. He'll understand.'

'So you always say. This time, put on your best show.'

'I will – I think he likes looking at my breasts.'

'It's his sinister little secretary you'll have to talk to. I hope she likes your breasts.'

'Maybe she does …' Miriam began to rub ointment into my blistered shoulders, her eyes turning towards Santa Margarita. Recently she had become intrigued by the admiring glances of other women. The admiration of her own sex existed on a higher and more intense plane than anything men could offer, like the romantic rivalries of sisters. Together, women formed a conspiracy of glances entirely exchanged behind the backs of their menfolk.

'We'll bring the girls tomorrow,' Miriam said. 'I want them to see this – it's like something straight out of television.'

'Miriam? What a thing to say …'

'Tell me, why don't we get our own place here? You've always said you wanted to live in Spain.'

'We will, one day.'

'Hemingway, Gaudi, Bunuel … you could work here, they're more your world.' Miriam turned my face towards her and pressed a finger between my eyes. 'Face it, dear, you're never going to feel at home in England.'

'Is that true? I feel at home in Shepperton.'

'Not even in Shepperton. You've been in England for eighteen years and you still look as if you've stepped off the wrong train.'

'Perhaps I need to go back to Shanghai. I should have taken up David's offer.'

'No, not Shanghai. You've finished with all that, thank God. Spain might give you just the jolt you're waiting for.'

'Am I waiting for a jolt?'

'Yes – like a rabbit in a Skinner box. You're getting bored with that one damned lever. Look how you come alive at those third-rate bullfights in Figueras.'

'That's tourist Spain. What about schools?'

'They have schools here. The Spanish may be mad, but they're literate. Think about your parents – they went out to China.'

'But they took a piece of Surrey with them. Spain would be a much bigger challenge. For you, anyway.'

'Balls. We've got to get you out of England ... you've found a small strangeness where you're comfortable, and that's dangerous. Anyway, Dali's here at Port Lligat. We might meet him.'

'And the mysterious Gala, his weird.'

Miriam bent down as if to kiss me, and bit my ear. She held a speck of blood on the tip of her tongue, and left it between my lips. 'Jim, you need to meet more weird women. A tussle with Señor Robles's secretary would do you a world of good. I might even arrange it.'

'I wouldn't know what to do.'

'Dear, you would do nothing – she'd quietly take your brain apart like a neurosurgeon. Poor love, I'll protect you ...'

She pulled my head on to her lap, with its scents of sea-salt, baby lotion and perfume borrowed from Mrs Nordlund. We watched Henry wading in the water beside the sea-wall. He lifted a stone and carried it across the patio, where the first flight of a simple staircase had been laid. He smoothed out a new shelf and carefully laid the stone, then surveyed his work with a child's pride.

'I'm coming, Henry!' Miriam pushed me aside and leapt up. She waded into the water and began to help Henry with the stones. I lay back under the awning, watching her assemble this modest stairway that in her mind already led to a new life. Eight years of marriage and three children had failed to dent her enthusiasms. From our earliest days she had always pushed me along, giving up holidays so that I could finish a book, taking the children to London Zoo to allow me a few hours of peace. Her confidence in me had never wavered, even during the time of endless rejection slips. She hid bank statements, quietly borrowed money from her mother and Dick Sutherland. In many ways she had remade me. I owed her everything, my children, my first published books, my refound confidence in the world.

But change would soon come, and I wondered if I was equal to it. She had taken part in the Shepperton Players' open-air performance of *As You Like It*, playing a spirited Rosalind like a feminist agitator. Already she talked of going back to her career in journalism. Watching her move impatiently around her kitchen, bored with the endless meals, I could see the mature and strong-willed woman in her forties that she would become. In a sense she would leave me far behind her, a problematical Peter Pan whose pockets were filled with a strange yellow earth …

For the moment she had set her heart on Spain. I guessed that Señor Robles had already shown her one of his villas in the hills above Rosas and Cadaques. The Dalis might prove to be more demanding neighbours than Miriam realised, but I was happy to see her revelling in the attentive gaze of the melancholy Spaniards as she strode around the supermarkets of Rosas in her black bikini. An economy of pleasure and possibility was about to rule our lives.

A new Europe had sprung up along the beaches of the Mediterranean, in effect a linear city 3000 miles long and 300 metres deep, that stretched from Gibraltar to Glyfada Beach beyond the eastern suburbs of Athens. The old Europe had shed its past, its hierarchies and snobberies. Here in this classless realm Lancashire typists shared bar tables with Stockholm accountants and Danish truck-drivers. The beaches of Spain were Europe's California, or at least its Florida. I liked its marina culture, its endless highways and apartment houses. This was the future that President Kennedy and the space race had helped to create, a residential zone laid down in advance for the science parks and high-technology projects yet to come.

In many ways there was something almost lunar about the white hotels, haunted by criminals running hash from north Africa, stealing antiquities or on the run from Scotland Yard. After the sombre light of northern Europe, the peculiar geometry of these overlit apartments seemed to lead us into a more abstract world where emotions were leached away. Even sex became more stylised. In the afternoons, while the children slept through the heat, Miriam and I would drink white wine in the kitchen. When she was pleasantly drunk, she liked to make love in the bathroom, taking up her positions against the mirrors and white enamel like a perverse gymnast. She watched me without expression, as if we were having sex in a space capsule hundreds of miles above the earth, conceiving the first of a new race of astronauts.

After a year on the Costa Brava we would be totally decorticated, with that blankness of mind I could see in the faces of package tourists after only a week. Before leaving England we had seen Hitchcock's *Psycho*, and the English secretaries in their bikinis behaved like so many Janet Leighs who had decided not to take that crucial shower but could no longer remember where they had left their lives.

'Jim, stir a leg!' Miriam called to me, arms covered with wet sand. 'While we're slaving away he's lying there like a pasha. Tomorrow we'll bring the dinghy here – the girls are going to be really impressed ...'

Building this simple flight of steps was Miriam's touching way of showing that she was serious about settling in Spain. Every morning the five of us set off in the inflatable, taking with us a picnic for the day. As I repaired the awning, stitching the ragged parachute silk, Miriam and the children cleared out the cabin and swept the patio. In the afternoon, after cold chicken and sangria, we dozed in the shade or swam with the children from the stone steps. The water-skiers sped across the bay, portable radios gleamed on the beach at Santa Margarita, and the mad ferryman aimed his bows at any passing swimmer.

A week later, when we landed on the island, new arrivals had occupied our beach hideaway. A small Citroën loaded with suitcases and camping gear had crossed the shallow water of the inlet and was parked on the sand. A bearded man and a young woman with a black shingle were swimming from Miriam's jetty, watched by a tall, naked man in his forties with shoulder-length hair, a book in one hand and a pipe in the other.

Uncertain, the children stopped by the car. Henry pointed to the sticker pasted to the rear fender above the French licence plate: 'Happiness is overtaking a 2CV'.

'What's a 2CV?'

'A kind of car – let's say hello.'

'Why is happiness overtaking it?'

Alice peered through her fringe and took Miriam's hand. 'Are they the cannibals? Is Daddy going to fight them?'

'Of course not. It's probably their house.'

The car was packed with bottles of Spanish wine, loaves of bread, and a clutch of paperbacks by Kerouac, Henry Miller, Ginsberg and William Burroughs. Lashed incongruously to the roof rack was an expensive pigskin suitcase covered with the labels of New York and Chicago hotels. Had they stolen the case from some distracted traveller at Perpignan station? As the naked man waved his pipe at the children I was visualising a new breed of beach criminal, reading *On the Road* or *Howl* as he slid the tourist's purse from her handbag.

The bearded man in the water was calling in French to the children. The door of the bathing machine opened and a blonde-haired young woman with an ivory-white skin came out to greet us. She wore high-heeled beach shoes and the bottom of a cream bikini. Her face had a look of slightly shop-soiled elegance, as if she had neglected herself for too long in some intimate way. When she smiled the sunlight shone against a set of immaculate American teeth, from which the left canine was missing, bridged by an inferior piece of English dentistry. But she had a rangy manner that I immediately liked.

'Hello ... I thought some little pixies had been cleaning the kitchen.' She swept Lucy into her arms and held the startled girl to her shoulder. 'Are you a pixie?'

'No! Mummy ... !'

'I think you are. You've been scrubbing and dusting and polishing ...'

She chattered on in a pleasant New England voice as the pipe-smoker ambled up to us. The children stared at him open-mouthed, even more intrigued by the star-shaped scars across his abdomen and thigh than they were by his penis and scrotum. I guessed that he had been badly wounded during the war.

Seeing that we were English, he introduced himself: 'Peter Lykiard. You're from London? Good. I teach at Regent Street Poly.' He pointed to the couple in the water. 'Robert and Muriel Joubert, from Nanterre. And this is Sally Mumford, one of my American students. She's probably going to steal your children.'

'I'm definitely thinking about it.' The young woman lowered Lucy to the ground and welcomed us into the shade. With a cheerful flourish she produced a jug of sangria, tapas and cigarettes. The French couple sunned themselves on the patio, their naked bodies inspected by the children with the measured eyes of experienced anthropologists. They had seen Miriam and me naked every day of their lives, but a different anatomy, however small the distinctions, held a universe of intriguing possibilities.

Sharing our hamper and wine cooler with this amiable crew, we sat drinking under the parachute canopy as Lykiard explained that he came down to Ampuriabrava every summer – though this, sadly, would be the last. The property developers' bulldozers would soon level the site.

'This island will vanish, literally turn into cement. They'll up-end the beach into half a mile of hotels and apartment houses.' He pointed to the pine posts like so many gibbets which the surveyors had staked into the dunes. 'There's a model of the whole complex in Gerona. They plan to consolidate the waterways with promenades of boutiques and bars, then sell off the housing plots to all those Dusseldorf dentists. Three years from now the place will be a film set, with a series of mock-antique Catalonian villages along the speed-boat canals.'

'Miriam wants us to settle here – she thinks it would be good for my imagination.'

'I can't see that there'd be anything left for your imagination to do. In fact, it's hard to visualise the lifestyles of these sober-sided Rhinelanders once they've set up their beach-head. When bourgeois life meets surrealism head on we know who wins.'

Children's squeals came from the beach, where Henry's sandcastle was holding out against the ferry-boat's bow-waves. Sally was on her hands and knees, constructing an elaborate double bed of damp sand with bolsters and eiderdown, under which she tucked a delighted Lucy and Alice. I dozed while Miriam helped Lykiard and the Jouberts to unload the car. Lykiard worked in his unhurried way, pausing to refill his pipe and read a page or two of the books packed below the seats. Watching him put a friendly hand on Miriam's waist, I realised how bourgeois we had become, with our rented flat, estate car and loyal inflatable bounding behind us on its trailer. Even our attempt to clean the bathing hut had shown the same bijouising suburban strain. I had always smiled at my parents for taking an intact piece of Surrey with

them to Shanghai, but Miriam and I were in the same export business. The real trapeze artists and dare-devils on the scene were the
Dusseldorf dentists.

At dusk the first marijuana smoke began to overlay the warm air,
pricking at the children's nostrils. Sorry to leave, we gathered our things
together and piled them into the inflatable.

'Bye-bye, pixies, come again tomorrow,' Sally told the children as
they sat in their life jackets. 'We'll do some more cleaning. We've got
to dust and polish the whole beach – just look at this untidy sand ...'

Miriam winced, but I warmed to this excitable American girl. She
waded out into the water, the smoke from her loose-packed cigarette
sending its scent into the evening. Holding it aloft in one hand, she
tugged at the inflatable with the other. As we motored away I could see
her generous, ironic smile following us across the waves.

'God, I feel so square,' Miriam told me as she gazed around our apartment, pastis in hand. '"Do some more cleaning" – that was a dig at me.'

'In a friendly way.'

'Am I square?'

'My depraved and respectable wife?' I pressed her reassuringly against
the refrigerator. 'Miriam, the Jouberts work at a left-wing lycée, and
he teaches modern literature at a fashionable polytechnic. They drive
a 2CV and smoke pot. What could be more square than that?'

'You're avoiding the point.' Miriam finished off the pastis and stared
at the sand-bar beyond the mole, a pale smudge along the shore of
Ampuriabrava. The blazing driftwood fire we had left behind was a
faint ember. 'Let's buy some pot.'

'Okay – I know you're dying to be arrested by those handsome
Spanish cops. Remember, Lykiard and his chums don't have children.'

'That amazes me – they look as if they're at it hard enough. Do you
think they sleep with each other?'

'Who cares? They're probably all celibate.'

'In a way, I care ...' Miriam nodded briskly to herself, mind already
set on an urgent recovery project, the retrieval of those possibilities
that marriage and motherhood had consigned to some cul de sac. I

often caught her staring at herself in the bathroom mirror, as if she sensed that her entire life, her husband and children, were a detour from the main road.

Every morning we returned to the island, leaving the crowded beach at Santa Margarita with its haze of sun-oil and deodorant that formed an almost visible microclimate. We berthed the inflatable on the sand below the headland, and joined the others under the tattered parachute awning. In the afternoon the French couple, keen bird-watchers, put on their saris and prowled the creeks and dunes of Ampuriabrava, sketch-pads and camera at the ready. Sally swam with Henry and the girls, while Miriam helped Lykiard to extend the patio, carrying stones from the sea-wall.

Watching Sally, I was surprised by her unforced pleasure in the children. She was forever down on her knees with them, devising games and conspiracies, mysterious errands that sent them darting off into the sand-grass. Miriam told me that her father was the owner of a Boston department store, and that she had achieved the distinction, rare for a rich man's daughter, of being expelled from both her private school and exclusive women's college. She had set off for the Mediterranean, crewing the yachts of her father's friends, and had come to England to meet the Beatles. Self-consciously a free spirit, she seemed deliberately to neglect herself, living on nothing but tapas, sangria and pot. I sensed that in some way she wanted to revenge herself on her own body.

Miriam also told me, in her most casual voice, that Sally slept with both Lykiard and Joubert, a piece of information that she swallowed whole and was digesting at her leisure. But it was only when we drove to Barcelona to see Cordobés and Paco Camino that she recognised the raw edge of Sally's mind and her uncertain grip on the world.

Leaving Lucy and Alice in our apartment with the Jouberts, the rest of us set off in our car. In honour of Cordobés, we sat in the primo barreras and bought thimbles of fundador to toast the Beatle of the bullring who scandalised the traditionalists with his bizarre stunts and reckless bravery. Henry sat between Sally and myself, clutching a huge plastic bull with a penis and scrotum, Sally whispered to me, larger than his own.

One of the early bulls, disoriented by the jeers and shouts of the tourist crowd, jumped the barricade and ran past us, spraying us with his saliva, ragged horns inches from our hands. Henry clutched his model bull, awestruck by the inflamed eyes of this violent and terrified creature, but Sally sprang to her feet and slapped its dung-smeared haunches. She was wearing a pale silk dress, and her excited sweat stained the bodice and armpits. She gripped Henry's hand, whistling and shouting as she worked herself up, while the band blared and the crowd screamed at every pass of the cape. When the banderilleros savaged the bull's shoulders with their ribboned darts she rose to her feet with a strange throaty cry, like a mad-woman in an abattoir.

Embarrassed by herself, she fell quiet when a handsome torrera, in elegant black jacket and flared breeches, fought a bull on horseback in the Portuguese manner. A commanding, strong-nosed woman with the maquillage of a glamorous bank-manager, she glared threateningly at the audience and noticed Sally standing at the barrera. The two women gazed at each other across the noise and the smell of blood and the reek of fundador. Time and again the torrera was about to be caught by the veering bull, but always accelerated away as the horns brushed the flanks of her horse. During one stand-off, while the bull choked on its tongue, bathed in blood and rage, she sat ramrod straight in her saddle a dozen feet from us. Sally and I could hear the stream of obscenities, the insults to the bull's testicles and paternity, spitting from the mouth of this imposing horsewoman.

When she dismounted to kill the exhausted beast, she first fed saliva from her scarlet lips onto the tip of her sword, making plain that she was advancing on the bull as more than a mere man, and that her saliva was the semen with which she would impregnate the creature as she struck it dead at her feet.

Dazed by the fundador and the screams of the crowd, I was trying to visualise how one would even dare to approach this terrifying figure, let alone have sex with her. But Sally had already decided. Sweat soaking her armpits, she gripped the wooden rail, and stared at the horsewoman as if she recognised all the headmistresses of her New England child-hood. I expected her to rip away her silk dress, leap the barricade and mount the horse with her white legs, arms clasping the torrera's waist as they galloped out of the arena.

While Cordobés was in the ring I forgot Sally, and marvelled with Miriam and Lykiard at this handsome street-fighter, part gangster and part film-star. As Lykiard pointed out to us through the hoots and applause, however close the bull charged the boy never moved his feet. For all his theatrical strutting and open insults to the decorum of the bullring, he took immense risks with his own life. After exhausting his second bull he began to play the fool, humiliating the gasping beast that staggered towards him, drenched in blood. As it stood on its shaky forelegs, Cordobés knelt with his back to the bull, its horns only inches from his shoulder blades, arms outstretched to catch the approving roars of the arena, which the older Spaniards were already leaving in disgust.

When he retired from the ring, through the delirium of the European and American tourists, I saw Sally clambering between the seats, her dress half-torn from her back. An hour later we found her in the mêlée around the bullfighter's black Mercedes, her make-up bruised, being pushed about by the jeering chauffeurs and bodyguards. Lykiard and I carried her to my car, watched by a shocked little Henry who offered her his bull. When we lifted her into the back seat she struck at us with her hard fists, still gripped by her unsatisfied need for some kind of violent climax to the afternoon. Miriam managed to calm her, holding her hands and wiping the streaks of mascara from her chin. The two women sat side by side, like sisters returning from a deranged funeral.

In the traffic back to Gerona I watched the flush in Sally's cheeks fading through the rear-view mirror. She sat in her torn silk dress, a delinquent schoolgirl caressing the coarse hide of Henry's plastic bull, forcing her lips together as she swallowed the aftertaste of some toxic emotion.

'I like her American spunk,' Miriam decided when we returned to the apartment. 'She knows what she wants, and goes out and gets it. Of course, she's completely mad.'

'Maybe she's completely sane – for people like Sally that amounts to the same thing.'

'Jim, she wanted to fuck those bulls! Never mind Cordobés and the chauffeurs. I bet they caught her trying to cut off the testicles. What do they do with them, anyway?'

'They're some kind of delicacy. Why don't you try a pair? We'll find a good restaurant in Gerona.'

'I might ...' Miriam stared in a determined way from the balcony. 'Sex is a branch of gastronomy – the best cooks make the best lovers. Every woman soon discovers that.'

I could see the 2CV trundling across the sand-dunes of Ampuriabrava. Sally was standing in the open roof behind Lykiard, the tatters of her silk dress floating like pennants between the poles of the property developers, an eager fury touring a field of gibbets.

Miriam put her arm around me. 'She's strange, but I like her. Do you wish you'd married someone like that?'

'I did.'

'I'd like to help her. She needs to have a child.'

'Only I can help her there.'

'You're going to be busy with Señor Robles's secretary, remember. Tomorrow could be tricky.'

I embraced Miriam, glad that Sally had charged her imagination. 'Dear, you always wanted to live on a desert island with three strange men.'

However, by the next day Sally's sunny humour had returned. She knelt on the sand by the bathing hut, straw horns tied to her head as Henry made passes with a beach towel. While Miriam fed Alice and Lucy, I took a handful of black olives and a bottle of beer, and walked into the scrub-covered dunes. I sat down in one of the hollows, trying to work out my route across the bay. Thinking of Cordobés and the maimed beasts waiting for the sword, I imagined a startled tourist on a pedalo crossing a wake stained with blood. Long after the ferry left for Cadaques, its waves rolled against the beach, as if Poseidon himself were reminding me of my close escape.

Smoking a cigarette, Sally climbed through the grass towards me. She still wore the straw horns around her white hair.

'Time for a rest.' She slumped down beside me. 'Jesus, I'm pooped. You and Miriam ... there must be a knack.'

'Tell us if you find it – we've been exhausted since 1957.'

She sailed the straw horns into the air. 'They're wonderful, take it from me. Everything turns into a party. I wish my childhood had been so much fun.'

She spoke wistfully, and flicked at the hair blowing into her eyes, almost trying to set the loose ends alight with her cigarette. Endlessly patient with Henry, Alice and Lucy, she was short-tempered with her own body, as if it had failed like a thoughtless child to respond to the problems on its mother's mind. She had chewed her nails to the quick, and her left nipple was raw and tender. A faint chemical odour rose from the gusset of her bikini, a hint of stale spermicidal jelly, and I guessed that she had been too distracted to change her cap for a few days. She helped herself to an olive from my hand.

'Where's your apartment? I can't see it today.'

'Next to the hotel with the sign ... if some developer hasn't moved it. We should have come straight here with a couple of tents.'

'It's great. I like Gozo best – Circe's island, I drank from her spring. And Ruanda. Last year I was going to live with the Watusi.' She patted the sand on her legs, as if readying herself for some husband painted in white dust. 'Miriam told me that you come from China.'

'Years ago. I've settled in England now.'

'Do you like it?'

'It takes getting used to.'

'That could be a good thing. Maybe you need to feel like a refugee.'

'What about you?'

She grimaced through the smoke, a gleam of American teeth. 'I keep waiting ... there aren't too many stars in the east these days. Sometimes I think that everywhere is pretty much the same. Miriam says you want to buy some pot?'

'Only if you have any to spare. She feels we're getting too bourgeois.'

'It's good for sex ...' Sally was lying on her side, her breast touching the bottle of beer in my hand. I could see the tender nipple magnified through the pale green glass. She passed her cigarette and watched as I took a draw on the loosely packed hemp and tobacco. The children were hidden behind the headland, Miriam was working on the patio, and the empty beach would give us all the warning we needed as we lay within the dune grass. Sally took another olive from my palm, her lips briefly sucking my thumb. She was waiting for me, but I felt curiously gauche, as if I were effectively a virgin with no experience of women. During the eight years of our marriage I had been faithful to Miriam, and knew her body far more closely than I knew my own. Another woman's body was an unfathomed mystery, let alone another woman's emotions and needs.

'Well, back to the monsters.' Sally stood up, brushing the sand from her thighs. She smiled quickly, erasing the offer of herself without any resentment, and strode down to the beach.

I followed fifty yards behind her, pausing to wash the guilty sweat from my face. I was surprised to find that I was shaking with irritation at myself – I was loyal to Miriam, though a little less loyal than I had realised.

When I reached the cabin the Jouberts were stepping from their Citroën, loaves of bread in their arms, more tapas and cheap wine from the bodega. Lykiard was holding a biology class for the children, who stood in a line, gazing fixedly at the lizard in his hand as Sally pulled a face over his shoulder.

The bow wave of the Estartit ferry struck the beach. Miriam strode across the patio, about to rinse the swimsuits in the sea. She skipped down the steps, stumbled and missed her footing on the polished stones. Her right leg skewed sideways, and she fell heavily on the staircase.

The crack of her head against the stone made everyone turn. When I reached the steps she was lying half-stunned, eyes staring at my face as if she no longer recognised me. Her leg was twisted under her hips, blood running from a deep graze on the ankle.

Lykiard was beside me, warning the children away with the lizard, which he threw into the sea. I lifted Miriam onto her side, trying to feel the broken bone. Still stunned, she held on to my shoulder and sat up, her face small and pale, inhaling shallow breaths.

'My, that was a knock.' She spoke flatly. 'Silly fool, where was I going?'

'Love, are you all right? Your leg …'

'Hurts like hell. Don't worry, Lucy. Mummy was silly and fell over. God, my head – I shouldn't have laid all those steps …'

Sally and I helped her back to the patio and settled her in the wicker chair. Miriam was shivering with the shock, her hair matted to her scalp, as she held Henry's hand. I tried to calm her trembling shoulders while Sally cleaned the ankle wound with a tampon soaked in mineral water. She turned to kiss Henry, and I saw the swollen bruise above her right ear, pushing against the unbroken skin.

Lykiard had put on his jeans and sandals. He spoke quickly to the Jouberts and brought out a bottle of fundador, but Miriam waved it away. She was reassuring the children, her face as small as theirs, her eyes staring at the staircase as if she had mislaid part of herself on the damp steps.

'I'd take her back to your flat,' Lykiard suggested. 'We'll drive the kids in the car. She'll be more comfortable in the dinghy.'

Sally and the Jouberts helped me to lift Miriam into the inflatable. We pushed off, leaving our hamper and beach equipment on the sand, where the waves were already soaking the towels. Miriam waved to the children climbing into the back of the Citroën, her awkward hands gripping the sides of the inflatable. During the short journey the sea air seemed to revive her, and she smiled at me confidently, raising her damp eyebrows to apologise. But she collapsed when I pulled the dinghy on to the beach, and had to lie down among the lines of parasols and the watching sunbathers until she recovered her breath.

She was strong enough to walk to the lift, but when I opened the door to the flat I sensed that only half of her mind recognised it. I called the bureau for the telephone number of a local doctor, and Miriam wandered on to the balcony, blinking at the crowded beach.

An hour later, when the Spanish doctor arrived, she was lying on our bed, smiling wanly at the sound of the children on the Nordlunds' balcony. The doctor examined her in a slow but scrupulous way. Afterwards he patted me encouragingly and spoke in Spanish to Lykiard. The practicante, a visiting male nurse, would keep Miriam under observation until the doctor called again that evening.

While the practicante sat beside Miriam in the bedroom I went into the kitchen and prepared the children's supper, then carried the tray to the Nordlunds' apartment. When I returned, the practicante was on the telephone. He spoke to the doctor, and then told me to be calm while he summoned an ambulance. I went into the bedroom and held Miriam's shoulders. She had lost all feeling from her left leg and arm, and was moving in and out of a shallow consciousness, smiling in a faint way as she seemed to recede from herself. She frowned at me with one side of her face, touching her numbed body with a small hand.

When the ambulance arrived I was already dazed with panic. The driver and his attendant were trying to assemble the collapsible wheelchair. While they argued with each other I lifted Miriam from the bed and carried her in my arms to the elevator. Her eyes stared vaguely at the falling lights of the floor buttons, and her body was cold, as if she had spent hours in the sea. We eased her into the ambulance, waving away the tourists returning from the beach, watched by the expressionless children on the Nordlunds' balcony.

Miriam could no longer see them. I heard the rear doors close behind me, and saw Lykiard smiling stiffly with a fist clenched in encouragement. I crouched on the jump seat behind the attendant as he secured Miriam under the blanket and readied his oxygen cylinder. We sped along the Figueras road, siren wailing, and began to swerve in and out of the traffic. I massaged Miriam's calves, trying to feel the pulse in her legs. The oxygen from the mask had driven the sweat from her face, which seemed as small as Lucy's at the moment of birth. Only her right eye was focused, moving across the lace curtains on the windows of the ambulance. She was forcing herself to breathe, but her rib-cage had collapsed.

We stopped behind a bus that blocked the road to the bullring. The attendant opened the rear doors and remonstrated with the driver, who slowly reversed out of our way. We reached the hospital ten minutes later, as the last crowds dispersed from the football stadium. The flower-sellers by the ticket office were wrapping up their unsold blooms, and the news vendors were taking down their metal racks. But by then Miriam was already dead.

8

The Kindness of Women

The kindness of women came to my rescue, at a time when I had almost given up hope. Within a few weeks of her death I discovered that I had lost not only Miriam but all the women in the world. An unbridgeable space separated me from Miriam's friends and the women I knew, as if they had decided to isolate me within a carefully drawn cordon. Later I realised that they were standing at a distance, in the nearby rooms of my life, waiting until I had faced my anger at myself. Then they came forward and did everything to help me. The kindness of women and the affection of my children steered me safely through those first long months.

During our final days in Rosas, as the Nordlunds helped me to pack, I looked down from the balcony at the tourists stretched out on the beach, playing their parts in the eerie imitation of reality that life had become. The sun shone on the same parasols and pedalos, but everything had changed. In the hours since Miriam's death the entire female race had mutated into a different species. The women eating their gambas in the beach restaurants avoided my eyes, talking among themselves as they licked their red-stained fingers. When I cashed the last of my traveller's cheques I noticed that the bodies of the women queuing at the counter had lost their scent. Even Mrs Nordlund, with her determined smile and affection towards the children, stared at me with the gaze of a relief worker from a foreign country.

Only Señor Robles's German-speaking secretary was still herself.

Checking the inventory, she peered into the darkened bedroom, clearly assuming that here Miriam had died at my hands. She opened the mirrored cabinet in the bathroom and ran her fingers along the tooth glasses.

'Nix kaputt?'

'Kaputt nix.'

She glanced at me in that way I would come to resent, a mixture of curiosity and distance, like a spectator at the scene of a crime. I wanted to take her wrists and raise her elbows so that I could inhale the scent of her armpits, press my fingers into her natal cleft. I disliked this cocksure young woman enough to have sex with her while the children waited in the car with the Nordlunds. I wanted to prove that at least one woman still existed. But she moved away from me to the hallway, and took the stairs rather than be alone with me in the elevator. In her mind my wife's death had let a rapist loose upon the world.

Rosas and the lizard-ridged rocks of Cape Creus fell behind us as we set off for Figueras and the French border. The resort beaches of the Costa Brava, the hotels and cafés slid past through a dream more lurid than any of Dali's paintings, a vision of the world's end seen in terms of polluted sand, the stench of sun-oil and terraces of over-exposed flesh. We passed the entrance to the municipal cemetery at Figueras, and the long corridor of cypresses leading to the white-washed walls and the ornate porticos of the family tombs. Miriam was buried in the adjacent Protestant cemetery, a flowerless bone-yard where a few anti-clerical Spaniards rested under modest stones beside an English youth drowned in a yachting accident. Looking back for the last time, I turned north towards the Pyrenees, France and home.

The children sat behind me, playing compulsive games all the way to the Channel. Henry was too stunned to speak, but Alice and Lucy soon took charge. Already they were more concerned for me than they were for themselves. Mile after mile, they helped me with the road maps and chose hotels for our overnight stops, and kept a careful watch on the whisky bottle I held between my thighs. Their good sense and cheer laid the foundation on which we rebuilt our lives together.

During the drive I could only remember my last moments with Miriam and the burial service at the cemetery. Nature had committed a crime against my young wife and her children, and I felt a deep, confused anger not merely at myself, for bringing Miriam to Rosas, but at the vine-covered hills, the plane trees and the grazing cattle. An hour after she died a fierce peace had come over Miriam as she lay in the emergency room at Figueras hospital. Her head was flung back, her chest braced upwards, and her lips gaped in a rictus that exposed the livid muscles of her mouth and throat. Her jaw thrust itself at me from the blue skin, teeth set in a scream of death. Steadied by Nordlund, I walked to the cathedral-like Figueras undertakers. We moved through the lines of ornate gothic coffins that resembled pews facing a profane altar of black marble headstones. Thinking of Miriam, it seemed only fitting that she should be consigned to the earth in a casket like a prop from a horror film.

But later that evening, when I returned to the hospital, a complete change had come over her. All the pain and fear of her last moments, as her stricken brain collapsed inwards upon itself, had passed. Her face had relaxed, and her skin was soft and white again. A nurse had combed her hair for me, and her cheeks and lips were as small and neat as a little girl's, giving me a last glimpse of her vanished childhood.

At the burial service the next day, the coffin was wheeled on its cart into the Protestant cemetery. The iron rims rang across the dusty rubble. The children stood beside me in their best party clothes, and I hoped that they would never hear the rage of death below the coffin lid. The young Spanish clergyman abandoned his broken English and spoke in a thick Catalan, once banished by General Franco, whose dark consonants were the language of the dead which Miriam would now be speaking. Sally Mumford stood with Lykiard and the Jouberts. None of them could look at me. Smoking her reefer, Sally stared at the graves as if she expected the stone lids to be flung back and the angry occupants to leap out and seize us.

The grave-diggers bent over their spades. The first stones struck the lid like a fist beating against a door. Nordlund handed a spare spade to me and I cast two blades of the nutty soil into the grave. Together we walked from the cemetery and drove through the football crowds, as if leaving a crime behind us.

After three days to cross a country and a sea, we returned to Shepperton. The long French roads helped me to straighten the perspectives of my mind. The past, on which I had turned my back on the day of my marriage, had rushed up and now stood behind me. Miriam's death joined me once again to all those nameless Chinese who had died during the Second World War. I remembered the dusty dead beside the crushed motor-cars in the Avenue Edward VII, and the straining jaw of the Chinese clerk at the rural railway station, first rehearsals for an afternoon at Figueras. Images of the bone-white paddy fields came back to me, like the pearly light that lay over Lunghua after the explosion of the atom bomb at Nagasaki. Kennedy had outstared Khrushchev during the Cuban missile crisis, but American bombers were still parked under the flat skies of Cambridgeshire, and the kingdom of light waited to be born from those concrete aprons among the fens.

Miriam's sister, Dorothy, and her husband were waving cheerfully by the gate when we arrived home. They had treats and surprises for the children, a cold roast lunch fit for a wake, and bottles of wine open on the table. I was grateful to them and held Dorothy tightly in my arms. But the echo of Miriam's bones in her sister's face, and the Cambridge crispness in her voice, made me feel that I and the children had returned to a parallel world that tried too hard to mimic its original.

While the children opened their presents I left Dorothy and Brian and climbed the stairs. The untidy rooms, strewn with toys and clothes, with favourite teddy bears rejected at the last minute, fixed the exact moment of our departure four weeks earlier. I stood by Miriam's dressing-table, looking down at the clutter of hairbrushes and cosmetics, and a discarded tube of the previous summer's suntan oil with its broken cap. Her finger-prints were set in the film of talc that covered the glass top, the ghost of her mouth in the red smear of a crushed tissue.

I opened the centre drawer, crammed with old phone bills, tampons and school reports, faded brassieres held together with safety pins, and her faithful Dutch cap, like an unreliable family servant, for years the home of the spare car keys. I tipped the waste-basket onto the floor, and sifted through the hair balls and tubes of contraceptive jelly, the torn suspender belt and fishnet stockings that she liked to wear at parties and later vamp around the bedroom. I lifted the stocking to my lips, smelling the scent of Miriam's thighs, the same body scent that rose from the pillows and greeted me when I opened the wardrobe on to the racks of her dresses. Her hundred presences filled the house like a chorus of ghosts.

I needed to let them go. I opened the windows and watched the clouds of talc and dust drift through the air, repatriating themselves to Figueras. In the garden the children were chasing their old toys while Brian mowed the lawn. Alice was rearranging the furniture in the tree-house, casting out the cardboard tables and chairs as if spring-cleaning before the arrival of a new domestic regime. Henry had found a still-inflated party balloon and was trying to stamp on it, while Lucy tested the swing, taking it up to a wild new altitude.

Watching them, I felt the first smile cross my lips. I knew that the children were braver than I was – during the long drive home they had never once mentioned their mother, the first of the many unspoken pacts which we made in the coming months. I sat on the bed, as the scents of Miriam's body floated on the summer air.

Dorothy was carving the cold roast in the kitchen. She was three years older than Miriam, the more serious sister, a partner in a firm of Cambridge solicitors. At our wedding she had smiled and shaken her head as I kissed the bride, clearly doubting whether I would ever be a match for the high-tempered Miriam.

I drank a tumbler of duty-free whisky, and hesitated before pouring another. Dorothy pressed my hand, refilling the glass.

'Go on – you've earned it. That must have been the most tremendous drive.'

'We were totally lost near Poitiers. I can tell you, Henry's French saved the day. For one moment I thought of turning back.'

'You should have done. No, what am I saying?' Dorothy checked herself, surprised by her tongue. 'Brian wondered if you were going to move?'

'From Shepperton?'

'From this house, at least – you ought to make a fresh start somewhere.'

'No …' I watched Alice and Lucy vigorously cleaning the tree-house. A flurry of leaves was followed by an old stuffed toy, loyal companion of years, that plunged headfirst to the newly mown grass. Women were ruthless from an early age, and needed to be. 'We've made a fresh start. It's best if we stay here and face things.'

'You'll keep the children?'

'Of course. It was part of the deal.'

'It's quite a challenge. Brian and I could have the girls.'

'Thanks, but no. We'll stick it out together.'

After lunch, when Brian had taken the children to Chessington Zoo, Dorothy and I began to tidy the rooms. As we put away the scattered toys and clothes I had the sense that we were scene-shifters changing a set of props. Everything tilted at an unfamiliar angle. Even Dorothy's resemblances to her sister, the echo of Miriam's broad cheekbones and small hands, strong walk and determined hips, made me feel that we were extras rehearsing a scene to be played by others.

'Would you like me to do the bedroom?' Dorothy was staring at the cluttered dressing-table and wardrobe. 'Heavens, it's sad. Jim, throw it all away. Clear everything out. Give the clothes to the jumble people.'

'I will, don't worry. I need a little longer. It's all that's left.'

'It isn't.'

Dorothy held my shoulders, trying to pull me back into the present. I put my hands on her waist, desperate to embrace her. After the spectral women of Rosas beach, Dorothy with her firm hips and comforting breasts was wholly alive. I pressed my hands to her shoulder blades, searching for the familiar contours that Miriam had trained me to recognise. Dorothy stiffened and moved away from me, unsettled by my trembling hands. Then she leaned against me, pressing her cheek to mine, calming my agitated face.

'All right. We'll go into Henry's room.'

'No … stay here. In Miriam's bed.'

Trying to control myself, I untied her apron and slipped my hands beneath her shirt, feeling the smooth skin of her back and her strong ribs. I sat on the untidy bed, the sheets still marked by the creases of the last night before the holiday, and placed my head against her thighs. Dorothy stood calmly in front of me as I undressed her, palms lightly on my cheeks, running her fingers into my mouth as I tasted their scent. An unfamiliar mole marked the skin of her left shoulder, but for a moment I could believe that she was Miriam. I kissed her labia and then sat her on my knees, caressing her vulva as if I had parted its lips on countless afternoons in this bedroom of a loving husband. When I pressed my mouth to her nipples she smoothed away the sweat on my forehead, and pushed me back onto Miriam's pillow.

For these few minutes her duty to her dead sister's children overrode her loyalty to her husband. She knelt across me, adjusting her knees to my heavier torso. Exhausted and over-excited, desperate for this kindly woman, I tried to press my limp penis into her vulva. Smiling in a distant but reassuring way, Dorothy took it from my fingers and began to massage the head between her hands. She forced a little spit onto her finger-tips and moistened the mouth of her vagina. She eased my penis into her, glanced through the window at a passing car and put her breast to my mouth, looking down at me like a wet nurse caring for a neighbour's feverish child. When I came, and sank back onto the pillow, she lay beside me and held my diaphragm until my breathing had steadied. I let my fingers into her vulva and tasted the sweet moisture, making sure that I would remember it in the empty months ahead.

She waited until I was ready and passed my clothes to me. Without speaking, she began to tidy the dressing-table, lining up the cosmetics and hairbrushes, and polishing the finger-smeared mirror. I gratefully embraced her before she left the bedroom for the last time.

From that afternoon I was celibate for nearly a year. Although the children and I often visited Dorothy and her husband, I never again made love to her. She had met her obligations to her dead sister, calming the widowed husband and reminding him that Miriam endured within our affection and shared memories. Greeting us, Dorothy would hold me briefly, keeping alive the link between her lost sister and the women I would know in the future.

But much as I needed other women, I found it impossible to approach them. My friends were careful to invite me to their parties, but a chasm of time and pain separated me from the women I met. Tongue-tied and clumsy, I moved past them in a daze of sexual desire.

Once, standing among the coats in David Hunter's bedroom, I found myself alone with one of his flying-club groupies, the young widow of an RAF sergeant killed in Cyprus. I guessed that he had assigned her the job of bringing me back to life. As David stood guard in the corridor, and pretended to discuss the Mercury space flights with an aviation journalist, she leaned against the door and drew me on to her thighs. I held her small shoulders as if she were one of my daughters, frightened after a fall in the garden. I pressed my cheek to her mouth, and felt her lips in my ear, teeth biting at the lobe. When I failed to respond she slipped her hand below the waist of my trousers, fingers probing between my buttocks. She tugged at my shirt and palpated me as she would have soothed a wounded lover. She waited patiently for my erection, but then gave up with a shrug, kissed me cheerfully on the forehead and slipped through the door.

Had nature, through long trial and error, decided that I had failed as both husband and father, and banished me before I could do any further damage? Certainly, many people thought that I should not be looking after the children. But Henry, Alice and Lucy were all I had to believe in, and I was sure that I could make them happy. We cooked in the crowded kitchen, following the girls' outlandish recipes, argued over television and did our homework together. With longer memories of his mother, Henry was sometimes sad, and in the evenings I carried the TV set into my study and sat with him on the sofa, an arm around him while he quietly watched his favourite comedy programmes. One evening at last I heard him laugh.

Every day was an Aladdin's Cave of schemes and enthusiasms. Alice and Lucy, seven and four, soon took charge of everything, deciding when we should go shopping or visit friends, whether I needed a rest from them or if it was time to hold a party. Already they were sizing up the mothers of their school-friends, urging me into little flirtations and blithely waving aside the minor problem of their husbands. I collected them from school in the afternoons and felt a thrill of relief when they clambered noisily into the car, as if we had been separated for months.

What they most resented was any hint that there was something freakish about our family. Too many people, swayed by folk wisdom or modish child psychology, took for granted that the loss of their mother was a wound from which they would never recover, and that no father, however loving, could ever take the mother's place. Even Peggy Gardner, now a paediatrician at Guy's Hospital in London, seemed to hold this view. Whenever she visited Shepperton she gazed tolerantly at the untidy rooms cluttered with the children's drawings and projects, as if the confusion reflected the deep crisis within this stricken family.

Peggy had never married, despite a long line of men-friends and an easy knack with children. Miriam had vaguely distrusted her, aware that Peggy was the first woman I had ever needed and that our relationship went far beyond the possibilities of sex. At the same time she was curious to see behind the handsome self-control that Peggy showed to the world. Bourgeois life had claimed Peggy – good sense, tolerance and understanding had totally corrupted her.

Six months after our return from Spain she called in to see us on the way back from a child-care conference in Bristol. Still in her professional mode, briefcase in hand, she sat smilingly on the sofa while Lucy made room for her. Surrounded by Lucy's full parade of dolls and bears, arranged in meticulous order of seniority, Peggy faintly resembled a stuffed toy herself. As always, I could see that my motherless children reminded her of our days together in Lunghua.

'That's nice, Lucy.' Peggy beamed at the row of dolls. 'I'm in the middle of a lovely little family.'

'You're not in the family,' Lucy warned her. 'But you're the oldest.'

'And the wisest,' I added.

Lucy straightened a battered kangaroo. 'Mrs Roo's much wiser – she told Daddy's fortune.'

'And what was that, Lucy?'

'He's going to live for a hundred years.'

'That's wonderful. I think he's going to live for ever.'

'No,' Lucy said, her eyes fixed on mine. 'He won't live for ever. But nearly for ever ...'

When Lucy had gone, Peggy smiled at the contingent of battered but cheerful dolls as if it were a model of my own family.

'Lucy's a dear – they all are. You've done an amazing job. How on earth do you manage to write?'

'They go to school.'

'But when they're home? It's a perpetual riot.'

'I like it.' I felt myself being pushed into a familiar corner. 'Some writers listen to Vivaldi. I like to hear my children playing. There's nothing abnormal in that.'

'It seems to work. You've been very brave.'

'Peggy!' Irritated, I pulled the glass of wine from her hand. 'For God's sake, men are capable of loving their children.'

'Not the ones I see at Guy's.'

'Men have never been given a chance. Every social convention you can think of is against them, believe me.'

'I do – but conventions are hard to change.'

'Women don't want them changed. It takes only one hand to rock a cradle, and they want that hand to be theirs.'

'The women I see are making a run for the nursery door.'

'Are they? Most women think it's wrong of me to look after the kids myself. They feel it's unnatural. Even you do.'

'It is unusual.'

'Look at men on a beach, where they're allowed to play with their children. You'll see all the care and affection in the world, while the women are busy fussing over their damn mascara.'

'I'll think of you here as on the beach.' Peggy sipped her wine, surveying the posters on the wall, wild drawings of aircraft on fire, dropping their nuclear bombs. 'How's Henry doing?'

'He's getting better. He's much happier. We read and play a lot together. I try not to go out too often.'

'You must get out sometimes.'

'I've been out. It looks pretty much the same old scene. Every day here is a new adventure.'

'Even so, you can't spend all your time mothering the children.'

I sat down on the sofa and took Peggy's hand. 'Peggy, I'm not "mothering" the children. I can't take Miriam's place, and I won't try to.'

'You still miss her – I can see that.'

'Of course ... there are so many things I wish I'd done for her. In many ways I was a lousy husband.'

'At least you loved her. You should think about her as much as you want.'

'I do. Take it from me, the death of a wife is all about sex. I keep dreaming about her in a weird way – walking around the bedroom in Rosas, or in the bullring at Barcelona. Dreams full of blood and dead bulls. I even saw her in Lunghua, strolling along the railway line to that little station. In some peculiar way she was involved with that. All those meaningless deaths that mean everything.'

'Do you think you'll marry again?'

'Not many women would marry a man with three children. Whenever I see a couple together in their car I really resent them. Almost as if they were to blame.'

Peggy put her hand on my arm. I looked at her capable fingers, unchanged since the days at Lunghua. During my fevers in the children's hut she had talked to me in her sensible schoolgirl's voice, trying to explain away the eerie visions of delirium. I felt the enlarged knuckle of her wrist, the condyle chipped when I darted into the hut and drove the door against her hand.

In the nursery the children were arguing over the Monopoly board, Alice delivering a magisterial lecture on the significance of passing Go. Henry was insisting on circling the board counter-clockwise. Peggy smiled, still holding my hand, but when I touched her thigh she pushed me away.

'Peggy ...'

'I know. Deep in the underwear something stirred. I have to go.'

'Stay the night. Why not?'

She picked up her handbag. 'I'm due back at Guy's. Besides, those dreams are just for you ...'

I waited while she said goodbye to the children. Had she guessed that I would be impotent and decided to spare my feelings? We had been too close to each other in Lunghua, forced into a child marriage that revealed too many flaws and limits.

She held my hand through the window of her car, one of the first Japanese imports, an engagingly odd choice. 'You're fine – the children have looked after you wonderfully. I've talked to Alice and Lucy and they're going to make sure you go out more often.'

I watched her drive erratically away. Of course she was right: it was the children who were bringing me up. They had come to terms with the past far more quickly than their father. I had emptied the wardrobes of Miriam's clothes, but I sometimes noticed that prying little fingers had teased the hem of a skirt through the lid of the suitcases where I stored them. One afternoon, while repairing the fence, I was aware that the children were unnaturally quiet. Climbing the stairs, I saw them in my bedroom. They had found Miriam's wedding dress, which Alice now wore, tottering on Miriam's high-heeled shoes as Lucy played a bridesmaid holding the train. Henry wore my old panama hat and dinner jacket. Bursting with glee, they paraded around the bed, bowing and curtseying through a mock marriage ceremony. Then Alice stretched out on the bed and closed her eyes, while Lucy and Henry folded the bedspread around her, solemnly laying her to rest.

Watching them without a word, I crept down the stairs, knowing that they had recovered. An hour later the dress had been carefully returned to the suitcase. A few flecks of confetti shaken loose from its hems lay on the bedroom carpet beside my slippers.

My own recovery took longer, delayed by the well-meaning refusal of almost everyone to refer to Miriam's death. A gentle conspiracy existed among my friends and publishing acquaintances, as they feigned not to notice that Miriam had vanished through a window of time and space. This silence reminded me of the cruel childhood game in which we pretended, without telling him, that one of our friends no longer existed – the poor victim would be ignored, stared through, excluded from any games. I envied the elaborate mourning rituals of the

Chinese, the public wailing of the widow on which Europeans so looked down. Watching the national mourning of a stricken America after the assassination of President Kennedy, I almost envied his bereaved wife. Every moment of her grief was endlessly replayed and anatomised on television. Her husband's death, like the murder of his assassin, was recapitulated in slow motion, frame by numbered Zapruder frame. She wore her blood-spattered skirt like a scream of rage at the world that had widowed her.

One evening, after eleven months of unbroken celibacy, I was taken on a tour of Soho's strip clubs by a London publisher then living in New York. The worst kind of Manhattanised Englishman, he wolfed down his sole and Chablis, and then dragged me from one back-street club to the next. At first I tried to slip away from him, but I was curious to see my own reactions. On minute boudoir stages the young strippers worked through their routines, smiling in their overlit way at the wan-faced men who packed the narrow seats. Caressing their breasts and buttocks, masturbating as they exposed their vulvas for a ritual few seconds, they mimicked the audience's lust in routines as formalised as the aircraft emergency drills rehearsed by air hostesses in the minutes after take-off. I waited for them to arouse me, but the strippers seemed to parade their sexual possibilities with all the fervour of anatomy demonstrators in a dissecting-room taking their students through the urino-genital system.

'How long since you had a woman, Jim?' the publisher asked.

'A long time.'

'Well, come on then. Cheer up.'

He told me that this tour of Soho clubs was our appetiser before we booked into an exclusive Westminster brothel he had been recommended by a British criminal whose memoirs he was editing. But I knew that he was too drunk to do more than go back to his hotel. Watching him as he gazed at a cobra-eyed teenager stroking her anus with a forefinger, I guessed that it was this stylisation of sex that most appealed to him, not the act itself. The atrocity exhibition was more stirring than the atrocity.

When I left him at the door of his taxi he put a heavy hand on my shoulder, searching for some insight into my sad condition.

'Perhaps, Jim, you just don't like girls any more ...'

I walked away from him under a cinema marquee advertising the first of the *Mondo Cane* films, bogus documentaries that cunningly mixed fake atrocity newsreels with genuine footage of human oddity. Next to the marquee was a newspaper billboard promoting a special supplement devoted to the Kennedy assassination, with a grainy enlargement of the Zapruder frame that recorded the last moments of the stricken President. Near Piccadilly Circus a group of CND members were canvassing support for an anti-nuclear rally to be held in Trafalgar Square. A well-nourished young woman pressed a leaflet into my hand bearing a photograph of a simulated nuclear attack, which showed hundreds of volunteers lying down together in a placid high street.

Fantasies of apocalyptic death fuelled the imaginations of these comfortable suburbanites. I was thinking of a different atomic bomb, which many of the Lunghua prisoners claimed to have seen above Nagasaki, the bomb that had saved our lives. In the rancid glare of the music arcades, as the hips of the young street-walkers shook to Trini Lopez, I could almost believe that a third World War might have saved Miriam, and that the war to come after that might resurrect her from her grave. A secret logic that I had yet to explore seemed to connect her death with the dead in the Avenue Edward VII, as if the unconscious needs of the human race could only be fulfilled in an obliterating sexual apocalypse, replayed in an infinity of slow-motion photography. Fragments of deranged dreams veered across the night air above the raucous neon.

The lurid glare still hung in my eyes as I walked the children to the school gates the following morning. When I returned to my car I began to chat to a mother of two boys in Lucy's class. We discussed the costumes for the children's Christmas party which she was helping to design. Keen to show me the patterns, she invited me for coffee at her nearby home.

As we sat at her kitchen table she explained that she and her husband had separated, but told me that he still brought his laundry home. Something about this admission seemed to amuse her. Without much prompting she added that they made love in the kitchen while the washing machine completed its cycle.

'Domestic routines survive everything,' I commented. 'I like that. It's rather touching.'

'Isn't it ...' Coming to the point, she switched on the washing machine. 'By the way, you haven't anything that needs washing?'

'No ... except this handkerchief.'

'It looks a bit grubby. Let me do it for you.'

While the machine circled and the white flag of my handkerchief waved to us from its drowned world, I sat her on the kitchen table, scarcely smaller than the strip-club stages. Her knees were held tightly against my hips by her short leather skirt. Her hands rested on my chest, as if she were measuring me for a new life on which I was about to embark. I was grateful to her for the unforced references to Miriam, whom she had known well, and for taking the lead so expertly. She had realised that only a frivolous approach, as divorced from real feeling as the Soho clubs and marquee signs, could ever have reached me.

Her fingers lowered my zip, and I said: 'I hope something happens ... it's been a long time.'

'Three weeks? Or three months?'

'Eleven months.'

'Time for a baby. Let's see what we can do about that.'

She unbuttoned my shirt and pressed her hands against my diaphragm. 'Heavens, you're tense ... deep breaths, now.' She laughed cheerfully, amused by herself. 'Still, at least we've met before. These days you have sex straight away and the wooing starts later.'

'I'll woo you.'

'Good. Something does seem to be happening. Now, can you remember what to do next?'

That night I dreamed of Miriam for the last time. I was walking down Shepperton High Street on my way to the shops when I saw her by the traffic lights at the crossroads. She was as young and beautiful as I ever remembered her, and I was filled with a deep sense of love for her, and relief that we would meet again. I was glad that the nightmare of the past months was over and that we would be reunited with the children in our little house. I called to her as she strode confidently across the road, her skirt swinging at her knees. She looked back, recognising me with a cheery smile, and walked on. I called to her again, but she strode past the shops, and I saw her disappear among the cars and pedestrians.

Waking from the dream, I listened to my children sleeping in their rooms. I lay in the darkness, and knew that Miriam had set me free.

9

Craze People

'We'll take the pixies with us! You can't leave them behind!'

With a noisy swoop Sally Mumford lifted Lucy into the air and held the excited six-year-old against her shoulder, while gathering Alice and Henry to the folds of her floor-length dress.

'Sally ...' I tried feebly to protest. 'They're too young for a pop concert. And I'm too old.'

'Rubbish! We're going together. We won't listen to him, will we?'

'No!' they yelled.

'Right! Coats and scarves, and ear-plugs for Daddy. I'll make a picnic for us, if I can find anything in that mouldy fridge ...'

Sally had taken charge. As always, I watched her with unstinted admiration as she rolled her skirt around her thighs, exposing her long white legs. She squatted, scowling, in front of the open refrigerator. Out came salami, Brie, two bottles of white Burgundy.

'Right. That's us. Now, what do you feed the monsters?'

'Beans on toast and all that jazz.'

'Too much of a fiddle. They can have salami.'

'They hate salami.'

'They'll love it! Washed down with a glass of wine? It's their first pop concert.'

'And mine.'

'Good. I'm going to get you out of here more often.' Sally licked and dabbed, making a quick survey of the refrigerator. She waved a cheese-tipped forefinger at me, flecks of coleslaw on her brightly painted mouth. 'Jim, you're spending too much time in Shepperton. It's like living on a small planet miles from anywhere. I'm moving you back to Earth.'

I loved to watch her, whether she was fuelled by amphetamines or plain American sass. She and Peter Lykiard had arranged to call for me, but Lykiard had left separately for the open-air concert, near Brighton on the south coast. The Arts Laboratory, of which Lykiard was now exhibitions director, was to stage a number of prose and poetry readings during the intermissions, and Sally had persuaded me to take part, against my better judgement. I found it impossible to resist her swerves of enthusiasm and good cheer.

'You'll enjoy it – Burroughs will be there.'

'The great man. But what do I read?'

'Anything. One of your sado-masochistic romps should go down a treat. The audiences are very conventional.'

'So am I. Sally …'

But nothing could stop her. As we drove away from Shepperton towards the south-east I felt my usual pang of uneasiness at leaving the Thames-side town. Sally was right – in the two years since Miriam's death the familiar gardens and water-meadows had come to my rescue, but at something of a price. I went up to London more often, but the quiet streets with their bricky villas, presided over by the film studios, formed the reassuring centre of my mind. Through the tranquil TV suburbs moved a light as serene as any Stanley Spencer had seen at Cookham.

At the same time, I was grateful to people who lured me away from it. Lykiard and Sally had arrived unexpectedly on the doorstep six weeks earlier. They carried presents and a cheery welcome for the children, who had almost forgotten them, and a bottle of Japanese whisky for me which Sally was opening as she stepped through the door. Lykiard wanted me to write the catalogue notes to an exhibition of Kennedy assassination photographs, but this was little more than the pretext for their visit.

I was happy to see them both, even though their island hideaway had been the setting for Miriam's fatal accident. Watching Sally whooping around the children, I realised how strong a memory she had left me of herself. Casually she filled the nursery with scented smoke that had the children's nostrils flicking like butterfly wings. She regaled them with baffling word games, concocted elaborate family histories for the tribe of plastic trolls that were their latest craze, scandalised them with media gossip from the television world where she now worked as a news programme researcher. Anyone within range was treated to her eccentric comments on the Viet Nam war, Carnaby Street fashions, the latest outrage committed by President Johnson and the British police. She was full of anecdotes about Dali, whose entourage at Port Lligat she had penetrated, and his voyeuristic delight in watching young couples have sex, without making clear whether she altogether disapproved.

Only when her last amphetamine tablet began to wear off would she become scratchy and silent, rubbing the coolness from her eyes until she could take her handbag and a glass of water upstairs to the bathroom. But I always looked forward to seeing her. She excited me in the way that Miriam had done, and I envied Lykiard his close hold over her wayward imagination.

The 1960s were tailor-made for them. In his office at the Arts Laboratory the pipe-smoking Lykiard logged onto his wall-charts the latest outburst of psychedelia, the newest drug craze or exhibition of concept art, like a contented meteorologist registering a summer of unexpected cyclones. Exhibitions of Viet Nam atrocities, posters advertising a self-mutilating cabaret performer or an Artaud revival moved beneath his tolerant eyes as if he had put aside all emotion or even, conceivably, not yet experienced this rare condition. For him the end of the world, the imminent nuclear armageddon against which protestors marched on every weekend, would merely be the ultimate happening, the audience-storming last act in the theatre of cruelty.

Sally, at least, still kept her feelings, though jammed into the wrong pigeon-holes in her mind. She thrived on the volatile landscape of the mid-60s, which made a virtue of psychic damage. Mediated by the TV documentaries which she helped to edit, the civil wars in Algeria, Viet Nam and the Congo became a never-ending group catharsis, a psychological life-support system into which she could plug between her amphetamine highs. Trying to sort all this out had brought her to Shepperton. In Sally's mind, a near-addicted Scotch drinker blessed with an ox-like liver and three children seemed a model of almost church-going rectitude. Once she had offered me her flat tin of amphetamine tablets, but then quickly withdrew them as if tempting me with the fruit of the second forbidden tree.

How could I manoeuvre her away from Lykiard? Her large, ramshackle apartment in an expensive Bayswater block was a museum of unmet needs. Dusty photographs of her mother, sitting stiffly in the garden of some private mental clinic near Boston, hung side by side with stills of jack-booted parade-ground troops from *Triumph of the Will*.

'Gorgeous men ... just *so* glamorous,' Sally commented wistfully, settling her icy heroes next to a magazine profile of Israeli kibbutz sentries, her other sexual dream. She attended Ouspenski seminars, had taken a parachute jump at Elstree Flying Club, loathed her department-store tycoon father, yet treasured her schoolgirl letters from him and wore his old silk smoking jacket as a dressing-gown, inhaling the ancient odours of sweat and tobacco like healing balm. Naively, I asked if they had committed incest. 'I wish we had,' she mused nostalgically. 'Jesus, I wanted him to – I know what a deprived childhood really means ...'

All the way to Brighton she played happily with the children in the back of the car. Was she, I wondered hopefully, trying to make herself one of my daughters? After ten years of Miriam's level commonsense it was difficult to hunt the zig-zag contours of Sally's mind. The Hell's Angels guarding the entrance to the concert site were wearing her beloved black leather and death's head insignia, but she gave them scarcely a glance.

We parked behind a tower of steel scaffolding high enough to launch a space-vehicle, and walked through the buses and location vans to the performers' canvas tent. Lykiard was holding court with his Arts Laboratory groupies – intense young women, concept artists all, with the intimidating stares of gangsters' molls. Anyone over thirty was a race enemy, and having three children instantly marked me down for retribution. Sally's presence gave me a temporary laissez-passer, to be revoked, I was made to feel, at the slightest betrayal of such bourgeois inclinations as wanting an ice-cream for the children or a hygienic lavatory. Lykiard informed them that I would read a text celebrating the perverse sexuality of President Kennedy's widow, and there was a momentary flicker of interest behind the heavy shades, soon replaced by a stony hostility. Class assumptions and exclusivities survived strongly amid the rock amplifiers and Warholiana.

Between the sudden bursts of rock music, as the engineers wired their circuits, the children were whispering to Sally.

'Me too,' Sally agreed. Entrusting the picnic hamper to Lykiard, she spotted a sign behind the stage, on which was printed 'Free Toilet'. An arrow pointed towards a wood of beech trees. Like characters in a Magritte painting, people wandered in a dislocated way among the trees, whose trunks steamed with urine. Burroughs hovered briefly into view, as formal as an undertaker in his natty suit.

I watched Alice and Lucy daintily pick their way through the moist grass after Sally, who had gathered up her long skirts. Henry was happily spraying every tree, and accidentally sprinkled the boots of a Hell's Angel too stoned to notice. Already the counter-culture was a revelation beyond all their childhood dreams.

Lykiard showed me his time-table and the ramp of wooden planks that led to the upper of the two stages. I gazed uneagerly at the tower of steel scaffolding.

'Is this thing going to hold together? If one bolt snaps we'll all be launched into orbit.'

'I think that's the idea. It may be our only chance. Let's face it, middle-aged America has hijacked the Apollo programme. Men older than your bank manager will land on the Moon.'

'But is it going up or down?' Trying to steady my nerves, I bought a whisky at the bar, then found that the plastic cup contained nothing but a brown stain.

'It isn't dirty,' Lykiard explained. 'That's your measure of whisky. Smoke pot, but don't buy any here. You'll find capitalist exploitation at its most ruthless.' He pointed to the seats in the VIP enclosure below the stage. 'Despite appearances, the old class structures survive intact. The best seats are reserved for the pop aristocracy – promoters, record company executives, TV people and the music press. Behind them we get the pop world's middle class, all those well-brought-up girls from the suburbs who just come for the day. But down at the bottom, as ever, is the proletariat of the drug culture ...'

Strolling through the fringes of the crowd, we reached a wide ditch that marked the edge of the field rented from a local farmer. Groups of shabby young men and a few sallow girls were camping in the ditch. Most of them had spent the night there, sleeping among the tree roots in makeshift tents of tarpaulin. Smoking their joints, they were cooking on small stoves from which a sweet pine-smoke rose into the air. They reminded me of the Chinese peasants I had seen clinging to life in the irrigation ditches of wartime Shanghai. One of them offered me a skillet of gruel. I squatted under the tarpaulin and ate the spicy oatmeal, sharing the plastic cup of wine I had taken from the picnic hamper.

Later, as I recovered from my reading, I lounged beside Sally and the children on the grassy slopes behind the concert stage. The entire terrain of trees and meadows resembled the aftermath of some harmless and cheerful Waterloo. Bodies lay in the long grass, singly and in pairs, as if they had fallen on the field of battle, while the survivors sat in their square below the stage, many of them wearing the scarlet tunics, gold braid and epaulettes of the classic English regiments. I envied them all their mastery of make-believe. I had wasted my own youth dissecting cadavers and training to be a military pilot, trying to match myself against the realities of the post-war world. But the 1960s had effortlessly turned the tables on reality. The media landscape had sealed a techni-color umbrella around the planet, and then redefined reality as itself.

Drowsy on the warm wine, I thought of myself on the swaying platform above the crowd, bellowing into the erratic microphones. Giant fragments of amplified prose had toppled away through the air like sections of a glacier. No one had heard a word. My dreams of Mrs Kennedy's sexuality had boomed across the placid downs, unsettling the grazing cattle a dozen fields away.

'It was a surrealist joke – on me,' I told Sally, shutting my eyes to the humiliation of it. 'Not the kind that Duchamp or Tzara would approve of ...'

'You were wonderful. Wasn't he, pixies?'

'Yes!' Their eyes were opening to a new world far richer than anything Shepperton could offer.

'Sally, the whole thing was absurd.'

'So? Nothing matters any more. Jackie Kennedy, Viet Nam, flying to the Moon – they're just TV commercials.'

'And what are they selling?'

'Everything you need – pain, fun, love, hate. You can make anything mean anything. Only the pixies matter.'

She seemed restless with me, smoking an endless series of joints that left her eyes blunted. Wine bottle in hand, she spent the afternoon striding around in her long gown, her neck and breasts turning pink in the sun, blonde hair like a white whip that she flicked from one shoulder to the other. The festival, which celebrated nothing except itself, already bored her. She wandered away from us, and an hour later I found her in a quiet field beyond the car park. She was running with a family of horses, a black mare and two foals, driving them round and round the field, her hands happily slapping their haunches, her eyes lit with some memory of childhood.

When she demanded that we visit the beach at Brighton I discovered what had unsettled her. Searching for Lucy in the performers' tent, we saw Lykiard and one of his concept artists lying in a deck-chair behind the bar. Ignoring Sally, they embraced each other, and both seemed to hide behind the single pair of sunglasses. Sally stared at them, the pink flush fading from her breasts. She took Lucy's hand and walked along the bar, scattering the paper cups with their brown stains.

Fortunately, she cheered up as soon as we left the festival behind and reached the beach. The incoming tide and strong black waves put an ironic gleam into her eyes. We parked on the hard shoulder above the beach and watched the waves splinter themselves against the wooden breakwater.

'Right!' Sally opened the door. 'I'm going for a swim.'

'Sally … the sea's too strong.'

'I'll tell it to behave … it's just a big puppy.'

I followed her across the shingle, as she kicked off her shoes and strode to the water's edge. The foam seethed at her feet, delighted to greet this beautiful and deranged young woman. I expected her to strip, but she stepped straight into the water, bare feet feeling among the stones. The waves smothered her legs, the sodden fabric of her dress clinging to her knees.

'Sally!' Henry had stepped from the car, model aircraft forgotten in his hand. The girls' little faces pressed to the windscreen.

Sally strode out as a larger wave launched itself at the breakwater. The violent black jelly slid around her, clasping her waist, and the undertow dragged at her feet. She was up to her armpits in the foam, her legs trapped by the weight of drenched fabric. She let the next wave carry her towards the shore, and stood unsteadily in the racing surf, waving to me with an apologetic grin. She was knocked from her feet in the surging water, pulled down and carried into the breaking maw of a huge Channel roller.

Warning Henry to stay by the car, I ran into the water, stunned by the wave as it struck my thighs. Wading out, I jumped chest high through the next roller and swam towards Sally as she lay helplessly on the surface. I seized her shoulders and held her against my chest, stood up and pulled her to the shore.

She sat exhausted on the shingle, teeth chattering while the foam seethed its disappointment against her feet, as if the sea were laying its eggs and hoping she would fertilise them. The shoulder straps of her dress had broken, and the bodice was around her waist, exposing the icy skin of her torso covered with shreds of sea-weed. Washed from her eyes, her make-up ran in blue stains down her cheeks. Her nose and chin were smaller, shrunk by fear and the cold, and she stared at the waves tugging at the train of her dress like a child remembering a drowning at sea.

Passers-by were watching us from the promenade. I covered Sally with my jacket and helped her back to the car and the silent, astounded children. Sally sank gratefully into the front seat.

'Well,' she said to the children, brushing away the flecks of sea-weed. 'How many lengths did I swim?'

Later that evening, when the children were asleep, Sally sat on the sofa among the stuffed toys, her good humour returned. During our silent drive she had slumped against the door inside my jacket, eyes fixed on the sodden dress between her feet. At the time I wondered if this had been a half-hearted suicide attempt, prompted by the glimpse of Lykiard in the deck-chair, or perhaps a bravura piece of exhibitionism by which she hoped to regain the centre of the stage. But when I mentioned Lykiard she scarcely recognised his name. Her near-drowning had been nothing more than an impulsive Channel dip.

Wearing my dressing-gown, she breathed the fumes rising from a tumbler of hot whisky. When I sat beside her among the stuffed toys she laid her head on my shoulder.

'Are the pixies asleep? I didn't mean to frighten them.'

'They're fine. They think you went for a swim.'

'I did! Until right at the end. When you reached me I was thinking what it would be like.'

'Drowning?'

'Those last moments before the end ... I had the strange feeling they would go on for ever.' She pulled away from me and stared hard at a stuffed toy. 'I want to live my whole life like that.'

'Sally, you do ...'

She opened my palm and carefully read its lines, then slipped it under the lapel of the dressing-gown and placed it on her breast. Despite the hot bath her skin still smelled strongly of brine. A depraved and innocent Miranda had been washed ashore on the island of Shepperton. When I caressed her breast she smiled at me in a conspiratorial way, as if we were two lubricous children in a tree-house.

'My nipples aren't very sensitive – probably less than yours.'

She watched me as I undressed her, curious to see how I would discover her body, beckoning me towards her with a ready smile. When I stroked her clitoris she lay back with her legs wide, her face between the soft toys. She took my fingers and moved them to her anus, rhythmically pumping her rectum like a soft accordion.

'Don't bother to fuck me. Just bugger me.'

She knelt on the carpet, her chest and shoulders across the cushions. Spitting on her fingers, she pushed the saliva into her anus with one hand, testing my penis with the other. I hesitated to enter her, nervous of tearing her scarred anus, but she pressed my penis into her, adding more spit between the gasps of pain. When I was fully inside her she at last relaxed, and her rectum was as soft as the vagina of a child-bearing woman. She buried her face among the teddy bears and brought her wrists behind her back, inviting me to force them to her shoulder blades. I moved carefully, trying to control her prolapsing rectum, gently forcing her arms as she wanted, picking the hairs from her mouth as she shouted to me, an eager, desperate child.

'Bugger me, daddy! Beat me! Pixie wants to be buggered!'

From that moment Sally Mumford became my guide to a new world. At the start she seemed keen to make a new life for us all in Shepperton, to be the wife and mother we had left among the Spanish cypresses. Part big sister and part friendly witch, and capable in the children's eyes of unlimited amazements, Sally brought all her good cheer and wayward flair to our suburban retreat. I tried to calm and steady her, as she relived her childhood like an exciting roller-coaster ride. Despite playing the role of her father, I felt surprisingly dependent on her, and hoped that I could give her the happy childhood that she was helping to give to my own children.

At the same time I knew that I could learn so much from her. Sally was a true child of the 1960s, and my guide to the secret logic that I saw unfolding. After years of domesticity in my marooned suburb by the Thames I had stepped into the middle of a decade that had started without me. I had woken from a dream of the Second World War into an England that seemed like the aftermath of the third.

In this overlit realm ruled by images of the space race and the Viet Nam war, the Kennedy assassination and the suicide of Marilyn Monroe, a unique alchemy of the imagination was taking place. In many ways the media landscape of the 1960s was a laboratory designed specifically to cure me of all my obsessions. Violence and pornography provided a kit of desperate measures that might give some meaning both to Miriam's death and the unnumbered victims of the war in China. The demise of feeling and emotion, the death of affect, presided like a morbid sun over the playground of that ominous decade, to which Sally seemed to hold a key. The brutalising newsreels of civil wars and assassinations, the stylisation of televised violence into an anthology of design statements, were matched by a pornography of science that took its materials, not from nature, but from the deviant curiosity of the scientist.

At an Arts Laboratory party launching an exhibition of work by a fashionable woman artist – a display of used sanitary towels – I proudly introduced Sally to Dick Sutherland, who had left Cambridge and now led a research team at the Institute of Psychology. In the hard months after our return from Spain he had been a generous friend. Often he drove to Shepperton in the evenings with bottles of bourbon and the latest traveller's tales from Cape Kennedy, Tokyo or Los Angeles. 'You'll bounce back,' he told me confidently. Television had kept him young. Roaming around the world with his BBC crew, he was one of the first of the airport thinkers, always available to give an executive-lounge interview.

Sally took to him instantly, and Dick could see that she was everything I needed: wayward, affectionate and perverse. When he invited us to visit his laboratory I remembered that I had first met Miriam while volunteering to take part in a bogus experiment. True to form, Dick was still playing games with illusion and reality. He took us on a tour of his laboratory, charmed Sally with a series of well-rehearsed optical tricks and paradoxes, all the while keeping up his smoothly practised patter. His real talent, I realised, was to make all those he met feel that they were on a television programme.

Dick's infatuation with television made him as much a true citizen of the 1960s as Sally and Peter Lykiard. He was fascinated by the way in which television theatricalised everything while anchoring it firmly to the domestic and mundane. Since leaving Cambridge he had jettisoned his own past and begun to float free into this electronic realm that, like a kindly sky, taught the audience to admire itself. In an unguarded moment, he told me of his childhood in Scotland, the son of a stony Edinburgh architect and his devout Presbyterian wife. Wartime evacuation to relatives in Australia had opened his eyes to the charms of a beach culture where affection and approval came, not from within the family, but from the world around it.

Not surprisingly, Dick had never married. Without the ever-present autocue and monitor screen, a close relationship would have seemed a little unreal. But his awareness of his own flaws made him an astute psychologist, and he was an endless fund of ideas, many at my expense. The house in Shepperton always intrigued him.

'You've been to Jim's place in Shepperton, Sally?'

'Of course. It's a shrine.'

'Absolutely. Freud's primal cave furnished with wall-to-wall carpeting and a million years of love. In the long run, suburbia will triumph over everything, though it's hard to tell if the suburbs are a city's convalescent zone or a kind of petting zoo. In fact, they may be where a city dreams – Jim's like a sleeper poised at the onset of REM sleep. But before he wakes, let me show you round the lab. Nothing is quite what it seems, rather like reality in a way ...'

In a darkened lecture theatre a volunteer panel of housewives, secretaries and off-duty firemen stared at the photographs of unnamed men and women projected onto a screen, trying to identify which were murderers and which victims.

'In fact, they're photos of the previous panel,' Dick whispered to Sally. 'People have remarkably strong prejudices about certain facial characteristics. The smallest cues convince them that they're looking at a child rapist or a Gestapo killer.'

In the laboratory next door a second group of volunteers were completing a confidential questionnaire about the effect of violent newsreels on their sex lives.

'Of course, there's no influence at all,' Dick assured us, 'and the footage we show them is much less violent than we tell them it's going to be. What's interesting, though, is that most people assume it does improve their sex lives. Everyone says there's too much violence on TV but secretly they want more.'

'So, thanks to TV, everything is the opposite of what it seems?' I commented.

'It does look like it.' We had returned to Dick's office, and he lay back in his chair, sneakers on the desk, letting Sally admire his long legs and actor's profile. 'It's obviously true in politics. We've studied the TV commercials put out by Governor Reagan of California. You can see that all this fierce right-wing stuff is the complete opposite of his reassuring body language. But people believe the body language – generally we've summed a person up long before he opens his mouth. We think Reagan knows this, thanks to his Hollywood experience. His whole political career is one long reaction shot with an irrelevant voice-over, as you can prove by deleting the sound-track and asking people to guess what he's saying. They trust the friendly sportscaster manner. On the other hand, once he's sitting in the Governor's mansion in Sacramento he has his mandate ...'

'You're saying that the Fuehrer shouldn't have ranted and raved but come on like ... the cowardly lion?'

'Exactly. The totalitarian systems of the future will be docile and subservient, and all the more threatening for that. Though there'll always be a place for out-and-out madness. In some way, people need the notion. The agnostic world keeps its religious festivals alive to meet the vacation demands of its work-force. By the same token, when medical science has conquered disease certain mental afflictions will be mimicked for social reasons – I'd put my bets on schizophrenia. It seems to represent the insane's idea of the normal.'

'And not the other way around?'

'Probably not – a disease that flatters our vanity has a huge advantage, like most venereal complaints.' Dick turned to the film projector behind his desk. 'Speaking of schizophrenia, we've been going through some wartime German film stored in the basement. One of the cans is a Waffen SS instructional film on how to build a pontoon bridge.'

Sally almost swooned at this. 'God, that's so weird – it just says everything ...'

'Doesn't it?' Pleased by her attention, Dick reluctantly lowered the blind, uneager to put himself in the shade. 'Perhaps we could show it at the Arts Lab? I'd be happy to introduce it.'

We sat sipping wine in Dick's darkened office, surrounded by American licence plates and photographs of him at the controls of his Cessna, while the SS film fluttered through his projector. Was the film yet another fake? It looked convincingly real, and Sally held tight to my arm, mesmerised by the strong, white-skinned young men good-naturedly singing their work-songs. Dick smiled to himself through the flickering light, murmured into the telephone when a BBC producer called, and watched Sally approvingly. He seemed glad that I had become the lover of this rapt and aroused young woman, and well aware of the rich and fierce sex we would have that evening as Sally replayed the film in her mind.

When we left he confided: 'She's right for you, Jim. Just what you need.'

Although Sally depended on me, in most respects I was her pupil, and the most important lesson she taught me came at the New Year's Eve party that she held at her flat in Bayswater. For some reason the place always unsettled me, filled with the debris of Sally's past, like those abandoned houses in wartime Shanghai where clock-time had been suspended for a little too long, and one returned to be confronted by the invisible stranger of one's younger self. I strolled around the Persian carpets stained with wine and cigarette ash, past the sofas with their unwashed covers reeking of stale incense, and thought of my children asleep in Shepperton as the middle-aged baby-sitter read her travel guide to British Honduras.

Yet the next day Sally would be washing Alice's hair and helping Lucy to stitch a miniature wardrobe for her trolls. Now she reeled about, amphetamines in her left hand, between the Marat/Sade posters and the blown-up photographs of Diane Arbus dwarves, shrieking at Peter Lykiard as he arrived with a po-faced Japanese artist who had recently filmed their buttocks.

Sally proudly held my arm, hiccuped and left a fleck of vomit on my shoulder. She recovered with a flourish, cleared her mouth into a glass of wine and kissed me happily on the lips.

'Jim, I've found some wonderful *crêpe-de-chine*! Lucy's going to adore it ...'

She careened away, swinging from shoulder to shoulder like a gymnast on the overhead rings.

Shortly before midnight, remembering the baby-sitter, I decided to leave for Shepperton. Searching for Sally, I pushed my way through the noise and smoke. Couples embraced among the unwashed dishes in the kitchen, and a party within a party was taking place as six guests camped on Sally's double bed. Two acolytes of the Japanese artist were taking a shower together in Sally's bathroom. I searched the other bedrooms and the second bathroom, filled with her friends' art school lumber, and then glanced into her little dressing-room.

When I reached the door Peter Lykiard asked me for a cigarette, clearly trying to distract me, as if I were a child about to stray into the adults' bedroom.

'Sally's busy, Jim – before I forget, I wanted to ask you about this Waffen SS film. Dick Sutherland is keen to do a presentation ...'

Pushing past him, I opened the door. Sally was sitting on the quilted seat of the laundry basket, her skirt raised to her waist. Her bare legs were crossed around the hips of a young Spanish photographer whom we had met briefly at the Arts Laboratory. His unzipped trousers had slipped around his thighs, and his strong hands had pulled down the bodice of Sally's dress to expose her breasts. With their awkward and almost abstract movements, he and Sally seemed to be rehearsing a pornographic circus turn in which they somehow swapped their clothes during an intense sex act. As he sucked at her right breast Sally kissed his forehead, her strong legs drawing his penis into her. Seeing me, she held the Spaniard's shoulders and gave me a frank and happy smile.

While I drove back to Shepperton I thought of Sally's affection for me, and her thousand kindnesses towards the children. Deep affection and the most casual disloyalty coexisted, separated by that tolerant smile. I remembered seeing the Vincents making love in their tired way on Sunday afternoons in Lunghua, and Mrs Vincent's knowing eyes when she saw me watching her through my curtain. I could almost believe that Sally had deliberately exposed herself to me, urging me to take the next step in my unsentimental education. I had been drawn to Sally because she offered a key to this strange decade, but the only stable element in Sally's world was instability. By isolating my emotions, by separating feeling from action, I might perhaps even learn to enjoy Sally's infidelities.

I thought of her near-drowning at Brighton beach, when she had allowed me to bring a second wife back from the waves. I could still feel the sombre power of the dark rollers striking my thighs and chest as I waded into the deep water where death ran, and the black foam through which I had dragged her on to the shingle.

Images of pain and anger floated free, like the billboards advertising the endless deaths of the murdered President, messages of violence and desire that alone could assuage the bereaved.

I sped on past the oncoming headlights, crossing the moonlit Thames to where Shepperton lay asleep in my children's dreams.

10

The Kingdom of Light

'Think of LSD as the kaleidoscope's view of the eye.'

While Dick spoke I sat in my study by the open French window, looking down at the glass of water in my hand and the sugar cube exposed beside the BBC tape-recorder. A sinister glitter rose from the foil wrapper.

'Dick, are we ready?' I asked over my shoulder. 'This is starting to feel like a suicide attempt.'

'Give me a moment – you *are* going to heaven …' Dick adjusted the tripod of his cine-camera, aiming its ferocious little lens at my face. Already I resented the camera, staring at me like a deformed robot. Summer light filled the garden, playing among the broken toys and the clothes-line with its waving pyjamas – the usual cheerful mess that I had offered to clear away. But Dick had been adamant that I change nothing.

Sipping at the water, I noticed the collapsed wigwam which Alice and Henry had built from an old tartan blanket and the cucumber frame. Banished from its dark interior for some breach of childhood protocol, Lucy had demolished the wigwam with her pedal-car. The others had threatened a terrible revenge, forgotten the moment that Cleo Churchill and her daughter Penny arrived at the front door. Friends of Dick, they would take the children down to the river while he and I embarked on a trip of our own, a short safari across the width of my skull.

'Dick, the garden's a mess – I ought to clear it up. Let's face it, your TV audience isn't going to be on acid.'

'Just what the ratings need. I'll suggest it to the BBC. They can put a gift-pack in *Radio Times*.'

The four children were shouting in the hall, clamouring for ice-cream, comics and bubble-gum wrappers. Cleo Churchill put her head around the door and grimaced cheerfully.

There's a riot brewing. I'll have to leave you to it.'

That's fine, Cleo. Jim's eager to go. Give us a couple of hours.'

'Two hours? You ought to be filming me.' She frowned at the camera and microphone, the blood-pressure kit and my straight-backed chair. 'Jim, it looks genuinely weird – are you going to be all right?'

'Don't worry. Dick's monitored a lot of trips.'

'Even so. Never trust the ferryman.'

I could see that she disapproved, taking the view that there were more than enough adult excitements in the world; the experiment that Dick and I were about to make with my brain chemistry was a boy's game scarcely different from those that Henry played in the garden, when he lit a cigarette stub inside the wigwam, or exploded a box of matches. Cleo, with her quick smile and shy glamour, was an editor of children's books whom I sometimes saw at Dick's parties. Aware, a little uneasily, of her concern, I guessed that she was worried about more than Dick's credentials. As she withdrew her hand reluctantly from my shoulder she glanced from the perspiration on my face to the untidy study and garden. Beyond any thoughts about the wisdom of experimenting with LSD was a thirty-second guess at my character and whatever flaws this potent hallucinogen might expose.

'Okay ...' Dick set a dial on his aviator's watch and started the tape-recorder. 'It's 15:05 on June 17, 1967 ...'

Meeting Cleo's warning eyes, I placed the sugar cube on my tongue and let it rest there in a small show of defiance. As the children flung back the front door and rushed towards the gate I hesitated for a last moment. When Cleo had gone, slamming the door after her, I swallowed a mouthful of water.

'Right,' Dick told me. 'You'll feel something in about half an hour, so sit back and relax. We can play chess.'

'I'll look at the garden.' I could usually beat Dick at chess, but this was one game he would enjoy losing, as the pieces turned into dragons. I listened to the children's shouts fading down the street, followed by Cleo's strong, cheerful voice. Herself a single parent, she had implied that I was stepping out of character, a responsible father taking this questionable drug, still legally available in England, though there had been frequent calls to have it scheduled.

I stared at the toy-cluttered garden, a moraine of happy memories that the past three years had deposited on this suburban plot. The glacier had moved on, Miriam sleeping calmly within its deeps. The children had almost forgotten their mother, something I had tried to prevent, mistakenly. If they remembered her it was on other levels, in their good humour, resilience and confidence in unearned affection.

Strangely, Miriam had begun to recede even from me, while at the same time standing out more clearly in my memory. She seemed like the statue of a madonna suspended above the nave of a cathedral, rising into the air as I stepped away from her. The perspective lines of my life still led back to Miriam, but I owed a great deal to the women I had known since her death, above all to Sally Mumford, who had helped me to face head-on the pressures of pain and obsessive sexuality. Curiously, Sally's open infidelities had helped to ease my memories of Miriam, as if her death had been an infidelity of a special kind.

However, Dick had not been keen on having Sally present when he offered to supervise my LSD experiment. Her sudden swerves of mood, her muddled enthusiasms, might derail the hallucinatory loco-motive. Eager to make the experiment, and explore the locked doors of consciousness, I agreed that Cleo Churchill should look after the children. The amphetamines and drinamyls I had sometimes taken seemed less mind-altering than the average double Scotch, but Dick assured me that LSD was pushing against the limits of the brain.

I remembered his presentation to the head of the BBC's science programmes, as he outlined the projected series in which I would take part. Confident as always that he held his audience's attention, he had prowled around his display charts of brain sections and ECG readings like a pitchman selling the human brain to a party of intrigued visitors from another planet.

'The central nervous system is nature's Sistine Chapel, but we have to bear in mind that the world our senses present to us – this office, my lab, our awareness of time – is a ramshackle construct which our brains have devised to let us get on with the job of maintaining ourselves and reproducing our species. What we see is a highly conventionalised picture, a simple tourist guide to a very strange city. We need to dismantle this ramshackle construct in order to grasp what's really going on. The visual space we occupy doesn't actually coincide with the external world. Shadows are far deeper than they seem to us; the brain softens out the sharp contrasts so that we can analyse them more clearly – otherwise the world would be a mass of zebra stripes ...

'Consciousness is the central nervous system's brave gamble that it exists, an artefact that allows it to make its way around the internal and external environments. In fact, we're beginning to think that time itself is a primitive psychological structure that we've inherited from the distant past, along with the appendix and the little toe. Yet we're totally trapped by this archaic structure with its minutes and hours trailing after each other like a procession of the blind. Once we get hold of a more advanced notion of time – let's say, time perceived as simultaneity – we reach the threshold of a far larger mental universe ...

'Why do the dying think they're floating through tunnels? Under extreme pressure, the various centres in the brain which organise a coherent view of the world begin to break down. The brain scans its collapsing field of vision, and constructs out of the last few rings of cells what it desperately hopes is an escape tunnel. Right to the end the brain is trying at all costs to rationalise reality – whether it's starved of input or flooded with sensory data it builds artificial structures that try to make sense of the world. Out of this come not only near-death experiences but our visions of heaven and hell.'

Everyone had been intrigued, but the BBC declined to buy the series.

'Dr Sutherland,' the head of science programmes had commented, 'your description of the dying brain rather resembles the BBC ...'

*

'Dick, my watch has stopped.'

'Let me see. No, it's 3.45.'

'It must be later than that …'

I stared at the motionless second hand, and tried to work the winder. My fingers felt as cool and sensitive as a jeweller's, but I had the sudden notion they belonged to someone else. The second hand moved again, then halted for a further indefinite moment. A deep ruby light filled the garden, as if the sun had begun to overheat. I leaned forward, almost falling from the chair, and peered at the vivid cyanide blue of the sky.

'Sit back and relax.' Dick stood behind me, reassuringly holding my shoulders. 'There'll be a little retinal irritation to start with.'

'Dick, I'm moving in and out of time.'

'That began some while ago. Look at the garden and see what you make of the colours – they're probably drifting down the spectrum.'

I pushed Dick's hands away, and wondered if he was playing another of his devious games. He had always been strongly competitive, and envied me both Miriam and my China background. There was a sly look on his face which I remembered seeing in his office at Cambridge, like that of a fisherman who had hooked an unexpected catch and was just out of reach of his gaff.

The spools of the tape recorder were turning, but I noticed that they were spinning towards each other. Assuming that this was another piece of antiquated BBC equipment, I waited for the unravelling tape to loop into the air. The black plastic case had separated from the frame, but before I could warn Dick he had stepped away from me to his camera.

Colours were floating free from the surfaces around me. The summer air had become a translucent prism and the blades of uncut grass were touched by a layer of emerald light. The giant Russian sunflowers that I had grown for Alice and Lucy wore crowns of gold that drew them towards the sky. A haze of dense ruby air suffused the foliage of the cherry trees. The scarlet paintwork of Lucy's pedal car was separating from the battered metal, a glowing carapace that some skilful technician had painted on the air, and which I wanted to press down onto the rusty shell.

The untidy garden glowed with chemical light. The apple tree and its tree-house formed a chalet-sized cathedral, its branches a stained-glass window in which the broken toys were set within their own haloes. The dragon-patterns of the Chinese carpet under my feet, the shaggy bark of the pear tree scored with Henry's initials, the creosoted panels of the fence were releasing the light trapped within themselves. The green veil of every leaf and stem, the scarlet of Lucy's car, were detachable skins below which the real leaf and car were waiting to be discovered. The sunlight and its generous spectrum were gaudy pennants celebrating the unique identity of the smallest stone and twig. Refracted through the prism of their true selves, the leaves and flowers were glowing windows in the advent calendar of nature.

'Jim, look towards the camera ...'

Dick sat in the armchair beside me, the tape recorder on his lap. Its spools still turned in opposite directions, but none of the tape had become entangled. As the light in the garden grew more intense I was struck by the remarkable lustre of Dick's hair – some over-eager makeup girl at the studios had fitted him with a shoulder-length toupee of copper fleece. Light coursed through its filaments, and I wanted to warn Dick that his viewers would see every fevered mole and freckle in his cheeks. The blood raced through the enlarged capillaries, turning his hands and face into a set of inflamed maps.

Stifled by the seething room, I stood up and stepped through the French window. I walked across the garden, my feet sinking through the electric haze that lay over the grass. The stones in the rockery shone like gems set in jeweller's velvet, and the soil in the flower-beds was warm with the glow of compost giving life to itself.

My arms and legs were dressed in light, sheaths of mother-of-pearl that formed a coronation armour. I looked down at the simple headstone that marked the grave of Henry's Dutch rabbit, waiting for the creature to reconstitute itself from its own bones and lollop through the glowing grass. In the waking dream of this illuminated garden, time and space no longer pressed their needs. The contingent world was rearranging itself, and serial time was giving way to simultaneity, as Dick had promised, where the living happily consorted with the dead, the animate with the inanimate.

I waited for Miriam to appear among the trees. She would walk in this garden again, while Alice and Lucy played with their younger selves and I met the youthful husband I once had been. I looked back at the house, but Dick had vanished, and his camera stood on its tripod beside my empty chair. Charlton Road ran through a nave of light towards the river, and I assumed that Dick had gone to collect the children, telling them of their new playmates waiting for them at home.

I followed the pathway around the house. The silver envelope of my car floated in the drive like a tethered blimp. My neighbour approached with her elderly retriever, whose frayed coat and white muzzle glowed like a lion's. Shepperton lay before me, a town of matadors and their families dressed in their suits of light. The traffic moved down the high street, the cars exchanging their vivid auras. A helicopter crossed the river, its blades throwing silver spears at the great elms.

I crossed the road by the war memorial and entered the riverside park. In the distance, under the willow trees, my children were playing with balloons they had bought at the sweet-shop. Globes of painted air hovered between their hands. Behind them a young woman walked through the forest. Her blonde hair floated among the leaves, shedding haloes on to the ground at her feet. Breathless, I was struck by the grace of her walk, as she calmed the trees with a gesture and settled the starlings with a smile. With her unguarded beauty, she reminded me of a princess in the jewelled caverns of Gustave Moreau. I waved to her, hoping that she would touch me with the same calm grace, but she was following the children towards the river.

Losing my way in the overlit foliage, I sat down on a bench and stared at the unmoving hands of my watch. The world paused as time held its breath. The light was now so intense that it bleached all colour from the foliage of the elms. The grass around me was a carpet of milled glass, the trees hung with pendants of ice carved from the crystallised air. My eyes were exhausted by the whiteness of the world. Alice and Lucy ran towards me, figures in an over-exposed film, all expression blanched from their faces as they played in their snow palace.

The river was a glacier of opal, moving past frosted banks. If time stood still, the water would fail to break under my feet. I walked towards it, ready to step on to its corrugated surface, aware of Cleo Churchill warning me away with her Moreau smile. She was pulling at my arm, but I knew that we could cross the river together and rest with the children in the meadow facing the park.

I called soundlessly to Alice and Lucy, who stared at me in a puzzled way, as if they had forgotten that I was their father. Then Dick Sutherland was running through the trees towards me, holding my shoulders and guiding me away from the water. I sat with him on the white grass, while the doors of the sun closed around me.

Three hours later I lay in my bedroom, a pillow under my back, and my neck aching from the strain of staring at the sky. An interior dusk had settled over everything. The garden was sombre now, the muted colours locked away within the trees and flowers, as if depressed after their brief freedom. I tried to shield my inflamed eyes from the sunlight reflected off the passing cars. My entire nervous system was irritable and exhausted, and I could neither sleep nor rest. After rescuing me from the river, Dick had driven me back to the house and left me to recover while Cleo cooked an evening meal for the children.

Distracted by a call from a TV producer, Dick had allowed me to slip away to the park. Already I regretted taking part in the experiment. Dick's carelessness, whether deliberate or not, had nearly led me to drown myself. Annoyingly, he was far more interested in my messianic attempt to walk on water than in my vision of Shepperton as a solar garden, a sleeping paradise waiting to be woken from every stone and leaf.

Trying to steady my mind, I stared at the bedroom ceiling. Whenever my gaze lingered for more than a few seconds a festering sore appeared in the old plaster, as if my eyes were transmitting a virulent disease, a Gorgon-stare that turned a minute insect stain into a throbbing infection. Soon the suppurating plaster was covered with a plague of boils. Trying to recapture their paradise vision, the optical centres of my brain were misreading the smallest cues in the play of light across the quiet room.

I covered my eyes and listened to the children enjoying an impromptu party with Cleo and her daughter. Their voices calmed me, but when I moved my hand I saw that flies covered every inch of the room. Their trembling wings seethed on the sheets and pillows, cloaking my hands in black mittens. Trying to drive them away, I touched my scalp and found that a piece of my skull was missing. The tips of my fingers dipped into the soft tissues of my brain ...

Hearing my cry, Cleo left the children and ran up the staircase. She sat on the bed and placed my hands in her lap, shaking her head over the afternoon's folly. Looking up at her concerned face, I could still see the nimbus of light that had followed her through the riverside trees. I remembered the benediction she had bestowed on every starling and blade of grass.

'Jim ... shall I telephone Richard? I ought to ring your local doctor.'

'No – but call Peggy Gardner. I'll come out of it soon.' The last person I wanted around was Miriam's sometime physician, still under the thumb of Midwife Bell and ready to cast doubt on my fitness as a parent. Short cuts to paradise and shamanistic visions belonged to the dubious realm of back-street abortions and nutmeg addiction. I moved my hands gingerly to my scalp, relieved that my skull was intact. 'My fingers are so sensitive – I thought I'd pushed them into my brain. Are the children all right?'

'They're fine – I've invented a new game for them. They think you've got sunstroke.'

'I have! That intense light – for a few seconds this afternoon I saw ... heaven and hell.'

'That *must* be one of Richard's overdoses.' There was a hint of criticism, as if she were well aware of Dick's ambiguous experiments, 'I hope it was worth it.'

'Yes ... yes, it was.' I held her hand, waiting as the termites faded into the walls. Somewhere inside my head Cleo was still walking through the riverside forest, waiting for me to join her in the palace of light. Its doors stood ajar among the homely elms. In that paradise vision all her shyness had gone, she no longer hid her eyes behind her long hair and ever-ready smile. 'It went to pieces at the end, but I saw something I'd never seen before, a dream of ...'

'The real world?'

'All the real worlds. Everything was its original self ...' Trying to explain myself, I reached out and touched her hair. 'I told Dick that you looked like an archangel.'

She moved my hand from her cheek, frowning at my foolhardiness. 'That should do wonders for my career. I hope you repeat that on the programme.'

'I will.' I raised myself and sat uncomfortably on the bed beside her. I wanted to embrace Cleo's broad hips. One day she and I would make that river crossing together. 'Cleo, tell me – was there any film in the camera?'

'I assume so – why?'

'People are easier to control when they think they're going on television. It's just Dick ...'

'Perhaps you've been too trusting – but I imagine he understands you.'

She paused at the door, looking at me as if aware for the first time of my real motives for embarking on this risky expedition across my head.

If Cleo was prepared to put aside her doubts, Peggy Gardner was resolutely disapproving. During the next days I prowled the garden, staring at the sunflowers and the broken toys, as I tried to understand why the light had left them. The whole of Shepperton was drab and inert, exhausted by the effort of briefly becoming its real self. While the children were at school I walked down to the river, searching the trees for any sign of Cleo's presence. As the sunlight pierced the foliage I caught hints of that magic glade where she had walked with the birds, dressed in light.

'You've let a Trojan horse into your mind,' Peggy told me, mustering a show of sympathy. 'What were you really trying to do?'

I conducted the air, thinking of a reply. '"Place the logic of the visible at the service of the invisible ..." It was stranger than I expected – I was actually looking inside my own head.'

'But, Jamie dear – we already know what's there. It's obvious to anyone who's read a few pages.'

'Shadows on the wall. Dick was right – I was watching the brain at work, seeing it assemble pieces of time and space into a workable dream of life.' I pointed to the walls of my study and the sunlit garden. 'All this is just as much a stage-set as anything in Shepperton Studios.'

'And what happens when you move the stage-sets out of the way?'

'To be honest, I don't know yet.'

'You're going to try again?'

'In a month or two. Dick is keen to film me.'

'Mad ... all this for a television programme?'

'I'm humouring him there. It's hard to describe the intense light, the sense that one's about to witness some huge revelation.'

'But what?'

'I'll find out. The same light lay over Lunghua on the day the war ended.'

'It never ended – for you.'

Peggy stood in the open doorway with her back to the garden, looking at me in the same kindly and tolerant way I remembered from the children's hut, when I had outlined some madcap method of finding food for us. The light touched her strong shoulders and the handsome hips I had never held. In a real sense we knew each other too well. Sex was for strangers, and as soon as one ceased to be a stranger desire died. Miriam had always been careful to keep part of herself veiled from me. Perhaps one day Peggy and I would become strangers to each other, as we grew older and apart ...

The light shifted, a retinal veer. For a moment I saw Peggy suspended in the air above the pear tree, angel of our suburb. I imagined this spinsterish doctor in her sensible woollen suit and court shoes, positioned at various points above the rooftops of Shepperton.

'Are you all right?' Peggy was staring at my eyes. 'You were miles away. What about the children – is Sally going to look after them?'

'Dick's asked a friend of his, Cleo Churchill. She brought her daughter and slept on the sofa. She's more level-headed – I think he's frightened that Sally might—'

'Poor Sally. You people use each other like deviant children.'

I kissed Peggy fondly, watched her drive away, and then helped the children with their homework and prepared our lunch. Deviant adults? The reproof stung, however much I reminded myself that Peggy's stance of responsibility and good sense was more at odds with the world than she realised. She might care for her deprived and abused infants, but she had never loved a child of her own, with all that love entailed. Spectres stalked the little garden of her house in Chelsea. It was not only in my mind that the four Japanese soldiers still waited at their wayside railway station for a train that would never come, as trapped by time as we were. War was the means by which nations escaped from time. Peggy and I and those Japanese soldiers had been marooned on that island platform, waiting for another war to set us free. They had tormented the Chinese to death in the hope that cruelty alone would release the mainspring of war.

Three weeks later, on another warm summer afternoon, I sat in my chair by the open French window. Dick's camera, with or without its film, sat on its tripod. While Cleo readied the children for a picnic, Dick was talking to his agent on the telephone, still in high hopes of selling his brain series to a regional channel.

At Dick's suggestion we had transformed the overgrown garden into a model of bourgeois family life. The children's toys sat on the grass like exhibits at a church fete. Rescued from the darkest cupboards, an older generation of bears and koalas sat in a circle like geriatric patients allowed to take the sun. The girls' brightest frocks, washed and ironed, hung from the clothes line, and Henry's bullfight poster, listing his name with those of Cordobés and Paco Camino, was pinned to the pear tree.

Hearing the children shouting by the gate, I left my seat and walked around the side path. Cleo was lifting a picnic basket through the kitchen door.

'Are you coming with us? Good.' She greeted me with a smile of surprise. She disapproved of Dick's experiments, and clearly thought I was being manipulated by him.

'No.' I helped her with the basket, 'I wish I was. We're starting in a moment.'

She brushed her hair from her cheeks, deliberately showing me her strong face. 'I hope you're all right. Last time …'

'There was something wrong with the dose. Don't worry. I'll see you as an archangel again.'

'See me as I am.' She stopped by the car and rested the picnic basket on the hood. Earlier she had helped Dick to set out the children's toys on the grass, striding uneasily around the garden on her strong legs like the reluctant member of a demolition squad. 'Why don't you come with us? You're the last person who needs to experiment with himself.'

'Cleo, I promised Dick ...'

Lucy skipped up to me, showing off her shiny belt. 'Daddy, are you coming?'

'Come on, Daddy,' Henry chimed in. 'We're going to Magic World.'

'Daddy, go on.'

Cleo hefted the basket onto her strong hip, leaving me to make my own decision. 'I've heard a lot about Magic World.'

'I hope it's still there. Old film props from TV commercials.'

'That sounds like fun. A lot more real than Dick's nonsense.'

I held the gate for her, and watched the children charge off towards the water-meadow, followed by the old retriever. Were they trying to recruit Cleo into their lost childhood, finding again that idyllic dream for which I was searching with LSD? I remembered the pale, spectral children who had gazed at me beside the river, as if watching me from the other side of death.

Alice held the retriever's collar, smiling as she waited hopefully for me to join her.

'You're right.' I took the basket from Cleo's hand. The warm scent of her body was more vivid than anything even LSD could contrive. 'Dick can find someone else. We'll bring a couple of bottles and see you at the splash in a few minutes ...'

Hallucinations sang on the summer air, skipping towards the water meadows and the magic glade by the film studios.

11

The Exhibition

The idea of staging an exhibition of crashed cars came to me in 1969 after the road accident near Fair Oaks airfield in which Sally and David Hunter were involved. Luckily, neither of them was hurt in any way, but the strange circumstances of the accident, and the behaviour of the witnesses, seemed to spring straight from the special logic of the Sixties. The exhibition at the Arts Laboratory, which intrigued some visitors and outraged a great many more, summed up so many of my obsessions at the time, and clearly foretold the car crash that nearly killed me three months later. Right until its end, the decade continued to unravel its lurid mythologies.

Sally, still determined to prise me away from Shepperton, had bought tickets for the Fair Oaks air show, where David was taking part in a formation flight of vintage Tiger Moths. Alice and Lucy were too frightened by the exploding exhausts to come with us, and were spending the day with Cleo Churchill and her daughter. Generous as ever, Sally insisted on a special treat for Henry. When she arrived he was assembling a model aircraft in the nursery, surrounded by his own air display of World War II fighters, exquisite replicas that seemed to contain more detail than their originals.
    'Come on, Henry! I'll ask David to give you a spin around Shepperton.'
    'Well ... David's scary. Will Neil Armstrong be there?'
    'He sent his apologies – he had to go back to the Moon.' Sally squeezed Henry's American football helmet, a gift from Dick Sutherland, over her white hair. 'Henry, I'm going to be the first woman astronaut.'

'Wow ...! A woman?'

'Hard to grasp, isn't it? One giant step for womankind, that's what we need.' When Henry went off to change, Sally soared around the model planes, blowing smoke from her Moroccan Gold through the silver propellers. 'They're so perfect, like hatched Fabergé eggs. The world's filling up with broken plastic, and little Henry sits here by himself, putting it all together again. That's the sort of thing you should write about.'

'I do, Sally. It's practically my only theme.' Glad to see her, I held her restless hips. 'Sally ... you're five miles high before the wheels leave the ground.'

'This is your captain speaking.' She placed her scarred forearms with their medley of sampler scents on my shoulders. 'The plane now crashing on Shepperton is the Mumford Express ...'

She was still wearing the football helmet when we set off for Fair Oaks airfield. Her visits to Shepperton, though less frequent, always calmed Sally. She landed like an eccentric Victorian balloonist, tethered to the ground by the children's affection for her. But once we left its gentle gravity she began to soar away. Blonde hair streaming through the open roof, she lay with her arms out of the window, waving to the extras leaving the film studios. The glowing end of her loosely packed cigarette blew a train of sparks into the rear seat and set fire to the ear of a faithful koala. As Henry choked, Sally lunged over the seat and slapped at the smoking embers. She shouted to the young policeman guiding traffic into Fair Oaks, who gazed in awe at her mini-skirt riding over her ice-pale buttocks.

When we reached the car park she noticed a television crew filming the air display. Sally pulled off the helmet and assumed the hard-eyed stare of her favourite amphetamine shades, gazing in a ravaged way at the parked planes and the handsome pilots. The anti-Viet Nam protest marches and scuffles with police, the drug busts and cooling-off trips to New York, had given her a terminal Manhattan tremor, part permanent jet lag, part overdose of heroin and time. Like so many others at the end of the 60s, that ten-year pharmaceutical trial, she thought of the media landscape as a life-support system, force-feeding a diet of violence and sensation into her numbed brain.

But sometimes I felt that it was Sally and a few thousands like her who supported the decade, which ruthlessly tapped their fraying nervous systems for the last pulse of energy and excitement. The carousel was spinning ever faster, driven on by Sally as she rode her exhausted unicorn. I hated the needle arms, but loved to see her sweep into Shepperton with presents for the children and endless King's Road talk. She was happy to camp for hours with Alice and Lucy in their garden tent, bake and ice a birthday cake for a long-serving teddy. Later, when the children were asleep, she lay back on the sofa with her heels in the small of my back, almost strangling me as she seized some slipping memory of her father that I had helped to return to her.

She would dress quickly and forget me, rushing into the night with shouts about a party, too impatient to burden herself with any needs of mine. A little deflated, I was usually relieved to see her go. I was nervous of the empty syringes I found in the lavatory cistern. Worryingly, she stole money from the children, as if trying to take back part of the affection she had given them. Alice and Lucy were too fond of Sally to care. When I tried to lend her money she waved her cheque books at me, and I realised that she needed to steal the small coins from the girls' purses. The carousel had tricked her into thinking that nothing mattered but its speed.

'Sally, sweet ... Jim, she got you out of that little Alcatraz of yours.' David stood glamorously by his Tiger Moth in a white flying suit, adjusting a fire extinguisher. He embraced Sally, treated me to a friendly but cool smile, and placed the extinguisher in my hands with a gesture implying that I might soon need it. 'Let's go, Henry – we'll sneak off and bomb Shepperton ...'

'Say, can we, David? Let's bomb my school.'

I had guessed for some time that Sally was seeing him. They shared nothing in the way of temperament or interests – David loathed hippies and bikers, and would try to run them down – but they could map their wayward needs on to each other.

Henry and I paused to peer at a Mignet Flying Flea, little more than an aerial skateboard, and Sally strolled towards the Tiger Moth, which David flew in a vermouth commercial. She peeled away her silk scarf as if they were about to make love under its wing. When he greeted Sally, David's eyes were filled with the easy humour he had turned upon the Moose Jaw whores. He held her to his shoulder, pressing her blonde hair to his lips, while giving Henry a cheery wave. Within minutes Sally was wearing a Bomber Command jacket, and an antique helmet and goggles, a fetishist's dream of a white-haired woman in flying leather. As she stood on tip-toe and kissed David, her crutch ruled the airfield.

Sally clung to his arm, glad to test this dangerous man. When they took off together in the Tiger Moth, David made a formal circuit of the airfield, and I sensed that he was exposing her to the entire air show, a naiad of the air he had brought down from the clouds. After they landed he lifted her from the cockpit, formally introducing her to the mortal earth. Sally's face was white with cold, her nose and lips as pointed as an arctic bird's, the wind still blowing through her roused eyes. The sky behind her was a dream of heroin. I wanted to stay with them, fearing that Sally might incite David to some mad piece of stunt flying, but he avoided my eyes.

David and I had seen less of each other in recent years. I liked him for his disruptive spirit and off-hand charm, and his fondness towards the children – Henry's entire passion for aircraft had been carefully instilled by David, who spent endless afternoons driving him to remote light airfields. But David had taken Miriam's death badly – far from forgetting her, he felt her loss more strongly as time passed. Sometimes he looked at me as if he thought that I was responsible for her death, and that he alone was keeping her memory alive. A week before the Fair Oaks air show he came up to me in a Soho restaurant, where I was having lunch with an American journalist, and stood silently by our table, ignoring my invitation to join us. While the waiters brushed past him he stared into my face, at last recognising me for what I was. I wondered if he was going to hit me, but he touched my shoulder without speaking and walked back to his friends.

Outwardly he was still the wise older brother, understanding my entire character and motives. He had never read anything of mine, saying that there was no need to – we had already lived through the most important story inside my head. His sense of humour had become more eccentric, almost mimicking the surrealists I admired so much. The increasing numbers of Japanese tourists who visited London he regarded as a conscious attempt to provoke him. Giving me a lift back from the premiere of *2001: A Space Odyssey* ('... a Pan-Am instructional film for space-hostesses,' was his comment), he stopped his Jaguar in Belgrave Square and smilingly watched one of the high stucco houses. I assumed that he had tracked down the home address of a favourite TV comedian, but as it happened this was the Japanese embassy. When some luckless attaché emerged, probably on the way to a British Council seminar on cultural relations between our countries, David raced the engine and hurled the Jaguar at the elderly Japanese, almost throwing him across the bonnet. To David this had been a lighthearted joke, which would have lost none of its point if he had killed the man. 'I have to remind myself of Shanghai,' he shouted as we cornered through Knightsbridge at speed. 'I'm starting to forget it ... the damn thing is, there's nothing else to remember.'

Fortunately, his service in the RAF had given him a support network of ex-military pilots, one of the strongest in the world. He was now an aircraft dealer, selling French two-seater helicopters to pop stars and style-conscious business tycoons. But his real passion was saloon-car racing at Brand's Hatch. He had twice been banned for dangerous track manoeuvres, the same dangerous driving to which he treated every suburban dual carriageway. He drove in a deliberately careless way, as if trying to express a casual nothingness. Cut off from his past in China, which both of us had begun to forget, and with no roots in England, he watched the few real elements in his life abandon him as his parents died and war-time friends retired to Australia and South Africa.

Concerned for David, I wanted to help him, just as I wanted to steer Sally away from her needles, but I was too busy with the children. When they strolled arm in arm towards the flying-club bar I began to follow them, and felt Henry tug at my arm. He had the sense to know that we should leave them alone, and was far more interested in the lines of vintage flying machines drawn up on the grass, each a conjuring trick to trump the wind. Glad to be together, we spent the afternoon roaming the air show.

At the end of the day, when we returned to the car park, David's Jaguar and Sally had gone. I assumed that David had given her a lift to her flat in Bayswater. The scent of her body still filled the interior of our car, imprinted on the seat beside me like an almost visible photograph of affection and desire. I thought of her as we pushed through the traffic returning to London. Tailbacks blocked both lanes, and warning beacons flashed from the roof of a police cruiser parked on the grass verge.

Two cars had collided in the approaches to Chertsey Bridge, and windscreen glass speckled the road. We moved forward, waved on in a theatrical way by a police patrolman, as if we were film extras late for the day's shooting. Through the oncoming traffic I could see the first of the damaged cars, a London taxi carrying two Japanese air stewardesses and their suitcases. Watched by a police sergeant, the cab driver was examining his crushed headlights and radiator grille. The young Japanese women stood beside him, squinting at the English sunlight in an almost guilty way.

I recognised the second car, and the white leg extended to the road through the open passenger door. David's silver Jaguar lay slewed across the road, its chromium bumper twisted into the right wheel housing. Sally and David sat together in the front seat. Neither had been hurt, but the Jaguar's windscreen had burst, covering the passenger compartment and the roadway with nuggets of glass. Sally lay back, her thighs spread, one hand resting on David's arm. She was looking down at the glass that covered their laps, which neither of them made any attempt to brush away. Watching them, I was struck by their self-conscious pose, like dancers arrested in an audience-catching flourish at the end of their performance. They were uninterested in each other's well-being, but only in the postures they assumed within the cabin of the Jaguar, as if they were memorising for future use the exact geometry of Sally's exposed thighs and the ribbed leather of the upholstery, the precise angle between David's crutch and the jut and rake of the steering wheel.

The police sergeant spoke to them through the window, but they ignored him, staring in a rapt way at their own hands. They seemed almost to be rehearsing themselves for a performance to come, some even more elaborately staged collision. There was no trace of shock in Sally's face, but a thin smile that was faintly sexual in its self-regard.

The traffic crept towards the bridge, but I stopped the car and opened my door, ready to offer my help before the ambulance arrived.

'Daddy ... !' Henry warned. 'The policeman's shouting at you!'

A fist drummed on the roof over my head. I acknowledged the patrol-man's signal, waved encouragingly to Sally and David and rejoined the queue crossing the bridge. A few pedestrians stood at the kerb, staring idly at the damaged cars. They stepped back, making room for a more appreciative audience that had now arrived. Spectators returning from the air show were leaving their cars in a side-street and in the car park of a riverside pub. They gathered around the Jaguar, inspecting the damaged bodywork and the pattern of tyre-marks scored into the road with the practised eyes of enthusiasts judging a display of aero-batics. Two cine-cameras recorded the scene, and the police made no attempt to stop them, so impressed were they by the knowledgeability of this sympathetic audience. Yet no one made the smallest effort to help Sally and David, and a man in a flying jacket even protested when an ambulance appeared on the scene and the attendants lifting Sally from the Jaguar blocked the view-finder of his expensive camera. As I watched, a new street theatre had been born.

During the next weeks, as I drove through central London, I noticed the same thoughtful gaze in the people who gathered at street accidents, as if the secret formulas of their lives were exposed by these random colli-sions. Office-workers on their way to lunch, drivers unloading delivery vans, stared at the damaged cars that materialised out of the passing traffic in a fanfare of ringing metal and sounding horns. An attentive audience would invariably form, calmly inspecting the stricken vehicles.

Often I stopped my car and walked through the crowds, struck by the spectators' quiet and measured response. Only ten years earlier everyone would have been pulling with their bare hands at the broken bodywork and crushed roofs, trying to free the injured occupants. Born out of an ecology of violence, acts of numbing brutality now ruled the imaginative spaces of their lives, leaching away all feeling and emotion.

Perhaps, in their thoughtful communion with the crashed car, they were trying to come to terms with the televised disasters and assassinations that enfolded their minds, and doing what they could to restore a lost compassion.

Where this perverse logic might lead I grasped for the first time when Sally drove me to the opening of the Arts Laboratory at its new premises in Camden Town. Usually I was wary of being a passenger in Sally's spirited but erratic MG, and always found an excuse to prevent her driving the children. On this evening, however, she was surprisingly sedate, driving well within the speed limit and keeping a steady eye on the rear-view mirror. Anxious for her, I wondered if she were still recovering from the collision after the air show.

'I didn't feel a thing,' she told me, clearly disappointed. 'I didn't even see it happen. Suddenly we were sitting there with all this glass and these huge policemen. Not even a scratch – I really feel cheated.'

'You could have gone through the windshield.'

'Jim, it was a bump! You would have enjoyed it. David pulled the wheel over without thinking.'

'I can't believe that ...' At the foot of Chertsey Bridge the Japanese stewardesses had stood blinking in the sunlight like hostages tied to a target. 'I bet he knew exactly what he was doing.'

'No, that's David. He felt like a shunt. I don't know why the Japanese were there.'

'Sally, he'll kill you.'

'Great! I might like that ...' We had stopped on the Westway flyover, and the traffic lights flared across Sally's sallow face and its wild smile. Seeing that she had shocked me, she pressed my hand to the steering wheel. 'Don't worry, David wants to get himself killed, he isn't interested in me. He's always trying to hit other cars. Every shunt reminds him of something – the war, I guess. You never talked about your camp, Jim. Did he have a bad time, physically?'

'Physically, nothing happened to him at all.'

'And what about you – mentally, maybe?'

'Sally, that was long, long ago.'

'Not for him. Car crashes bring it all back for David. They mean for him what bull-fights mean for everyone else – sex and death ... Jim, you didn't mind me going off with him? He's your oldest friend, in a way it's not like my picking someone you didn't know.'

'I suppose that's true ...'

'I love the pixies. They helped me to grow up. And you. Now you're writing all the time, and I'm so busy with things ...' She spoke softly, as if to herself. 'Everyone changes, and we're always moving away from each other. Just for once I wish we could all stand still and remember the way things were. There's so much happening, and I want to be part of it all. I want to live everyone's dreams, be right inside them ...'

'Sally, you are. But—'

'Jim, I'll always let you fuck me.'

She brushed her ungroomed hair, aware that I might not always want to. Her fingers fiddled with her scarred upper lip, where she had been punched by a casual lover, an evil-tempered underground film-maker. Looking at her, as she bravely tried to draw herself together, I realised how much she had lost any centre to her life. Shepperton had been the axis of her carousel, where she had warmed herself by the cheerful calliope she had helped to play with my children; but she had moved away to the whirling lights and the rushing air far out on the rim. I was too dull for her, too immersed in the children's games and homework, too steeped in the tumblers of whisky and soda that cheered me and calmed the world, a trade-off that Sally found too limiting. She needed the world to rush up to her like the waves seething around her waist at Brighton beach.

We drove on, crossed the Marylebone Road and strayed into the maze of old commercial properties off Camden High Street. As Sally fumbled with the rear-view mirror, I sensed that she had deliberately lost her bearings, as if waiting for someone to find us. I searched the skyline of derelict buildings. The Arts Laboratory had moved into a one-time pharmaceutical warehouse; its open concrete decks were the perfect setting for its brutalist happenings and exhibitions, its huge ventilation shafts purpose-built to evacuate the last breath of pot smoke in the event of a drugs raid.

As we turned into a one-way street I saw headlights flash from a waiting car parked in a slip-road. It moved towards us, accelerating with the roar of a supercharged engine. I forced the wheel over while Sally stamped at the brake pedal, but the car had swerved past us, its windscreen pillar clipping the mirror from a parked van. In the rush of speed and danger I recognised the silver Jaguar and its deformed fender. Without pausing, it careened out of the one-way street and headed into the night.

'Sally – pull off the street. He may come back.'

Sally lay against the head-rest, white hair across her face like a lace of death, stunned by the moment of violence that had opened and closed with the roar of a furnace door. In the darkness the broken mirror rang for a last time against a fender. Depressing the clutch with my foot, I started the stalled engine and steered the car into the loading bay of a disused warehouse.

We sat in the silence, listening to the distant moan of the Jaguar's engine as it hunted the streets, a lover's cry in the night.

'Was that David?' I asked. 'Sally, did you see him?'

'He'll be back.' Sally held my arm. 'He was trying to warn you.'

'How long has he followed you around?'

'Only sometimes. Then I follow him.' She pressed her hand over mine as I gripped the steering wheel. 'It's a game of hide-and-seek. We pretend to crash into each other. Keep out of his way, Jim – once he said you were really Japanese …'

She sat in the darkness, looking at the faded sign on the wall beside us, advertising sets of Edwardian crucibles and alembics. She had spread her thighs, imitating her posture in David's car after the Chertsey Bridge collision. She was sedated and aroused at the same time, adrift within a dream of violence and desire.

'It's snug here. Car crashes always … Jim, you'll have to …'

She took my hand and placed it between her thighs. The cotton gusset was damp with moisture that soaked her skirt, a fluxus brought on by the swerving Jaguar. Arching her back, she pulled the G-string down to her knees, and kicked it away among the pedals. She steered my hand to her vulva, settling my ring-finger over her clitoris, and spread her arms across the back of the seat, as if reclining in the car after a spectacular accident. When I caressed her thighs, trying to soothe the needle ulcers on her veins, she followed my fingers with her own, searching for the outlines of the wounds that would set their seals into her white skin.

'Jim, one day we'll be in a crash together. I'd like that ... think about it now for me.'

She moved diagonally across the seat and raised her thighs to expose her anus, caressing her vulva with her forefinger. I embraced her tenderly, thinking of the years we had spent together. I remembered her running with the horses in the field near the pop festival, her white hair lifting among the horses' tails, her eyes flushed with thoughts of her childhood.

I knelt on the floor of the passenger well, aware of the dashboard panel gleaming against my shoulder, the instrument binnacle jutting forward in the darkness. The stylised interior of the car embraced Sally as intensely as any lover. When my penis entered her vulva she took my hips in her hands, holding me so that only the glans lay between her labia. She pulled the black shoulder straps from her dress, and lowered the bodice to free her breasts.

When I caressed them she watched me in an expressionless way, as if she wanted to be violated by a machine. She held my head a few inches from her nipple, tracing out a sign on her breast, the diagram of an undreamed mutilation. She was exposing herself not to me but to the designers of her car, to David Hunter, whose proxy I had become, and to the unknown man who had shaped her childhood. Her fingers scratched at my chest, trying to draw the bandages from a wound, and she tapped her nipple like a nurse drawing blood from a vein. When I came she pressed her breast to my mouth, as if returning to me all the blood that I had lost in the sex-death that filled her dreams.

We lay together as David's Jaguar hunted the streets, a beast pursuing its strange courtship. When the headlamps flared against the walls of the warehouses Sally pressed her head to my shoulder. Sucking her infected arms, she clung to my chest, afraid that she might leave me and run towards the oncoming light.

My exhibition of crashed cars was held for four weeks at the Arts Laboratory, and throughout that time came under continuous attack from visitors to the gallery. One of the few who wholeheartedly approved was Peter Lykiard. When, at Sally's urging, I suggested the exhibition to him, he instantly accepted the project.

'Excellent, Jim ... in its way, emotional minimalism at its purest. Warhol would approve.'

In fact, my intentions were the exact opposite. For me, the crashed car was a repository of the most powerful and engaged emotions, a potent symbol in the new logic of violence and sensation that ruled our lives.

In my catalogue notes I wrote: 'The marriage of reason and nightmare which dominates the 1960s has given birth to an ever more ambiguous world. Across the communications landscape stride the spectres of sinister technologies and the dreams that money can buy. Thermonuclear weapons systems and soft-drink commercials coexist in an uneasy realm ruled by advertising and pseudo-events, science and pornography. The death of feeling and emotion has at last left us free to pursue our own psychopathologies as a game ... "Crashed Cars" illustrates the pandemic cataclysm that kills hundreds of thousands of people each year and injures millions, but is a source of endless entertainment on our film and television screens.'

Contrary to expectations, setting up the exhibition presented few problems. The automobile graveyards of north London were a treasure house of exhibits, the outdoor store-rooms of a technological Louvre. In a Hackney breaker's yard we selected a telescoped Peugeot and a Mini that had rolled down a motorway embankment, whose grass was still growing in its roof sills.

By chance, we found a Lincoln Continental that closely resembled the open-topped limousine in which President Kennedy had met his death. This huge American car had been involved in a massive front-end collision that had driven the radiator grille deep into the engine compartment while leaving the remainder of the car in virtually pristine condition.

Without doubt it was this crushed Lincoln that excited the strongest reactions. The immense black car sat under the clear gallery lights, surrounded by the barest white walls. Although none of the cars would have prompted the slightest concern had they been parked in the street outside, or a moment's grief over the tragic fate of the occupants, within the gallery they became the focus for nervous laughter and angry comment. Visitors who wandered into the gallery and found the cars unexpectedly in front of them began to titter to themselves or swear at the vehicles.

These responses confirmed all my suspicions of everything that an aberrant technology was threading through our lives. Further testing the audience, I hired a topless young woman to interview the guests at the opening party on closed-circuit television. She had originally agreed to appear naked with her microphone, but on seeing the cars decided that she would only bare her breasts – an interesting response in its own right.

Needless to say, all this provoked the guests beyond endurance. No gallery opening in my experience had ever degenerated so quickly into a drunken brawl. Egged on by Sally and David Hunter, the guests poured wine over the cars, tore off the wing mirrors and began to break the few intact windows. David leapt around the gallery, supervising the mayhem in high good humour. His restless hands hardly left the damaged cars, as if he had at last found his natural habitat.

Towards the evening's end the party took an uglier turn. Sally was nearly raped in the rear seat of the Continental by an over-boisterous tableau sculptor for whom she was mimicking the postures of the President's widow. Carried away by the excitement, David urged the topless girl to interview her during the heat of the assault.

'Sally, this is live TV! Tell the viewers how you feel!' David dragged the camera-man after him, snatched the microphone and rammed it through the passenger window into Sally's enraged face. 'Over to you, Sally! Let's have a commentary in your own words ...'

By the time Cleo Churchill and I had rescued Sally the party was spilling into the street, the guests searching for an even larger exhibition. Straightening her torn dress, Sally lunged at the drunken sculptor with her shoe and hobbled away on a broken heel through the scattered wine-bottles. She grimaced at the image of herself on the television screen and disappeared with a cry into the night.

'Is Sally safe?' Cleo avoided the wine dripping from the roof of the

Lincoln, and slammed the passenger door with relief. 'You've proved something, Jim – though I don't know what. Was it worth it?'

'As an experiment? I think so.' I knew that she disapproved of the exhibition, and had gamely come along to give me support. 'At least they never stopped looking at the cars, which is more than you can say for most gallery openings. Dick Sutherland wants to film all this for his new series. When he gets back from the States they'll stage the party again at the Television Centre, with studio extras playing the guests.'

'Heaven forbid ... Don't let him use you all the time.' Unsettled by the violent evening, Cleo wiped the wine from her hands. She pointed to the monitor screen transmitting a picture of the empty gallery. 'You're on TV now – isn't that enough?'

'Broadcast TV, Cleo – Dick feels the idea deserves an audience of millions.'

'I thought it had one. You know, out in the streets, the real thing?'

'Cleo, this is the real thing ... But I'm glad you came. Can I give you a lift home?'

'Jim, dear, I think not. This is one evening when I wouldn't trust your driving ...'

Cleo stood in front of the camera, using the screen as a mirror as she checked the wine stains on the sleeves of her dress. The electronic colours had separated slightly, and reminded me of my acid vision when I had seen Cleo robed in a train of light as she strolled through the trees beside the river. My Moreau princess, who turned the starlings into peacocks and calmed the air with her graceful hands. I wanted to invite her to Shepperton again, drawn by her intelligence and forthright mind.

But Cleo was nervous of me, aware that I was doggedly following a dangerous logic of my own. If death had outstared life, which the world seemed to believe, I could rest my case. In a desperate sense Miriam would be alive again, Kennedy would drive triumphantly through Dealey Plaza, the casualties of the Second World War would rest in their graves and a Chinese youth at a rural railway station would at last have conveyed his desperate message to me.

*

The exhibition ran its four-week course. During this time the cars were continually abused by outraged visitors. A hare krishna sect stormed into the gallery and threw a tin of white paint at the Lincoln. Meanwhile Sally and David continued their courtship, hunting each other across the city in the same way that David and I had once played hide-and-seek in the streets of Shanghai, a game too important to be brought to an end.

On the evening that the exhibition closed I was driving back to Shepperton along the Hammersmith flyover, when I saw Sally's MG speeding down the exit ramp in front of me. I had spent the afternoon at the gallery, supervising the removal of my battered exhibits, whose distressed condition – they were covered with paint and graffiti, their seats soaked in urine – shocked the hardened car-breakers when they arrived with their tow-truck. At first they refused to accept the vehicles, their eyes opened to the barbarities of modern art. The cars might be destined for the compactor and the blast furnace, but as they dragged them into the street they were already cleaning them protectively.

While I drove along the flyover I wiped the last of the white paint from my hands, and watched Sally's sportscar speeding through the traffic, a defective tail-light winking at the dusk. In the past, whenever I saw her on the roads to the west of London, I was sure that she was on her way to Shepperton. Now I guessed that she was off to see David at Fair Oaks airfield, and for a moment I felt a small part of that loss I had known after Miriam's death. Sally at least would smile at me again; we would make love and remain as fond of each other as ever. But the last things she wanted were sympathy and affection. She needed David's unresolved aggressions, and his outbursts of erratic humour when he would slap her face for her if she played the difficult child.

Beyond Twickenham the traffic began to open out. As we passed the rugby stadium Sally moved into the fast lane, forcing an overtaking car to brake. Headlights flared against the bounding tail of the MG, and Sally pushed a derisive finger through a tear in the canvas hood, sending a shower of embers from her cigarette into the night air. Reluctantly, she moved over to allow the faster car to pass her, then swerved back into his slipstream, her headlamps flooding the driver's mirror.

Left behind in a line of slower cars, I waited until we reached the next roundabout, accelerated past an idling truck and set off after Sally. She glanced in the rear-view mirror, and I wondered if she had seen me, but she was repairing the make-up to her eyes and lips.

I thought of her with David, making love on his air bed, as she had often told me, under the wings of his Cessna in the silent hangar. A reverie of jealousy and desire filled my mind, regret that I had lost Sally to this winged man, anger at myself for being so prudishly afraid of her needle ulcers and thieving ...

Escaping from my hands, the car leapt across the road and touched the tail of the MG. Our fenders locked as we careened along the carriageway. Startled, Sally crouched away from the wild headlights and the hurtling mass of the car that had leapt out of the night. Cigarette in her mouth, she pulled away to my left, overran the soft shoulder and then swerved in front of me as she lost control of the small steering wheel.

Trying to avoid a collision, I braked sharply into the fast lane. As the car veered to the right I felt a front tyre burst and deflate. The wheel wrenched itself from my hands. The car side-slipped across the dual carriageway, and the flattened tyre struck the central reservation, hurling the vehicle onto its side. It demolished an illuminated traffic sign, rolled on to its back and carried on along the on-coming lane.

Hanging from my seat belt, I saw the asphalt rush past a few inches above my face, a ceiling of racing gravel lit by my headlights. The windscreen exploded in a burst of glass chips. The roof collapsed, and the rear-view mirror struck my forehead.

The car had stopped, and lay in the centre of the oncoming lane a hundred yards beyond the demolished traffic sign. I listened to the wheels spinning in the night air. Around me cars were slowing, horns competing with each other. Already I could smell the fuel dripping from the engine on to the glass-covered road. Drivers were running from their cars towards me. I switched off the engine and tried to free myself, but the collapsed roof had locked the door into its frame. Fuel pooled against the window as a dozen people rocked the car, trying to loosen the door. A man's fist drummed against the pillar. I wound down the window, released my seat belt and sank on to the warped ceiling.

Hands seized my shoulders and dragged me from the cabin. Stunned by the blow to my head, I lay on the grass verge as a crowd gathered around my car. I could still see the rushing asphalt in the glare of headlights, as if death itself were speeding towards me, passing a few inches above my eyes.

An ambulance man knelt beside me, frowning over his first-aid kit. He seemed uninterested in me, and complained to the driver about some missing piece of equipment. A police vehicle, its beacon flashing, stopped within thirty feet of my car, which a group of young men were rocking from side to side. Two teenage girls in party frocks looked down at my face, moving from one dance slipper to the other on the cold night grass. They hummed the melody of a recent pop song, gazing at me as if I were a drunk at a party who had fallen at their feet.

A cigarette lighter flared in the night air. Before I could speak Sally Mumford pushed between the girls. Drawing protectively on her cigarette, she peered over the head of the ambulanceman, and lowered the lighter flame to my face, curious to see the driver of the car which had nearly killed her.

Four months later, in the last days of the 1960s, I stood with the cheering crowd in a disused soccer stadium in east London, watching the battered saloon cars of a demolition derby lumber around the muddy track. In the centre of the arena, helmet on her hip, Sally stood in white jeans and a crimson rally driver's tunic. She was shouting angrily at David Hunter, now out of the race and resting behind the wheel of his demolished car. As Sally urged him on, whistling through her broken teeth, he lay back in his silver suit and stretched his arms, gazing contentedly at the rusty impacts around him.

Watching these desultory collisions, I remembered my own crash and the exhibition at the Arts Laboratory. I still assumed that the exhibition had been designed to test the psychology of its audience, but David took for granted that its sole purpose had been to incite myself. Was my accident, in which I was lucky not to be killed, an attempt to die in an erotic death-pact with Sally?

David had suggested as much, when he and Sally visited me in Roehampton hospital. Looking up from my bed at this deteriorated couple, of whom I was so fond, I realised that I had exploited them in the same way that Dick Sutherland and Lykiard had exploited me. I wanted to help them, but the insane roller-coaster of the Sixties had seized our lives and swept us headlong between its screaming rails.

The last cars on the circuit heaved against each other like the bored bison wallowing in the mud-pit beside the railroad bridge at Moose Jaw. I thought of the hell-drivers in Shanghai before the war, and the spectacular collisions staged by the casual Americans. Across the years their spirit seemed to hover over this modest track, and over the greatest of all motorised tragedies, Kennedy's death by motorcade. I could still remember individual frames of the Zapruder film, endlessly anatomised on television and in a thousand magazine exposés. Had the events in Dealey Plaza been no more than the most elaborate of a series of staged accidents prefigured on that Shanghai race-course of my childhood?

Chilled by the winter air, the spectators shuffled their feet on the wooden stands. Nostrils quickened in the drifting smoke and engine fumes. The advertised highlight of the afternoon was the recreation of a spectacular road accident, a multiple collision on a Manchester overpass in which a dozen vehicles had been involved.

As a curtain-raiser, there would be a women's event, and the crowd moved forward for a closer view. Sally and a group of women drivers, all in striped silk jackets, faces made up like streetwalkers, were gripping the roof sills of their cars and sliding their legs through the drivers' windows. The spectators, heavy men in leather coats, pushed past me to the rail. They settled their hands deep in their pockets. They had only come for the women's event, a figure-of-eight destruction course filled with jolting impacts, when every penis in the arena would be clenched within a hand.

12

In the Camera Lens

'A film festival,' Dick Sutherland remarked over our third rum collins at the Copacabana Palace Hotel, 'gives you a fair idea of what the future will be like.'

'Beautiful but unapproachable women, frazzled men, and a million dreams held together by hype?'

'That sort of thing. Lang's *Metropolis* re-shot in Las Vegas. It's not that illusion takes the place of reality, but that out-and-out hallucination takes the place of illusion. Activities of the human brain it's needed the whole of evolution to control are here let out to play. I love it.'

'Dick, I thought you might. And what about our congress of science films?'

'The same thing applies. In many ways, more so.' Dick smiled knowingly, always happy when he could provoke me. 'Sooner or later, like everything else, science is going to turn into television.'

'Does that sound sinister?'

'Very. Exciting, though. What's that idea you're always trotting out …?'

Dick liked me to repeat this weather-worn prophecy of mine whenever his confidence flagged or he found himself in a place where no one recognised him, the ultimate in sensory deprivation for the TV personality.

'I forget … that you might be responsible for the first major scientific discovery to be made on television?'

'That's it. It could happen here. Rio is a total media city.'

From the air-conditioned bar he gazed contentedly at the procession of giant floats that moved along the Avenida Atlantica advertising the star film of the festival, Stanley Kubrick's *2001*. Through the crowded traffic edged a fleet of silver space craft, resembling the demonstration models of an interplanetary nightclub. In their abbreviated foil space-suits, the crews of hip-rolling young women flashed cocktail-waitress smiles at the crowds of tourists. For some reason, only the beggars and cripples squatting outside the beach hotels bothered to watch them. Waves of amplified music rose above the clamour of police sirens and the cries of lottery salesmen. Two light aircraft flew above the beach, and towed pennants advertising rival film attractions. Challenging them, giant fragments of 'Also Sprach Zarathustra' drummed against the facades of the hotels and rolled out to sea to wake Poseidon himself.

The carousel disappeared into the din and haze, instantly forgotten. Apart from Dick and the families of beggars, no one had paid any attention to the floats. Everything in Rio was dominated by the beach. This was no strip of basking sand on the Mediterranean model but a linear, open-air city in its own right, filled with thousands of sunbathers, kite and watch salesmen, ice-cream vendors and marauding beggar troupes, and a complete league of football teams playing on almost full-sized sand-pitches. No one swam. The morose Atlantic breakers hurled themselves against the Richard Strauss crescendos, wave for wave, daring the film executives and festival organisers to match their epic reach.

As Dick and I had noticed soon after flying in from London, Rio happily embraced the film festival and at the same time completely ignored it. Everywhere the crowds jammed the movie theatres, and the hotel terraces were packed with television crews, starlets and producers. Fleets of limousines and buses ferried the delegates from one lavish embassy party to another, while gangs of prostitutes and their pimps so packed the streets of Copacabana that they squeezed out any hope of finding a customer.

But the city absorbed all this, as if the illusory visions of the festival scarcely matched the vastly greater illusion of Rio itself, a city that reminded me of pre-war Shanghai in so many ways, but a Shanghai of tiled sidewalks ruled by the most confident and beautiful women in the world. Watching the bored policemen white-washing the windscreens of illegally parked cars, I could almost believe that they were protecting the drivers from a blinding glimpse of this extraordinary sex.

And above all this were the people of the favelas, the shanty towns crowding the dozens of large hills that rose from the streets of Rio. Where the poor and destitute of most cities occupied its nether regions, in Rio they lived up in the sky, coming down from the clouds to exhibit their undernourished and crippled children and pluck at the tourist sleeve. Had these impoverished people found the door to heaven open one morning, taken possession of its misty peaks and discovered too late that they had been tricked by those with their feet on the firmer ground far below? 'On you it looks great,' I heard a film executive remark to a beggar woman, carrying a bony child asleep on her dry breast, who dared to raise her withered arm to him outside the Copacabana Palace.

However, it was easy for Dick and me to buy off our consciences with a few conference cruzeiros, and perhaps equally naive. The gangs of confident pickpockets and the cripples viciously defending their pitches against any rivals reminded me again of Shanghai, with its rich beggars protected by their bodyguards. Shanghai, too, had been a media city, perhaps the first of all, purpose-built by the west as a test-metropolis of the future. London in the 1960s had been the second, with the same confusions of image and reality, the same overheating.

In Rio fiction and reality still played their games. At a party given by the American Embassy we found ourselves in a reception line shaking hands with the crew of the Starship *Enterprise*, a group of grey-haired actors like venerable morticians. Famous faces surrounded us, older and unsuccessful impersonations of themselves. Struggling to make small talk to a producer's wife, I felt that I, too, was an impostor, masquerading as myself in an unconvincing way. I was grateful for the light-show and the amplified music that raised all conversation to an unintelligible shout.

Rescuing me, Dick pushed through the throng and seized my arm. 'Jim – come and meet Fritz Lang ...'

He plunged into the press of dinner jackets towards a group of some twenty guests gazing down at what seemed to be the scene of a small accident. An elderly man in an oversize tuxedo sat on a straightbacked chair turned sideways to the wall. He slumped in the chair like an abandoned ventriloquist's dummy, buffeted by the noise and music, the light show dappling his grey hair a vivid blue and green. He looked infinitely weary, and I thought that he might have died among these garish film people. When I shook his hand, and briefly told him how much I admired his films, there was a flicker of response. An ironic gleam flitted through one eye, as if the director of *Metropolis* had realised that the dystopia he had visualised had come true in a way he had least expected.

Lang's resigned humour came to mind as we finished our rum collins at the Copacabana Palace and set off for the congress hall where the festival of scientific and documentary films was being held, an adjunct to the main festival which the organisers had decided to sponsor as a tribute to Kubrick's science fiction epic. A crowd of film fans pressed around us when we climbed into a taxi, and Dick momentarily brightened until we realised that almost all of them were pickpockets, brothel touts and voodoo pitchmen.

'Hey, mister, you want voodoo? Real good voodoo?'

'Mister, you want to watch a guy fuck a chicken?'

'Only ten years old, mister. Real clean girls.'

We shut the windows on a forest of arms. 'Well, Dick,' I asked. 'Do you? It's not exactly your everyday BBC wildlife film.'

'Wait and see – you may be surprised, Jim. Even you.'

Offering Dick my moral support, I sat in on his lecture and the panel discussions which he chaired, fascinated as ever by the sight of him working his audience like a seasoned music hall trouper. Yet his performance seemed oddly subdued, as if he were trying to shrug off the repertory of television mannerisms he had cultivated so carefully since the Cambridge days. Now and then, as he acknowledged the audience's laughter, he glanced at them in the same weary way that Fritz Lang had accepted my handshake. Rio was filled with old actor-managers trapped within their images of themselves.

Dick's laboratory at the Institute of Psychology was now little more than a public relations bureau, and Cleo told me that he had secretly borrowed bench-space in a colleague's lab so that he could return to original research. Sometimes he would sit there for an hour, in this shrine to his younger self, unable as yet to come up with an original project. Then he would return to his own laboratory and become the reluctant fugleman of popular psychology, feeding news of the latest breakthroughs to his coterie of TV producers. I admired Dick, and regretted that I had always encouraged him to think of the media world as his true laboratory. Sometimes, when I asked him about his own research, he became almost testy.

Later, wandering around the wide corridors where the out-of-competition films were screened, I was surprised by the variety of documentary films being produced, only a fraction of which would ever reach the general public. Zoos, schools of dentistry, agricultural research stations, international hotel chains, hairdressing colleges, and a consortium of undertakers and embalmers all had active film units.

In the glowing half-light the shirt-sleeved delegates stood by the lines of monitor screens, watching studies of the nose-wheel housing of the Boeing 707, the stress-fractures of ice-hockey players, the life-cycle of the cane-toad, the architecture of brothels. As I turned from a close-up of an exposed nasal septum to another about the curing of sable skins the two seemed to merge in my mind. Were all these films moving in their reductive way towards the same undifferentiated end? Drained of emotion and value-judgement, the lens of the scientific camera anatomised the world around it like a patient and pensive voyeur.

The medical and psychological films showed the process most clearly at work. In the competition section of the festival I watched Dick introduce the afternoon's programme on the theme: 'Aversion therapy – desensitisation in the perception of sexual imagery'. The three films described work in Sweden, Japan and the United States with habitual sex offenders, in which these doomed and gloomy men were exposed to endless images of their notional victims – small children, vulnerable women, racial targets and fellow sex-offenders. Doses of emetic drugs, surges of electric current, noise and other aversive conditioning supposedly turned the subjects against the objects of their desire.

As the succession of harrowing images passed by, I looked away from the cinema screen to the members of the audience. For the most part documentary film makers and professional psychologists, they gazed at the screen with the same steady eyes and unflinching expressions of the men in the Soho porn theatres, or the fans of certain kinds of apocalyptic science fiction. Whenever the criminal subjects winced with pain or vomited into their sick-basins, ripples of appreciation would move across the audience at some particularly striking camera angle or expository close-up, as the Soho patrons might have applauded a telling crutch shot or elegant anal penetration.

Later, when we returned to our hotel on Copacabana Beach and our first frozen daiquiri of the evening, I said to Dick: 'I need this. We should have gone to the voodoo. That was quite an afternoon.'

'Gruelling stuff?'

'I was watching the audience. The future may be like a film festival, but which one? Yours, or the one at this end of the beach? They had the eyes of tourists at a death camp, the kind of tourists who keep going back.'

'We've shocked you, Jim – that was worth coming to Rio for.' Delighted to catch me out, Dick glanced at me slyly over his glass. The rivalry between us, which for reasons of his own he had always encouraged, had become more open in Rio. 'It's interesting that scientific films unsettle you more than hard-core porn.'

'But pornography is really very chaste – it's the body's unerotic dream of itself. Your films come straight from the psychopathic ward. Imagine how you'd react if you found them in the film-library of a sex-criminal.'

'So …? Take a set of surgical instruments – innocent in an operating theatre, but in Myra Hindley's handbag? You're seeing them out of context.'

'Nothing is seen in context any more. Switch on your TV set, Dick, and you find a murdered prime minister, a child eating a candy bar, Marilyn lifting her skirt – what sort of scenario is the mind quietly stitching together?'

'It might be interesting to know. Tell me.'

'One of Cleo's fashion magazines showed some models prancing about in front of a blow-up from the Zapruder film – the Kennedy assassination as a fashion accessory?'

'Of course. In the future everyone will need to be a film critic to make sense of anything.'

'Not a psychologist?' His remark surprised me. 'Surely, you ...?'

'No, I think the psychologist has had his day ...'

Dick stared coolly across the crowded terrace of the Luxor, at the relaxing delegates and the photographers waiting by the lobby in hope of a passing celebrity. Despite his success that afternoon he seemed dissatisfied, as if he accepted that the epoch of popular television, in whose secure playground he had thrived, would soon be replaced by a harsher and more open world, an ever-changing media landscape in which fame was as transitory as a may-fly. Like an astronaut unable to tether himself to the Moon's surface, he longed for a stronger gravity. The need for attention had sent him bounding ever higher through the airless dust of celebrity, and there was nothing now to pull him down. He often asked me about the children's school results, glad to hear of their success, and clearly envying me my family ties. He had never married, and his women-friends moved through his life like game-show panellists, cheerful, optimistic and unremembered. Even their fascination with Dick was never enough.

'Dr Sutherland – we saw your interview. Without doubt, the most handsome psychologist in Rio ...'

An avuncular voice hailed Dick across the terrace. Señor Marcial Pereira, a leading film critic on a Rio newspaper, approached our table, accompanied by two of Copacabana's ambling beauties. He recognised Dick from the interview he had given the previous evening on a local TV station. He joined us at our table with his companions, who surveyed us with the eyes of empresses. Like all the women in Rio, they were filled with such character, elegance and hot beauty that only some inexplicable oversight had prevented them from achieving Hollywood careers.

'We have a party tonight, in my apartment at Ipanema,' Pereira told us. 'A festival car will collect you at ten. Each day we must relax a little more. I leave you with my actress friends – Carmen and Fortunata. They are most anxious to meet visiting Englishmen.'

When he had gone the women settled themselves at our table, eyes conferring as they swiftly surveyed the crowded terrace. Both wore the same loose silk frocks that revealed their thighs and shoulders. They were scarcely older than my daughters, with an equal command of the space around them. Carmen's dark hair sprang from a sharply sloping profile that was part Portuguese and part Indian. Her forehead was perpetually creased, as if she were fretting over some misplaced clue to the world. Her friend, Fortunata, a passive, heavy-breasted blonde, was waiting for the signal to leave, but Dick, excited by the heady body scent of the two women, was already ordering drinks and practising his pidgin English.

'You live in Rio? Here?'

'On the beach? No.' Carmen was ticking off Dick's television smile, his gold medallion and credit cards. 'São Paulo. We come for the festival.'

'Like us. We come from London – in England.'

'London, oh … Carmen and I go to London.' Fortunata stared down some Carnaby Street vista inside her head, at the end of which stood the Beatles and the Rolling Stones. She spoke wistfully, as if unsure whether Carmen would agree.

'Rio is much better,' Dick assured her. 'Many beautiful women. Like you two.'

'Yes … many women in Rio.' Carmen sounded like a commodities dealer in a slow market. 'You prefer beautiful women?'

'Of course. Especially in Rio.'

'You're an actress?' I asked. 'Have you made any films?'

'Yes. I act in films. With Fortunata.'

She spoke matter-of-factly. I assumed that we were with two São Paulo prostitutes visiting Rio on a speculative trawl. I waited for Dick to realise that there was only one way to impress them. Carmen was strumming at the table top with one hand, while the other flicked at her shoulder strap. She was exposing her breast to me, at the same time letting the hem of her silk dress ride up her thigh.

I remembered Marilyn Monroe's early years on the fringes of

prostitution. I had shaken hands with the great Fritz Lang and with the crew of the Starship *Enterprise*, but this stony-faced beach whore would be my real contact with the international film industry. Perhaps she had appeared in TV commercials advertising dog-food or a valet-parking service.

I looked up from her breast. Dick was ready for me to make the first move. Since our arrival at Rio airport he had scarcely taken his eyes from the women who strolled along the sidewalks of this extravagant city, but I knew that the idea of sex always excited him more than the event. He needed me to complete the circuit of desire and fulfilment. For years I assumed that he and Miriam had been lovers at Cambridge, a suspicion she had always denied but Dick had subtly encouraged.

Carmen was flicking at her shoulder strap, like a bored guitarist trying to think of a tune. Fortunata primly smoothed her skirt with the broad hands of a docile child.

'Where do you stay?' I asked. 'Here in Copacabana?'

'We go to our apartment.' Carmen pointed to a nearby side-street. 'You have American dollars? One hour, two hours ...'

'Dick? Money for time? Shall we go?'

'Of course. Money is the original digital clock ...'

We left the Luxor and set off through the crowds in the Avenida Atlantica, past the beggars and jewellery salesmen, the nightclub touts with their waiting taxis. Carmen led the way on her long legs. She stepped into the traffic when we reached the side-street, avoiding the hundreds of pimps standing on the pavement, each with his woman. Prostitution powered Rio, provided its engine. When I first walked down this side-street on the evening of our arrival I had been struck by the charm of these countless couples talking amiably on the wide pavements, a tribute to the marital bliss of this benign city. But the husbands were touting their wives' wares, like so many bales of cloth. Freelancers and festival-hunters such as Fortunata and Carmen had to run the hazards of the traffic-filled roads.

We dodged through the passing limousines and entered the lobby of a huge block of low-rent apartments. Beside the annunciator buttons hundreds of mail slots ranged like all the addresses in hell. A minute elevator carried us to an upper floor where a low-ceilinged corridor ran for ever into the gloom past dozens of doors. The perspiring tenants lounged outside their cramped apartments. Children played under the dim light, and a damp corridor life survived like fungi in a cavern. Men in vests and undershorts leaned against the walls, mothers dressed their daughters' hair, old women worked at trestle tables.

At the door of her apartment Carmen turned, hand on key, and peered at me. During the short walk from the hotel she had forgotten my face. She waited for a curious old man to drift away.

'Okay, now we see. Fifty dollars.'

'That's a lot.'

'For two. As long as you like. Afterwards we go to Señor Pereira's party in Ipanema.'

'Fine by you, Dick?' He already had his arm around Fortunata while I searched for my wallet. He was romping playfully with her, as he did with my daughters.

Carmen stuffed the notes into her purse, and opened the door on to a crowded room. Three middle-aged women and a small child were working at a trestle table, surrounded by piles of plastic sacks. They were producing cheap mementoes for the film festival, stitching cardboard-backed photographs of film stars into gilt papier mâché frames, assembling festival kites from ready-made components which they snatched from the sacks. Hundreds of belt buckles with movie motifs, 2001 lapel badges and other geegaws lay in open cardboard boxes on the shabby sofa, lined up in rows by the methodical child. Bags of spare components filled the small kitchen and were piled around the lavatory in the bathroom.

'Wait a minute …' I turned to Dick. 'Let's go back to the hotel.'

'No.' Carmen tugged my arm with surprising force. She pointed to the bedroom of the apartment. 'We go in – it's just for us.'

A woman with a stapling machine glanced at us without interest, and drove a staple through the forehead of Elvis Presley. As Carmen unlocked the door I assumed that she and Fortunata rented the room during the day. Beyond the double bed, unwashed windows looked out on to the rear balconies of a vast apartment block, more low-rent housing in this city where the poor were pushed away into the sky. Every balcony was crammed with bird-cages and cardboard cartons, washing lines and abandoned furniture.

'Okay – nice time now.'

Carmen tried to close the door, but Dick and I were staring uneasily at the room. The rumpled sheets were stained with sweat and lipstick, the pillows covered with a blue glaze of mascara and vaginal jelly. Underwear hung across the pine dressing table, and on the floor beside the bed were a dozen paper tissues, each crushed around a smear of phlegm. Impassively surveying this scene was a small cine-camera on a tripod. Nearby, boxes of Kodak film were stacked on the wall unit.

'Jim, you'll catch something ...' Dick frowned at me, turning towards the door. He held Fortunata by the waist, but his interest in the escapade had cooled. His eyes had retreated behind his handsome face, and he seemed to have aged since setting out from the hotel. The cheap cine-camera threatened him in a way he had never known at the BBC Television Centre, with its soft and accommodating lenses. I was surprised to find him so obviously out of his element, and wondered why he had urged me into the hands of these two prostitutes. Perhaps he hoped to see me humiliated in some small way that would do no damage to our friendship but would leave him in the dominant position.

Behind us, the stapling machine stamped through the faces of the film stars. Undisturbed by our presence, the women hunched over their table, now and then snapping at the child. An old man in a vest wandered into the apartment, tried to remember something, and faded into the corridor.

'Jim, we need another room, we can't all ...'

'Yes ...' Fortunata brightened up, drawing Dick towards the bed. 'It's nice ... all together.'

Pointing to the women in the sweat shop, I said to Carmen: 'Ask the women if we can use their room – just for an hour.'

'They must work, it's very busy.'

'I'll give them ten dollars. They deserve a rest. Tell them to go to the movies.'

'Sure. I tell them.'

Carmen spoke to the women, who together peered at me, baffled by this show of modesty. They downed tools, stowed the money into a shared handbag and moved into the corridor. As Carmen closed the door I saw them leaning against the dingy wall outside the apartment, lighting their cigarettes as they waited for us to finish.

Dick had pushed a tray of film badges onto the floor and sat back on the sofa cushions with Fortunata, who had slipped the shoulder straps of her dress. With a thin smile he pretended to admire the weight and curvature of her heavy white breasts, like a greengrocer assessing a new variety of albino melon. When Fortunata flicked at her extruding nipples with little gasps I shut the bedroom door.

Carmen stepped out of her high-heeled shoes and hung her dress on the wardrobe, brushing the silk with housewifely concern. Using her free hand, she reached out and expertly released my belt buckle.

'Okay. It's very nice.'

I undressed beside her, aware of her jollying me along. Time, not money, dominated the prostitute's life. To enjoy sex with them required a special knack of its own. A teenage girl with a cat in her arms was watching me from a balcony thirty feet away. While I drew the curtain Carmen took a spermicide dispenser from the dressing-table drawer. Screwing it into the open tube, she squeezed three inches of jelly into the dispenser. She lifted a leg onto the bed, parted her labia with her fingers and eased the shaft into her vagina. She pressed the plunger, withdrew the dispenser and wiped her fingers on the sheet.

Waiting for her, I turned the camera and pointed the lens towards the bed.

'You like for me to make·a film?' Carmen asked.

'You'll film us here?'

'It's good, for four minutes. Only one hundred dollars. Perhaps you show your girl-friend. Or your wife.'

'My wife?'

'Yes! It's popular, it's really good.'

I sat on the bed, staring at my reflection in the camera lens. Beyond the bedroom door I could hear Dick laughing as he chased Fortunata

around the work-room, and the women in the corridor shouting to
the straying child. By comparison, the bedroom was a stage set. This
earnest young prostitute, the stained sheets and the tissues with which
she had wiped her clients' semen from her vulva, an enticing spoor for
future customers, together seemed like film props. The presence of the
camera transformed and even dignified this seedy bedroom.

As we lay together on the waxy sheets I asked: 'Have you been in
other films?'

'Sure! Many films …' She screwed up her face, dismissing the bedside
camera with a contemptuous wave. She held my limp penis in both
hands, tugging lightly at my scrotum. 'I make many films – I'm acting
for real director.'

'That's good.' I could guess the kind of studio. 'For Señor Pereira,
maybe?'

'Señor Pereira … ugh!' She grimaced at the mention of the film
critic. 'His films … not clean!'

I moved the hair from her fierce forehead, admiring her determina-
tion. 'You'll work for other directors. You'll be a star one day.'

'Yes …' Ignoring the doubts in my voice, she licked her fingers and
smoothed her eyebrows, gazing fiercely at the future that lay beyond
the walls of this rented bedroom. As she searched her lips for a small
sore, the muscles of her arrow-shaped face were set with a touching
confidence.

She noticed me lying beside her and returned to work, shaking her
head over my feeble erection. She took her left breast and teased out
the nipple, tapping it with her sharp nails until it grew erect. Raising
it to my mouth, she pressed the warm body of the breast against my
nose and chin, placed my hand against her buttocks and steered my
fingers down to her anus, pushing the tip of my ring-finger into the
soft pad. She reached down to the root of my penis, searching for my
prostate. When my penis came to life she nodded encouragingly, made
sure that my eyes stayed on her breasts and my fingers on her anus.
With her strong arms she turned me on to my back and squatted across
my hips, sitting on her haunches so that the only part of her body to
touch me was her vulva.

Like a fisherwoman at an angling hole, patiently waiting for a bite, she moved about on her heels, the tip of my penis between her labia. At last, when the rake of both penis and pubis had matched to her satisfaction, she settled down and let my penis enter her vagina. She bobbed away energetically, glancing briefly at herself in the dressing-table mirror, and now and then blowing the hair from her eyes.

I held her strong thighs, aware that she was working as hard as the older women assembling their trinkets. All of us, myself certainly included, were working to make the film festival a success. Even the empty camera in whose lens we were reflected had helped to shape our sex act. As she smoothed her eyebrows Carmen was measuring her profile against the lens, preparing herself for the even more elaborate sex films in which she would appear. Lying between her thighs, I was little more than an extra recruited from the hotel terraces of Copacabana. When she raised herself, teasingly holding the tip of my penis between her breasts, I almost felt that we were extemporising a small variation on a fixed routine.

With its passive and unobtrusive despotism, the camera governed the smallest spaces of our lives. Even in the privacy of our own homes we had all been recruited to play our parts in what were little more than real-life commercials. As we cooked in our kitchens we were careful to follow the manufacturer's instructions, as we made love in our bedrooms we embraced within a familiar repertoire of gestures and affections. The medium of film had turned us all into minor actors in an endlessly running day-time serial. In the future, airliners would crash and presidents would be assassinated within agreed conventions as formalised as the coronation of a tsar.

When I came, my cheeks pressed to the spermicidal pillow, Carmen nodded matter-of-factly. She took her breasts from me, and disengaged her vulva from my penis, a technician turning off a life-support system. Her body shining with my sweat, she stepped from the bed and opened the door into the next room, where Dick and Fortunata were playfully throwing the plastic mementoes at each other. Dick, I noticed, had not undressed.

Carmen watched them bleakly and closed the door. She plucked a tissue from the carton on the dressing table. With a jerk of her thumb, she confided: 'He no fuck.'

Deftly she scooped my semen from her vulva, wiped a streak from the inside of her thigh, then crushed the tissue and threw it carefully on to the floor below the camera, a small offering to this one-eyed inquisitor.

Later that evening, I saw Carmen under the lens of a very different camera. As promised, the festival limousine arrived at the Luxor to take us to Pereira's party at Ipanema. Another guest, a Dutch film distributor, shared the car with us. He and Dick kept up an animated commentary as we drove down Copacabana Avenue, pointing to the movie theatres besieged by the eager crowds, the gangs of whores and pimps striding arm in arm through the flashing strobes, and the passing tourists stunned by the sight of the Rio police holding up six lanes of traffic while they knocked about some pickpocket or parking offender.

Throughout dinner Dick had been in unflagging good humour, while I felt vaguely depressed. Missing the children, I telephoned Cleo Churchill, who had volunteered to look after them while we were away. I spoke to each of them in turn, thrilled to hear their voices telling me of the day's triumphs and excitements, a model aircraft lost in the river and a tame squirrel in the garden. Listening to them, I wanted to put the receiver down and head for the airport. Cleo spoke last, reassuring me that all was well and that the children scarcely remembered me.

'Don't hurry back – they're having the time of their lives. I hope you and Dick are thoroughly misbehaving yourselves.'

'I am, but Dick's been too busy giving TV interviews. Everyone agrees he's the sexiest psychologist in Rio.'

'And in London – bring him back in one piece.'

I remembered Dick romping in the women's workroom, and Fortunata with the medallions of Jane Fonda and Bardot clipped to her nipples, Robert Redford's face pressed to her pubis. Dick would look but not touch. Yet I was depressed and he was in ebullient form. A certain reserve now marked his attitude to me, as if I had failed an important test. I had always been reluctant to appear on television, a shyness that amused him and which he put down to an old-fashioned strain in my character. Clearly I was too bound to the mundane, to the contingent realities of a wife, children and desire, to the fear of death and the anguish of space-time. Dick had side-stepped all these, accepting that the electronic image of himself was the real one, and that his off-screen self was an ambitious but modest actor who had successfully auditioned for a far more glamorous role. He might interview Carmen and Fortunata, but he would never break the spell by touching or needing them.

Watching as he enjoyed himself in the limousine, I guessed that he was the forerunner of an advanced kind of human being. If one day the world became a film festival, its inhabitants would all resemble Dick Sutherland. Television had made him impotent, but perhaps its real role, in evolutionary terms, was to depopulate an overcrowded planet. The camera lens was our way of disengaging from each other, distancing ourselves from each other's emotions. Looking out from the limousine at the veering, over-exuberant streets, it occurred to me that everyone in Rio was having, not a good time, but the image of a good time.

Except, unmistakably, at Señor Pereira's party. The terrace and reception rooms of the duplex apartment seemed to rotate like a satellite nightclub in orbit over Rio, filled with lavish buffet tables, roulette wheels and a light-show. Hundreds of guests danced to a maracas band, celebrating new year's eve in the year 2000. Elderly bankers who seemed to be impersonating distinguished film extras, sleek Rio gangsters more handsome than any film star, and fashionable property tycoons looking like expensive call-boys mingled with a lower echelon of film agents, journalists and television executives who formed the proletariat of the super-rich.

Above the cocaine voices and firework display on the terrace, I shouted to the Dutchman: 'This party must have been going on since last year's festival. Rio film critics live in some style.'

'Pereira is much more than a film critic. He has a stake in a local TV station, all sorts of businesses and even his own production company.'

Just what Pereira's film company produced I saw later that evening. Dick was dancing with the most glamorous woman at the party, somewhere between sixteen and sixty, whose costume had ransacked a Las

Vegas casino. The Dutchman and I had fallen in with an American casting director and her husband, who were imagining the impossible task of casting the party's guests from the world's stock of supporting actors. After a buffet supper together we went in search of Dick.

Outside the disco in the dining-room I caught sight of a familiar stocky blonde climbing the stairs to an upper floor.

'You know Fortunata?' the Dutchman asked. 'She's trying to get into Pereira's films.'

'Can't she act? What's the problem?'

'No, she's stupid, but she can act – that's the problem. His films need obvious amateurs. They employ a new kind of realism.'

A glass verandah fronted the upper floor of the duplex. Guests thronged the rail, looking out over the sea towards the lights of Copacabana, the Sugar Loaf and the great illuminated Christ of Corcovado. But Fortunata had turned into a small corridor that led past a kitchenette and bathroom into the rooms at the rear of the duplex. A uniformed security man stood by a locked door, talking to one of Pereira's gangster friends. He let Fortunata through, pointing out some defect in her make-up. When she smiled at me, snapping her compact, he assumed that we were with her and beckoned us forward.

We had entered a private suite within the duplex. An office equipped with desks and filing cabinets served as temporary storage space for the furniture moved from the rooms used for the party. Film equipment, lights and silver umbrellas stood in the corner with a set of stage props – two plastic sofas, a roll of turquoise nylon carpet and a tawdry bedspread, like the decor of a cheap motel.

Fortunata opened the rear door and stepped into the corridor beyond, where powerful, ice-white lights flooded through an archway. Two men in tuxedos and a woman in a ball-gown with a drink in her hand were staring into the lights. Fortunata joined them, frowning as a dog barked in pain and its handler shouted angrily.

When the dog calmed itself, whimpering plaintively, Fortunata stepped into the room. Over the Dutchman's shoulder I could see the dim faces of a film crew through the harsh lighting. Guests in evening dress leaned against the walls, watching as Pereira signalled to his cameraman. He gestured impatiently at the sound engineer who crouched forward with a boom microphone, trying to pick up the dog's pathetic barks. The nervous German Shepherd was being alternately comforted and abused by its handler, a small, shirt-sleeved man in his sixties with a pencil moustache. The glaring lights, the soundman's nervous thrusts and the handler's fingers fondling its testicles had unsettled the large dog. It tugged at its leash, eager to go home, paws slithering on the tiled floor.

In front of the dog the crew had assembled a miniature film set, a garish double bed with a quilted headboard, a cheap dressing table and a red plastic lamp. Kneeling on the floor beside the bed was a naked woman, muttering to herself as she moved from one tired hand to the other. The fierce lights had bleached all the tones from her skin, which seemed like the latex on an inflated dummy. When she shook her long hair and glared angrily at Pereira I recognised Carmen's arrow-like profile. The dog struggled against its handler and she slapped her hand on the floor, shouting some obscenity in Portuguese. Pereira tried to calm her, but she stared at him with unconcealed distaste, as if regretting that she had been persuaded against her better judgement into an ill-considered career-move with this incompetent producer.

The dog's ears pricked forward, its nose scenting Carmen's exposed buttocks. The handler warbled into its ears, one hand massaging its penis, the other pushing its bushy tail from his face. With a look of mock resignation, Carmen glanced at the spectators along the wall. There were nods of sympathy, heads shaken over the incompetence of the handler and his beast's lack of virility.

The sound engineer moved forward with his microphone, and the cameraman adjusted his eye-piece. The lights intensified, blanching out the faces of the spectators. The dog approached, paws slipping on the floor, the handler steering it by the testicles. Carmen raised one palm and brushed away an annoying piece of grit, then stared self-critically at the black pool of her shadow.

Three days later I stood on the steps of the conference centre, waiting to say goodbye to Dick Sutherland before catching the flight back to London. I had missed him when the audience dispersed after the televised panel discussion he had chaired. Giving up, I was about to walk to my taxi when I saw him emerge from the building with Señor Pereira. The film critic spoke effusively, thanking Dick for his presentation to camera and the few words of Portuguese he had memorised.

In the doorway behind Pereira, her silk dress lit by the TV monitors and their scientific films, Carmen was practising her English with one of the women simultaneous translators. Pereira saluted Dick, and she strode up and smilingly took the film critic's arm. Together they stepped into a waiting car.

'Dick, I'll see you in Shepperton. Carmen seems happy – I thought she loathed Pereira.'

'She did. But she feels her career is taking off – apparently she's made some film with a dog. Pereira wanted to show me the rough cut. It's been a big hit with the distribution people.'

'Lassie come home, all is forgiven ...'

'Is that the title? I'll give it a miss.'

'I would, Dick.'

Dick gazed at the statue of Christ on Corcovado. He squared his shoulders, not unhopefully, measuring himself against the TV ratings of the ultimate media personality. Along Copacabana Beach the salesmen were flying their festival kites above the heads of the footballers, hawking their movie-star lapel badges and belt buckles. The beggar woman from the favelas and her crippled child were hiding among the limousines outside the Copacabana Palace Hotel, ready to startle an unwary film executive. In the air-conditioned corridors of the conference centre the scientific films filled the monitor screens with their close ups of nose-wheel housings, nasal septums and pain-registers, a vast dormant pornography waiting to be woken by the magic of fame.

13

The Casualty Station

Mental asylums, like the prisons they resemble, are so often burdened with the least appropriate names. As I drove through the gates of Summerfield Hospital I wondered who had christened this sombre Victorian pile. Immense red-brick walls like a perpetual headache rose to the shabby eaves, broken by barred windows that had never been cleaned, as if to protect the patients from the gloomy micro-climate that hovered over this forgotten corner of south London. Faded lawns struggled in the shadows of the tall fir trees, but on my visits to David Hunter I had never seen even one of the two thousand patients taking the air.

Anyone, I found, could drive through the gate-house without being stopped, and the endless internal roads that wound past the great buildings gave the impression that Summerfield was open to the world. In fact, the gate-house, like the dead lawns and the visitors' car parks, was part of a decoy. The central enclave of the asylum, the citadel of the insane, remained securely sealed within itself. From the windows of David's ward, through one clear pane that had replaced the original frosted glass, I could see the internal courtyards attached to the high-security wings. Into these bleak stone pits, walls topped by steel claws, the deeply insane were occasionally released to stare in their haunted way at the mystery of the open air. Puzzlingly, the exercise yards were all of different shape, some triangular, others rectangles or gnomons, with small recesses that served no conceivable purpose, as if they together formed a jigsaw of a fractured mind, to be completed before a patient's release.

Two vehicles occupied opposite corners of the car park, breaking that companionable rule by which drivers arriving at an empty car park place themselves alongside each other. Most of the patients, I noticed, were visited only by the poorer of their friends and relatives, who had to make the long walk from the gate-house and were too tired to do more than sit and listen. A signpost pointed to the short-term wards – 'Narcissus', 'Rosemary', and 'Hyacinth'. Carrying my chessboard and a bag filled with fruit, aviation magazines and newspapers, I set off towards the entrance lodge. As always, however hard I tried to repress the sensation, I felt that I was arriving with my luggage to begin my own stay at Summerfield. These impassive buildings possessed a moral authority far more intimidating than the tired psychiatrists who worked within their wards.

While the superintendent checked my name against the roster I rattled the chessboard, and guessed that it would soon be lighter by a piece. The battered chess-sets at Summerfield had lost half their men. In his matter-of-fact way, David explained that these destitute patients, often abandoned by their families, possessed nothing, and would treasure a stolen piece like a precious doll. Usually, as I sat in the day-room with David, one of the old men he had befriended would be staring at his private pawn on an open board. A former accountant at the Church Commissioners, he had tried to suffocate his invalid wife. After an hour of thought he would at last embark on a cautious move.

Closing the board at the end of my visits, David always palmed one of the pieces, usually the black bishop, which he had identified with me. This was partly to irritate me, and partly to ensure that I played with no one else. While I searched for him I could hear his gentle voice outside the women's ward, as he gallantly steered one of the old women towards the lavatories. He greeted me cheerily, closing the lavatory door.

'I hope she knows what to do,' he confided. 'Most of the time she just stands there, trying to remember her daughter. She calls it her memory box …'

Affable and good-humoured as ever, he surveyed the day-room, looking for something new to tell me. Patients in dressing-gowns sat on the leather chairs, talking to their subdued relatives. On the sofa beside us a young woman lay with her knees pulled up to her chin, lost in her deep sleep of largactil. Her open eyes were tilted into their upper lids, as if she were trying to see something inside her skull. At the dispensary hatch a line of patients queued for their thimbles of tranquilliser.

'They'll bring some tea in a moment.' David leafed through the aviation magazines, and held my arm, glad to see me. His confinement had brought us together. 'It's good of you to come – how are the kids?'

'They're blooming, passing all their exams. Henry's built an aircraft for you – the Wright Flyer. Alice and Lucy wanted to come with me.'

'Not a good idea, actually.' David tore at an orange and treated me to a knowing smile. 'They can visit you, Jim, when it's your turn.'

I let this pass, and watched another of the older women, wearing nothing but a faded nightdress, carry a vase of daffodils to the window-ledge. She held the flowers to the light, introducing them to the sun.

'It's restful here,' I commented. 'All the sunlight, and these sleeping women. You could be in a private hotel on the south coast.'

'Of a rather special kind, dear sport.'

'I know – it always amazes me that they let the men and women wander around together.'

'No one's got pregnant yet.' David stared at the young woman asleep on the sofa beside him, the hem of her nightdress around her plump calves. As he set out the chessboard I noticed that the black king had failed to appear, a modest penalty I had incurred. 'Besides, the medical staff trust us completely. For them, we're the normal ones. They know our names and faces and little ways of doing things. It's you people who seem genuinely weird.'

'We probably are.'

David hunched over the chessboard, watching me through the pieces. He was waiting for me to catch up with my real self. He regarded my visits to Summerfield as an educative process; gradually I would accept my responsibility for the events that had brought him to this grim institution. At the end of my visits, when he accompanied me to the staircase, he clearly expected me to decide to stay. I would move into a spare bed in Hyacinth ward and our games of chess would continue until all the pieces had been stolen from the board.

'Have you seen Sally yet?' he asked off-handedly. 'I think she'd like to hear from you.'

'We talked on the telephone – she's staying in Scotland with some rich woman-friend of her father's, while they try out this new methadone treatment. She sounded a lot calmer.'

'She ought to go back to the States. I can see her strolling around Haight-Ashbury …' His hand was trembling over the board, as he fixed his eyes on some wayward dream of the past. When I reached out to reassure him, touching his wrist, he pulled away from me, and I saw that he had replaced the black king.

'David, all that's over now – the GIs are back from Viet Nam, and Nixon's gone to China.'

'I know. Thank God I'm here, everything's so earnest. You'll miss Viet Nam.'

'Will I? Why?'

'All those newsreels every night? I used to wonder why you never came back to Shanghai with me. You didn't need to – they started the Viet Nam war for you instead.'

'I wasn't ready to go back.' I watched the old accountant hovering over his solitary pawn. 'It would have been too much like returning to the scene of a crime.'

'I know what you mean, Jim. I looked for that little railway station of yours.'

'On the Hangchow–Shanghai line?' I tried not to sound sceptical. 'I'm surprised you never told me.'

'Well … Miriam had died. You had enough things on your mind. Anyway, the damned taxi-driver couldn't find it. Those tourist guides are doing their best to turn Shanghai into a riddle.'

'It's probably gone, I shouldn't worry. Let's play some chess – black or white?'

'No, it's there.' David ignored my raised hands, his eyes fixed on mine. 'It's marked on the Greater Shanghai Transit Company map. And inside your head.'

'Not any more.'

'No? Your crashed cars exhibition – no one realised it, but that's what you were staging there.'

'At a few removes.'

'At no removes. Jim, I understand ...'

Not for the first time he had linked his own last accident to my exhibition, implying that I had served as the catalyst for his erratic driving. But, if anything, the exhibition had been inspired by David. I remembered him hunting the streets of London, driving in the same dangerous way that he had practised for the first time on the long, straight road from Moose Jaw to the air-base. At the demolition derbys in the shabby stadiums of east London he and Sally had willed themselves towards death.

One-way streets excited them to play a desperate roulette. Late one evening, two years after the exhibition, David had driven the wrong way down the westward lane of the Hammersmith flyover, headlamps flashing as he forced the oncoming cars against the safety rail. A middle-aged cellist and her husband, confused by the siren of the pursuing police car in the parallel carriageway, had failed to stop in time. The wife had been killed over her steering wheel, and only David's deranged behaviour after his arrest, and his active RAF service in Kenya, had saved him from a manslaughter charge.

Under a section of the Mental Health Act he had been sent, first, to the special custody unit at Rampton, and then to Summerfield for observation. Six months later, as he crouched with his largactil shudders in this sunlit room filled with entranced and grumbling women, the memory of the cellist's death still pushed at the door of his mind. I felt nothing but concern for him and his younger self, now the same age as Henry, who had emerged from his Japanese camp into the post-war world. David had understood my needs but failed to read his own. He had tried, hesitantly at first, to recreate the cruelty he had known in war-time China, not realising that the post-war world was only too keen to do this for him. The psychopath was saint.

When I first visited him at Summerfield he had said, setting out the rules of our relationship: 'Remember, Jim – all I did on the flyover was what you did in your exhibition ...'

Now the casualties of the Sixties were coming home, to the veterans' hospitals, the mental institutions and private clinics. In a drawing-room above a cold Scottish lake Sally Mumford was measuring out her days in methadone. When I telephoned her she sounded flat but rested, unlike the confused and hyper-irritable woman who had arrived at Shepperton one evening two months earlier, needing my help but refusing to speak to me. Fortunately the children had been away, staying with their aunt. I tried to sleep on the sofa as Sally spent the night weeping and striding around the empty bedrooms, ransacking the cupboards for old toys which she stuffed into her bag.

The next day she allowed me to take her to our family doctor, who referred her to an American physician at the London Clinic. She then moved to a specialist nursing home on the Thames near Marlow, one of those private prisons in which the rich, with the connivance of the medical profession, confine their elderly or embarrassing relatives. When I visited her there she was calm and sedated, smiling from a waking sleep as she spoke of our first meeting on the sand-island near Rosas ten years earlier. She seemed a child again, the kindly and generous young woman who had come to the help of my own children when they most needed her. Only when I mentioned Dick Sutherland did she frown and turn away from me.

Dick, alone, had made a triumphant exit from the Sixties. As I guessed, science and pornography at last made their long-awaited rendezvous under the lens of his laboratory camera. His successful TV series on the paranormal – ESP, astrology and telekinesis – was sold to an American network and brought him to the attention of a progressive New York magazine tycoon who had recently founded an institute of sexual research. On its governing body sat many of the gurus of the counter-culture – evangelists for LSD, trend-hunting neurologists, zen philosophers and Marxist popularisers. With much fanfare, the tycoon announced that the institute would continue the pioneering work of Masters and Johnson, Kinsey and Havelock Ellis.

At first, its researchers devoted themselves to scientific films of heterosexual intercourse, using the latest fibre-optic technology and miniaturised body-orifice TV cameras, all in pursuit of the white whale of modern sexology, the female orgasm. Soon, however, as graphic stills from these exploratory films were published in the parent company's magazines and pushed the circulations to record heights, the research broadened to include more wayward forms of sexual activity. The institute was discreetly relocated in London, avoiding the scrutiny of the US Justice Department and any possible threat to the professorial tenure of its academic board-members.

Dick became the institute's scientific director at its new headquarters, in a former hotel overlooking the Regent's Park canal. Here, under the neutral gaze of the rostrum camera, a recruited force of volunteers had explored every legal permutation of lesbian, homosexual and hetero-sexual intercourse. The cans of undeveloped film were air-freighted to the magazine offices in New York, and selected stills appeared beside the gate-fold nudes with Dick's scientific commentary.

When I mildly suggested to Dick that he was producing something indistinguishable from pornography he had readily agreed.

'Except for one thing – our aim is to analyse, not arouse. Think of this vast human activity, common to the whole biological kingdom, and you realise that surprisingly little is known about it. What actually happens when a woman fellates you? Do you know, Jim?'

'Dick, you make me doubt it ...'

'Well, what more is there to say?'

'But why do I need to know?'

'Because sex is the last great frontier.' Dick had gestured at the hori-zons of Regent's Park like Cortez grasping the immensity of the Pacific. 'One thing we can say for certain about the future of sex – there's going to be a lot more of it. Already we can see that new forms of social structure will emerge to cope with the sexual imagination. What you and everyone else think of as the pornographic mind may well allow us to transcend ourselves and, in a sense, the limits of sex itself.'

'Your new series should be fascinating, Dick.'

'You've already heard about it? Good.'

I hadn't, but I saluted him ungrudgingly. Thinking of our journey to Rio, I realised that the evening with Carmen and Fortunata had been his brave attempt to step down from the television screen into a lost world of emotion and desire. He had discarded the image of the hoodlum scientist – part rock star, part Robert Oppenheimer – that had sustained him since his Cambridge days. Out went the leather jackets and gold medallions, in came tweed suits and woollen ties. He was at ease with me now, happier and more confident, at last engaged on the original research that had always eluded him, and unaware that he himself was the victim of a bogus experiment.

But Sally had been hurt. Along with the other volunteers who worked at the institute, she had been beguiled by Dick's evangelical ardour. She told me that she had been amazed by the unedited films screened for the volunteers in the institute viewing theatre, of the cathedral-like interior of her own vagina, moisture beading on its cavernous walls like jewels dripping in a grotto. As she lay with her laboratory partner, a remote-controlled camera recorded the involuntary movements of her facial musculature, the flushing of her breasts and abdomen, the skin tremors on the backs of her thighs.

Seeing these abstracted portions of herself had led to a growing numbness, a fading sensitivity of her skin to pain and feeling, as if her nervous system had been connected, not to the familiar nerve endings of her hands and lips, but to the screen in Dick's viewing theatre. She would turn the pages of the men's magazines in the waiting room before the laboratory sessions and find detached parts of her anatomy between the covers, the moist escarpment of her pubis like a remote mountain range viewed from the window of an airliner.

A progressive dismemberment of herself was taking place, until she reached the point where she expected to find the skin of her breasts and thighs stretched across an advertising billboard or upholstering the seats of a modish nightclub. When, like most of Dick's volunteers, she dropped out of the programme, she never fully reintegrated herself, and would wander the streets in her heroin daze searching for the lost parts of her face and lips.

Soon after, the Home Office became interested in the institute, and its work was suspended. Across the Atlantic, the magazine tycoon announced that the sexual revolution was over, and that he had donated the miles of cine-film to the Kinsey Foundation. Leisure industries represented the wave of the future, and investment would be moved to new vacation sites in Hawaii and the Caribbean. Sex, with every regret, was left to fend for itself.

The set-back was a blow to Dick. As he admitted in a moment of surprising frankness, he had naively hoped that the institute's original work would be accepted for what it was. He knew that his reputation in the scientific community had been damaged, and that the doors of most laboratories would be closed to him. Trying to help him, I introduced him to an interested publisher, and at my suggestion Dick quickly wrote the text of a pop-up guide to human psychology. Later, reading through this colourful best-seller, which seemed to have strayed from the back of a cornflakes packet, I was struck as always by Dick's shrewdness, intelligence and wit. Since its sales far exceeded those of my own books, Dick could continue to patronise me in his friendly way. I was still his gauche student, making the coffee in his laboratory and allowed to flirt with his secretary.

But had the rat in the Skinner box always controlled the experimenter? When I thought of David Hunter, of Dick and Sally, I sometimes wondered what part I had played in plotting the course of their lives, steering them towards goals that I had set many years earlier. I had never consciously manipulated them, but they had accepted their assigned roles like actors recruited to play their parts in a drama whose script they had never seen.

Peggy Gardner had no doubts about my responsibility. I visited her small Chelsea house after seeing David remanded in custody at the magistrate's court, hoping that she might later testify as a character witness. She sat away from me in a straight-backed chair, surveying me as if I had been at the wheel of the Jaguar and she were a police psychiatrist called to give her assessment.

'Poor David. The last of your troupe. First Sally, then Dick ...'

'Dick? I've had nothing to do with him.' I lowered my tumbler of whisky with such force that I cracked the enamel of her blackwood table. 'Peggy ...?'

'That tawdry institute, and all those TV programmes.'

'He's an actor at heart, who happened to stray into psychology. Dick's ... a shaman for the TV age.'

'For years you've been encouraging him to buy all those American cars, telling him – what was it, some nonsense? – that he'd make the first scientific discovery on television. How could he resist?'

'He never wanted to resist. Can't you remember him at Cambridge?'

'I tried to avoid him. He was always so attentive and flattering.'

'He was just waiting for television to come along.'

'He was waiting for you.' Peggy paced over to the mantelpiece and stared at me through the mirror, as if the reversed image might give a clue to my sinistral dreams. 'Sometimes I think he set up that bogus experiment just to meet you.'

'He didn't know I existed.'

'Someone like you. Obsessed with the Third World War, your head full of all those American bombers and Lunghua …'

'I never talked about them.'

'You didn't have to! You were desperate for violence! It made sense of everything, but you needed television to fill the air with it, play all that horror and pain over and over again. That really excited Dick. He gave you Miriam as the only way of holding on to you.'

'Isn't that a little callous? He'd have found his way to television if he'd never met me.'

'The Viet Nam war, the Kennedy assassinations, the Congo, those ghastly *ratissages* … they might have been invented for you.'

'Peggy, that makes me sound like a war criminal.'

'Miriam used to say you were. And you love your children.' Peggy pressed her hands against the mirror, touching the secure glass. 'Before we left on the *Arrawa* you took me to a film in Shanghai, about an American aircraft carrier …'

'*The Fighting Lady* – a collection of newsreels.'

'I thought you might get carried away in the dark, but I needn't have worried. Your mind was up there, moulded against that screen. I was so amazed I couldn't stop watching you.'

'It was the only film in Shanghai. Anyway, I was fascinated by flying.'

'You told me you'd seen it ten times!'

'The Americans brought it with them, and gave us all free tickets. I had nothing else to do.'

'Nothing else? In the whole of Shanghai? You'd been locked up for three years and all you wanted to do was sit in the dark and watch those suicide pilots crashing into American ships?' Peggy turned from the mirror, ready to face me. 'Tell me, you know that Dick has a copy of that film?'

'I think he does.'

'You know he does. Miriam told me that you used to watch it together in his garage at Cambridge.'

'Once or twice. Dick had a pilot's licence and I'd flown in Canada. Besides, it's a remarkable film – those American pilots were brave men. And the Japanese.'

'Of course they were. No braver than the Russian pilots or the British pilots. What the Americans had was more style and more glamour.'

'Like everything American. So?'

'And that's exactly what you've always needed – glamorised violence. That terrible afternoon on the railway line near Siccawei – you'd seen dozens of atrocities by then.'

'We all had. That was Shanghai.'

'But for once you were too close. A part of it actually happened to you. All those car crashes and pornographic movies, Kennedy's death, they're your way of turning it into a film, something violent and glamorous. You want to Americanise death.'

'Peggy ...' She had spoken with surprising force. Patiently, I followed her as she carried the drinks tray into the kitchen. 'As a matter of interest, Dick's institute did come up with some original research. I never watch pornographic films, and I've had a single car crash in my entire life. You have one every year.'

'I know. You live in Shepperton and you've brought up three wonderful and happy children. How, I don't know.'

I leaned against the refrigerator, looking around the little kitchen with its elegant spice jars and expensive French saucepans, so different from my own, where scarcely a piece of crockery matched and half the glasses had been given away at filling stations. Peggy's house was a boudoir designed for the charm and excitement of men. She had been through many affairs, but had kept herself untouched by them. There were no holiday photographs to remind her of the men who had taken her to Florence and San Francisco, shared villas over the years with her at Venice and in the Lot. Not a masculine gift stood on the immaculate desk in her office.

She had never married, as if afraid that she might bear a daughter who would one day grow to be twelve and remind her of the years of separation from her parents. Curiously, the one person who had helped to sustain her had never been allowed to share her bed, and was the person whom she continued to reprove and reproach in the way she had done when I played pranks in the children's hut.

'And what about you, Peggy?'

'Me?' She stowed the glasses in the dishwasher. 'Are you trying to recruit me into your repertory company?'

'I was thinking of the dedicated paediatrician who's never dared to have a child.'

'I've left it a little late.' She dried her hands and placed them forbearingly on my shoulders. 'Besides, I had you. I think I looked after you rather well.'

'You still do – is that why you became a paediatrician?'

'Christ, don't say that!' Without thinking, she slapped my mouth, then caught herself and winced at my bruised lips. 'Oh, damn – there's blood on your teeth. Jim, I didn't mean to upset you over Miriam ...'

I kissed her, for the first time since we sat alone together in the circle of the Grand Theatre in the Nanking Road. I could feel her tongue tasting the blood in my mouth. The scent of her body had changed, and her greying hair reminded me of her mother's as she stepped from the American landing craft after the journey from Tsingtao. I placed my hands around her, feeling for the thin bones of the girl I had known in Lunghua. The soft arms against my chest were those of another woman.

Then I felt her shoulder blades, and the strong ribs of the hungry twelve-year-old who had firmly lifted me from my sick-bed. I slipped my hands around her waist, touching the familiar broad crest of her pelvis. Kissing her again, I ran my fingers along the shy chin that had lengthened as the war progressed, always set to one side as she pondered my latest scheme for finding food. She smiled at me in the kitchen mirror, trying to apologise for my bruised mouth. I gently raised her upper lip with my forefinger, feeling a rush of memory and affection for her worn but still even teeth, now marked with my blood.

'It's stopped bleeding.' She slipped between my hands. 'Jim, you're not demonstrating the skeleton to a class of freshers – let's move upstairs.'

She drew the curtains, folded back the bedspread and began to undress at a leisurely pace, neatly hanging her clothes on the chair beside the wardrobe. I expected her to be shy, but she was staring proudly at her handsome body in the mirror. Still smiling to herself, she stood in front of me as I struggled with my cufflinks, and massaged away the pressure lines below her breasts. She held in her stomach, hiding her plump abdomen and teasing me with the reminder of a very different body that had once hung from these bones.

Sitting on the bed in front of her, I placed my hands on her hips and began to kiss the small freckles on her abdomen, and the spiral scar whose pearly silver curved around the small of her back and ended below her appendix. This marked her kidney operation ten years earlier, the Anderson-Hinds resection of the renal pelvis. When I collected her from the Middlesex Hospital she had walked unsteadily with me down Charing Cross Road, and in the medical section at Foyles I had bought for her the surgeon's monograph, the book of her operation. I felt the eroded surface of the scar, trying to catch up with the thousand small bumps and bruises her body had known. I could see her clasping the monograph as we stepped from the bookshop, smiling at me with all her hot temper and exasperation.

I held her tightly, sucking back the blood from my mouth, unsettled as if I were embracing a sister. She calmed me with a hand, and began to caress my chest as we lay together, settling the movements of my diaphragm. Decades of need and dependence surged from me to her breast as I held it to my mouth. I moved her knee on to my hip and eased myself between her legs, wishing that we had once conceived a child together.

She wiped my blood from her nipple and raised it to her lips. 'Quiet blood ... that's good, Jim. Now I can remember ...'

I moved inside her, in that deep interior embrace, glad that I could no longer feel her bones.

'Peggy ... I wanted to do this thirty years ago.'

'Poor boy, you couldn't have managed it then.' She kissed my forehead, cleaning her lips and leaving a damp bow of blood that I could feel on my skin. 'This is the last time – you'll have to wait another thirty years.'

'I'll wait …'

I rested within her as she began to make love on her own. Her eyes watched her breasts as they rose and fell, and she touched her nipples to excite herself and then steered my fingers to her pubis, letting herself into some reverie of lust as private as a dream. Her mind was far away, beyond this little house and the King's Road rooftops. She gazed at her strong ribs against my chest. Her brisk interrogation in the sitting-room had been her devious courtship of me, and the blood in my mouth allowed me to play the sick child again. For a few moments we were lying on my bunk in the children's hut. In her roundabout way she was making her own return to the war, to her first desire for me. Now that her parents had died, she and I had taken their place and we were free to go back to Shanghai. Once again we were 12-year-olds who had made a small marriage of need among the rags and malarial straw.

When we had dressed she straightened my tie and jacket, brushing away a fleck of dandruff in a wifely way. She said goodbye on the doorstep and kissed me robustly, sending me out into the world.

'Talk to David's lawyer,' I reminded her. 'He'll telephone you.'

'I'll see what I can do – I can tell the magistrate he was abused by the Japanese.'

She embraced me for a last time in front of the passers-by. A window into our childhoods had opened and closed.

'Tea-time – thank God.' David sat up, our chess game forgotten. 'The biscuits are good here, the best in Summerfield.'

Pushed by a tall Jamaican nurse, the trolley bearing the tea-urn advanced towards the polished table, on which some forty cups and saucers were laid out in ranks. Five minutes earlier, a barely perceptible movement of patients had begun. Dressing-gowns fastened, spectral figures appeared from the lavatories and dormitories. Other patients stood up without a word and drifted away from their relatives, pausing to shake the shoulders of the sedated men and women asleep in their chairs. None dared to approach the table, waiting as the nurse, with much officious rattling of the tea-urn, set out the biscuit plates.

'It's kind of you to come, Jim.' David held my arm, but the black king had temporarily left the board. 'To be honest, I don't get too many visitors.'

'David, I'm glad to come. Peggy and I are doing everything we can. We're trying to get you released as an out-patient.'

'The old Shanghai firm – never escape from that. It's interesting here – I thought it might give you a few ideas.'

'It has …'

Beside us, the young woman with the plump calves and everted eyes slept in her deep largactil stupor, unaware of the wraith-like figures advancing past her. They froze whenever the nurse glanced imperiously over her shoulder, as if all the ordeals of their lives obliged them once again to play a childhood game. Still unaware of the tea-urn, the elderly woman in the nightdress was laying a row of daffodils along the strip of carpet that separated the recess of the bay window from the rest of the day-room. Watching her, I tried to guess at the significance of this floral threshold, perhaps a gateway through which her lost children might one day appear.

'Doreen! Stop messing with those daffs!' The nurse banged the lid of the tea-urn, glaring at the row of dripping flowers taken from their vases. 'Now help me with these teas.'

Reluctant to leave her handiwork, Doreen began to line the cups beside the urn. David leaned back in his armchair, stretching towards the tea trolley, as if about to put his hand up the skirt of this imposing Jamaican woman. He was looking at the tray of biscuits, his hand moving to and fro like the head of a cobra. Every eye in the ward was fixed on him, and even the drowsing young woman had straightened her eyeballs to watch him.

'Doreen, you're getting behind.' The nurse stepped forward, her massive legs putting an end to David's dream. Doreen was holding a cup filled with tea, eyes fixed on the brimming liquid. She stared at the trembling surface, clearly struck by the unbearable contrast between the infinitely plastic fluid and the polished hardness of the table. She held the cup at arm's length, unable to bear the contrast between these opposing states of geometry. At last, testing a desperate hypothesis, she inverted the cup in a defiant gesture.

'Doreen ... !' Tea was splashing everywhere, soaking the biscuits and racing across the table to pour in a steaming torrent on to the carpet. The nurse indignantly turned off the tap, her skirt and starched apron damp with the flying drops. 'Doreen, why did you do that?'

'Jesus told me to.' Doreen spoke matter-of-factly. She gazed happily at the mess before her, pleased that she had been able to resolve these irreconcilable natures. Her moment of insight had seemed divinely inspired.

'Get to your room!' The nurse bore down on her. She seized Doreen's wrist and elbow, and pitchforked her violently across the floor, shaking the old woman so severely that I feared she would break an arm. No blows were struck, but a dose of corporal punishment was being administered. Doreen stumbled to the carpet, and I rose from my seat to help her, ignoring the outraged nurse and the shocked stares of the relatives. Doreen's body was as light as a child's. She clung to her injured arm, sobbing to herself. When I left her at the door of her dormitory she stared at the rows of deserted beds, and spoke to them plaintively: 'Jesus *told* me to ...'

After saying goodbye to David I made my way down to the lodge, glad to see the empty lawns and the car park. 'Twenty-nine, thirty, thirty-one,' David had counted as he returned the pieces to the box. He locked the catch and added: 'Thirty-two.' He smiled at me, fully aware of the game we were playing. Find the key was David's game, but he had never found it, and the search had led him to Summerfield, while Doreen had found her own in a moment of faith and imagination. I thought of this simple woman protecting herself from the world with her cordon of flowers, solving a pressing mystery of time and space with a brave gesture.

I gave my name to the orderly and stepped into the sunlight. In a curious way I felt that I was being discharged from Summerfield.

David and all the patients in this Victorian asylum had put their heads together, trying to solve the puzzle from whose board an essential piece had been stolen.

I walked to my car, across the damp asphalt that never dried after the night's rain. Before I started the engine I made a note to visit David in the following fortnight and to bring daffodils for Doreen. Summerfield fell behind me, an empty labyrinth hoarding its exits and entrances.

PART III

After the War

14

Into the Daylight

The telephone call from Sally Mumford surprised me. Four years after returning to America for good – she had sent farewell postcards from Berkeley, California, and a retreat somewhere in Idaho – she was in England again, with a young husband, a small daughter and a house in the Norfolk countryside. In a cheerful, almost matronly tone she told me that she had been back for six months, squirrelled away in what sounded suspiciously like a hippy commune left over from the Sixties. She had invited David to visit them and suggested, on hearing of his life-time driving ban, that I come too and give him a lift.

'We have a goat, I grow beans and cauliflowers and bake our own bread. You'll be amazed!'

My heart couldn't decide whether to sink or soar.

The trip, three weekends later, got off to a confused start. David failed to appear as agreed in the lobby of the Heathrow Penta Hotel, delayed by a late flight from Brussels. After waiting for an hour I headed towards the North Circular, wondering if David shared my second thoughts. I was glad to be seeing Sally again, at last with a child of her own and expecting her second – or so she had seemed to mention in an earth mother's vague afterthought, as if she now intended to be permanently pregnant for the rest of her life.

But the thought of returning to an intact piece of the Sixties was as daunting as trying to re-enter the previous weekend's hangover. Eight years after the decade's end there were all too many Sixties casualties still around, a walking wounded like the veterans of an unpopular war, who had no compunction about nagging at the public conscience. They clung to the fringe-life of provincial universities, edited books on the occult or alternative lifestyles, or sat entombed in remote offices of the BBC, always ready to waste a lunch-hour with talk of programmes on some 19th-century herbalist or forgotten friend of the Pre-Raphaelites.

The dream of the Sixties lay dead in their eyes, and probably in my own, along with the hopes for a millennial world of peace and harmony – hopes, curiously, that had been propelled aloft by the cruel excitements of the post-Kennedy era and a million drug overdoses. My children had set off for their universities, leaving a vacuum in my life that would never be filled. The house in Shepperton was like a warehouse discarded by the film studios, along with the plywood candy bars and toilet roll of Magic World. The old toys and model aircraft that crammed the cupboards were the props of a long-running family sitcom which the sponsors, despite its high ratings and loyal audience, had decided to drop.

The sense of being pulled out of the schedules pressed on me as I mooned around the empty bedrooms, looking at the old holiday snapshots lying in the debris. Wiping away the dust, I stared at these pictures of the girls cutting a swathe through the Greek and Spanish waiters, Henry arm-wrestling with a captain of pedalos and learning to water-ski. I missed our shared childhood that had once seemed to go on for ever. When they came home on their brief visits – eerily like cast reunions – I knew that I was the last of us to grow up. They accepted adult life, while I was still thinking of our happy days watching the televised Moon-landings and Miss World contests, anachronisms that belonged to a vanished decade.

As I left London I ran deeper into the past than Sally's commune near Norwich. I could have chosen a more easterly route, avoiding Cambridge altogether, which I had not visited for twenty years. But the old university town, where I had first met Miriam and Dick Sutherland, was worth a detour, if only to see if my mixed feelings towards the place had survived intact.

Fortunately, any uneasy memories were forgotten in the roar of heavy traffic that filled the approaches to the city. Cambridge had expanded into a complex of industrial and science parks, ringed by monotonous housing estates and shopping precincts. At its centre, like the casbah in Tangier, was the antique heart of the university, a stop-over for well-disciplined parties of Japanese tourists stepping from their TV-equipped German buses. As an undergraduate I had prayed for a new Thomas Cromwell who would launch the dissolution of the universities, but mass tourism had accomplished this, overwhelming the older European universities as it would soon destroy Rome, Florence and Venice.

I parked my car near the backs, crossed the Cam and joined a column of Japanese as they wound through King's. Undergraduates lolled in their punts like bored film extras hoping to catch a producer's eye. Dons with their faux-eccentric manners posed outside the chapel with the self-consciousness of minor character actors, waiting as a Spanish TV crew set up its lights. The spirit of the Disney Corporation and the ethos of the theme park hovered over the gothic stone. Listening to a tour-guide's commentary, I waited to be told that the entire chapel was a fibre-glass, tourist-resistant replica, and that the original structure was now in the more enlightened care of the Ford Foundation in some warehouse on Long Beach.

The Cambridge of old, of Rutherford, Keynes, Ryle and Crick, had long since departed to the American universities that had superseded it, leaving behind a TV academia with its eyes on its script-consultancy fees. Meanwhile, the more real world that I had first glimpsed on my motorcycle rides still existed. Away from the tourist cameras and the posing dons presided the enduring realities of American power. Beyond the hedges and the chain-mail fences the nuclear bombers stood at the ends of their runways, guarantors of the civilised order upon which the university so preened itself.

Hearing the sound of American engines, I turned off the road near Mildenhall as a huge bomber swept over the trees. A car passed me, carrying an off-duty American airman and his family. They wore civilian clothes when they ventured from their bases, like the keepers at a nature reserve maintaining a discreet watch on their unpredictable charges. I parked in a narrow lane and stared through the perimeter fence at the worn concrete beside the nuclear weapons silos. The unsung and unremembered cement was more venerable than all the primped and polished stone of the university. The runways were aisles that led to a more meaningful world, gateways of memory and promise.

'Jim! You haven't changed ... you should have warned me!'

'Sally ...? Dear, you've—'

'*I've* changed. My God, yes!'

She embraced me fiercely, arms strengthened by tethering goat, child and husband. Her hair was cut short, swept back to reveal a plump, cheerful face that might have belonged to Sally's sensible younger sister, married to a Philadelphia surgeon. Her skin gave off a rainbow of scents that set my mind reeling back to the first years of marriage – baby lotion, disinfectant, kitchen herbs, a recently potted geranium, warm breasts and armpits, topped up with a dab of best perfume brought out to greet the occasion.

I put down my presents and surveyed her fondly, amazed by the sight of this robust Anglo-American housewife. She was only three months pregnant, but seemed to have doubled her weight, a handsome, strong-legged woman with a warm flush of a complexion.

Surrounded by this pleasant farmhouse overlooking the tidal mud-flats of the river, I had the feeling that I had strayed into another film set. A few minutes earlier, driving up the rutted farm-track towards an old metal barn, I had expected to find an encampment of teepees, with a troupe of former account executives and record industry drop-outs picking the fleas from their caftans as they mumbled mantras and smoked their pot. But the farmhouse, with its Chinese carpets and deep sofas, seemed more like a dream of the Eighties. Even its coffee table was stocked with genuine coffee-table books and not with highbrow biographies. Its comfortably lived-in air and children's toys heaped in a corner might have starred as the backdrop to a wholemeal bread commercial.

'Well, what do you think?' Sally was watching me with a look of her old mischief.

'Sally, it's bliss – I'm thrilled for you. It certainly isn't what I expected.'

'Of course it isn't. But do you recognise it?'

'In a way. Don't tell me it's been on television?'

'I hope not. Think hard.' When I gave up, she cried triumphantly: 'It's just like Shepperton!'

'Where? My old dump?'

'Yes! Don't look so stunned. I thought of you and the pixies when we furnished it.'

'Sally ... I can't believe it. So all along I was a complete suburbanite without realising it.'

'Of course you were. If you're going to bring up children there's only one way to go about it.'

'Yes ... the children decide that, all right. I can't wait to see little Jackie.'

'She's a love, I'd die without her. Edward's bringing her back from a kiddies' party.'

'And Edward too.'

'You'll be impressed. He's years younger than me but he's so mature. Sometimes I think he's my father.'

'I'm glad ...' She had spoken without any thought of the past, as if all memories of her Bayswater flat and the stock-car tracks of east London had vanished for ever. 'Sally, it's wonderful here.'

'I've bought the whole package – station wagon, big dogs, sheep-skin jackets, church fetes. I should have moved in with you years ago. Now, tell me about the pixies.'

She poured tea, happily showing off her mother's silver tea-set. We settled back on the sofa and brought each other up to date. She had met Edward, a physics lecturer at the University of East Anglia, while he was on a year's sabbatical at Berkeley. I imagined Sally as one of the morose, chain-smoking ex-hippies sitting on the kerb along Telegraph Hill, but in fact she had been the manager of a small bookshop, and had begun to settle down long before meeting her husband. Watching her, I felt that the past years had slid away down some chute in her mind. She was young again, confident of herself and the world, the sunlight and this cheerful, untidy room. In her middle thirties she had been able to rendezvous with the 18-year-old self she had last seen at Idlewild airport in 1962, catching a plane to Europe.

Another Sally Mumford had gone off to join the Sixties, had taken
too many overdoses and fallen into the doubtful company of arts
administrators, TV psychologists and impresarios of car crash exhibitions. Happy for her, I listened as she described Jackie's latest crazes.
At the same time, I wondered how long all this would last, whether it
was another momentary fantasy, a dream that would founder when it
struck the first hard wave ...

A battered Volvo estate car had turned into the drive, rolling in the
deep ruts. A boyish-looking man with a shock of pale hair and strong
footballer's shoulders stepped from the car. He opened the rear door,
released a harness and swung out a little girl in a party frock.

'They're here. Just look ...'

Eyes bright with pride, Sally beckoned me to the door. She hoisted
Jackie on to her shoulder, rubbed noses and quizzed her about the party.
She kissed her husband, who greeted me pleasantly but warily. When
we followed Sally and her daughter into the sitting-room he told me
that David Hunter was due at Norwich station within an hour.

'I'll collect him from the station, and we'll join you at our site –
we're digging out a wartime Spitfire. Sally thought you'd be interested.'

'I am – my son should have come along.'

Sally had mentioned that Edward was a member of a local group of
aircraft enthusiasts, excavating the remains of old planes that had come
down in the estuary. Photographs of the aircraft stood on the mantelpiece – an ancient Heinkel and a wingless Messerschmitt encrusted
with peat being lifted by crane from a mud-flat. An almost intact
Hurricane had pride of place. Edward and his team posed beside it
with the curator of an aircraft museum to whom they had donated
the Battle of Britain fighter.

But there were more important matters at hand than these forgotten
aircraft. I took Jackie's present from my bag and handed the box in
its bright tissue and ribbon to the serious-faced little girl. I thought
affectionately of the hundreds of hours that Sally had happily given
to my own children. Jackie stood beside her mother, now and then
raising her arms stiffly to remind herself of her taffeta dress, watching

me with her sweet but empty smile. Her prominent knees and elbows, the hands that flexed so sharply that their palms touched her wrists, and her toneless face made me realise that the clouded mind of this handicapped child would never be aware of the loving home that Sally had created for her.

Already I regretted the over-elaborate toy I had bought, a model kitchen with battery-powered lights and cooker far beyond Jackie's grasp. She seemed almost to understand this, as Edward set out the toy on the coffee table and connected the batteries. She stared at her father with her trusting, fixed smile, as if she were crossing the world at a slight angle to the rest of us. Now and then she reached out in a tentative way, and then gravely withdrew when Sally held her hands, a child of nature who would for ever play alone in a twilit garden walled by shadows she could never touch.

Throughout our cheerful lunch Sally beamed fondly at her daughter. Pouring the wine, Edward reminisced about his year at Berkeley, and their meeting, quite by chance, when Sally's car broke down on the Bay Area Bridge. I was sure that this decent and responsible man had never even speculated that his life would have taken a different turn had he chosen not to drive to San Francisco on that particular morning. Watching them, I was confident that this loving house was not a facade. If anything, the daughter had strengthened the family, and Sally's dream would endure.

The tide had begun to run through the estuary, slipping between the mud-flats. Stranded by the falling water, sailing dinghies sat above us on the draining pedestals of silt. A cabin cruiser creaked against its mooring line, waking from its deep riverine sleep into the open air. When we set off in the rowing skiff the last of the tidal water ran into the channel, carrying away the reflection of the house.

I lay back comfortably among the cushions while Sally pulled on the oars, scarcely glancing over her shoulder as she navigated expertly through the maze of waterways. Two hundred yards from the house we left the main channel of the river and entered a parallel realm of small islands and tributary streams. Edward and Jackie had driven to the railway station at Norwich, and would join us at the excavation site, which we could reach more easily by boat.

'Where are we?' Sally rested on the oars and shielded her eyes from the gleaming mud. 'They only dig at low tide. If you can manage to stand without falling in, try to spot a church spire. It should lean to the left.'

'I see it.' I stared across a lake of grass. An entire air force could have disappeared into this world of forgotten creeks. 'There's some kind of crane on a barge.'

'Norfolk Lighterage. One of the directors is an aircraft buff.' Sally pulled away with strong arms, knees spread beneath her swelling abdomen. Her smock rose in the shifts of air to reveal her long brown legs. Minute pearls of scar tissue were all that remained of her old needle ulcers.

'What sort of plane is it? Are they sure it's a Spitfire?'

'Edward thinks so – because of the engine. Usually that's all there is left. You'll be impressed, Jim.'

'It could be a Mustang ... that used a British engine.'

Watching the mud-flats slide past, I listened to the plash of Sally's oars, and wondered why Sally was so keen that David and I visit the excavation site. I thought of the Mustangs that had strafed the airfield next to Lunghua camp, and the downed pilots hunted by the Japanese soldiers in their dilapidated trucks. In some ways the banks of mud reminded me of the Whangpoo and the crashed aircraft lying by the irrigation ditches.

'I'm beat.' Sally decked the oars and let the skiff drift on the water. 'Time for my rest.'

'I'll take over.'

'No. Too risky. It's good for me, anyway.'

Taking my hand, she left her seat, stepped along the trembling boat and sank beside me on to the cushions. She wiped away the sweat that matted her blonde hair to her forehead. We drifted on the ebbing water, sealed off from the world by the wild grass and the slopes of silky mud.

'That sounds like Jackie.' Sally raised her head to the warning hoot of a disturbed water-fowl in the reeds. 'No, too far.'

'She's gorgeous, Sally ... you're very lucky.'

She leaned her head against my shoulder and held my hand, tracing my palm-lines with a cracked finger-nail as if to remember my strange life. 'She's great. Edward adores her. She's getting on really well at the remedial classes and made masses of friends.'

'And she'll have company soon. Is it a boy or girl? You can choose these days.'

'No, thanks! I don't want to know. Boy or girl, *it's* going to decide.' She pressed my hand to her belly, and chortled when I felt the child kick. 'Beware of pregnant women, Jim. You've spent a lot of time with them.'

'I loved every minute – let me know if you ever get bored with Edward.'

'I won't get bored.' She closed my hand around my life-line. 'Do you remember when Miriam was pregnant?'

'I never knew her when she wasn't. Believe me, she was twice your size.'

'Happy to hear it. I'm going to be thrice my size. Do you think I've changed?'

'Completely. David's going to be amazed.'

'It was time to change. For you, too, Jim. Those were wonderful years, but ... I keep looking at Edward and little Jackie and I'm so glad. We must have been very, very sane to act so crazily and get away with it.'

'Not everyone did.'

'Like David? I know.'

'You'll be surprised. David's a lot better – he runs his air-freight company in Brussels. He and his girl-friend are trying to adopt an Asian child ...'

'David's dead.' Sally dropped her hand into the water. 'I heard it in his voice. He died years ago.'

'That's unfair. And it's not true – you could say that about me. Peggy Gardner frequently does ...'

'No – everyone knew what you were looking for. But David? Still, I'm glad he's all right.' She smiled to herself, avoiding my eyes. 'I tried to call Dick Sutherland – we keep seeing him on a children's programme. He's Jackie's favourite doctor.'

'He's the same matinee idol he always was. People who go on television never grow old – or they grow old in a different way. Some sort of kidney trouble has slowed him down; he wants to give up TV and become a serious psychologist again.'

'Hey, you always said that television was serious! Don't tell me Dick's started to think for himself. I used to feel that he was totally under your thumb ... Now, tell me about yourself. All those books?'

'There's nothing to tell – that's the problem. I spent the whole of my adult life with children. Suddenly, when I'm fifty, there's this colossal vacuum. Mothers feel the same way. Nature hasn't provided a contingency plan – or, as Dick would say, nature's contingency plan is death.'

'Rubbish. You're not going to die. Not this afternoon, anyway. Besides, you've got the children, even if they're not at home. It must be a bit of a relief – how you coped with teenage girls I'll never know.'

'I always did exactly what they told me. Actually, fathers can be better mothers than you think. It's mothers who make a hash of their teenage daughters – some of Alice's and Lucy's friends went through hell.'

'Well, think about it – all these young men ringing the bell, daughters on the pill, the poor mother finds she's practically running a brothel. No wonder Peggy disapproved of you. Besides, she wanted to keep you for ever in that awful hut... but Miriam would have been proud of Henry and the girls. Do you still think about her?'

I drew my name on the surface of the water. 'Now and then – the damned thing is I've started to forget what she looked like. Sometimes I try to remember her and it's like watching someone else's home movie. I know I shouldn't say that. Memories of the people you love are supposed to last for ever, but often they're the first to go ...'

Sally moved my hand to her breast. She held it there for a moment, and then placed it on her lap. The women I had loved were saying goodbye. We lay together in the sun, as the water carried us through the clicking reeds.

The diesel tapped against the deck plates of the lighter, sending its smoky exhaust into the clear estuary air. Cables unwound from the winch and the crown block descended from the sky. Sally and I sat in a saddle of dry sand between two hillocks of grass, the picnic hamper open in front of us. Still wearing her party frock, Jackie squatted between her mother's legs, smiling in her straightfaced way at the swaying boom of the crane.

Below us, in the bed of the drained creek, Edward and his team were digging out the last silt from the fuselage of the entombed aircraft. Sections of flat steel piling had been driven into the bed, forming the walls of a metal chamber. Their interlocked edges held back the silt from the remains of the aircraft six feet below the surface. When the estuary flooded, the excavation site filled with water, which drained away at low tide and allowed the team a brief two hours to resume their patient work.

I stood up and searched for any sign of David, who had become bored with the slow preparations. Delighted to see Sally again after so many years, and bemused by her transformation from Sixties hippy into career housewife, he happily played hide-and-seek with little Jackie among the dunes. He ignored the excavation site, clearly disapproving of this morbid interest in old war wrecks.

'It's like your bloody car crash exhibition – Jim, you really started something there ...'

'David, hold on. They were digging these planes out during the war.'

'Maybe – the next thing they'll be hiring Olympia, and laying out the debris of a 747 for everyone to pick over ... You could help to arrange an Arts Council grant.'

Morosely, he wandered off to a small inn four hundred yards across the mud-flats where the cars were parked. Since leaving Summerfield he had become almost puritanically strict towards himself and the world, with all the zeal of the recent convert. I sensed that he disapproved of his entire past life, and felt that he was responsible, not only for having spent his childhood in Shanghai, but for my being born there as well. No penance could atone for this historical crime; a logic triggered in that cruel city had led inevitably to the death of the woman cellist on the Hammersmith flyover.

Leaving Sally, I strolled to the edge of the sand-cliff and looked down into the pit. Buckets of silt were being hoisted from the watery bed, and Edward stood knee-deep in the dark ooze, ready to hose away the last debris from the engine and canopy of the aircraft. Most of the wings and tail were missing, lost when it plunged into the creek, but I could see the typical nose-heavy bulb of a single-engine World War II fighter.

As it emerged for the first time into the daylight everyone fell silent. Edward hosed the intact canopy, watched by the small group of locally recruited workmen and the two-man crew of the lighter. Even after nearly forty years it was easy to imagine the immense force with which this stricken machine had plunged into the creek. The exposed engine block, a black bull's head of unrecognisable metal, was a fossil of pain. We waited for it to give its last cry as Edward hosed the silt from the valve-jacket and propeller boss. His boyish face revealed a clear-eyed seriousness that must have swept everything from Sally's heart when he parked behind her on the Bay Area Bridge and changed the flat tyre of her VW.

A warped propeller blade appeared, bent into a graceful arc. Edward wiped the mud from his arms and chest. Leaning against one of the ladders lowered into the pit, he ran his hands over the engine, searching for the carburettors and exhaust ports. Behind us, David had left the inn and was wandering across the mud-flat, a tray loaded with beer glasses in his hands, attention distracted by a child with a large dog.

'It's a Spitfire,' someone said. One of the excavation team, a Norwich surgeon, turned and gave a thumb's up to Sally and nodded encouragingly at me. I waved to David, who approached through the grass, watching the froth on the glasses. Edward was hosing away the mud from the top of the fuselage, exposing the cockpit canopy and the ragged metal plates where the tail had been torn away. He was frowning at something he had discovered, and turned off the hose, shaking his head to himself.

There was a shout, followed by a further moment of silence as everyone stared into the pit. The Norwich surgeon signalled to the lighter-men, and the diesel ceased its tapping. The workmen stepped closer to the pit.

'What is it?' Sally asked. 'Is Edward all right?'

'He's fine. The canopy's closed.'

'And? Does that matter?'

'The pilot's probably still in there.' I lowered my voice. 'If he'd baled out the canopy would have shattered on impact.'

'Dear God.' Sally grimaced, holding tight to her daughter as David arrived with the tray of drinks. 'Jim, I'm sorry, we shouldn't have come. I thought you and David might—'

'No ...' I touched her shoulder, trying to calm her. 'I'm glad we did.'

'What's going on?' David stepped past us, and made his way down to the site. 'Is someone hurt?'

'No, but ...'

I followed him to the edge of the pit. Pints of ale were passed round, but no one drank. Wrenches in hand, Edward and the surgeon straddled the fuselage, like sailors unfurling a shroud. The canopy, its black panes intact, lifted without any effort, revealing a solid mass of ancient silt moulded to the glass and windshield.

I waited as buckets of water were lowered, and the suction hose drew off the liquefied silt. David stood beside me, face set, sipping his pint. His fair hair raced across his forehead in the breeze, a frantic semaphore. I watched his lips tasting the malty foam. White beads clung to the fine scars, miniature balloons celebrating these residues of his accident.

Dials had appeared in the cockpit, their last readings registered after all these decades. The trim wheels and throttle mounting emerged, a few fragments of blackened leather and the pilot's harness straps.

'The cockpit's empty – he must have baled out,' I said to David, but he shook his head and put his glass into my free hand. Edward was pulling at a leather parcel, bound by rotting straps, that lay below the seat on the floor of the cockpit, perhaps a spare parachute left behind by the pilot.

Reaching into the cockpit, Edward eased the parcel on to the seat and applied water and suction hose. Calling to him, David pushed through the watching workmen. He climbed over the steel palings and stepped on to a ladder, still wearing his grey worsted suit. One of the workmen pointed to the mud that already smeared his trousers, but David ignored him and sank to his knees in the wet silt that filled the bottom of the excavation pit. Arms inside the cockpit, he helped Edward to release the contents of the leather parcel. I realised that they were holding the remains of a flying suit, jacket and helmet. Already I could see the notched teeth and nasal bones of a small skull. Without thinking, I sipped at David's beer, surprised by its coldness.

They buried Pilot Officer Pierce two weeks later, in the churchyard below the tilting steeple, within sight of the creek into which he had plunged on a June morning 38 years earlier. His grave lay among the worn memorial stones of the local villagers, and of six RAF aircrew who had been interred during the war. None of Pierce's relatives was present; the only surviving member of his family was an elderly cousin living in New Zealand, but the RAF provided the honour guard that attended the burials of recently discovered wartime aircrew, and two former pilots from his squadron made the journey to attend.

Standing behind these elderly men, their blunt and polished medals on their dark lapels, I found it difficult to believe that P.O. Pierce, had he parachuted safely from his Spitfire, would now be over sixty. The small skeleton in the leathery parcel of his flying suit seemed to be that of a teenage boy, some child pilot who had bluffed his way into a wartime fighter base.

I remembered how Edward and the Norwich surgeon had laid the flattened parcel on the wet floor of the excavation pit, beside the exposed mass of the Merlin engine. As they carefully prised away the mummified leather they found a few small bones, a shoulder blade and several ribs, scarcely enough to constitute a grown man. Wearing his mud-drenched suit, David had climbed into the cockpit and sat in the pilot's seat, searching with his hands through the silt on the floor of the fuselage.

As he felt under the instrument panel and between the brake pedals, I imagined him at the controls of this Spitfire, sitting on its grass airfield somewhere in southern England in 1940. Had he or I been a few years older we would have returned to England to fight in the war, and our bones might well have been brought to light by these weekend archaeologists. I thought of the crashed Japanese and Chinese planes at Hungjao aerodrome, and of how as a ten-year-old I had often climbed into the cockpit of a forgotten fighter lying in the long grass. I had played with its rusty controls at about the same time as Pilot Officer Pierce sat in his Spitfire at the bottom of this Norfolk creek.

With luck, the burial of his bones had laid to rest more than one young pilot. David had been reluctant to leave the excavation pit. Sitting in the cockpit, his arms black with mud, he had looked up at the daylight as if newly born into the fresh air of the Norfolk estuary from the deep memories of decades. He stood beside me through the service, wearing his RAF uniform for the first time in twenty years. Head back in the light breeze, he was smiling and handsome again, mouth working in the ironic way I remembered from the japes of our childhood. He had looked at the Lunghua commandant, Mr Hyashi, with the same insolent grimace.

I worried that he might create a scene, but I realised later that his real recovery dated from that chance moment when he had returned with the tray of drinks across the mud-flats. He had brought with him a friend from the aviation world, a burly South Korean who had once been a JAL pilot and now worked at London Airport. I was puzzled why David should have invited this impassive, middle-aged executive all the way to a modest churchyard in Norfolk, but it then occurred to me that a retired Korean pilot was as close as David could come to asking a Japanese to witness the interment of all his resentments of the past forty years.

15

The Final Programme

From the start, everyone I knew felt uneasy at the very thought of Dick Sutherland's last television project. Cleo Churchill urged me not to take part – the proposed documentary struck her as ghoulish in the extreme, pandering to the exhibitionist strains in Dick's character. More tolerant of Dick, and admiring his courage, I had tried to sidestep his invitation for different reasons. In later years, countless similar programmes were to be shown on television, and the making of these films became part of the therapeutic process by which the dying prepared themselves for their deaths. But in 1979 the idea of an explicit filmed record of the last weeks running up to one's death seemed virtually pornographic.

However, as I pointed out to Cleo, the film satisfied the logic of Dick's life. He had only felt fully alive on television, and in a macabre way would only be fully dead if his last weeks, and even the moment of his death, took place under the camera lens. A BBC producer had already shown an interest in the project, and a format had been devised which would incorporate Dick's film into a documentary series about the taboos surrounding this most unmentionable of topics.

'Taboos?' Cleo scoffed at the word, when we talked it over at her publisher's office, careful to separate herself from me behind a barricade of wholesome children's books. 'He's actually going to make a snuff movie. Jim, he's staging a sex-death in which he's raped out of existence by the whipped-up emotions of all those peak-time viewers. And you're going to take part?'

'Cleo ... that's unfair. Think beyond the film. Aldous Huxley took

LSD as he died – perhaps this is Dick's way of coping with a challenge he can't face. The film will probably never be shown, and I dare say he knows that.'

'But do you know it? Piffle!'

Three weeks earlier, after an exhausting struggle against his thyroid cancer, Dick had discharged himself from hospital. A make-up girl preparing us for a late-night discussion programme had first noticed the goitre. I remembered waiting to take Dick's chair in front of the mirror, and how he sat surrounded by all the lights and cosmetic jars, his throat bobbing as the make-up girl pointed out his enlarged Adam's apple. He caught my eye in the mirror, as if aware that a dimension had entered the script for which all his years in television had never prepared him.

He was subdued during the recording, though outwardly his confident and charming TV self. I thought, unkindly, that it took only this modest swelling, probably a cyst or mild iodine deficiency, to touch his one vulnerable point – his own body. As he smiled and spoke to camera his familiar repertory of gestures and mannerisms suddenly seemed like so much decorative armour breaking loose from a stumbling warrior. When I drove him home to Richmond, before going on to Shepperton, he was already complaining about his sore throat, almost needing to punish his body. I knew he had been slightly ill during the past year, and urged him to see his doctor.

Soon after, Dick entered hospital for observation, passing into the paradoxical world of modern medicine, with all its professional expertise, ultra-high technology and complete uncertainty. As Dick pointed out on my first visit to Kingston Hospital, the qualities traditionally ascribed to patients – self-delusion, a refusal to face the truth, irrational hope and a despair born of underlying pessimism – in fact were those of their doctors.

'You have to realise,' he whispered to me when a nurse had declined to answer a direct question about his suspected cancer, 'that the first and most important job of medical science is to protect the profession from the patients. We unsettle them and make them feel vaguely guilty. We ask questions they know they can't answer – the one thing they really want us to do is go away, or pretend that there's nothing wrong with us. What they like best of all is to admit us to hospital and then hear us say we feel fine, even if we're at death's door.'

Despite the prospect of exploratory surgery, Dick had already recovered his spirits. He flirted with the nurses and tamed the formidable senior sisters, promising them parts in his next TV series. But the reductive and grinding logic of hospital life began to take its toll, and he was astute enough to see behind the facade of ward-level optimism.

'The nurses are amazingly sunny,' I commented. 'I feel as if I ought to climb into the next bed.'

'Not a good idea, on the whole. Remember, they're like hostesses in a nightclub who know the customers aren't going to enjoy the floorshow.' Dick leaned against the big pillows, his keen eyes scanning the ward. 'It's interesting that the higher you move up the professional ladder the more depressed the doctor becomes. Your local G.P. and the junior housemen are reasonably cheerful – they can pass on the serious decisions. But as you meet the senior consultants you find this deepening gloom, because they realise there's almost nothing they can do to help you. Serious cancers are the worst thing they have to face – they remind them of how helpless medicine really is.'

But Dick's good humour had passed when I next saw him. He had woken after surgery in acute pain, unable to swallow and convinced that another throat had been transplanted into his own. Lowering the loose cotton dressing, he showed me the wound running from ear to ear, held together by a score of metal clips and covered with dried blood. He was discharged three days later, and within a week returned to the specialists to learn the results of the biopsy.

Far from clarifying the real nature of his condition, the operation had only served to confuse it. A specialist had eventually seen Dick, and embarked on an enthusiastic account of the educational benefits of TV medical programmes. Dick described, with grim relish, how his use of the word 'cancer' was met with a silent rebuke, followed by a disquisition on the meaninglessness of the term in the context of modern medicine. At last, as an afterthought, the specialist recommended the complete excision of the thyroid gland, reassuring Dick that he would re-open the old scar, and so preserve his neck for the TV cameras.

'The remarkable thing,' Dick confided to Cleo and myself, 'is that no one will tell me I have cancer. It's as if they want to hide the news from themselves, just when I've been able to face it. Now I feel almost guilty. A brain tumour with lots of secondaries in the lungs and liver would have been the decent thing …'

Cleo and I admired Dick's courage and humour, which sadly deserted him after the second operation. The complete removal of his thyroid lowered his metabolism, and he became lethargic and dispirited, despite the large doses of calcium. His appearance radically changed. A long pointed jaw jutted from his eroded neck, and we both noticed that he no longer glanced at himself in the hand-mirror that a nurse had given him.

When we arrived he stared at us as if we belonged to an alien species and his true companions were his fellow-patients in the ward. I sensed that he regretted his own self-delusions, of which the greatest had been his apparently sincere attempt to discover the truth about his cancer. This was a bluff that had now been called. His attitude to the nursing staff had also changed. All irony and humour had gone, and he was far more docile and cooperative, like a rebellious prisoner at last accepting the unwritten rules of an institution.

Exhausted by the radiation therapy, Dick lay against his pillows, his bald head covered by the NASA baseball cap that Cleo had found in his computer room at Richmond. He had lost interest in himself, and neither the nurses nor the registrar to whom we spoke seemed to have any clear idea of his real condition. Concerned with its own needs, the hospital moved in a parallel world to that of its patients.

After three weeks of radiation therapy, Dick learned that the last of the malignant tissue had yet to be eradicated. He was now completely hairless, and no longer bothered to wear his NASA cap or conceal his ravaged neck. Leaning on my arm, he walked with difficulty to the ambulance that would take him to what, in a moment of brave but tired humour, he described as the 'Caesar's Palace of cancer therapy' – the Royal Marsden Hospital to the south of London.

As it happened, this ultra-modern hospital might well have been a hotel-casino on the Las Vegas strip. Its airy corridors were hung with

Pop art posters, and Dick was given a ward to himself, with telephone, television and disposable toilet. In fact, this room was an isolation cell, in which he was imprisoned for nine days, watched by the geiger counter above his bed, until he had excreted the last of the radioactive iodine. When he spoke to us on the telephone, as Cleo and I stood by the lead-glass windows under the warning neon sign, his voice seemed to lift from a tape played at wavering speeds. The nurses who entered his room to take his blood and urine samples wore heavy gloves and protective overalls, and left him as quickly as they could, like conspirators setting a lethal device with the shortest of fuses.

Despite some success in eradicating the tumour, malignant cells had rooted themselves in his spine and liver. Too weak to bear any further treatment at the Marsden, Dick was returned by ambulance to Kingston Hospital and the chemotherapy ward of last resort.

Here, left to recover and without medication, he began to improve. I felt a surge of affection for him as he rallied himself, sitting up in bed to try on his new wig, shuffling along the landings with us as he craned through the windows for a distant view of the river and his Richmond house, even asking Cleo about her publishing career. When he was strong enough to submit to chemotherapy he would be moved to a sterile room which would give his depressed immune system the best chance of fighting off any passing infection.

Making sure that the nurses were elsewhere, he showed me briefly into the small, sterilised cell that was being prepared for him, a cubicle stripped of all furniture and fittings that might harbour bacteria, with a sealed door and windows, and a ventilation system that resembled a midget submarine's. Eerily, the screen of a TV set was set into the wall behind a thick glass plate, as if even television was withdrawing from Dick.

'Cosy, isn't it?' Hunched inside his dressing gown, Dick straightened his wig and beckoned me away. 'Just the place to take your last view of the world. Did you notice the TV screen? Like a retina seen from the rear.'

'Dick, come on …' I held his arm as he hobbled away, aware how much stronger he was, like a wiry and determined old man. 'You're so much better – you may never move there. I can feel it.'

'I can feel it, all right ...' He let me help him on to a settee in the patients' day-room, then pulled up a wooden chair for me. As he stared around the room I realised how much he had changed. He had lost all illusions about himself – he had always enjoyed being recognised in public, but no one now, neither the nursing staff nor his fellow-patients, remembered the handsome presenter-psychologist who had fronted so many popular science programmes. Dick appeared not to care. To show his indifference to his earlier self, he had selected an oversize golden wig, almost a caricature of his sandy hair.

'You'll have time to read,' I commented. 'Cleo has the keys to your house, she can pick anything you want from the shelves.'

'No – I'm too busy watching everyone here.' He pulled my arm and whispered: 'You have to admire people. Most of them are far worse off than me – yards of gut cut out, half their jaws gone, ribs and God knows what. Yet they look like film extras ready to play a party scene.'

'Perhaps you should bring a camera in here?'

'It's a thought. In fact –' Dick glanced at me, as if recognising me for the first time. 'They say factory production always goes down after a film-crew visit. Here I'd expect the opposite effect. Perhaps there are too many TV screens in hospitals and too few cameras. Jim, tell me about Cleo and the children. It's good to see you, by the way.'

My suggestion had taken root. He was rallying himself, trying to be interested in our inconsequential world. Looking at his long, jutting jaw, I sensed his gathering will, if not to survive, at least to impose himself on whatever time was left to him.

The following Sunday, when I visited the hospital, I learned that he had discharged himself and returned home.

'It looks as if I have three or four months, possibly six,' Dick explained as we sat in his computer room. '*Omnibus* and *Horizon* are both very interested ...'

'Dick, are you sure?'

'They'll set up the lights and equipment for me, and some kind of static video camera we can talk into. The idea is to show what actually happens as we approach the end, and break through all the taboos and

preconceptions. No high-flown stuff about life and death, but as close
to our ordinary talk as we can get. We'll start with something easy to
get the ball rolling, the ten best films ever made, our last trips to New
York, Chomsky versus Skinner. Most of it will be taped down here, but
we'll move upstairs towards the end ...'

He spoke in a confident and matter-of-fact way, sitting comfortably at his desk as if he were back in his old office at the Institute of
Psychology. I was impressed by his easy command of his situation – he
had found a role for himself, which I considered to be quietly heroic,
but which he saw as merely the most interesting way of using the time
left to him. He had lost even more weight, and wore a high-collared
shirt and silk scarf to cover his chin. A smaller and neater wig allowed
him, in a certain light, to resemble his former self, but I felt once again
that he had begun to reject the affable and good-humoured personality
I had known for so many years.

Altogether he had made a marked recovery from the months of
medical treatment. Was he enjoying one of those periods of remission
that give false promise to the victim or, as I still hoped, had he made a
genuine return to health? As for his macabre documentary, at its worst
this was a last gamble that his own survival would invalidate the project.
Or, perhaps, having rid himself of all illusions in the radio-iodine room
at the Marsden, he was now free to choose whatever maverick notion
he needed to fill his last days.

As we soon learned, the improvement in Dick's condition was a
brief upward tremor on a steadily downward graph. The specialists at
the Marsden had arranged with Dick's doctor in Richmond to provide
the drugs that would hold back the metastasising tumours. Now the
cure, rather than the disease, would kill him. The cancer would not
spread, but the increasing doses of chemotherapy would destroy his
immune system, so that the smallest respiratory infection would turn
into a fatal pneumonia.

But Dick was beyond the reach of these ironies. He was conserving
what strength was left to him in order to carry out an important psychological experiment that would test his audience as much as himself.
During our first recorded conversation, a trial run of the equipment,

I found it difficult to speak at all, as if my throat was trying to mimic Dick's ravaged larynx. Our second appointment was cancelled when I developed a heavy head cold. But Dick was insistent; for reasons of his own he had decided that I should be the moderator, in part because I had first suggested the documentary to him, but also because he wanted to involve me directly in his death.

Sitting in his study as we prepared for the first episode, I regretted raising the idea. When Dick at last settled behind his desk I could see that he was almost exhausted by the effort of calming himself for the interview. The youthful actor-psychologist had become a shrunken and wounded old man, visibly fading under his powdered wig, and I hoped that the BBC team would pull the plugs on the entire spectacle. But everything was now grist to television's mill, like the razor-toothed rollers in abat-toirs that stripped the last shreds of gristle from the bones of a carcase.

While we waited for the sound engineer to check his levels, I noticed that Dick had taken down the California licence plates on the walls of his study, the Cocoa Beach beer mats and Cape Kennedy press badges. During the course of our interviews more of these snapshots of his past were to disappear, as if he were consciously dismantling a carefully constructed myth of himself.

But when he spoke to camera he soon rallied.

'... Many people have left detailed accounts of how they ended their lives, from the Greek Stoics to the Jewish doctors in the Warsaw ghetto who kept careful records of how they starved to death. In the past, of course, everyone knew what happened when a human being died – relatives sat around the death-bed, doing their best to comfort the dying, and most people died in their homes. Today, though, death is something we experience for the first time when it happens to us ... most people die in hospital, surrounded by machines, and watching someone die, especially a person very close, is more than we can face. Why? What is it about death that so unsettles us? In this series we're going to look at death through the eyes of a single dying person – me. I'm Dr Dick Sutherland. Three months ago my doctor told me that ...'

While Dick rested from his introduction, I noticed the digital desk clock recording the date, September 23, 1979. The green rice-grain letters blinked through the minutes and hours, unmoved by the camera or Dick's commentary. He sat in a deck-chair in the bathroom while the director and the series producer discussed the few fluffs and verbal slips. They decided that, given the nature of the documentary, these would only enhance its authenticity, despite the problems they posed for the dubbing of foreign-language versions sold abroad. My own role, thankfully, was limited to asking Dick a number of general questions about his state of mind.

'... How do I really feel? Does the thought that all this is going to end in two months' time – as it happens, before the last episode of my favourite TV series – throw me into a complete panic? Do I walk around all day with a feeling of terror, like a victim in a horror film? Surprisingly, the answer is no. If anything, I feel cool and detached, as if all this is happening to someone else. The brain seems to have developed a way of standing back from itself, like a locomotive uncoupling the carriages behind it. To tell the truth, the biggest problem faced by the dying is how other people feel, especially their friends. There's a real sense in which the dying have to die twice, once for themselves, and once for their friends ...'

Did Dick believe this? His sister and her husband, a retired Dundee accountant, had moved into the house to look after him, but they were unobtrusive, sensitive and reassuring. As I drove home it occurred to me that Dick had many acquaintances but virtually no close friends other than myself. Did he resent my concern for him and my visits to his hospital bed? Or were the friends for whom he had to die the invisible TV audience that had invested its admiration in him for so many years and now needed to be placated?

But all sense of an audience had gone by the time of our second interview. The first recording had left me light-headed. Unable to work, I roamed from room to room. Time seemed dislocated, like an endless afternoon in a strange city. When I arrived at Richmond, an hour early, Dick scarcely seemed to recognise me, and consulted his diary as if to remind himself. During the recording he sat stiffly at his desk with a brave if bleak smile, and described his activities in the past week, which seemed, eerily, to resemble my own.

I noticed that more mementoes had left the walls, the ticket stubs of the Rio premiere of *2001* and photographs of himself with the American astronauts at the Houston Space Center. I guessed that he was clearing away these remnants of the past twenty years so that he could return to his youth. Steadied by the camera, he reflected on his Scottish childhood and his wartime schooldays in Australia, where he and his sister had been evacuated.

'... Thinking about the Japanese during the first years of the war was rather like thinking about death. Everyone in Australia was vaguely frightened of the Japanese soldiers and knew they were approaching, but no one had ever seen one. Of course, our idea of the Japanese was a complete caricature – very different from your case, Jim, as a boy in wartime Shanghai. You knew exactly what the Japanese were like, and you'd also seen a great deal of death. Looking back, how do you think that affected you?'

I watched the sound engineer's tape-deck turning, and looked up to find Dick watching me with surprisingly clear eyes, his long jaw raised to reveal his ravaged neck.

I replied clumsily: 'I did see a lot of dead people – as you'd expect during a war. In some ways I think it was very corrupting ...'

'Go on – you say corrupting, but how exactly?'

'Well ... it wasn't the dead who were devalued, but the living. Our expectations of life were lowered.'

'Is that because they were too high in the first place?' Before I could reply, Dick continued in a last surge of breath: 'Perhaps we have exaggerated ideas about life, expectations that we see are unrealistic only as it draws to an end? It may be that we've allowed life and death to become polarised, when they're really much closer to each other than we realise. As I get nearer to my own death the distance seems to shrink ...'

After the recording Dick held my hand in a friendly but absent-minded way. He walked stiffly into the dining-room, which overlooked his high-walled garden. Had he begun to forget me, along with the beer mats and the American licence plates? Yet his apparently impromptu question had made a telling point, addressed more to me than to the television audience, a brief but acute inquiry into my own motives and character.

The days between our recordings seemed to lengthen, as if I were applying some unconscious brake to time in an attempt to hold back the approaching end. A different man was emerging through Dick's wasted features, far more self-reliant than the television performer he had seduced himself into becoming. At our third and fourth interviews he spoke to camera in a short-breathed and almost impatient tone, describing his pleasure in the everyday world around him, in the garden and fish pond, his sense of triumph at winning the affection of his neighbours' cat. But these pleasures seemed as abstract as the moves in a chess-game. I guessed that he was entering a realm where, seeing everything with absolute clarity, he no longer cared to be distracted by pleasures of any kind.

Our fifth recording was cancelled, and I assumed that Dick had decided to end the series. But his sister told me that he had briefly returned to the Marsden, to be introduced to a new regime of drugs that would stabilise a secondary tumour in his knee. By now, two months after discharging himself, he breathed with continuous effort, his diaphragm forced into his rib-cage by the enlarging lobes of his liver. On the day of our interview his sister and I knocked on his bedroom door, unable to get a reply. We entered to find the French windows open to the cool November air. Dick was sitting in his woollen dressing-gown at the bottom of the garden, staring at the house without noticing us. I had seen the same fixed eyes in my neighbours' golden retriever when it had crept into the garden to die. Only when Dick rose from his deck-chair and stepped slowly towards us did time begin again.

Without any greeting, he led me to his computer room, where a small editing suite had been installed. Before the arrival of the BBC crew Dick began to run through the film of our earlier conversations. Shifting the clips of film with his impatient fingers, he stared at himself as he addressed the camera. Until then I had been glad that the TV screen was helping to ease his last days. The medium that had trivialised his scientific career had appeared to come to his rescue, but now its magic had dimmed.

The BBC crew arrived, and we could hear their lowered voices in the hall. Usually their appearance provided Dick with a slight lift, and the expression would return to his face like a bucket drawn from a dark well. But he ignored them, staring at the empty screen of the editing machine. I touched his arm, thinking that he had lost consciousness, but his eyes were alert.

'Dick, they're here ...'

'You can tell them to wait.' He gestured dismissively at the screen. 'The producer's lost his nerve – he wants to change the "direction" of the series. Can you believe that? A little late in the day. Bring in other topics, what do I now think of abortion? Abortion – do-it-yourself genocide ... He didn't like that.'

He laughed thinly, massaging his knee through his pyjamas.

'Dick, can you walk? I'll bring the wheel-chair.'

'No – it's just down the hall. The surgeon at the Marsden talked about a prosthetic limb. The wonders of modern prosthetics, dear God – the castration complex raised to the level of an art form. He explained that they're close to "understanding" disease – they don't realise that they're soon going to be overwhelmed by an epidemic of *imaginary* diseases. The one thing we treasure most is a corrupt version of ourselves.' He held my wrist, aware that I was trembling. 'Now, this experiment ... Someone else will have to take over. Perhaps one day, who knows ...'

These were the last words that Dick spoke to me. He stood up and stepped quietly into his bedroom with a backward wave of the hand. He closed the door, leaving me to apologise to the film crew. He had spoken matter-of-factly of our 'experiment', and I realised that he had taken part in the documentary with one end in mind. The series had been a desperate stratagem that alone might have saved him. He had literally put his faith in my ironic prophecy that he would make the first great scientific discovery on television, and had gambled against all logic that the scientific discovery would be his recovery from inoperable cancer.

What was to have been our last interview never occurred. When I arrived at the house a fortnight later an ambulance was parked outside. In the hall were Dick's local doctor and the district nurse, his sister and her husband, all lit by the glare of the television lights through the door of Dick's bedroom. He was to have taped his last reflections on his life before being taken to hospital, but it was clear that he was now too exhausted to speak. The producer had persuaded the reluctant doctor to allow a last shot of Dick lying on his bed in the dining-room, beside the dark mahogany table and its straight-backed chairs, a scene set for a tribunal.

Standing in the doorway behind the cameraman, I waved to Dick as he lay with the oxygen mask over his face, a glucose drip in his arm, a catheter draining into a glass flagon under the bed. He no longer wore his wig, and his face seemed to have been sucked into the mask, as if his wasted body was about to drain away down these encircling tubes, their coils like the telephone wire looped around the chest of the young Chinese on the railway platform.

16

The Impossible Palace

A funfair was visiting Shepperton. As I walked along the river I could see the chromium-panelled caravans through the trees, driving into the park beside the war memorial. There were trucks loaded with dodgem cars and sections of merry-go-rounds, a dismantled dream that these taciturn circus folk reassembled each weekend in one of the small towns of the Thames Valley, reminding the inhabitants of a forgotten corner of their imaginations. Already the children playing by the river bank had left the water. Whooping to their mothers, they ran towards the park, where the dozen vehicles were drawn up in a circle, a magic fortress that only children could storm.

I remembered how Alice and Lucy would ride their unicorns side by side, sixpenny treats that bought a fortune of excitement as they moved up and down, ribbons flying, arms clasped around the unicorns' necks, wide eyes cutting the air. Henry would sit stiffly in his silver aeroplane, embarrassed at being too large for the cockpit, then stand up like a stuntman and grip the leading edge of the wing, a lordly, three-year-old Lindbergh.

I strolled through the trees, almost expecting to see them waiting for me by the entrance to the funfair. They had left for the start of the university summer term, but in my mind they were always playing in the park. Alice's bright eyes, a swirl of Lucy's white frock, Henry's excited shout at some new idea, conjured themselves from the eddies of air and light. Generously, the park released its hoarded treasures. Stirred by the summer wind, the great elms were shedding their memories. I shielded my eyes from the sun and looked up at the shifting hampers of foliage, searching for a troupe of children perched on the branches, younger selves of the housewives and office workers of Shepperton. Perhaps I would see my own youthful self, bony cheeks under a strange haircut, whom I scarcely recognised in our snapshot albums.

As if cued by these memories, a young man in a pinstriped business suit and tie was standing in the car park beside his Triumph sportscar, watching me as he folded back the canvas hood. I followed the children towards the caravans in the centre of the park, not quite able to make out his expression, though he seemed to recognise me. From its licence plate I realised that his Triumph was twenty years old, the same age and model as the car that Dick Sutherland had once let me drive.

Chattering to herself, a neighbour's daughter overtook me. When she held my hand, urging me towards the funfair, the young man left his Triumph and began to walk in a deliberate way towards me. Was he a friend of Alice and Lucy? There was an edge to his jaw that reminded me again of the photograph of myself before my marriage. As the elms stirred over our heads, dappling the hair of the child pulling at my hand, I had the absurd notion that this young man was myself. He was calling to me, a hand raised in warning.

'I say – are you the parent ...?'

I turned to greet him, and bumped into the girl's older sister, who had followed us from the river. I helped to pick up her bucket and spade that I had knocked onto the grass, but by the time we had exchanged apologies the young man had returned to his car. He locked the canvas hood, avoiding my eyes as he stepped into the driver's seat. I guessed that he had seen me following the children, too old to be a parent and too young to be a grandfather, and suspected that I might have some illicit interest in them.

I watched him drive away, exhaust roaring as he swerved past the war memorial and the crowded lunch-hour pubs. When he had gone I felt that I had narrowly missed meeting myself.

This sense of an imminent rendezvous somewhere in Shepperton had been growing within me during the six months since Dick Sutherland's death. I woke each morning, looking forward to the day's work, buoyed by the warm spring light and by a mysterious elation that had overtaken me. I had expected to be depressed by Dick's death, an ordeal made all the more harrowing by the uncompleted documentary, but I felt an immense sense of release. The air outside the crematorium was so bright and pungent that I scandalised Cleo Churchill by searching the chimneys for any signs of combustible flesh.

The non-denominational service, with its recorded organ voluntary and mock-solemn trappings, had resembled the rites of a new religion still in its development stages, an effect only stressed by the large contingent of television producers who were present. Behind their heavy shades, forever dreaming of 12-part series, they perhaps saw Dick as a mana-personality for the age of global TV. We were attending the funeral of someone who, with the shrewdest foresight, had already interred himself within the film archives of the BBC.

I had taken care to grieve for Dick while he was still alive, aware that repeats of his old programmes would soon be returning to our screens. Much as I disliked the documentary film in which we had taken part, I was grateful to Dick for choosing me as his interviewer. By demystifying his own death he had freed me from any fears of my own. For the first time since the birth of my children I felt that I was wholly done with the past and free to construct a new world from the materials of the present and future.

Time itself, bundling us headlong towards destinations of its own choice, had begun to loosen its grip. A day would last as long as I chose. Leaving my typewriter, I could spend an hour watching a spider build its web. On my walks by the river I stood among the elms and waited for time to calm itself, listening to its measured breath as it settled itself over the forest. I recognised the mystery and beauty of a leaf, the kindness of trees, the wisdom of light. My small house, the domestic streets and gardens glowed with the same vivid air I had seen during my experiment with LSD, and in that unending summer when Henry, Alice and Lucy had been born.

At the entrance to the funfair, while their mothers gossiped and searched their handbags, the children waited impatiently by the ticket booth.

They rushed squealing towards the merry-go-round, leaving behind the solitary, copper-eyed son of the Pakistani newsagent. He watched me shyly as I bought our tickets and darted away to join the others.

The carousel was turning, and the children shrieked as the ancient calliope chuntered out its brassy tune. Horses and unicorns rose and fell. Small hands tugged at the horses' manes, pig-tails streamed in the air and cries of alarm gave way to frowns of deep seriousness.

Watching them sail by, I stepped closer to the rotating canopy. The lights swirled past, borne on the jangling music that drew memories from the wind, a dream of my own children when they had ridden these shabby unicorns. A two-year-old boy solemnly piloted the miniature aircraft, too frightened to cry, eyes charged by the steaming hoots of the calliope.

As I gazed at this enchanted scene, the carousel seemed almost stationary, preserved for ever in a single moment. For the first time I could see beyond the little riders, through the silver forest of spiral pinions and the rotating mirrors above the calliope. Everyone I had known was riding the unicorns, Miriam and Dick Sutherland, a teenage Sally Mumford, boyish David Hunter. I stepped forward, waiting for an empty mount ...

'Jim! Look out! What are you doing?'

A wooden pillar struck my hand. The carousel whirled past in a rush of noise and light, a raucous tumbril of chipped paint and peeling gilt. I fell backwards, steadied by two men watching their sons. A woman's firm arms held me as I stumbled across the veering air.

'Jim – you nearly fainted!' Cleo Churchill pressed my cheeks, concerned eyes peering into my face. 'I thought I'd find you here. You looked as if you were trying to climb on board ...'

Sunlight filled the garden below the windows of my study, cheering the brambles and elders that crowded the edges of the lawn.

'I'm glad you don't drive like that ...' Cleo brought two tumblers of gin and ice from the kitchen. 'Jim, tell me – were you trying to join the children?'

'Not really ...' I managed to laugh at myself, and massaged my bruised hand. The rosy glow of angostura suffused the gin like a blood-stream glimpsed through a butterfly's wing. The carousel owner and his muscular sons had ordered me away, suspecting that I was up to no good. 'I'd forgotten the thing was moving – a trick of the sun. It turned the carousel into a kind of stroboscope ...'

'Well, I believe you ... try not to stop any speeding cars – I'd hate having to explain that to Lucy and Alice.'

The fan on the mantelpiece was turning, and the reflected sunlight through her blonde hair reproduced this curious effect. The same aura hovered over Cleo's bare shoulders as over every leaf in the garden. I was sorry to have worried her – for months she had been telling me that I was marooned in Shepperton, and the accident at the funfair must have seemed to her like another of my attempts at internal escape.

Old friends by now, we had never become lovers – in a boozy and reflective mood I had once described this to her as a technical omission, to which she had replied with a raised eyebrow, a shrewd smile and silence. But we had been separated by our shared friendship with Dick. Our different perspectives on this remarkable but ambiguous man had kept us apart, along with a certain wariness that Cleo felt towards me. Now that Dick had gone we had only ourselves, that shock of recognition sensed at so many funerals, and the cue to so many realignments.

I wanted to embrace her, but I found it difficult to get to grips with anything around me, the realm of desire and even the world of everyday objects. Cleo's sensitive hands and shy lips, the leaves in the drive, the rainbows on the windshield of my car, had all become idealised versions of themselves. The housewives shopping in Shepperton High Street, the extras leaving the film studios, the children on the carousel had been transformed by Dick's death. Distanced from their everyday selves, they seemed to hover beyond the contingent world of time and space, exiled from the paradise of the ordinary.

I stood by my desk, where Cleo had placed two heavy manila envelopes. They contained those mementoes of Dick which his sister had offered to us. While Cleo watched from the safety of her glass of gin, I drew out the California licence plate, the fading photographs of Dick in the cockpit of his weekend Cessna, posing alongside astronauts and space scientists at the 1960s Cape Kennedy. There were coasters from the Tropicana Motel in Hollywood, chips from a Las Vegas casino, and name tags of forgotten psychological conferences.

I arranged them in chronological order, as far as I could remember. The photographs and mementoes were clips from the film of his life, in which he had been both star and director. The artless vanity of the young Richard Sutherland only prompted my affection for him. I was glad that he had died quietly and without pain, in the deep peace of the hepatic coma.

Cleo wiped her eye, taking my arm. 'It's like a shrine. The bones of a saint. Are you going to keep everything?'

'I don't think we need to. Let's each of us take just one thing.'

I was looking at the sunlit sky over Shepperton, and remembering how Dick had talked about our perception of time. If our sense of time was an archaic mental structure, one we had inherited from our primitive forebears, perhaps Dick had made a first move towards dismantling it?

Cleo leaned across the desk, sunlight on the pale crown of her scalp. She was one with the children of the carousel, motionless but forever moving past me. I had scarcely touched her, aware of the distance she had set between us, but I put my hands on her shoulders, embracing her in the light.

Later, Cleo watched me while I undressed her in the bedroom, her hands on my forehead, as if watching my temperature.

'We don't want you to explode. I'm glad we came upstairs – those beer mats are a bit unnerving. Like that terrifying film the two of you made.'

'Poor man, he was trying to pull off a miracle. I saw him edit the thing, moving pieces of himself back and forth, trying to solve a jigsaw. He was literally editing his own life.'

'Are you going to edit me?'

I kissed her strong wrists as she tried to pull them away from me. 'Absolutely. All arguments and disagreements will be wiped from the tape. Left profile only to be shown—'

'But I like my right profile – it has more intellectual integrity ...'

'– flattering glances to be stressed, with deferential pauses …'

'God, I never *stop* being deferential …!' She helped me with the zip. 'Is this part of the editing?'

'Absolutely.' I carried the zip down to the base of her spine and let the dress fall forwards from her shoulders on to the floor. 'Think of it this way – I'm really dressing you, but you're seeing the film run backwards.'

'So it's all the fault of the projectionist? If only I'd told my mother that …'

She reached out and adjusted the wings of the dressing-table, then opened the wardrobe door so that its full-length mirror multiplied our reflections. Satisfied, she glanced at me slyly to see if I approved.

'I feel at home,' I commented. 'It's like *The Lady from Shanghai.*'

'What have I done? She got shot!'

We stood naked together, surrounded by the images of ourselves, lovers who had found each other during an orgy in a house of glass. Naked couples stood around us, immersed in themselves, half-hidden behind the doors. We were watched by the lenses of a dozen cameras, multiplied and dismantled at the same time. I held Cleo's breasts in my hands, touching the blue veins that ran past her broad nipples, and caressed away the pink grooves left by the wiring of her brassiere. I kissed a small scar in her armpit, relic of a childhood I had never known, and ran my lips through the shoal of silver stretch-marks, like seeds of time spilled across her abdomen by Ceres herself as she sowed her fields. She held my penis in her hands, rolling it gently between her palms, her fingers drawing on my scrotum. Phallic corridors receded from us, an erotic labyrinth in an impossible palace. When I kissed Cleo's nipples a battalion of lovers bent their heads. I sat on the bed as she knelt on the carpet between my knees, her forearms resting on my thighs. She took the head of my penis in her mouth, touching the tip of my urethra with her tongue, then sank deeper to hold the shaft between her teeth, biting lightly on the swollen muscle.

I drew her beside me, kissing her thighs and hips. With her firm hands she pressed my shoulders to the pillows and knelt astride me, long hair falling across my chest. I lay back, happy to share Cleo with the mirrors, but she stretched out and kicked the wardrobe door with her heel. The house of glass vanished into the cupboard, a collapsing concertina of light.

'Just you and me, Jim … I think that's all we can manage now …'

She returned to the pillows and lay beside me, brushing the hair from her eyes, knees raised in the air as I caressed her vulva. Engorged with blood, her labia rose like coxcombs around her clitoris. My fingers parted the mottled crests and moistened the stiffened nub. I soothed the hot pad of her anus, pushing back the soft upholstery of a small pile. Lying beside her, I masturbated her affectionately. When a sudden fluxus drenched the sheet she gasped at the ceiling and bit my shoulder, embarrassed by herself. She rested for a few breaths, held my hips and drew me between her legs.

Watched by a single mirror, we made love through the afternoon. As I lay deep within her, I was certain that this act of sex would endure far beyond these summer hours. Time had refused to yield to Dick Sutherland, a Janus locked within his own relentless self-regard. Cleo had been right to seal away those silver screens. With every glance in the mirror a small part of us died. Images of ourselves formed the real walls of our lives. The tyranny of the lens shored its fragments against us, an infinity of recorded selves that shut out the world beyond. I held Cleo tightly, trying to fuse the scent of her body into my skin. One day we would find the key to the mirror, and enter it together.

At the end of September, Cleo telephoned me from her office to say that the documentary on Dick's death would be shown on television.

'I thought they'd scrapped it,' she said, sounding unsettled. 'Are you going to watch?'

'No.' I knew that she had always disapproved of the film, suspecting that Dick had invited me to take part as a means of binding me to him for ever. 'We'll remember Dick when he was alive.'

'Good. I feel a lot better. Let's take a boat for the weekend and sail up to Henley. You haven't been out of Shepperton for months.'

This was literally true. Cleo had been happy to leave London at the weekends, cook in my third-world kitchen, and drink double gins in the gardens of the riverside pubs. Sitting with her at the water's edge, as she tore up her sandwiches and threw pieces to the aggressive swans, I felt more contented than I had been for twenty years. Sally had given birth to her second child, a healthy daughter, and bombarded us with invitations. Peggy Gardner's surprise marriage to an architect young enough to be her son (a fourteen-year gap, Cleo noted, Peggy's age when I had left the children's hut in Lunghua), and the orphaned Malaccan boy whom David and his Belgian wife had adopted, together convinced me that the past had been laid to rest.

Before we collected the rented cabin cruiser Cleo asked the marina operator to remove the miniature TV set in the saloon. Filled with riverside gin, we would be sleeping soundly when the late-night documentary was transmitted. As we moved through Shepperton lock, Cleo at the helm, I stood beside her with my arm around her waist.

'Cleo, we've never done this before. Why?'

'Why, indeed? You've been a prisoner in Shepperton.'

'We'll stop at Cookham and see if it's changed.'

'Not Cookham – and it won't have changed.'

'Why not?' I was surprised, knowing that she admired Spencer's visionary paintings. 'You always liked Cookham.'

'Too many angels dancing in the trees. Be honest, do you really want to hear Christ preaching again at the regatta?'

'We'll have lunch at Runnymede. We can visit the Kennedy Memorial.'

'Do I approve of *that*? I'll think about it …'

These talismanic zones disturbed Cleo. She distrusted their hold on me, for the soundest reasons. My decision not to watch Dick's documentary struck her as a promising first step in my rehabilitation, a return to the contingent world. I looked back at Shepperton, at the great elms in the park by the war memorial, at the film studios and the riverside hotels, receding from me like the Bund at Shanghai.

'Jim!' I felt Cleo gripping my arm. 'Relax, the place will still be there when you get back.'

'I know. I'll get a drink for us.'

'We don't need a drink. You always behave as if Shepperton only exists thanks to an act of will on your part.'

Laughing, I embraced her, almost sending the cruiser into the bank. 'Cleo, I dream the place …'

'And a wonderful dream, too. Alice and Henry and Lucy. Now and then, though, wake up.'

'I will …'

Two hours later we moored at Runnymede and walked across the meadow towards the hills that rose through the woods. In a sentimental gesture, a British Prime Minister had bequeathed an acre of soil to the American nation, and the limestone monolith of the memorial to John F. Kennedy overlooked the site of Magna Carta. During the Viet Nam war the memorial had been continually defaced and vandalised, and on one occasion cracked by a bomb.

Arm in arm, we climbed the pathway towards the memorial. The crack that divided the limestone was freshly cemented. Ancient graffiti had left their blurred traces in the face, overlaid by slogans and swastikas aerosolled in day-glow paints. Litter and beer cans were strewn about the site, and the remains of a takeaway meal in silver foil had been pushed under the memorial stone. Fifty feet away, partly concealed by a magnolia shrub, a middle-aged man with a shock of pale grey hair was copulating with a twenty-year-old woman. Trousers loosened around his waist, he lay between her raised legs, moving in hurried spasms as if urged on by the presence of this morbid stone.

Cleo lowered her gaze and frowned at the litter. 'Doesn't anyone ever clean the place? You'd think Kennedy was completely forgotten.'

'I suppose he is – in a way, that's a good thing.'

I thought of the role that Kennedy and his assassination had played in my own life, and how his televised images had shaped the imagination of the 1960s. Stills from the Zapruder film had seemed more poignant than a Grunewald crucifixion. Now only the graffiti endured, like the bird-droppings on the statues of Victorian generals and statesmen in the squares of London.

We walked down to the gate and crossed the meadow to the car park beside the jetty. Groups of people leaned against their cars, watching a family recover a motor-boat from the river. A father and his teenage daughter manoeuvred a two-wheel trailer down a stone ramp. When they had submerged the trailer in the shallow water the father released the speed-boat from its mooring by the bank and steered the craft on to the metal cradle. Above them, on the ramp, his wife sat at the controls of their car, waiting to tow the trailer from the water. A younger daughter sat behind her, eating an ice-cream and engrossed in a comic.

The current pulled at the speed-boat, trying to draw it into the centre of the stream. The father struggled with the metal cradle as his wife raced her engine, watching him through the rear-view mirror. When he signalled, she engaged bottom gear and edged up the ramp in a blare of noise and exhaust. The tow-rope tightened and the trailer moved forward, its tyres emerging from the water. But the speed-boat had floated away, and the man shouted to his wife, who switched off her engine. Oblivious of all this, the girl in the rear seat read her comic, now and then remembering to lick her ice-cream.

A youth in swimming trunks strode down the ramp and helped the man to pull the speed-boat on to the trailer. The wife reversed a few feet, releasing the tension in the rope. As Cleo and I boarded our cruiser they were fastening the craft to its cradle. The wife restarted her engine, released her hand-brake before engaging gear, and fumbled with the controls when the car rolled backwards down the slope. Everyone began to shout in warning, and the car park attendant left his ticket booth and remonstrated with the hapless driver.

'What's going on?' Cleo asked, as I waited to cast off. 'Are they driving into the river?'

'It's starting to look like it...'

The car's rear wheels had disappeared below the water. Flustered by the attendant and the shouts of the onlookers, the woman had lost control of the car. The girl in the rear seat cried out and lifted her feet from the water covering the floor. Her mother opened the driver's door, allowing her impatient husband to take the controls. But as she stepped into the shallow water there was a shout from the young man in the swimming trunks.

Buoyant now in the deeper current, the speed-boat had floated into the stream, dragging the trailer with it and pulling the car down the ramp. People were leaving their parked vehicles, cups of tea forgotten in their hands. Two men waded into the river and gripped the door pillars of the car, trying to hold it against the current.

'Cleo, wait here!'

As I stepped into the water I could see the white-faced child screaming in the rear seat, the water already up to her armpits. Trying to reach her, the mother floundered into the river, the skirt of her cotton dress floating into her face. Her husband seized her arms and pulled her on to the ramp. Already exhausted, he plunged into the water, face below the surface as he tried to disconnect the tow-rope.

I gripped the left-side door pillar, trying to reach the girl, who held the ice-cream over her head. Her shoulders were covered by the water, and she screamed at her mother, surrounded by loose tissues and aerosol containers, road-maps and cigarette stubs that had risen from the ash-trays and glove-pockets.

Before I could seize the child, the car began to tilt to one side, dragged back by the speed-boat. Everyone was shouting as the water swilled over the roof, a white spiral of ice-cream floating on the surface. Knocked from my feet, I found myself swimming beside the father as he fought his way to the speed-boat. He released the metal catches on the cradle and the craft swung away across the stream, bumping into the hull of a passing cabin cruiser whose crew stared at us from their sun deck, glasses of wine in hand.

Finding our footing, we pushed the car on to the stone ramp. The father pulled open the door, releasing the last of the water, only to find that the rear seat was empty. He plunged through the water beside the bank, slapping the waves with his hands as he searched for his daughter, but the car park attendant had found her lying on the floor below the steering wheel.

Cleo joined me as they laid her on the wet grass.

'Dear God – do you know any first aid?'

'No, but I think ...' The cold river-water streamed from my chest and legs. When the attendant lifted the child, her body hung from his hands like a dead rabbit, her eyes unfocused, her blue arms trailing across the grass. The sobbing mother smoothed the child's hair, and the

attendant began to move her arms rhythmically across her chest. Soon
tired, he lowered his face to her blanched cheeks, trying to detect her
breath, and then resumed his to and fro motion as if exercising a doll.

Stunned by the suddenness of the tragedy, Cleo was weeping into her
hands. I held her head against my shoulder. Trying not to look at the
child, I searched the Windsor road, hoping to see a passing ambulance. A
coach loaded with Middle East tourists sped past, but too late it occurred
to me that at least one doctor would have been among the party.

Fifty feet away, a tall man in hiking boots strode along the footpath,
approaching us at a brisk pace. He carried a bulky haversack on his
shoulders, and his bare knees brushed aside the long grass. Between
his heavy beard and the hair that crowded his forehead was a narrow
face with red-rimmed eyes, as if he had spent too much of his hiking
holiday reading in an unlit tent. A paperback guide-book to Eton and
Windsor protruded from the pocket of his tartan shirt, and he seemed
more interested in finding the historic site of Runnymede than in this
tragedy on the river-bank.

As he neared us, he caught sight of the little girl. Before anyone could
speak he slipped the haversack onto the ground, asked a middle-aged
couple to keep an eye on it, and stepped through the circle of onlookers.
He ignored the sobbing mother and knelt on the grass, taking the arms
of the inert child from the exhausted attendant.

His bony fingers moved like a conjuror's over the child. He lifted
her shoulders, so that her head fell back, forced apart her jaws with his
thumb and with a deft hooking movement of his forefinger released
some obstruction in the back of her throat. One hand held her ribs
and the other compressed her diaphragm. Instantly there was a gush
of water from the child's mouth. Carefully smoothing his beard, he
bent down and placed his lips over her mouth and nose. He began to
breathe slowly but strongly, stopping to pump the child's breastbone.
As he worked, the crowd of some thirty people was silent around him.

'She's breathing ... oh, my God.' Cleo's fingernails had torn the fabric
of my shirt. The girl was coughing. She choked and spat out the water
in her lungs and windpipe. The bearded man watched her calmly with
his blood-shot eyes, then sat her up with his strong hands and steadied

her breathing. The girl gasped at the air, and her eyes focused on the circle of people. She leaned against her distraught mother, coughed and rubbed her nose, sucking great gasps of air over her swollen tongue.

Two cars had backed to the edge of the stone ramp, the drivers discussing the fastest route to the hospital at Windsor. As the water streamed from her cotton dress, the mother carried the child to the nearer of the cars. Cleo smiled at me through the tears that blurred her mascara. Everyone followed the child, but I was watching the bearded man who had saved her. He made sure that the child was breathing comfortably in the car, then slipped through the crowd and reclaimed his haversack, thanking the couple who had placed it on their card-table. Before the convoy left the car park he had already resumed his walk along the bank.

We passed him an hour later, striding towards Windsor. I wanted to thank him, which no one had managed to do, but I found it difficult to come up with the right words. I steered the cruiser close to the bank and reduced speed so that we kept pace with him. He strode along in his heavy boots, checking some detail on his map. On his tartan shirt I could see the dry stain of the ice-cream that he had expressed from the child's stomach. I guessed that he was a school-master or civil servant, but I knew that he might just as well be a ship's purser or a day-release psychiatric patient. The heavy knapsack cut into his narrow shoulders, but he seemed unconcerned by the weight. Tied to the back of the knapsack was a pair of drying socks that I had not seen before and which I assumed he had washed in the river soon after saving the child.

Cleo waved to him, and he gave her a friendly but quick smile, lengthened his stride and moved away from us. He was enjoying his holiday and preferred his own company. Cleo's contingent world, the bare knees and the ice-cream stain and the drying socks, moved past the cabin cruiser and the dozing swans. I had thought of asking him who he was, but I realised that, for all practical purposes, I already knew.

17

Dream's Ransom

Guests were arriving in fancy dress, for a party of a very special kind. Hundreds of vehicles lined the quiet Buckinghamshire lane, and as I searched for a parking space I was overtaken by a studio van carrying two Marie Antoinettes, a pirate chief and a trio of Roman senators. Their rouged cheeks and painted lips gave them a look of plague victims on their way to a fever hospital.

My dream of Shanghai had materialised, like all dreams, in the least expected place, among the imposing houses built around the golf course at Sunningdale, little more than a fifteen-minute drive from Shepperton. I had lived for thirty years within sight of the studios, but had never stepped inside the huge sound-stages, and was unprepared for the scale of a major Hollywood production. A genie had sprung from the pages of my novel, and was busily conjuring the past into life, working with an extravagance more than a match for the original Shanghai.

The city of memory whose streets I had redrawn within the limits of the printed page had materialised in a fusion of the real and the super-real. Memory had been superseded by a new technology of historical recovery, where past, present and future could be dismantled and reshuffled at the producer's whim.

I had set out from Shepperton at seven that morning, expecting to find a small location crew at the Sunningdale mansion. Rented by the film company, the house would play the part of my childhood home in Amherst Avenue. Much of the film had already been shot in Shanghai, where the banks and hotels along the Bund stood unchanged since

the Communist seizure of the city in 1949. But the houses in Amherst
Avenue were semi-derelict, turned into tenement apartments crammed
with Chinese families and makeshift offices. No. 31 Amherst Avenue
now contained the New China Electronic Import and Export Agency.
Its drive was overgrown, its rotting window-frames were supported by
bamboo scaffolding, and the swimming-pool had been roofed over to
provide a damp-proof warehouse.

Fortunately, a reasonable replica of Amherst Avenue lay to hand on
the other side of the world, a few miles from the studios at Shepperton.
These handsome, half-timbered mansions, built in the 1930s beside the
golf course, had served as the models for the houses which the British
émigrés like my parents had built in the suburbs of Shanghai – houses
whose Tudor exteriors were themselves facades, hiding American bathrooms, kitchens and air-conditioning.

There was something odd in the notion that the home of a near-
neighbour could serve so plausibly as my childhood house, as if these
Thames Valley towns formed part of Greater Shanghai. While I followed
the studio van carrying the party of costumed extras I looked up at
the familiar mullioned windows and realised how shrewd an eye the
art director had brought to his job. He had convincingly recreated the
exotic city of memory from materials far nearer to me than I cared
to accept.

In place of the small location crew that I expected, a fleet of vehicles had taken over this quiet corner of Sunningdale. At first sight
the scene resembled the evacuation of London – dozens of trailers sat
in the surrounding fields, huge marquees stretched their canvas over
miles of duck-board, double-decker coaches, restaurant buses and
lavatory trailers were parked in lines, generators drummed at the cold
morning air, sending their current through a maze of cables to the
location three hundred yards away. A private police force controlled
the traffic, and a bus service ferried cast and crew from the trailers
and make-up vans.

Not one house, I discovered, but four of the mansions had been
rented by the film company, each contributing a segment of my childhood home – one provided a drained swimming-pool, another the

reception rooms and lawn where the fancy dress party on the eve of
Pearl Harbor would be held, while the third and fourth would recreate
the kitchen, dining-room and my own bedroom. Later that day, as I
walked around the site, I stared through the windows of the mansions
around the golf course, wondering what other segments of my childhood were hidden among the bridge tables and billiard rooms.

I parked my car on the edge of a commandeered tennis court, and
watched a team of scene-shifters unloading the 1930s props – Chinese
screens, art deco lamps, tiger-skin rugs and white telephones. All these
technicians, I realised, from the barber who had given me a period
short-back-and-sides, to the carpenters, lighting specialists and costume
designers, were working to construct a more convincing reality than
the original I had known as a child.

The clock of my life had come full circle, in all sorts of unexpected
ways. In a kindly gesture, the director had invited me to play the part of
a guest at the costume party. Grateful to him, I had accepted with all the
nervousness of a passenger volunteering to parachute from an airliner.
A benign conspiracy was already in motion. Many of my neighbours
had worked for years as part-time extras, and had been hired to play
internees at Lunghua Camp. Only the previous afternoon, leaving the
wine store in Shepperton High Street, I was greeted by the mother of
a girl who had gone to the same school as Lucy and Alice.

'Jim, I've just heard. We're in the camp together! Tim Bolton and
the Staceys are going to be there ...'

Not only the mother but her daughter, now 25, would play a
Lunghua prisoner. I almost believed that I was dreaming, and that
my sleeping mind was recruiting my Shepperton neighbours into the
narrative of the dream. Walking home, I wondered why I had come to
live in Shepperton in the first place. Thirty years earlier, Miriam and I
had picked the town at random, but perhaps I had known even then
that one day I would write a novel about Shanghai, and that it might
well be filmed at these studios, using my own neighbours as extras
and the nearby mansions that had inspired the houses in Amherst
Avenue. Deep assignments ran through our lives; there were no
coincidences.

'Jim, you made it!' One of the American producers waved to me through the electricians and lighting men who were moving in and out of the house. She held my arm, as if suspecting that I might lose my nerve and escape. 'We weren't sure if you were going to turn up.'

'How could I miss it? I don't mind saying, Kathy, it feels pretty strange ...'

'I bet it does. It's a good thing you decided against coming to Shanghai with us. How does the house look?'

'Uncanny.' White pigeons released during the shooting of the children's party the previous day still strutted on the lawn, and a security man sent them fluttering into the roof. 'I should have bought it 30 years ago.'

'Then you'd have had nothing to write about. And we wouldn't be here ... We're shooting the party in about an hour, so you'll have to change. The dresser's waiting for you upstairs.'

'I need a disguise ...'

While we spoke I became aware that a three-man film crew was quietly recording our exchange for a documentary about the production, a film within a film that took its place in the corridor of mirrors. This sense of illusions trapped within illusions persisted as I entered the large bedroom on the first floor. Here the principal actors were changing into their costumes, a cheery group whom I recognised from scores of films and television plays. Their faces seemed oddly different, but when they put on their make-up they grew more real. By contrast, I felt an impostor inside my John Bull costume of red tail-coat, top hat and Union Jack waistcoat.

Later, in the long drawing-room overlooking the garden, I stood with the party guests in a virtual replica of the house at Amherst Avenue. On the table beside me were copies of *Time* and *Life* dated December 1941, a week before the Japanese attack on Pearl Harbor, and I almost expected the white telephone to ring with a warning that we should leave on the next passenger steamer for Singapore.

Standing with a glass of whisky in my hand, I felt curiously like one of the intruders who sometimes gate-crashed my parents' parties – Axis agents posing as real estate dealers, professional bridge-players with a sideline in morphine, ex-nightclub hostesses on the look-out for my mother's jewellery box – whom Boy and Number 2 Boy would escort firmly to the door. I waited for my parents to appear and ask me to leave, failing to recognise me in this caricature costume.

'Hello ...' An engaging 12-year-old with a slim face and mature eyes stood in front of me, wearing Turkish slippers, spangled vest and trousers. He introduced himself confidently:

'I'm you ...'

As he extended his hand I could see him doubting if this overweight figure could ever have resembled himself.

'... and we're your mum and dad!'

An attractive couple in their early thirties, he in pirate costume, she dressed as a milkmaid, greeted me laughingly. While we spoke the lights filled the drawing-room with a powerful glare. The dream was about to dream itself. The camera crew were ready for a tracking shot through the party. After talking to each other about the threat of war, the guests would say their goodbyes and step through the hallway into the drive, where a second camera would record our departure.

The director came up to me with a friendly word.

'All set, Jim?' He nodded encouragingly. 'Just relax – put a hand on your hip. You look as if you know how to hold a glass of whisky.'

'I've had a little practice – but that's as far as it goes.'

'What about a line of dialogue? You can give yourself one right now.'

I stared at him, too tongue-tied to even say my name. He patted me reassuringly and walked back to the monitor. Everyone fell silent and the camera began to turn. I felt myself drifting into a trance, trying to imagine this line of dialogue missing from my earlier life, which I had spent my entire career trying to define.

Followed by the camera, we moved towards the hall. Lights were shining in the driveway, reflected from the polished roofs of the cars into which we would step. Drawn up on the raked gravel were a Buick roadster of the 1930s, a high-roofed Packard like my parents' car, a black gangster's Chrysler with running boards and white-wall tyres, and a 1940 Lincoln Zephyr convertible. Beside them stood Chinese chauffeurs in pre-war Shanghai uniforms, caps under their arms as they opened the rear doors for the departing guests.

Staring at the scene, I tried to focus my eyes on the camera and the watching crowd beyond the gates. I stepped into the rear seat of the Packard, remembering in time to remove my top hat. The actor playing my chauffeur closed the door and took his seat behind the wheel. As the cars moved across the drive between the departing guests I felt that I was being carried away from this quiet Buckinghamshire lane, across another world and another time to the Shanghai of half a century earlier, towards the lights of the Bund and the department stores of the Nanking Road, through the French Concession to the tramline terminus at the end of the Avenue Joffre, to the barbed-wire checkpoints that led to the western suburbs and the high-gabled house where a small English boy played with his German toys, surprised by the white pigeons that had taken shelter on his roof.

The cabin stewards cleared away the last drinks before we landed, moving nimbly through the debris of the 12-hour flight from London. Sitting beside Cleo in the front row, the cockpit of the 747 far above us, I peered over her shoulder at the north-east suburbs of Los Angeles. Vast highways busy with cars stretched across the sun-filled landscape, covered by a yellow haze as if the sand had begun to evaporate from the desert.

'Swimming-pools ...' Cleo pointed below. 'Thousands of them. When the rains fail these people will survive. How do you feel?'

'Fine. I'll recover. As if I've taken too many amphetamines.'

'You have. Don't worry, you'll land in about three days, when it's all over.'

'I hope so. It's a long way to go to a movie.'

'But what a movie.' In fact, neither of us had seen the film. 'It's a shame you're in fancy dress – no one will recognise you.'

'It's hardly a major role.'

'Rubbish – it's modest, but crucial.'

'Cleo, I may have been edited out altogether.'

'Of course you haven't! How could they?' she huffed, indignant at the very idea. 'You're the only one who was really there.'

'I'm not sure that's true – I think the actors felt that I was the odd man out, the only one who wasn't real. Most of them had been back to Shanghai.'

'You could have gone with them.'

'I know, but I hadn't the nerve. I wasn't ready to face everything again – I've spent my whole life trying to sort it out. This is the right way to go back to Shanghai, inside a film. In a sense they started shooting it fifty years ago ...'

The world premiere would be held in three days' time, at a theatre in Westwood. Seatbelt fastened, I waited as the plane turned over the sea and swept in across the idle waves. Despite the long flight from London, and what I had said to Cleo, I felt remarkably at ease. I looked down at the deserted beaches, with their isolated palms standing on the edge of the Pacific Ocean that I had last seen in 1946. I had never visited Los Angeles, but it seemed right that my childhood should meet its end in this desert city whose limitless imagination had re-mythologised the past and invented the future.

An hour later we rolled along the San Diego freeway in the studio car, looking at the landscape of Los Angeles that neither of us had seen before, but which was instantly familiar. Thousands of films and television series had installed an intact replica of the city in our minds, far more accurate than the preposterous beefeater and pearly queen image conveyed by the British tourist board. Vaguely garish bungalows and store-fronts stretched for miles under the tangle of overhead wires, a terrain of ticky-tack and painted glue fading in the sun, as if the entire city was a dusty film set waiting to be refurbished in some as yet to be financed production. I loved every inch of it, and felt instantly at home.

Then, as we left the freeway and joined Santa Monica Boulevard, I saw the first anomaly, a jarring intrusion from another level of reality. A billboard the size of a tennis court stood beside the road, advertising the film we had come to see, my own name below those of the producers and director. For a moment the dream had woken and summoned its sleeper.

Identical signs reared over the rooftops of Los Angeles, and even over Sunset Boulevard, where another writer, Joe Gillis, had become entangled in the Hollywood dream. In our hotel I switched on the television set to find commercials for the film filling the screen with

low-flying Mustangs, a real Shanghai burning again as Japanese soldiers
marched down the Bund and my boyhood self was swept up in a panic
of coolies and office clerks. Arm in arm, Cleo and I stared from our
terrace at the billboard over Wilshire Boulevard. My past had escaped
from my head and was clambering across the rooftops like some doomed
creature in a Forties monster movie.

Happily, the irony of all this was not lost on Cleo.

'How did Sinbad get the genie back in the bottle? Think.'

'God knows – some piece of low cunning, I suppose.'

'You've spent years writing about the media landscape, and now it's
escaped and stood you in the palm of its hand.'

'I'll rent a car tomorrow. We'll find the real Los Angeles.'

'Dear, wake up. This *is* the real Los Angeles.'

The next morning we set out on a circuit of this mysterious city.
Entire districts sat in the musty sunlight like intact fragments of television episodes, as strangely familiar as the revisited streets of one's
childhood. Far from being the youngest, Los Angeles was the oldest
city of the 20th century, the Troy of its collective imagination. The
ground-courses of our deepest dreams were layered into its past among
the filling stations and freeways.

On the day before the premiere, while Cleo was visiting English friends
in Santa Barbara, the reception desk rang to say that a Mrs Weinstock
had called to see me. Assuming she was a local journalist, I asked the
desk-clerk to send her up to our suite. Moments later, I opened the door
to find a handsome American woman in her middle sixties, strikingly
dressed in a Persian lamb coat and silk hat. Her commanding eyes rose
instantly to the challenge when I failed to recognise her.

'James, you're too busy to remember me?' She stepped forward, in a
heady aura of perfume and expensive fabrics. She seized my shoulders
and pressed my face to her smooth cheeks. 'Olga! Olga Ulianova from
Shanghai!'

'Olga …?' I was pinned against the television screen by my childhood governess, who had materialised from the Hollywood sky like the
billboards and TV commercials. 'Olga … I can't believe it …'

'So you'd better start now.' She glanced around the suite, taking in every detail of the books on the table, Cleo's clothes hanging in the bedroom, the open suitcases and presentation photographs. As she sized me up, deciding that no more than a few seconds' inspection was needed, I tried to remember the edgy young woman I had last seen in the Del Monte nightclub. Despite the years, her features were almost unchanged, the lips as cutting as ever, the hectic eyes carrying out an inventory of my clothes, self-confidence, integration into the real world. But her face wore a curious mask, as if a child's cheeks, nose and chin had been slung from her temples, through which glared the penetrating eyes and sharp teeth of an old woman.

'You haven't changed, James. Not even a little. You're still riding your pedal-bike.' She smiled shrewdly, slipping her coat across a chair. 'But now you remember me?'

'Olga, yes ... I'm still amazed to see you. Did the studio arrange this?'

'The studio? Everything isn't a film, James. My daughter and I are staying with our friends in Van Nuys, so I thought, let's see how my James is.'

'I'm glad you did. But you got out of Shanghai?'

'Of course! Once the Americans left. Believe me, James, I'm not designed for communism. I'm living in San Francisco for many years now ...'

'And you're married ...?'

'Mrs Edward R. Weinstock – my husband is a nose and throat surgeon, very influential.' She nodded darkly, scrutinising with only marginal approval a photograph of Cleo and myself. 'But you were nearly a doctor yourself? I read an interview – I couldn't understand ...'

'I gave it up after a couple of years – I wanted to be a writer.'

'A writer?' Her nostrils twitched doubtfully, as if only the plushness of this Beverly Hills hotel suite prevented her from criticising a disastrous career-move. She was wearing an expensive gown with a gleaming lamé thread that she might have worn to the opening of a Las Vegas casino, but as she turned to and fro on her rapier heels I found myself glancing under the arms for the tell-tale tear. I remembered the brief glimpse of her breast that had so dazed my adolescent mind. Despite her expensive hair and jewellery, there was still something slatternly about Olga, as if her body was a disposable tool to be used as necessity dictated. I thought of her in post-war Shanghai, a tank-trap full of vodka, lying in wait for the young American servicemen.

'So this film, James. Is it good?'

'I'm sure it is. They say it's his best. I haven't seen it yet.'

'You haven't?' This was clearly a serious omission, one I should have rectified before signing the film contract or, more sensibly still, before writing a line of the book. She shook her head, as if I was still the odd little boy who had cycled all over Shanghai in search of a war. 'Anyway, it's a big help for your career. You were always telling stories. Your poor mother didn't know what was coming next ...'

'This is the only book I've written about Shanghai – for some reason, it took a long time.'

'Too much to forget, people don't realise ... the things I could tell about Shanghai. You and I should write a book, James, a real best-seller. My ideas and your—'

'One is enough, Olga. I might write a sequel about my life in England.'

'England?' Doubtfully, Olga sniffed her Scotch. 'Is it so interesting? I read about your wife – that's sad for you.'

'That was a long time ago. I'll treat you to lunch, Olga, and you can bring me up to date.'

'Listen, it's never long enough. When my mother passed away ...' As an afterthought, she added: 'My second husband died. An English dentist in Hong Kong, so I understand.'

On our way to the rooftop restaurant she held my arm in a genuine show of sympathy, evoked almost entirely by her feelings of pity for herself. Responding to the attentions of the restaurant, she was soon as animated as a teenager, showing off her smooth cheeks and trimmed nose. The young Olga I remembered, whose body I had tried to glimpse as she undressed in the bathroom, seemed to beckon across the years from this ageing but still glamorous woman. She spoke with scarcely a pause for breath about her years in Hong Kong and Manila, battling her way to the top of the social hill as husbands died under her like horses under a cavalryman at Austerlitz.

When we returned to the suite she said: 'James, your book made a lot of interest in San Francisco – many people from Shanghai are living there. Perhaps you could give a talk to us. You could say I was your family's friend. Maybe in the diplomatic service ...'

'Olga, I'd like to, but even writing about Shanghai was difficult enough.'

'Of course. I know your feelings. We were always close, James. You never told your mother about those things I took – the silver and the jade horses ... I always wanted to thank you for that.'

'Olga, I never knew.'

'Maybe you forgot. They had so much, and my parents were hungry every day. My father lost all his hope, sitting in that little room. It's lucky he died before the war came. My mother forgave me – women understand – but a father? Never ...'

Olga held my arm, the scent of her hair, throat and breasts overrunning my senses. She stood beside me, staring at the mansions of Beverly Hills as if seeing the vanished facades of Amherst Avenue. I remembered how, forty years earlier, I had felt her strong hip pressed against mine as we stood in the glass-strewn ballroom of the Del Monte nightclub. During the dark days at school in England I had often thought of Olga. We would have made love on one of the roulette tables if I had been less intimidated by her, and particularly if I had offered a short cut to my father's office.

I embraced this exotic female chimera, with her dream's ransom of a face-lift. Her body was even older than mine, but her face was that of the White Russian teenager who had first looked after me.

She smiled to herself, perhaps amused by the memory of some childish exploit in the garden at Amherst Avenue.

'And your friend, James?' Her fingers loosened my tie and shirt. She ran her nails across my chest, making sure that my nipples were still there. 'Is she back soon?'

'Not till tomorrow – she's gone to see publishing people she knows in Santa Barbara. Olga, this has nothing to do with her.'

'Publishing? Then it's okay ...' She raised her face in front of me, a small screen on which was projected the image of a young woman.

I wondered why she had bothered to see me – perhaps out of pride, and to remind me that she could still dominate my life. Certainly, she would have felt no debt of honour for stealing from my parents before the war. But she knew that we were both victims in our different ways of western rule in Shanghai, which my parents represented for her. We had once been wounded and corrupted by Shanghai, in so far as children could be corrupted, and by making love in this California hotel we would prove to each other that the wounds had healed.

'Good ... you know, James, I never waited long for a man. This could be a bad example for me ...'

She held my wrists in the same firm grip she had used half a century earlier to steer me towards the bathroom. Standing beside the bed, she closed the wardrobe mirrors so that no reflection of her back would reach my eyes. She began to undress me as if preparing me for a party, her fingers never leaving my skin as they moved around my body.

Delaying herself deliberately, she stood against me, playing the moody governess unsure whether to accord some trivial privilege to her charge. I kissed her affectionately, glad that she had come through and was happily married to her influential surgeon.

The film of our life rushed backwards through the projector, devouring itself as it hunted for some discarded moment that held the key to our earliest selves.

On our final day in Los Angeles, a week after the film premiere, Cleo and I decided on a last visit to the ocean. Waiting for our car, we stood in the entrance of the hotel, looking up at the black skyscrapers of Century City a few hundred yards away. This cluster of sightless towers emerged through the low-rise sprawl of the city like a harsh, obsidian Manhattan.

Cleo stared at the razor cornices, and gave a shiver. 'Is it all going to look like this when we come back? Please, God ... what sort of heaven circles those spires?'

'None I want to wake into. But face it, Cleo – modernism is the gothic of the information age. Dreams sharp enough to bleed, and no doubts about man's lowly place in the scheme of things. Let's head for the beach ...'

Venice, by contrast, was ramshackle and comforting. An intact fragment of the Sixties survived along its promenades. The wide sands stretched past roller-skaters and muscle-builders, break-dancers and beggars posing as Viet Nam psychos. Its modest stands were hung with flower-power T-shirts and mystic jewellery. Driftwood fires were burning on the sand beside the shelters which the groups of hippies had erected. The sea seemed far away, a glimmer of waves along the horizon, as if the Pacific had decided to withdraw for the day. I could almost believe that we were walking on the bed of a fossil sea, with ancient cigarette ends, ball-point pens and beer cans embedded in its scarred surface, all that remained of some earlier race.

I slipped my arm around Cleo's waist, happy to be with her and glad that we would be going together to New York. The premiere had been a great success, presented with effortless Hollywood professionalism, like a vast good-natured hallucination – the hundreds of limousines, revolving searchlights and sealed-off streets lined with red carpet and security guards. The audience of film actors seemed to have absconded from reality for the evening, ambling down the aisles of the theatre with their sable coats and pop-corn cartons.

As it happened, my small role had been edited out of the finished film, much to my relief, though I survived as a brief blur seen as the camera followed my younger self playing with his model aircraft. But this seemed just, like the faint blur which was all that any of us left across time and space. Besides, the film had served a deeper role for me – seeing its masterly recreation of Shanghai had been the last act in a profound catharsis that had taken decades to draw to a close. All the powers of modern film had come together for this therapeutic exercise. The puzzle had solved itself; the mirror, as I had promised, had been broken from within. In my mind the image had fused with its original, enfolding it within its protective wings. Looking at the great hotels along the Bund, unchanged after fifty years, I could almost believe that my memories of Shanghai had always been a film, endlessly played inside my head during my years in England after the war.

*

'They're launching some kind of ship.'

Cleo pointed to the crowd of people at the water's edge. A caterpillar tractor backed across the sand, pushing a trailer loaded with a bizarre sailing vessel. A single mast rose above a cabin that resembled a thatched hut. As we approached across the sand we could see that the hull was built entirely of papyrus reeds, bound together at stem and stern like the handle of a wicker shopping bag.

A square-rigged sail floated from the mast, bearing a half-familiar red emblem.

Cleo stopped and squinted through cupped hands.

'It's Heyerdahl's papyrus ship – *Ra*. We published the book.'

'I thought it sank in the Atlantic …'

'He must be trying to cross the Pacific. Jim, you ought to volunteer. It's the original slow boat to China.'

'I don't think it's an original of anything …'

Crew-men knelt in the shallow waves, examining the underside of the craft. We stepped through the children and dogs playing in the water around the tractor. The mock-papyrus superstructure, assembled from moulded plastic and fibre-glass, was bolted on to a sturdy steel hull.

'It's the replica of a replica.' Cleo laughed at herself for being taken in. 'They must be using it in a film.'

'It looks like a real ship, though. If they're making a TV commercial they'll need something more seaworthy than Heyerdahl's original. This one's going somewhere.'

'Jim, now's your chance to get aboard.'

A black labrador ambled through the waves, licking our hands and ready to shake its coat over us. I patted its head, admiring the easy expertise of the American crew. A man in swimming trunks and straw hat filmed the launch with a hand-held video-camera. At least this vessel would not sink, and a trial cruise among the weekend yachts of Marina Del Rey might uncover more truths about the performance of crew and vessel than its original's abortive mock-voyage across the Atlantic.

I thought of Olga, sailing serenely through the lobby of the Beverly Hilton after we said goodbye. As she pressed her cheeks against my own I kissed for the last time the face of my childhood governess. That youthful and ageless mask was her true self, which time had stolen from her, the innocent and unlined face she had never been allowed to know as an adolescent.

The war had postponed my own childhood, to be rediscovered years later with Henry, Alice and Lucy. The time of desperate stratagems was over, the car crashes and hallucinogens, the deviant sex ransacked like a library of extreme metaphors. Miriam and all the murdered dead of a world war had made their peace. The happiness I had found had been waiting for me within the modest reach of my own arms, in my children and the women I had loved, and in the friends who had made their own way through the craze years.

The waves struck sharply at our ankles. A strong wind was gusting across the beach, and the papyrus craft had broken free from its crew. With only the camera-man aboard, fumbling at the mast as he ducked the swinging boom, the craft confidently rode the waves. The launch crew leapt through the deeper water, pulling on the mooring lines but unable to restrain the boisterous vessel. The replica of a replica it may have been, but it was buoyant and well-founded, more than capable of taking on the sea and setting its own course across the Pacific, with only its shanghaied camera-man as crew, perhaps ending with a last triumphant heave on the beaches of Woosung.

'New York tomorrow. Then home to the children.' Cleo held my arm tightly as we walked back to our car, past the hippies and the fragrant beach fires, embers glaring in the freshening air. 'Tell me – when they show the film in London, will they put back your little cameo?'

'I hope not.' I watched the papyrus craft, cresting the breakers that rolled in from the Pacific, its bows set towards the China shore. 'Cleo, think where that might lead …'

The Ballard Tradition

by Will Self

Why is J. G. Ballard rated by many (including myself) as the most significant English novelist of the second half of the 20th century? His fusions of 1920s surrealism, 1960s science fiction and contemporary suburbia can appear not merely dystopian but perverse. His prose, when not clunking along as if daring you to find it prosaic, can veer into imagery at once bluntly technical and comically transcendent: eros and thanatos browning on a gas-fired barbecue. But Ballard's prose is daring, because it can seem like a form of mass spectrometry, as western society is incinerated to reveal what it is really made of. If you can be bored while love, hate, sensuality and received values flare up, then you are as numb and rudderless as a typical Ballard character.

Ballard's books are not pretty; nor are they obviously 'literary' in that hammy way whereby a writer conveys between the lines that he is exceedingly well read and that you may be as well. Ballard belongs neither to the academy nor to the book group. His characters cry out neither for sympathy nor identification from the reader; they stand in a null moral ground, staring balefully towards a long-suspected future, defined usually by little more than their profession and a few rags of memory.

Ballard is a writer more prized than prizewinning. True, his aficionados have something of the cultish about us, a legacy perhaps of his origins within the SF genre (and those of us over forty most likely encountered his work first under this guise). But ever since Steven Spielberg filmed *Empire of the Sun* (an experience of which Ballard himself has remarked laconically 'it lifted my income from that of an English to an American GP'), the mainstream has made its claims on him as well. Sitting in his Shepperton semi, screamingly ordinary (a devoted single father and now a grandfather), Ballard has issued a series of bulletins on the modern world of almost unerring prescience. Other writers describe; Ballard anticipates. To paraphrase the title of one of his short-story collections, he has provided us with our own myths of the near future.

His public pronouncements have been gnomically ambivalent: pro-pornography, pro-sadomasochism, half in love with American braggadocio, half in hate with the sell-by date of technology. In a typically prissy edition of Radio 4's *Book Club*, Ballard didn't demur for a second before his middle-English audience. 'I loved the Japanese soldiers,' he said of his time as a child spent in an internment camp outside Shanghai. 'There's nothing more attractive to a boy than the side that's winning.' Is he satirist or seer? A consummate English ironist or quietly in search of the genuinely irenic?

One thing is certain: his mutant science fictions (explorations of 'inner space', as he once put it) have enabled Ballard to sustain the attack and rigour of the avant-garde while all about him have succumbed to the process whereby everything formerly counter-cultural becomes consumable, so long as it has that seductive 99p price point. By anticipating the very form of the death of Diana Spencer (in *Crash*), the social fallout of postwar urban planning (*High-Rise*), the impact of global warming (*The Drowned World* and the short story 'The Terminal Beach'), as well as taking sideways trajectories into the surreal (*The Atrocity Exhibition* and *Vermilion Sands*) and limning in the society of the spectacle (*The Unlimited Dream Company* and *Hello America*), Ballard has justified his own adjectival status. To speak of anything from a popular delusion to a deranged political démarche as 'Ballardian' is not merely to pay the writer his due, but to acknowledge the genuinely minatory nature of his vision. Indeed, the time has come to entertain the notion that one of the new seasons we are experiencing – dry spring, warm winter – should be named, simply, 'Ballard'.

This article originally appeared in Prospect *magazine in 2003.*

The Worst of Times

by J. G. Ballard and Danny Danziger

I was born in Shanghai in 1930 and brought up there by my English parents. I spent the war in a Japanese civilian camp, all of which I describe in my novel *Empire of the Sun*.

I came to England in 1946. My father stayed on in China so I was travelling with my mother and younger sister. I remember standing at the rail of the converted troop ship that brought us back from China, looking down at the port of Southampton as we moored against the dock. I was amazed – I genuinely thought we had come to the wrong country.

I had an impression of England, which I had drawn from my childhood reading, of a sunlit, semi-rural land with beautiful rolling meadows and village greens and ivy-clad rectories, a land almost entirely middle-class. Everything was much greyer and grimmer and darker and colder than I had been led to believe, there were no village greens and no cheerful Constable skies as I looked down on the backstreets of Southampton under a low grey sky. Even the sun seemed to be grey, and it rained perpetually; I'd come from a hot climate where the sun shone, and there is every difference between the semi-tropical rain in Shanghai and the kind of rain that fell on Southampton in 1946.

Shanghai had been a cross between Las Vegas and ancient Rome, full of American cars and American exuberance – and I remember looking down from the ship at a country that was so poor and so spartan. I had never seen an English car, and the docks were lined with what looked like little black mobile coal scuttles.

We took the train from Southampton to London, and I remember travelling across London and seeing this total devastation – I mean hundreds of acres of the city had been levelled to the ground, the whole place had a shattered look. And everyone looked small and tired and white-faced and badly nourished, they looked like people who had suffered a particularly ugly enemy occupation. The British I met talked as if they had won the war but acted as if they had lost it.

We then travelled to Birmingham where my mother's parents lived, and one never saw the sun, and every chimney-pot belched out clouds of coal smoke. People were obsessed with their tiny butter ration and the tiny portion of stewing steak they were allowed each week. I had spent three years in a Japanese camp, so I could cope with the physical deprivation, but the psychological deprivation from which the English suffered unsettled me far more.

Within about a year my father came back on a brief trip, and he took us on a motoring holiday through France and Italy in the spring of '47. I remember being amazed by the abundance that one found in France – there was no rationing and people looked more confident, lives were brighter and more cheerful.

Those early years were totally dislocating. I found the English attitudes towards the world utterly incomprehensible. The whole country seemed at complete variance with its situation. Everyone believed that Britain was still a world power ruling a world empire, and we had an obligation to maintain large forces at every point of the atlas. Even in the Sixties, people were still debating whether Britain should maintain forces east of Suez.

Everyone believed in a kind of social harmony, which was sentimentalised in Ealing comedies – whereas the reality was that the country was harshly divided between the have-nots, who were basically the working class, and the middle class, who weren't exactly the haves but they had just a little bit more.

I found their mindset completely mysterious. All these middle-class people, my parents, friends and relations and the like, were seething with a sort of repressed rage at the world around them. And what they were raging against was the post-war Labour government. It was impossible to have any kind of dialogue about the rights and wrongs of the

National Health Service, which was about to come in, they talked as if this Labour government was an occupying power, that the Bolsheviks had arrived and were to strip them of everything they owned.

There was enormous resistance to change. Everyone clung to this narrow band of state-controlled programming, the Home Service and the Light Programme, whose main task seemed to be to maintain all the myths about England's importance.

There was a lack of belief in enterprise, it was very difficult to spend more than a few days abroad because you weren't allowed to take more than £100. All this seemed to be a kind of Eastern European approach to things. I can remember people being hostile to the first supermarkets, and defending the little corner shop with its stale pieces of bacon and cheese exposed to any passing breath. People were hostile to the first motorway, there was a tremendous amount of debate about the M1, whether it should even be built; there was a feeling that mobility wasn't a good thing, that getting from A to B as quickly as possible was somehow rather unBritish.

The upshot of all this was that I felt a complete outsider and never really integrated into English life until I got married in the mid-Fifties, and had my children, and began to put down roots. Curiously, now that my children have grown up, I feel a sense of strangeness coming on again.

It wasn't until the early Sixties that prosperity in any sense came to this country. Middle-class people used to sneer at the working class with their washing machines and their Cortinas, and the consumer-goods society that was targeted at the working-class population. But in fact those washing machines and second-hand Cortinas transformed this country for the better. The consumer society that came into existence and provided the engine of affluence for the Sixties was the best thing that ever happened to this country; it liberated us in all sorts of ways, and helped to break down the class barriers.

I admire the English very much, I think they are a remarkable people. They are pugnacious and very fair-minded at the same time, they have a great civic sense, they take responsibility for each other, and I think there is a strain of kindliness in the English that is quite rare. There is a great respect for eccentricity, for the individual.

One doesn't want to sentimentalise these things, but they are part of the fabric of English life and they are admirable. It is sad that these admirable qualities are straitjacketed into a class system that doesn't really give them full expression. The English cling to that straitjacket, they are happy wearing it, now and then they pull down one or two zips and breathe a bit more deeply, but they are quite capable of pulling the zips up again.

This article originally appeared in the Independent *in 1991.*

Printed by RR Donnelley at Glasgow, UK